Evernight Publishing

www.evernightpublishing.com

Copyright© 2015

Heather Hambel Curley

Editor: Melissa Hosack

Cover Artist: Jay Aheer

ISBN: 978-1-77233-444-9

ALL RIGHTS RESERVED

WITH ME NOW

DEDICATION

Nothing I write could be accomplished without my core support team, Billy, Tommy, Jimmy, and Mom—you guys keep pushing me and are enthusiastic over every semicolon. I love you!

To Sara Lower, Jocelyn Allenby, and Lindsey Loucks: You're more than friends, you're sisters! I value your encouragement and friendship—and sense of humor—every day.

And, as always, to Dad: I miss you.

WITH ME NOW

The Lazarus Society, 1

Heather Hambel Curley

Copyright © 2015

Chapter One

The man next to her might have been dead.

Madison Monroe rubbed her bleary eyes with her fist, the grinding pain of her contact lens against her cornea enough to partially jar her out of the alcohol induced haze. Had that frat bastard mixing drinks slipped her something? Probably.

She balanced her red plastic cup on the armchair behind her and scooted closer to the man beside her. His eyes were half open, his stare fixed in the general region of his belly button. Was he breathing? She wasn't a med student. Even if she was, her eyes felt like they were swimming in her head and she couldn't tell for sure if his chest was actually rising or falling, or if it was her head drooping and lolling from all the shots of Jim Beam she'd thrown back.

She decided to ask him. "Are you dead?"

He didn't answer.

Madison giggled. Christ, she couldn't even remember his name. It wasn't liked she'd fucked him—she hadn't, had she?—so it probably didn't matter, especially if he was dead. Well, it might matter to someone if he was dead. She remembered making fun of his shoes, ridiculous plaid loafers with a clashing plaid shirt. Alternating patterns of plaid; fucking hipster engineering student. And his name was Arty. That was it, Arty.

She shook him. "Arty. Arty, are you dead?"

He groaned. Good, not dead.

She slumped back against the wall next to him and fumbled for her drink. The music was still pounding, the thump of the base reverberating in her skull. Going to a frat party was a bad idea, obviously, but this was finals week. Mild mannered Madison—everybody should be able to cut loose once in a while, right? She was really only worried about her Skeletal Forensic Anthropology final, but it wasn't until Thursday. Or was it Wednesday?

The music downstairs shut off.

The sudden scream of silence was jolting. She squeezed her eyes closed and opened them, as if that would somehow help her hear more efficiently. People were yelling about something, about the mops. Who the hell cared about mops?

The dim light of the bedroom was pierced by alternating blue and red flashes from the window. Shit, they weren't saying mops. They were saying cops.

Someone had called the cops.

"Damn it." She slid back over to Arty and shook him harder. "Dude, it's the cops. We've gotta split."

She jumped to her feet and careened toward the door. The room tipped and turned; overwhelmed by dizziness, she stumbled sideways and slammed against the footboard of the bed. Now was not the time to pass out. *Come on, Madison, get with it.*

Cops were yelling downstairs. Christ, they'd be upstairs any minute. She kicked Arty again, panic welling up in her chest. She couldn't get arrested for underage drinking, not with the trip already planned. No. No, this was bad. The summer trip to France was going to be the crown in her double major history/anthropology undergraduate degree. This was the ticket to get her in the accelerated and combined Master's slash Doctoral program. The history department frowned on underage drinking. Hell, the history department frowned on everything fun.

She dropped to her knees and squeezed under the bed, pressing herself as far back against the wall as she could. They'd see Arty. Maybe they wouldn't see her.

The sound of footsteps echoed down the hallway; a figure paused outside the open bedroom door. "Got one, looks like he's out cold."

She could see a second pair of black boots in the doorway. "I'll take him out to the truck. Come on, buddy, wake up. Can you hear me, son? Wake up."

"Just drag him out." The first cop spoke from the doorway. "I never get tired of frat busts. Check out those shoes, man. Kids these days."

Madison shrank back, almost as if she thought by doing so she could disappear into the baseboards. *That's it, Arty, distract them with the mind boggling power of plaid.*

As the cop leaned over to hoist Arty to his feet, Madison felt a strange vibration from her back pocket. She froze.

Her cell phone.

Before she had time to fumble for the phone, the melodic sound of Mozart's Eine kleine Nachtmusik rang out. The ringer sounded thirty times louder than it did when the phone was next to her face. She moved her arm backwards to shut off the phone, slamming her elbow off the mattress's metal box spring. *Shit.*

She squeezed her eyes shut and pressed her face to the cold tiled floor. The scrape of boots crossing to the bed shrieked in her ears. It felt like it seared into her brain and through the alcohol to jab her and announce, "Busted."

The cop's voiced seemed like it boomed from the heavens, the voice of God himself. "Why, hello there."

She didn't look up. "Hi."

"How about you come out from under there? I think we have a few things to talk about."

He stepped back from the bed to allow her room to maneuver. She slunk out like a pitiful muskrat slinking from a hole. Rumpled. Sweaty. Pathetic in her inability to execute a coordinated movement.

The cop reached out to help her to her feet. "I'm Officer Jamison. This is Officer Burke. Can I see your driver's license?"

She had to think. Frat parties didn't typically require people show identification to be served alcohol.

The cop leaned forward. "I'm going to need to see your identification, Miss."

Jamming her hand in her back pockets, she withdrew her cell phone and her driver's license. She handed him the license and waited.

His response was almost immediate. "Looks like you have a birthday coming up."

"Yes, sir."

"Not going to turn twenty-one for a few more weeks, huh?"

"Yes, sir."

"Okay, Miss Monroe, party's over." He handed her the license back. "Let's go downstairs and have a little chat. Do you need medical assistance? Are you okay to walk on your own?"

"I'm fine." She shoved her license back into her pocket and rested her hand on the doorframe, steadying herself before creeping down the hallway. Her ankles twitched and quivered as she strained to walk in a straight line over the dull wood floorboards. The thought of tripping in front of the cops made her feel even clumsier and dizzier. Brain overload. At this rate, she would probably stumble over an empty floor, fall down the stairs, and break her neck.

At least she wouldn't go to jail.

The front yard of the fraternity house was boarded by thick hedges, now being utilized by the police to corral students who were too slow—or drunk—to get away. The cop who'd examined her license circled around her and rushed up to another cop with a clipboard. She raised an eyebrow and giggled. It certainly hadn't seemed like a race when they started downstairs.

It was impossible to make out what he was saying. She caught a few random comments, mostly remarks pointedly made in her direction: "…hiding under the bed…" and, practically guffawed, "…will be twenty-one in like, four weeks!"

Awesome.

The cop beckoned her to him with an over-exaggerated wave and she shuffled forward, feeling like a six-year-old stubbornly refusing to go to bed. She dragged her feet and resisted the urge to pout. Pouting probably wouldn't help at this point.

"This is Officer Richards." The cop flashed an obviously forced smile. "Do you consent to a breathalyzer test?"

"I think we all know I've had too much to drink." Madison winced. *What a dumb thing to say.*

Officer Richards calibrated the breathalyzer device. "Can you tell me a little about what happened tonight?"

"It was a fraternity party. I had too much to drink." Madison shrugged. "Am I going to need an attorney for all this?"

"Do you want an attorney? You have the right, you know."

"Yeah, uh, I'd rather keep this as easy as possible."

"Do you consent to the test?" Officer Richards held up the device. "It only takes a few seconds. Then we can see where we're at and go from there."

"Okay."

He held the device up to her mouth and waited while she positioned her lips over the mouthpiece. "When I tell you to, start blowing as hard as you can. Ready?"

She grunted.

"Okay…blow. Blow. Keep going." He studied the end of the gage. "Keep going. Stop."

The other cop peered over his shoulder. He shook his head.

Officer Richards put the breathalyzer down and filled out a few lines on a form. He circled something and then signed the bottom, clipping the pen to his front pocket with a flourish. "Very good. Now, Miss Monroe, why don't you just head to the officer set up by the cruiser—yes, that's right, just over there—and he'll get everything processed for you."

Madison pursed her lips together. She was drunk. She wasn't a child; she couldn't miss the folding table and chair set up next to the police SUV. "Aren't you supposed to give me some kind of percentage? Or fractionated decimal? Some kind of hardcore, quantifiable objective finding of how drunk you presume me to be?"

"Officer Godwin will go over all of that with you. Do you need help getting over there or can you make it on your own? If you need medical assistance, I can call the paramedics."

"I think I'll survive." She jammed her hands into her pockets as far as the tight denim would allow. *Or I'll trip and kill a cat.* Wobbly, but in a reasonably coordinated manner, she picked her way across the yard to the seated officer.

He cocked his head to the folding chair set up across from him. "Go ahead and take a seat, Miss. Name?"

"Madison Monroe." She slumped down in the chair and almost slid off the edge. She groaned; her sudden inability to master the art of taking a seat was not going to win her case against underage drinking. Obviously.

"Oh, like Marilyn Monroe." He held up a digital camera and leveled it in front of her. The whirling shriek of the zoom adjustment irritated her more than his apparent incompetence at using it correctly. "You can smile if you want."

The last thing she wanted to do was smile.

The flash was blinding. She blinked, the negative-like apparition of the flash floating across her line of vision. "Um, not actually like Marilyn Monroe. Like James Monroe."

The cop looked at her.

"You know, James Monroe. The fifth president of the United States?" She rubbed the back of her neck. "Obviously you weren't a liberal arts major."

"Madison is nice. You ever been to Madison, Wisconsin? Nice place." He slowly penned her first name on a form. Even through her quickly sobering haze and reading upside down, she could make out the bold printed word on the top: Citation.

"Yeah, no, it has nothing to do with Madison, Wisconsin. It's like James Madison, the fourth president of the United States..." She let her voice trail off. "My parents were kind of like studious hippies...I guess."

"What's your address, Miss Monroe?"

"Eighty-four Montpelier."

"Is that on campus?"

"Yes."

"And what about your parents? Where do they live?"

"In Greengate. Fourteen sixty-one Grace Crest Court."

"Their names?"

"Richard and Joyce Essington." Madison leaned forward, resting her fingertips on the edge of the table. "Are you going to call my parents? Seriously?"

"No, you're going to call your parents." He glanced up. "Seriously. What's your current age and date of birth?"

She'd let him do the math. "My birthday is May 10th. I'm twenty."

A smiled spread across his lips, but this time he didn't look up. "All of this and you would have been twenty-one in a couple weeks?"

"Tell me about it."

He shook his head. After a few more swipes of his pen, he flipped the paper around and pushed it across the table to her. "Okay, Miss Monroe, you're being cited for underage drinking. You are required to respond to the citation within ten days. At which point, you will be required to appear before a Magisterial District Judge. Underage drinking is considered a 'summary crime' in the state of Pennsylvania. However, it is still listed in the Pennsylvania Crimes Code and therefore is considered a crime. It will be listed on your record. Do you understand everything I just told you?"

"Yes."

"Since you're over the age of eighteen, it's up to you to notify your parents of your citation. Did you drive here tonight?"

"No. I walked from my dorm."

"Good, that's one less thing to worry about. Do you have someone you can call to come pick you up? We can't let you leave on your own." He slid a granola bar and a bottle of water across the table. "You can take as much time as you need."

"I'm feeling pretty sober now as it is." She folded the citation in half and carefully stood, holding on to the table with one hand as she gathered the snacks in the other. It was humiliating enough to be cited for underage drinking less than a month before she turned twenty-one. The last thing she needed was the humiliation of tripping and face planting on the sidewalk.

"Maybe try and make better decisions next time."

She ignored him, instead shuffling down the sidewalk and easing down into a sitting position on the curb. Unscrewing the cap from the water bottle, she took a quick swig and then pulled her cell phone out of her pocket. The light flashed on: one-thirty in the morning. Her roommate was not going to be happy.

Tapping the face of the phone, she dialed Cora's number and waited. The rings seemed endless, longer than normal. Voicemail.

Madison swore under her breath. Scrolling through the contact numbers in the phone, she tapped the number for her dorm room. Where in God's name was she? She'd refused to come to the party, insisting she had to cram for her Advanced Tax Calculations final instead. Anyone who was willing to skip out on the always entertaining gentlemen of the Tri Chi Fraternity was no doubt snug and warm in bed at that hour—alone.

"Hello."

"Cora?" Madison peeled the wrapper back from the granola bar. Oatmeal raisin: disgusting. Her bad luck continued. "It's Madison."

"What time is it?"

"One-thirty, look, I need you to come pick me up." She took another swig of water and judged the steadiness of her hand. Her coordination seemed fine; who was to say she couldn't walk back to her dorm?

"Pick you up? Where are you?"

"I'm, ah, funny story actually, I'm still at the frat house. I kind of got a citation for underage drinking."

There was silence on the other end of the line. Cora was silent for so long that Madison thought the call dropped, but finally, she responded. "You don't 'kind of' get a citation. Your birthday is next month."

"Yeah, that's been pointed out a couple times already. I just really need you to come and get me."

"Did they call your dad." It was a statement, not a question.

"Step-dad." Madison balled up her fist and pressed it to her forehead, pounding it in time with her pulse. "That's what I'm trying to avoid. Can you just come get me? It's like, a thirty second drive."

"You seriously want me to drive three blocks to frat row? Just walk."

"I'm fairly sure the police won't let me walk."

Cora huffed into the phone. "You owe me. I'll be there in a couple minutes."

The call disconnected.

Madison took another swig of water and rubbed the back of her neck with her hand. God. The last thing she needed was her step-father to find out. It was inevitable and when he found out…she didn't want to think about it. She was also fairly sure she had, in fact, fucked Arty the hipster douchebag and she didn't want to think about that either. Hopefully she'd had some semblance of sobriety to at least point out to him it was a one-time thing.

Fucking hipster. This was somehow his fault, it had to be.

A familiar white Volvo crept down the street and slowed to a stop in front of her. It took several moments for Cora to roll down the manual crank window; her brow was knitted in a frown. "Do I need to sign something to bail you out?"

"For a citation?" Madison eased to her feet and checked her balance. Not bad. "As far as I know, I'm free to go. Well, at least for ten days."

"Then what happens?"

Madison shuffled around the car and crawled into the passenger's seat. "Then I have to respond. Oh, and go to court. I'm sure my step-father will be especially pleased with that part."

"Jesus Christ."

"It's been a pretty epic night of failures. Oh, and I fucked an engineering student."

"Typical."

Madison unfolded the citation. She was still tipsy enough that the words wobbled and swayed in front of her. Her step-dad was going to see words like *citation* and *crime* and go through the roof. Hell, he could see her name listed in conjunction with terms like "citation for meritorious service for the prevention of crime" and freak out. Richard Essington was the human equivalent of boiled oatmeal. He liked structure. He liked schedules. And he especially liked being President of Monongahela University of Western Pennsylvania, where he could monitor her academic achievements and ensure nothing remotely resembling "fun" or "shenanigans" happened in her social calendar.

Shit.

Chapter Two

The voicemail from her step-father was to the point: "My office. 10:00am."

There were no extraneous threats, no "If you know what's good for you, you won't be late." There didn't have to be—she knew that tone. She'd heard that tone a lot since she was twelve. Richard Essington was never an abusive man; he was the king of guilt trips and revenge, Mr. "It's a shame I have to be so disappointed in you" parenting fail.

His secretary, Mary Beth, was staring at the doorway when Madison slid into the outer reception area. She raised her hand in a half-wave. "Good morning, Madison. President Essington is just finishing up with a conference call. He asked me to have you take a seat until he's ready. It should only be a few more minutes."

President Essington, for Christ sake. She was surprised he didn't decorate his office like the Oval Office or issue school currency with his picture on it. Douchebag.

Ten minutes into her wait, she knew he was proving a point. Despite the fact he'd been married to her mother for nearly eleven years, she wasn't entirely sure what the man's occupation entailed. When he became President of the University, she knew even less. All she knew for sure was that he wrote an article for the alumni magazine. Sometimes he made phone calls. Other than that, she assumed he sat in his office, doing as she did now: playing mindless games on an iPhone.

"He'll see you now, you can go on in." Mary Beth nodded to the still closed door. How did she know? Text? Instant message? Mind chip?

Madison shoved her phone in her pocket and hoisted her bag over her shoulder. It was about damn time. If he pissed around any longer, she'd be late for class.

He didn't look up as she entered the office, instead keeping his focus on his computer screen. His hand rested delicately on top of the wireless mouse. He moved it back and forth over the mouse pad with conviction—probably difficult moves in solitaire or something equally unimportant.

"I have class in eleven minutes." She consulted the clock on her iPhone. "It's going to take me four minutes to get to Ferris Hall, so…how exactly can I help you?"

"Close the door," — he still didn't look up — "and sit down."

She complied, setting her bag on the floor. *And we're off.*

"Your mother and I are disappointed in you."

"Okay."

"You couldn't even be bothered to discuss it with us? At least let us know something happened?"

"It happened about eight hours ago. I hardly think we're outside the statute of limitation for letting you know I got a citation."

"I hope you don't think you're going to get away with this. It's a serious concern, both academically and ethically." His eyes remained transfixed on the computer screen. "Your future is at stake, especially if you think you're going to move forward toward graduate school."

"It's not a big deal—"

"It is a huge deal."

"Look, I have class I need to get to. If you insist on reprimanding me, can we do it later? I have a paper to turn in and a speech to give in seven and a half minutes."

"You're treading on thin ice, Madison. I will not permit this type of behavior on my campus and certainly not in my family."

"Are you threatening me?" She narrowed her eyes. Bastard. The fact he couldn't comprehend why she hated him so much was mind boggling.

He double clicked the mouse and then pressed his fingers to the keyboard; slowly, impeccably, beginning to type. "You can go."

She rolled her eyes, throwing her bag over her shoulder as she trudged to the door. She wanted to slam it, to punctuate her disdain for him. He was infuriating, from the way he used a keyboard to the way he thought he could run her life. "No preferential treatment just because you're my stepdaughter." She wanted to give him a newsflash: being a jackass was not preferential treatment.

And he wondered why she drank.

* * * *

A fifteen minute wait for a chicken salad sandwich on a croissant instead of a hamburger bun was preposterous, yet Madison was willing to let it slide this time. What other pressing matters did she have? There was only one final left to worry about—WWI Comparative Perspectives—and her mother's telephone calls to avoid. Somehow it seemed easier to roam around the Barista and debate what flavor of potato chips best accompanied chicken salad and diet Mt. Dew.

She swung her bag to her other shoulder. Now that classes were over, she'd have to start packing up her belongings in preparation for moving home. Thank God summer would be busy with the Normandy trip. Her step-father would no doubt make life unbearable...at least, more unbearable than usual.

"Madison. Hey."

She wanted to slam her hand in the refrigerator case door. Repeatedly. "Anthony. How delightful."

He flashed his impish, crooked smile. It'd seemed so adorable when they'd started dating. Now she wanted to smash a bag of chips in his face. "Are you okay, Maddy? I heard what happened last night."

"I'm fine, Anthony, thanks for asking." She snapped a bag of chips from the display and stormed to the counter. How long did it take to scoop chicken salad onto a croissant?

He was right behind her. "How did your step-dad handle it?"

"Okay, you know Tricky Dick." She avoided looking into his chocolate hued eyes. She wouldn't fall for his Italian charms—again. "He was a real peach."

"Maddy, can we go somewhere and talk? I think we have a lot to talk about."

"We have nothing to talk about, Anthony."

"Maddy, please. Give me another chance." He touched her hand. "We were good together."

She ignored the surge of electricity in her veins. "I gave you about four chances, Anthony, and despite that, I still caught you fucking Sarah Radford in the parking lot. The *parking lot*, Anthony. She sounds like a God damned wildebeest."

"I know, I know, it was a mistake." He paused and took a deep breath, as if he was grounding himself. She felt herself leaning forward. "And I'm sorry."

"Anthony, no." She debated throwing the chips down and just leaving the Barista. No sandwich was worth this. "I told you before, obviously I have to tell you again. There is no 'we' anymore. There's you. There's me. You can't keep doing this."

The hair netted Barista girl moseyed to the counter. "Chicken salad on a croissant?"

Madison pushed past Anthony and snatched the Styrofoam container out of the girl's hands. She barely mumbled a thank you, instead throwing herself into the line at the register.

It wasn't that easy to lose her ex. He was right beside her, again, blathering on about change and regrets and love.

Ha—love. Yes, there'd been a point when she would have dropped out of school to marry Anthony Bautti. But Anthony had the persistent habit of always making her third to everything else: usually right behind hockey and other girls.

She wasn't about to put up with that shit.

"Look, I'm flattered you feel this way, but you need to get over it. We're through. Over."

"I can't lose you."

"Anthony," she groaned, pawing through her bag in desperate search of her student ID/meal card. "I can't do this right now. I'm stressed. I'm hung over. I'm just not in the mood to be a spectacle in front of half the student body."

He reached around her and handed his ID to the cashier. "I've got this one."

"You don't have to do that."

"I want to."

She sighed, uncomfortable with his sudden show of generosity. It didn't feel genuine, not entirely. She was fairly sure he was just trying to buy her affection. She wasn't that type of girl, but if she was: chicken salad and chips? Really?

The cashier loaded her lunch into a plastic bag and slid it across the counter. Anthony adjusted the handles, deliberately running his fingers across hers as he handed her the bag. "Call me if you need me, especially if things get ugly with your step-dad."

"Thanks." She watched him saunter away, the fabric of his black t-shirt smooth across his broad shoulders. There was no denying he was gorgeous. He knew he was gorgeous; he reveled in it. And he also knew part of her was struggling getting over him. Anthony was like a pair of old shoes, albeit expensive Italian old shoes. He was comfortable. He'd been through everything with her. They were a match set.

Unbelievable. Things couldn't possibly get any worse.

Chapter Three

She received her court summons in the mail the next morning. And, ten minutes into her last final, she received a voicemail message from her academic advisor, Dr. Ruzich.

Much like her step-father's was the day before, it was short and to the point: *Madison, please come to my office as soon as you can. I'll be available until noon.*

As she climbed the steps of the student center, Madison exhaled with the vehemence of a charging bull, so loudly a nearby student glanced quizzically in her direction. Nothing good ever came from a spur of the moment advisor meeting. No good was going to come from this one—she was fairly sure of that. It could only be about one thing.

Dr. Ruzich's office was the "dorm room" of tenured professor's offices: small, cramped, and with room dimensions too strange to adequately hold a standard size desk and chairs. Even so, she managed to cram two bookshelves on either side of the desk and a small one behind her, working solely from an iPad. Books were neatly stacked on the shelves and on her desktop. Not a paper was out of place, despite the lack of space or storage.

She didn't look up as Madison edged in the room. "Hello, Madison. Thanks for coming in on such short notice."

"It's bad, isn't it." She said it as a statement, not a question.

"It's bad." Dr. Ruzich pulled a file folder from a stack and opened it in front of her. She flipped through the papers clipped inside and ran her finger down a familiar form. The citation. "I'm sure I don't need to say anything else about what happened. The department head reviewed the case this morning."

"Dr. Emerson reviewed it or my step-father asked Dr. Emerson to review it?"

"Madison." Dr. Ruzich momentarily closed her eyes. When she opened them, she looked back at the file folder. "Dr. Emerson reviewed the case this morning, and the department decided to revoke your acceptance into the Normandy program."

She felt her stomach lurch to one side, as if she'd just plummeted face first from a plane and onto Omaha Beach. Her mouth ran dry; she licked her lips. "Are you kidding me? I wasn't the only one at that party who was given a citation. A citation, may I remind you. I wasn't arrested. I didn't run someone over with my car. I was given a citation for underage drinking."

"You're right. There were other people cited at the party. But none of them were the so-called 'golden child' of our history department. People had expectations for you, Madison. You were well on your way to being accepted into the masters/doctoral program this fall, but now that's put on hold. They wanted to throw you out of the program completely. It was recommended you be placed on academic probation."

"I assume the recommendation came from my step-father, who no doubt also recommended I be kicked out of the doctoral program before I was even accepted." She could feel her pulse pounding away in her temple, a cadence she felt like replicating with her fist against the desk. This couldn't be happening.

"I'm not going to lie. Dr. Essington had a lot to say at the meeting today." Dr. Ruzich held up her hand to silence her before she could speak. "Dr. Emerson was strongly against throwing you out of the program. The department as a whole doesn't want you thrown out of the program."

Madison huffed, digging her fingernails into her knuckles until she left crescent shaped indentations in her flesh. "So what does that mean?"

"Right now it means you won't be going to Normandy with us."

Madison stared down at the file folder and crossed her arms over her chest. There was nothing to say.

"The good news is, your application to the joint masters/doctoral program will still be reviewed in the fall. Your citation won't be mentioned in the official department recommendation, pending your completion of the court's determined sentence. Besides, by the fall you will be twenty-one, and you can petition the court to wipe your official record clean."

"So, basically my step-father has assured I won't get accepted into the program." Madison hunched forward in her chair and pressed her palms to her forehead. She then sat upright and wildly motioned around the room, as if talking it out in pseudo-communicative dance would help solidify her point. "I needed the Normandy trip to get me in. You said so yourself; a dig backed by the French government and the American Monument Association was a rocket launch in. I worked my ass off to even get put on the Normandy trip. I sorted and documented nail fragments at Fort Necessity for seventy-two hours straight for god's sake. My qualifications are pretty slim to none—Normandy was going to *be* my qualification. What I am supposed to put on my application now? Trust me, I'm really good at what I do despite being a drunk?"

"I know, Madison, I know." Dr. Ruzich held her hands up as if in submission. She leaned back in her chair and plucked a pen off the desk, twisting the cap around. "Dr. Emerson and I discussed it at length. His recommendation was a different project. It's obviously not on the scale of the Normandy dig, but it's good. It's extremely good."

"Okay."

"The Gettysburg Foundation acquired the Spangler Farm several years back and, despite the fact renovations aren't even close to being complete, they're ready to open it up to the public. Before they can do that, they want to conduct a small archeological survey of the area. Nothing fancy, just a few small test pits and a brief write up. The dig team is set, but lucky for you, Dr. Emerson's nephew is heading it. He offered to add you to the roster."

"You say that like there's a catch."

"The only catch is that we don't know what your sentence will be and if the court will allow you to go to Gettysburg. From what I can tell, most of those cited for underage drinking in the state are sentenced to community service, a fine, or alcohol rehabilitation classes. I don't see why you couldn't complete those in Gettysburg, but ultimately that's up to the court to decide. When is your hearing?"

"Two weeks, on the twenty-fourth."

"Dr. Emerson needs a solid answer by next week. The dig is scheduled to start the first of the month." Dr. Ruzich leaned forward and tented her fingers in front of her, delicately resting her chin on her fingertips. "Can you give me a tentative answer? Because, worst case scenario, you go down and start working the dig, come back for the hearing, and see what your options are from there."

"I want this."

"I knew you would." Dr. Ruzich leaned back in her chair and picked up her iPad. She ran her fingers over the screen, obviously composing an email. "I'll let Dr. Emerson know so he can get you set up with housing and hopefully some kind of stipend. You need to call me after your court date in case there're any issues we need to work around. Are you utilizing a lawyer?"

"I hadn't really thought about it."

"It might be something to consider."

"It was a citation for underage drinking. Not a DUI."

"I know. Hopefully that works in your favor."

Madison swallowed hard. Of course Dr. Ruzich sounded ambivalent—it wasn't her name on the citation. Or on the history department's hit list. "You know, Alonzo Cushing—who died at the Battle of Gettysburg— said that although he didn't expect to last the war, he expected to make a name for himself. Similarly, I don't expect to get into grad school. But I've already made a name for myself."

"Just be honest." Dr. Ruzich smiled with such warmth that Madison almost felt better. Almost. "Stop worrying, Madison. It doesn't accomplish anything. You'll get this straightened out and you'll move on. We're all allowed one screw up."

"Tell that to my step-father." Madison stood and hoisted her bag over her shoulder. "Thanks, Dr. Ruzich."

"My door is always open."

The walk back to the dorms always seemed to take forever. Today it seemed twice as long. Kicked off the Normandy dig. Her step-father was playing his hand and trying to prove some ridiculous point. What better way to do it than take away what she wanted most? She had suspicion he wasn't making a show of his superiority because of a moral aversion to her drinking. More likely—and more true to his character—was that he was doing it to show he could. He always got his way. He always won.

Fine. Let him have Normandy. She had Gettysburg.

She pursed her lips together. Gettysburg. Great. Not that she didn't love the Civil War as much as the next history major, it just didn't seem on the same par as Normandy. Not as elite. And, in turn, despite what Dr. Ruzich implied, it didn't really seem like it would be enough to get her into the Masters/Doctoral program.

Jamming her key into the lock, Madison shoved her dorm door open and stalked inside. Cora was gone—probably for the best—and it took every reasonable sinew in her body not to chuck her backpack across the room. *Son of a bitch.*

The court summons was where she'd left it: discarded at the foot of her bed. She snatched it up and scanned the instruction form. Two weeks. It amounted to fourteen days of too much free time, time to sit and ponder if she'd ruined her career before it even started.

It was going to be a long two weeks.

Chapter Four

The court room was stuffy, an interior room tucked in the bowels of the county court house. It was evidently long overdue for the upgrade to central air conditioning. The benches were uncomfortable, the stain worn off from nearly sixty years' worth of fidgeting civil servants and irritated accused. She fell into the latter category. After nearly forty-five minutes of waiting, the backs of her knees were starting to sweat. She wondered if sweat stains would be visible through her black dress pants. Was that something that would diminish her already shaky credibility?

"Madison Monroe."

Time to find out.

She stood from her bench and tugged on the hem of her silky blue blouse, holding her chin high as she walked to the front of the court room. It was like some kind of bizarre game show. She was making her way to the platform for the Russian roulette of court appearances. No lawyer. No well-wishing parents in the audience. Just a rapid internet search on underage drinking laws in the state of Pennsylvania and the input of a former roommate who had switched to pre-law.

You got this, Madison. You'll be fine.

The judge looked bored out of her mind, so much so that she'd obviously gotten to the point where she no longer felt the need to feign interest. She shuffled through a stack of papers and glanced at her over the tops of bright turquoise glasses. "State your name for the record."

"Madison Elizabeth Monroe."

"You received a citation for underage drinking on April 11th?" The judge paused and looked up at her for a moment. "I see your birthday is May 10th."

"Yes ma'am, that's correct. May 10th is my twenty-first birthday."

The judge shook her head and looked back at the citation. "Do you plead guilty or not guilty of your charge?"

"Guilty, ma'am."

"I trust you've learned a valuable lesson here." She again peered at Madison and then back down at the papers, carefully lettering information on a form. "But I think some community service might help reinforce that lesson."

Madison had hoped maybe the judge just had a giant "guilty" stamp she could slam down on all citations. How disappointing. "Ma'am, I'm taking part in an exclusive archeological dig in Gettysburg starting May 1st. I was wondering if I could take Alcohol Education classes in lieu of community service. The local college in Gettysburg offers a program through the Adams County Court system for Alcohol Rehabilitation and Education."

"So, what you're proposing is," —the judge glared at her— "you want me to let you enjoy your summer."

"Well…an archeological dig is actually a lot of work. It's manual labor: digging, cleaning, cataloging. And…it's school sponsored. I have these printouts from the Adams County Court system." Madison looked down at the printed pdf file she'd brought with her: *So You Got Caught Drinking: Now What?* Suddenly this didn't seem as good of an idea as it had before. "It's…well, the program still requires I plead guilty and pay the fine. But I'd also go through the classes as laid out by the court. I know similar classes are offered through my college and are often recommended by this court—I'd just be doing the same thing in a different county."

The judge looked skeptical, but despite any reservations she may have been formulating, she held her hand out and twitched her fingers. "Bring them here."

Madison awkwardly shuffled to the front of the courtroom and handed the papers to the judge.

Her eyes scanned them, her face as emotionless as Mt. Rushmore. After a few moments she spoke. "Miss Monroe, I am well versed in our county's underage drinking rehabilitation classes. I think it's an excellent program. This program seems to be of similar requirement and curriculum. I'll grant it, however, with the stipulation that your dig supervisor also act as sponsor and sign off that you attend the classes as designated. Is that reasonable?"

Madison slowly exhaled. "Yes, ma'am."

The judge handed the papers back to her and then scribbled her name on her paperwork. "With the guilty plea and your agreement to partake in rehabilitation classes, I'll set a reduced fine of two hundred fifty dollars. You can pay in the clerk's office on the first floor. I caution you, Miss Monroe. You seem like you have a good head on your shoulders. Let's see that this is just a juvenile mistake."

"Yes, ma'am. Thank you, ma'am." Madison accepted the forms back, feeling as if she'd just earned a knighthood from the Queen of England. The dig was a go.

Chapter Five

The trip from the suburbs of Pittsburgh to Gettysburg took nearly five hours, due to the fact she hit an obscene amount of traffic through 'The Steel City' and her 1995 Dodge Neon had a hard time getting up over sixty-five miles per hour. Although she called her car, among other things, "a tank" and "The Blue Meanie," the truth was the car was one hiccup short of a scrap heap. But it was paid off. It got her where she needed to go. And it had two white racing stripes up over the hood and over the roof—it was a Neon desperately trying to be a Mustang. She loved it.

She did not love, however, the lack of information Dr. Emerson had given her on what precisely she needed to do once she got to Gettysburg. "Don't worry about it." He'd sounded so confident on the phone. "My nephew will meet you at the hotel and get you checked in. You're going down the night before so you'll have plenty of time to get settled in. I told him to take you to dinner. No drinks though, Madison, remember that." He'd laughed, a humorless giggle that alluded to a shared joke, when obviously there was absolutely nothing funny about it.

"Hilarious." Madison turned The Meanie onto Steinwher Street, the main drag through commercialized Gettysburg and evidently the location of her hotel. She hoped she wouldn't be getting lost anytime soon, as she was fairly certain she couldn't pronounce the street name.

Her hotel was a chain hotel, a giant sprawl across from several normal looking chain restaurants. Aside from an ostentatious looking "General Pickett's Buffet", to the untrained eye, it looked like any other town in

Pennsylvania. She turned the car off, craning her neck as she peered down the street. It was kind of depressing, actually, that the battle that supposedly changed the course of the war seemed to have more t-shirt shops than museums. Maybe it was just this street.

As she turned back around in the driver's seat, she noticed a man ambling down the sidewalk in the direction of the parking lot. He was dressed in oddly muted tones and had a strange hitch to his step, like the joint of his hip didn't work correctly. The distance between them was still too great to adequately make out his features, but when she looked towards his face, the man stopped. He seemed to gape at her, his feet planted firmly as if he'd taken root in the sidewalk.

She shrugged to herself and leaned over to collect her bag from the passenger's seat. Either The Meanie's engine was on fire, or that was Dr. Emerson's nephew, Brad. Brad Emerson. She mentally practiced what she'd say, *Mr. Emerson, thank you so much for asking me to take part in this dig. It's a great opportunity. Letting me take part in this dig.*

She straightened up and looked out the window.

The man was gone.

Madison groaned. Perfect—maybe the word was already out that the drunk was in town. Lock up your sons.

Someone knocked on the car window. She jumped, slamming her hands down onto the steering wheel. Turning her head to the side, she saw a man peering into her car. Dammit, she'd run the bastard over! She fumbled to turn the engine in the ignition. Why in God's name had she turned the car off in the first place?

"Madison?" The attacker looked quizzical. "You're Madison Monroe, right?"

She hesitated. "Uh. Yes."

He cocked his head to the rear of the car. "I saw you pull in. You have a Monongahela University parking sticker on your bumper."

She stared at him.

"I'm sorry. I'm Brad Emerson. My uncle is Charles Emerson?" His face broke into a smile. "I didn't mean to scare you."

"No, I'm good." As she opened the car door, she glanced over her shoulder. Brad Emerson was dressed in a garish yellow polo shirt, nowhere near the muted color of the gaping pedestrian. Weird. But dismissible. She opened the car door and stepped outside, extending her hand to shake his. "It's nice to meet you, Mr. Emerson. Thank you so much for allowing me to join the dig. It's an honor."

His touch was gentle, but his eyes were somewhat too probing. "Brad—please. I'm sure I'm not all that much older than you."

Creeper. "Dr. Emerson told about the case of unfired rounds you found at a garage sale. That's pretty neat." Madison inwardly groaned. Neat? What was this, 1953?

"It was a surprise! And from the Allegheny Arsenal nonetheless. That's in Pittsburgh, isn't it? I'm sure you've been there."

"Uh, no." She followed him toward the front lobby of the hotel, inexplicably self-conscious. Something just didn't feel right. She tried to dismiss it. "It's not in the best part of town and, from what I've heard, there's nothing left. The city put up a plaque or something but, for a complex that was a major supplier of ammunition and blew up under pseudo-suspicious circumstances in 1862, it's pretty much forgotten."

"That's too bad." He didn't sound like he was actually listening. He sidled up next to the front desk and flashed a smile at the spectacled red head checking guests in. She visually melted. "Reservation under Emerson."

"Bradley?"

"Yes." He leaned against the desk, resting his chin on his hand. "The room name needs transferred to Madison Monroe."

The red head's eyes flicked over to Madison, a glare of unconcealed disapproval.

Madison waved and smiled with what she hoped translated as pep. "Hello."

The red head responded to Brad. "I'll need to see some ID."

Madison plucked her driver's license from her bag and slid it across the desk. The red head regarded it, but didn't touch it. "Fine."

Madison resisted the urge to roll her eyes.

Brad pulled his wallet from the pocket of his cargo shorts and withdrew a credit card. "Charge the room to my card...Jill."

The red head—Jill, evidently—picked up the card, again shooting a look of disapproval in Madison's general direction.

Madison ignored her. "You don't have to do that."

"My Uncle Charles is doing it, actually. I'm sure he told you about the stipend." Brad shook his head and flashed a smile at her. It didn't have the same effect as it did on the front desk girl. "It's his way of making up for it."

"I'll be sure to thank him." The "stipend" Dr. Emerson had managed to convince the Gettysburg Association to pay was seven dollars per day. Seeing as how her step-father had refused to chip in any money to help her while she was gone, she had a feeling her credit card bill was going to be insane after the dig was complete.

Jill slapped a printout on the desk. "Sign here. You're in room 255. It's on the second floor, but the designated parking space is in the back. You'll have to walk upstairs and back toward the front of the hotel. Continental breakfast starts at 6am, bar opens at 6pm."

Madison scribbled her name on the paper and snatched up the key. This was the kind of thing that drove her to drink. "Thanks."

Jill didn't respond.

Brad motioned to the front door leading from the lobby. "Okay, so, why don't you get settled in your room and meet me out front? I thought we'd just walk down the street to a local diner for dinner, if that's okay. Nothing fancy, but my treat." He paused and smiled at her again. "I know your stipend doesn't start until tomorrow."

"Sounds good. I'll just drop my suitcase off and be back down." Madison trudged back to the Blue Meanie and jammed the key into the ignition. After a subpar parking job, she dragged her oversized and over packed suitcase up the two flights of stairs and around the exterior of the hotel for what seemed like miles, until she found Room 255. It was pleasant enough, with a large king sized bed and flat screen television. There were a bizarre amount of chairs in the room, which she found odd, but it was clean and comfortable. What more did she need?

She shoved her room key into her back pocket and retreated back to the front of the hotel.

Brad was waiting next to a newspaper box. He smiled as she walked toward him. "Ready? I hope you're hungry."

"Actually, yeah. I just had a cheeseburger at a rest area on the turnpike like, six hours ago."

Awkward.

He led her down the sidewalk and across the street, stopping in front of a brick building with a chipped stone front façade. The sign overhead read: *The Gingerbread Man.* Opening the door, he motioned her inside. "After you."

The interior was dark. It took her eyes a moment to adjust. Brad had already made his way to a booth and was taking a seat. She followed suit, sliding in across from him. "I'll be honest, I expected the town to be busier than it is. I mean…this is Gettysburg. I thought everyone came here."

"They do, but usually more towards July." He flipped open his menu. "This place is a madhouse in the summer months, but it's a ghost town the rest of the year. I prefer it that way; it's more intimate."

She resisted the urge to gag. "Can you tell me about the dig? Dr. Emerson really didn't have many details other than it's at the Spangler Farm. Are we looking for anything specific?"

"There's always the hope we find 'The Major Find' but in reality, I think it's more going through the motions. The plan is to open the farm to the public for limited viewing by the middle of June, regardless of what we find or don't find. The main farmhouse and the barn still need extensive renovation, so once the tourist season is over, it will close again."

Madison idly flipped through the menu, searching for the item she was least likely to end up dripping or spilling on herself. Grilled cheese sandwich it was. "You don't sound overly excited about the plan."

He ran his hands through his sandy brown hair. "Not really. I mean, don't get me wrong, the opportunity to do a test dig anywhere at Gettysburg is an honor. So, as a student of history, I'm kind of overwhelmed. But as a professional, there's always the desire for more time."

"There's never enough time. College has, if nothing else, taught me that much."

"You should enjoy your time in college."

"I think we both know I've enjoyed my time just a little too much." She smiled awkwardly at him, heat flushing her cheeks. "No doubt Dr. Emerson filled you in on my...court appearance."

"My Uncle Charles is actually a champion of yours. Believe it or not, he's pretty crushed the history department took Normandy away from you." His voice trailed off as the waitress approached the table. He handed her his menu. "Pot roast sandwich and fries, gravy on the side please, and a water with lemon."

Madison handed her menu to the waitress. "Grilled cheese and fries, with a Mountain Dew."

Brad watched the waitress leave the table with enough interest to make Madison feel uncomfortable. He pulled a cell phone out of his pocket and slid his thumb against the screen. "A lack of field experience, yeah, but that comes with time. Your publishing credentials are mind blowing."

She flushed. "Research and I share a mutual fondness for each other."

"Well, you're being modest. I could name off twelve archeologists in our field who would kill for that kind of resume. No wonder Uncle Charles says you're what the field needs."

Madison blushed again. "Well...thank you."

"You are welcome." He smiled. "And look, the whole citation thing. It's really not a big deal to me. It's obviously a giant rod in someone's ass, but really, as far as I'm concerned it has no bearing on your career."

"I can tell you exactly whose ass it's up. My step-father. He's unfortunately also the president of my college, so I'm fairly certain he's just making an example out of me."

"Don't even worry about it."

"I still need to go to the rehabilitation classes. I have to turn the paperwork into the court system at the end of the summer. I'll be utilizing my time as best I can and simultaneously petitioning to have my record wiped clean." She paused as the waitress set her glass of pop in front of her. "I guess the college is right outside of Gettysburg?"

He nodded. "I called and got all the class information for you. Tuesday nights, from six to seven. No big deal. I'll sign whatever you need me to sign, just remind me."

"Sounds fair enough." She studied his features as he focused on his cell phone. He was attractive, maybe mid to late 30s, but there was something about him she flat out didn't like. Maybe it was the way his eyes seemed just slightly too close together or the way that they seemed to focus in on any female in a six mile radius. "So…the dig starts tomorrow? I haven't missed anything?"

He shoved his phone in his pocket. "The only thing you've missed is us trying to get permits in places permits should have already been issued. I had no idea I'd have to go through so much red tape to get park service heavy equipment to come and dig test pits on park ground for a park sponsored project. It's still not done."

"How many people are on the team?"

"Including you? Four. Plus me, but I have a feeling I'll be running interference between the site and the park service. I handpicked everyone. I've worked with them all before and consider them more my core

41

team of diggers. I think you'll get along with everyone. It's hard to be the new kid in town, especially when you're coming onto a team that's already set in its ways."

"So everyone has worked together too?"

"When we can. Our last dig together was about four months ago; we were working outside of Baltimore where they'd proposed extending the light rail system. It was a similar circumstance to this: get it done fast, turn in your report, and call it a day."

"Seems as frustrating as living with my step-father."

"No doubt." He smiled at her. "I can pick you up tomorrow and drive you to the site. I'm coming from this direction, anyway."

"That sounds good!" *No it didn't.* "I am notoriously bad at directions. Even with a GPS system in my car, I still would need printed directions and a walkthrough on google maps. And I'm still sure I'd get lost."

"Good things are going to happen with this dig. I just know it." He looked so hopeful, so excited, that for a brief moment he lost his creeper aura and instead looked like the excited, young archeologist she desperately wanted to emulate. At that moment, his eyes dropped to her breasts and then back up to her face. She inwardly groaned. Feeling passed.

"What time do I need to be ready?"

"I'm aiming to get there by 8am. So, be ready to go at 7:30. It won't take us the full half an hour to get out to the farm, but I'm doing my best not to be late." He smiled again, running his hands through his hair in a mirror image of his earlier movement. "I'll bring donuts."

"You've got a deal."

"I know we weren't your first choice, but trust me. We're thrilled to have you." For a brief moment, there was a crack in his bravado. He almost looked sheepish; almost, but not nearly enough for her to let down her guard.

"It's going to be epic." Epic seemed a safe enough description for whatever it was she was in store for. Brad Emerson seemed perpetually two steps away from a restraining order. It was either going to be an epic disaster or epically awesome.

And either way, it was far better than sitting at home being shunned by her step-father.

Win.

Chapter Six

He pulled into the hotel lot at 7:30am on the dot, so precise, in fact, that she wondered if he waited at a parking meter down the street and then just rolled up to her room on time to impress her. She wasn't impressed. Not completely.

Swinging her bag over her shoulder, she pushed her sunglasses back into her hair and headed out to his oversized pickup truck. "Good morning."

"Hey." He cocked his head to the backseat. "Put your bag back there and help yourself to a donut. Get your pick now before Liam and Mike decimate them at the site."

She climbed up into the passenger's seat as if she were climbing Mt. Everest and tossed her bag in the back. The bakery box was nestled in between her seat and Brad's. She lifted the lid back to reveal oversized golden donuts topped with a thick layer of chocolate frosting. "These look phenomenal."

"They taste even better. I could care less what everyone likes in their donut selection. These are the best you'll ever have."

She plucked a donut from the box and gingerly took a bite, trying her best not to get the frosting all over her face. She had a feeling it was a futile attempt, but the potential mess was worth it. The flaky donut melted in her mouth, the chocolate frosting mixing with a delicate, whipped vanilla cream overflowing from the center. It was heaven in pastry form. "Oh my God."

He laughed. "I told you. I had to drive forty-five minutes out of my way to get them, but they're worth it. It's this little, tiny hole in the wall shop named DeLuca's.

Anytime I'm working a dig even remotely close to there, I stop."

"I can see why. Taste why?" She shrugged. "I hope you won't think me piggish if I insist on having two."

"Help yourself! You'll need the sugar rush to keep you awake. The heavy equipment won't get to the site until 9:30. We're going to have a lot of down time before we even get started."

"Time to form your game plan."

"Something like that." He eased the pickup around a sharp turn and onto a road through a residential area. "We've been given pretty specific instructions on very specific places we're allowed to dig and not allowed to dig."

"The park service frowns on relic hunting; even at Ft. Pitt in Pittsburgh we had signs hanging up prohibiting it." She paused, the corners of her mouth twitching up into a smile at the thought of previous summers working at the pre-Revolutionary War block house. "And since the fort is located in the middle of a major metropolitan area, I'm sure relics are few and far between. But, you know. Just in case."

"You have no idea. I had to sign and initial paperwork promising we'd stick to our allotted area and not trip and fall onto the battlefield and accidentally pull out a shovel full of dirt."

Madison glanced out the window. "Isn't the battlefield like, three miles from the site? I'd think the difference in area would be somewhat noticeable."

"You'd think. But as you said, you know. Just in case."

The silence between them as they ate their donuts was surprisingly comfortable. She had no idea where they were at and somewhere, in the back of her mind, was the nagging concern he was dragging her off into seclusion to kill her. Surely not. If he was that kind of creeper, Dr. Emerson would have had some kind of inkling and, in turn, concern for her safety, right? The donuts couldn't really be a ploy…right?

It would have been a good ploy. *Death trap donuts.*

He slowed the truck down and carefully turned onto a gravel road. It was transected by a wooden fence. Tacked to the leftmost side was a large white sign with red letters. *Area Closed: National Park Service Battlefield Reclamation Program. Authorized Personnel Only.*

Nice.

The gravel gradually gave way to a simple dirt road leading up to an enormous red barn. The structure was flanked by a vinyl sided farmhouse and small stone structure, most likely a summer kitchen. The surrounding fields were overgrown with thick grass and patches of wild wheat—obviously the main focus of "reclamation" was on the buildings and, maybe, the archeological dig.

Vague panic welled up in her chest. Was anyone else actually there? Was it just going to be the two of them, awkwardly sitting around until a heavy equipment operator strolled to the site to dig the pits? Shit, she couldn't think of anything worse. Fifteen minutes in the car with him and she was already out of things to say.

Cars! Thank God, two cars were parked across from the barn, tucked back against the wooden fence and blocking a blue port-a-john. Great…outdoor toilets.

"Fuckers beat me here." He parked the pickup next to a white Jeep Wrangler. "They're just in it for the donuts."

Madison felt like she'd swallowed a sparrow. Her nerves had been reasonably calm prior to that point, but the prospect of meeting the rest of the crew launched her heartrate into over drive. She retrieved her bag and slid out of the pickup, following Brad toward the barn. The structure was fire engine red, which seemed blindingly out of place.

Two men strolled around the summer kitchen, the taller of the two waving his arms at Brad. "Did you get the donuts, man?"

Brad motioned at him with the bakery box. "It's the only reason you showed up, isn't it?"

"You don't pay shit. There's got to be some kind of perk to getting up at six am and then sitting in the sun, doing nothing."

"Mike, you were in the Army. It used to be your job to get up at six am to sit in the sun and do nothing." Brad handed the box to them. "Madison, this is half our crew. Probably the less desirable half: Mike Caldwell and Liam Stanish."

She let her gaze linger on Mike longer than she should have. He was tall and toned, his jeans and olive t-shirt ably accentuating his frame and muscular shoulders. Obviously former military, his hair was cropped close in a modified, "high and tight". His eyes were brown bordering on black; they locked on hers almost instantaneously. "Hey."

Hey. It was a disappointing start. "Hello."

The shorter man, Liam, snatched a donut from the box. He adjusted his weight from one foot to the other, regarding her with noticeable criticism. "Aren't you cute?"

"I do my best." She shrugged, taken aback. Liam was short and compact, the length of his plaid button-down shirt making him look strangely long waisted. He looked young—probably roughly the same age as Mike—but had a deeply receding hairline. "I like to

47

think I can rock a pair of jeans and a black t-shirt like no one else."

"Stop hitting on the new girl, Liam." Brad was smiling, but his tone was less than jovial. The closer she studied him, though, the smile was more of a grimace.

"I don't do girls."

"We know." Brad handed the box to Mike and started back to the truck. "Did you two start plotting out the pits? The excavator will be here in two hours, give or take."

"Nothing like pinpoint accuracy." Mike flipped back the lid of the bakery box and motioned to Madison. "Want one?"

"No thanks, I've already had one." Madison quickly ran her hand across her mouth. She felt like she had chocolate frosting all over her face. Shit, maybe she *did* have chocolate frosting all over her face. That would explain Liam's quizzical stare.

Liam spoke up as he helped himself to a pastry. "You could stand to eat another one, Slim. We all have to throw our weight equally around here and you are…how do I say it? At a severe disadvantage."

"I'm 120 pounds of coiled steel." Madison snagged another donut from the box. "But I'll see your challenge and accept it."

"That's a girl."

"Mike, where's Cianna?" Brad slammed the driver's side door shut. "She knew what time she had to be here, right?"

Mike shrugged his shoulders, a movement Madison found to be way more distracting than it should have been. "You know Cianna. She's late."

"Call her."

"I'm not calling her." Mike glanced at her and then cocked his head toward Liam. "You call her."

"Hell no, I don't like talking to her in person. Why would I want to call her?" Liam rolled his eyes toward Madison and, with great effort, sighed. "You'll love Cianna. She's all grace and charm and sophistication."

"So, you're saying she's a bitch."

"I like you." Liam elbowed Mike in the side. "You're sassy."

"Liam. Call her." Brad took the box back from Mike and handed him a plastic bag. "Save her a donut, guys, Jesus Christ. Look, I've got to run to the park service headquarters. There's some kind of issue with the excavator. Plot out the sites for the test pits. You remember where they're going?"

"I have it written down."

"Try and have it done by the time I get back." He ran his hand through his hair and glanced at Madison. "Do you want to come? I can use the company."

She hesitated. "I think I'll stay here and start pulling my weight, so to speak. Thank you, though."

He looked crestfallen. Shoving his sunglasses on, he turned from the group and headed toward the truck. "Try not to destroy anything while I'm gone."

"One time, man, one time!" Mike chuckled and peered into the plastic bag. "Twine and stakes, but no hammers. Typical. Good thing I brought my own. So, have you been here before?"

"Nope." She peered over her shoulder to the immense red barn. It was actually two floors, the larger upper area inaccessible from the back where they stood. The lower level was cut into separate storage areas and stables. A walkway ran between the two halves. From the distance she was at, the interior of the rooms were no more than open, gaping holes. Though light filtered in, there wasn't nearly enough so she could see anything in the shapeless dark. The blackness seemed darker than it should have, almost oily. She looked away.

"Well, allow me to give you the grand tour." He handed her the plastic bag and yanked open the door of the Jeep, withdrawing a medium sized toolbox. He rummaged through the box and withdrew two hammers. "Welcome to the Spangler Farm, the 1863 home of George Spangler and site of the 11th Corps hospital. Confederate General Armistead may have died in the summer kitchen to your left. Either that or he died in the kitchen inside the house, we don't really know. Union General Francis Barlow was also treated here. And fun fact, the barn is a Pennsylvania bank barn. Wounded occupied it from July first through the afternoon of the fifth."

"I'm guessing we're not allowed to dig inside the barn."

"You'd be right." He flexed his shoulders, the muscles in his back taut against the thin cloth of his shirt. "I'm not sure I'd want to, anyway. The lower level seems pretty sturdy, but that roof looks like it's made of matchsticks."

She glanced back at the barn. The shadowy interior seemed to pulsate against the sunlight, as if it was drawing it into its inky depth. *Stop it, Madison. If it's not a guy distracting you, it's the dark. Grow up.* "The, ah, outside is pretty…vibrant."

"Plywood. It pulls right off. They put it over the outside until they can redo the actual timber siding." He cocked his head toward the summer kitchen. "I left my bag in there, with our fancy schematics and log books. We only have four pits to plot out: one way to the back of the house, one way to the side of the barn, one way to the side of the summer kitchen, and one way back there by the woods. You know, close enough but not too close."

"Last summer I was on a dig at this historical house, Woodbridge, in Pittsburgh. We were allowed to dig just so deep in an area only over to here—not there—and damn it if we even went a millimeter too far in either direction, the curator almost had an aneurysm." She rolled her eyes. His last name was Quimby, his body shape so spherical she was afraid if he tripped he'd bounce across the property and into the road. "Despite his attempts to keep us from actually getting work done, we pulled up some pretty cool stuff."

"I read your paper on it." He said it casually, like he was reporting to her how many hammers he was holding. "That's insane you found a clay pipe in such good condition."

She blushed. "Thanks."

Liam stormed toward them, gesturing with his cell phone. "I'm not even going to describe what that filthy bitch said to me. But she's fully aware she's running late. She doesn't care."

"I didn't think she would." Mike rubbed his temples with his fingertips and groaned. "Tell me again why she signed on? Especially after last time?"

"She thinks maybe Brad will change his mind." Liam rolled his eyes, fluttering his eyelashes dramatically. "You see, Sassy, Cianna Simon is obsessed with our fearless leader, Bradley Emerson. She likes the way he smells. She likes the way he walks and brushes his hair back from his face. We know this because she's told us this. She wants to hump him. He's not interested in her, which is surprising because Brad usually is interested in anyone of the female gender."

Mike chimed in. "We did this dig down in Baltimore not too long ago, just a quick survey at a historic structure. I got poison sumac. She hooked up with Brad and got rejected afterward. Harshly rejected."

"It was awkward. The look on her face, God, you'd think he'd just stomped on a kitten or something. I still don't know what she was thinking, he's her God damned boss. Maybe it's because she has herpes."

Madison nearly choked.

"You don't know she has herpes." Mike reached over to take the plastic bag from her. As he did, his fingertips brushed across her knuckles. She flushed, her pulse racing in her temples.

Madison. Get. A. Grip.

His eyes lingered on hers for a beat, but then he quickly looked away. "Okay, look, Brad's going to punch one of us if we don't have at least one pit roped off. Liam, you measure. Madison can tie the twine between the stakes. I'll do the hammering because...someone has to do it."

"And when Cianna gets here, she'll wait in the car until Brad gets back." Liam rolled his eyes. "Come on, Sassy, count them out. What are the dimensions supposed to be? I'll be honest. I didn't listen to a word he said this morning. Last week. Whatever. "

"Four by four, but they have to start five feet away from the side of the buildings. The one by the woods can be wherever." Mike stood against the outer wall of the summer kitchen and offhandedly gestured to the open lawn beside it. "So, I don't know. About there?"

Madison exchanged a glance with Liam. "That's a pretty precise measurement."

"Oh, for Christ sake." Liam handed Mike the end of the tape measure and stormed across the lawn. He turned back. "Five feet, prick."

Mike ignored him, instead picking up a notebook with his free hand. "Brad wasn't really specific where he wanted the pit positioned. So…your guess is as good as mine."

"I'd put it there." Madison gestured toward the open area across from the summer kitchen's door. "It's logical to assume if they tossed anything out that door, they'd have tossed in that direction. If they'd tossed it the other way, it would have landed on the path and they'd have to walk through it."

"Oh, Sassy!" Liam clicked his tongue. "She out nerded you there, Mikey."

Mike smiled at her, two deep dimples punctuating his cheeks. "That's okay by me."

She watched him cross the lawn to where she'd indicated and lean down, hammering the first stake into the dirt. His biceps were intense, not the overwhelming size of a man who worked out to be buff, but the well-toned upper arms of a man who wanted to stay in shape. And she liked his shape.

He straightened and stepped backwards, surveying the stake placement. "Looks good to me."

"It's crooked." Liam handed him the end of the tape measure and strolled off in the opposite direction.

"I wasn't looking for a critique."

Madison secured the end of the twine to the stake and followed Liam the requisite four feet. As Mike hammered in the next stake, Liam huffed and jammed his balled up first to his hip. "Jesus Christ, she's here already."

Madison watched a well waxed red car slowly ease down the dirt driveway and even more slowly pull into the spot next to Mike's Jeep. The woman who stepped out didn't look like any of the archeologists or history majors she'd ever met. Her blonde hair was cropped short, in an almost pixie style. Her eyes were hidden by huge, round sunglasses. She was dressed in black skinny jeans and a hot pink tank top layered over a white tank top. In one hand she clasped what appeared to be a plastic cup of iced coffee and in the other was a hot pink cell phone. She wasn't smiling.

Liam leaned closer to her. "Looks like she got a manicure."

Madison snickered, but glanced down at her own fingernails. They were clipped short and already had dirt underneath the tips. Attractive.

Cianna stopped in the shade of the summer kitchen. "Why are you putting that there? Shouldn't it be closer to the building?"

"No." Mike didn't look up from hammering in the stake. "This is where it's supposed to be."

"According to…" Cianna's voice trailed off. She pursed her lips together and looked between Liam and Mike. "Where's Brad?"

"He went to park headquarters." Liam scampered down the yard to measure out the next four feet, obviously not able to get away fast enough. "He left you a donut."

"I'm on a diet." She pulled her sunglasses off and smiled at Madison. "You must be Madison. I'm Cianna Simon. I've been working with Brad and the boys for years."

"Okay." Madison walked over and extended her hand to Cianna. "I'm Madison Monroe."

Cianna stared at her and, for a moment, Madison thought she was going to ignore the handshake. She finally reached out and limply squeezed her fingers, wiping her hand on her jeans as soon as she released her. "Charmed. So, you didn't stop them from putting the pit there?"

"I actually like it there."

"Is this your first dig?"

"No. I've worked around the Pittsburgh area and also did some work at Elmira Prison in New York." Madison paused, not entirely sure Cianna knew where Elmira Prison was, let alone that it was a Union prison.

"But not Normandy." Cianna's lips twitched as if she were suppressing a smile. "Right?"

"Right." Madison clamped her teeth down on her tongue. She wasn't going to get mad—getting mad would let the bitch win. "I'm apparently too good a time to go to Normandy."

"I'm surprised Brad let you on the team."

"I'm sorry." Madison leaned down to attach the twine to the stake. "Did I fall asleep and wake up back in high school? I'm not really sure how this is pertinent to anything."

"Just stating the obvious."

"Okay. Well, thanks." Madison strolled after Liam, stretching the twine taut. "Did you want to help or something?"

"I'm waiting for Brad to get here to tell me what I should do."

"Good talk." Madison leaned down and tied off the twine. She heard Cianna huff and, out of the corner of her eye, watched her stomp across the field and back to her car.

Liam snickered, quickly attempting to cover it with a cough. He cut the twine free. "That was hot."

"Her pants were inappropriately tight."

"You're a catty bitch like me. I love it."

Madison straightened. The feeling someone was watching her washed over her back and shoulders, leaving a trail of raised gooseflesh. She turned toward the barn and its black, pulsing lower level rooms, her heightened pulse leaving her dizzy.

Mike was standing in the gravel path leading up to the barn, watching her. He flushed when her gaze met his and he looked away for a moment. When he looked back, he smiled. "Want to help me out over here?"

Liam sucked in a sharp breath next to her. "Girl."

As she walked up the path, she noticed a figure leaning against one of the barn's lower level support beams. He seemed to be watching her, but from the distance she was at, it was hard to tell if his gaze was leveled on her or was looking past her to the summer kitchen. Weird.

Chapter Seven

When Brad returned to the farm, he arrived without an excavator.

"Where's the equipment?" Mike dragged his forearm across his brow, wiping away the sheen of sweat. The humidity was starting to rise and, although it wasn't overly warm, it felt oppressive when combined with the direct glare of sunlight. "If they don't want to run it, I can."

"How many pits did you get roped off?" Brad yanked open the truck's tailgate and pulled out a case of bottled water. He set it on the ground and then reached back in, withdrawing first one shovel, then a second.

"We got them all roped off but the one by the woods." Liam tilted his head toward Cianna's car. She was still in there. "We had a small disagreement over where we should put the pit by the house. Why are you unloading shovels?"

"Because it's the Gettysburg Foundation's opinion that we don't need heavy equipment and, in fact, they strongly feel that between the five of us, we can dig the pits in no time flat." He pulled out the last three shovels and tossed them to the ground. "That said, we'll need to revise our game plan."

Liam and Mike exchanged a look. Liam loudly cleared his throat and glanced back towards Cianna's car. "Do you really think there will be five people digging?"

"I'll make sure there are five people digging." Brad pulled a Leatherman from his pocket and sliced open the case of water. He withdrew a bottle and tossed it Mike. "You were in the Army. Doesn't that make you count as two?"

"Seriously, dude? She has to help sometime."

"She's got plenty of work to do." Brad handed a bottle to Madison. "I hope they didn't torture you too much while I was gone."

She stared past his shoulder toward the lower level of the barn. Though he'd disappeared for a while, the man was back, still leaning against the support beam. She looked away. "We had a good time."

"I had some time to revise our dig schedule while I waited at park headquarters. I think the easiest thing is splitting up into two teams. We've got the four pits and, ideally, four weeks to get this finished. We could put four of us on a pit and do a pit a week, but I think it will be better in the long run to have two diggers per pit and just split the month. Thoughts? Objections?"

"Yeah, just one." Liam took a swig of water. "Her name is Cianna. Whoever gets stuck with her is going to end up doing all the digging and all the work. I'm not digging a pit, sifting all that dirt, and cleaning all the artifacts while she sits and bitches that she chipped her nail polish."

"Liam. This time is going to be different."

"Brad. That's what you said last time."

"Work it out." He slammed the tailgate shut. "Get the last pit roped off and then get started on digging. I want the pit here by the barn and by the summer kitchen started today."

Madison picked up the plastic bag containing the twine and measuring tape. "As much as I love digging, I'm going to volunteer to finish plotting out the pit and let the men handle the manual labor."

"It's really a two person job." Mike flipped the hammer around in his hand and took the bag from her.

He headed back down the path to the summer kitchen. "Maybe by the time we're done, Cianna will have decided to finally get out of the car."

"I'm timing you." Liam raised an eyebrow. "Seriously, I know how long it should take."

Madison winked at him. "It being the operative word."

"Down girl."

She heard Brad make some sort of gurgled noise in his throat, but hustled after Mike well before he could comment. She didn't care what he had to say because, no doubt, it was going to involve the phrase *No no, let Liam do it.* They'd only be away from the group for a few minutes, anyway.

Mike cupped his hand above his eyes to block the sun. "Having fun yet?"

"I live for this, dude. Digging in the dirt and being up to my elbows in nail fragments is my happy place. Besides," — she reached out and snagged the bag back from him — "it's better than sitting at home remembering that I officially have a record other than my academic record."

"It's not like you killed someone."

"I pointed that out as well."

"Their loss is our gain." He stopped at the edge of the walking trail and looked out over the unmowed field leading up to the tree line. The grass was scrubby, interspersed with long shoots of wild wheat and thick, heavy boulders. It didn't appear to be the best ground for growing crops. "I have no fucking clue where he wants this one. This is what I've got written down: over by the trees. That could mean anywhere."

She strolled along the edge of the trail, touching the shoots of wheat with her fingertips. "Does he mean in the woods or here by the path?"

"I'd assume by the path. The park is going to put up waysides and signage back here for a self-guided walking tour. This whole farm was crawling with the 11th Corps. I think they even dragged artillery through these fields at one point. There's always the chance we find something."

"Yeah, always that chance." She abruptly stopped walking. For a moment, no less than a split second, she'd sworn she'd heard someone say her name. It was a whisper, a sound more like a tired exhale, but the cadence was there. Three muffled syllables without enunciation, trailing off into softly sighed silence. She turned and looked back toward the barn. Maybe it was Liam. Or Brad.

Mike caught her eye. "What?"

Or maybe it was nothing at all. "I think we should put the pit here."

"Why?"

"Why not?" She shrugged and pulled out a stake. "It seems like as good a place as any. Not a lot of big rocks on the surface. The trees are there. Criteria met."

"Makes sense to me." He took the stake from her and took a step backwards, surveying the area. "Maybe the far corner there, by you? Then stretch it out parallel with the barn?"

"I think it should go towards the woods."
Forward, not back.

"You sound pretty convinced."

"I'm usually right."

He shrugged again, his lips pursed in an obvious effort to hold back a smile. "Hey, you're the published professional. I mean, you know, we can just defer from my years of experience."

"If you'd like play the age before beauty card, you feel free." She crossed her arms. "But I still think I'm right."

"Twenty-eight is not old."

"I'm not saying it is, but if you're going to throw it out there, I'm going to point out the fact I was ten when you were eighteen. Take it as you will."

He tapped the hammer against his hip a few times and then pouted as he drove the first stake into the ground. "I'll concede, but only because I'm a gentleman. And because you're professionally ravishing."

"Hate me because I'm hotter than your girlfriend or because I drive a cooler car than you." She crouched down and tied the twine around the stake. "Not for my ability to be in the right place at the right time. Or inability, depending on your point of view."

He tossed her the measuring tape, holding it against the top of the stake as she paced out the requisite four feet. "What kind of car do you drive?"

"A 1995 Dodge Neon."

"I'm not going to qualify that as a cool car."

"You obviously have no taste in cars."

"I must have subpar taste in women too, because I don't have a girlfriend either."

She had to bite the inside of her lip to keep from smiling. Good to know. "It's not a socially awkward condition, I assure you."

"This coming from someone who no doubt has a boyfriend."

"Negative. I'll admit to being socially awkward, but I dumped my douchebag ex-boyfriend months ago." She abruptly shivered, gooseflesh spreading across her bare arms. "It's a lot cooler over here near the woods."

"You think?" He studied her. "I hadn't noticed."

61

"I'm freezing."

"Weak."

"If I get put on this pit, I'll be wearing a parka. This is ridiculous." The cold seemed to seep down her shoulders and coat her arms like thick oil. She rubbed her forearms in an attempt to generate warmth; it didn't help. "Maybe it's just an adverse reaction to thinking about my ex."

He pressed his fingers to her forearm. His hand was hot against her cool skin. "Jesus Christ, you are cold. Do you want to…stand in the sun or something? Maybe chip in and hammer this last stake in? Because, honestly, I'm a little concerned you're going to get hypothermic on me. I was in the Army. You can trust my judgment on this kind of thing."

The cold seemed to edge away at his touch. She flushed, feeling heat rise in her cheeks. "I think I'll survive."

"If you get this cold standing in the shade, God knows how much I'm going to have to egg you on to keep hydrated in the heat." He caught her hand in his and turned her arm over to better see her wrist. "That's a nice tattoo."

"I got it in New Orleans when I was sixteen. A guy named Voodoo Johnny did it for me. I told him I was markedly older and he didn't really seem to care." She glanced down at the watercolor fleur de lis inked on the inside of her wrist. "It was a gateway tattoo. I couldn't stop with just one."

"How many do you have?"

"Nine. They're all hidden, except for this one."

"So…what you're saying is, that a scavenger hunt is in order?"

Her breath caught in her throat. Hell, yes, a scavenger hunt was in order.

"Seriously, you two still aren't done?" Liam's voice broke through the somewhat cloudy thoughts in her brain. He glanced between them. "Why are you looking at her like that? Did I hear you say scavenger hunt?"

"Don't worry about it." Madison smiled encouragingly. "He was just openly mocking me for being cold."

Liam didn't look convinced. "How can you possibly be cold?"

The feeling was gone—for the most part. The lingering sensation of icy pinpricks on her skin made her shiver again. "I'm hard to explain."

"Obviously." He glanced between them again, his gaze markedly more critical. "Did you offer to warm her up?"

"Is there a reason you came back here, Liam?"

Liam clicked his tongue. "Brad's going to be jealous."

Mike hammered in the final stake. "So you didn't come back here for a specific reason."

"Getting away from Cianna is reason enough, but believe it or not, Brad has put her to work. She's currently in charge of ordering lunch for us. Yes, I too was surprised he'd give her an assignment so critical and important, but there you go." Liam rolled his eyes dramatically. "She was concerned she'd get her shoes muddy if she trekked *all* the way out here. So, instead she made me stop documenting soil samples for the reports and come fetch you. So, fetch, bitches. I'm starving."

"Sounds good to me." Mike's eyes slid back to her. "Ready?"

"I'm not one to argue with the suggestion of planning out our lunch break four hours early." She fell into step with them. "You both realize it's a ploy to get us to dig the pits after we eat though, right?"

"I think that's the only way we can get that bastard to pay for it."

Madison laughed. She glanced over her shoulder toward the pit, the nagging sensation she'd left something behind tugging at her to turn around. Her eyes flicked to the wood line—the man she'd seen earlier at the barn was leaning against a tree, his arms crossed casually across his chest. He was watching her, there was no doubt in her mind this time. His dark gaze was fixed on her movement.

Panic fluttered up in her chest. She and Mike had just been standing at the tree line; they'd practically stood next to him, yet, she'd never seen him. Never heard him.

Mike caught her eye. He leaned toward her, his arm brushing up against hers. "Is something wrong?"

"Nope." She forced a smile. "Just making sure I didn't leave anything back there. I'm notorious for that."

"Yeah, because you know we'll never be back there." Liam looked behind them. "I think you're good."

Madison glanced behind her again.

The man was gone.

Chapter Eight

The monotony of digging test pits was quickly replaced by the monotony of sifting dirt. Madison picked through the sifter tray. Just more rocks. Most likely they were still too close to the surface, but still, every shovelful of dirt had to be sifted and examined for artifacts. If—when—they hit a cache of artifacts, they'd expand the pit outwards or further down. Every movement was dictated by what they found, but the process would be the same: always a grid, always four by four.

"Brad, how deep do you want these starting out?" Mike eased a shovelful of dirt into a blue bucket and pushed it toward Liam. Despite Brad's earlier instructions, they were all working on the barn pit, dubbed Alpha Pit Bank Barn. "I feel like I'm digging a foxhole right now."

"Put Liam in, if he can't see over the top then it's too deep."

"Hilarious." Liam shook the contents of the blue bin onto the sifter and then collected the "clean dirt" from underneath. He emptied the sifted dirt onto a pile at the far end of the pit. "You're the first person to point out that I'm short. I'm fun size. I'm a stocking stuffer."

"Two feet should be fine." Brad made a notation in a notebook and headed back toward the pickup. "Look, I know this isn't how we do things. It's usually more meticulous and you know how much I prefer meticulous. The Park Service's ramp up schedule is tight. We have to be out of here in four weeks, like it or not, so they can open it to the public."

Madison picked through the objects on the sifter screen. Rock. Clot of dirt. More rocks. It seemed to her there wouldn't be a time crunch if Cianna would do more than sit on a blanket, crouched over a notebook. Shovel test pits were made to be small and things didn't get complicated until artifacts were pulled up. For as long as they'd been working, with as many diggers on the pit, they should have had all four started.

But, no. They had one.

She huffed into a loose strand of hair that had worked its way out of her messy bun. *You're lucky to be on this dig. Don't be critical.* No, no, she was still going to be critical. The distribution of tasks on this dig was like nothing she'd ever seen before. Whiny blonde in tight jeans gets to sit in the shade and watch while the other three worked. "So, Cianna, where'd you go to school?"

"I went to art school in Philadelphia."

"Art school?" Madison brushed her hands on her jeans. "That's…a unique way to get into archeology. Was it art history?"

"No." Cianna didn't look up from her notebook. "I took some art history classes, but I'm much more interested in process and technique. Watercolor, charcoal, pencil, oil. You know."

"Not really."

Mike snorted.

"Ultimately I'd like to work in an art museum or work as an art broker. I'm going through a watercolor phase right now, actually. I've collected some nice pieces, but I like working on my own." Cianna blew on the notebook and held it out in front of her, critically reviewing the face of the page. She placed it back on her lap. "I've been in some shows."

"Cianna Simon: Best in Show." Liam made no effort to lower his voice. He chuckled.

"I had some pieces in a gallery in Harrisburg." Cianna paused. "And countless pieces in Philadelphia galleries."

"Don't take this as bitchy," — Madison also paused, mimicking Cianna's dramatic speech pattern — "because admittedly, it's bitchy. But, why are you here? Do you like history? Do you like archeology."

"I like it. It's just not my passion."

"Okay…so, again, why are you here? I know kids at school who would sell a kidney to get on a dig like this." Madison stopped shaking the sifter and stared at her, suddenly transfixed on her crouched figure like she anticipated her to spontaneously combust. "You're just here to kill time or something?"

"Yeah? So?" She was defensive. "You're here because you're a drunk."

Mike and Liam simultaneously stopped working.

"True, but I'm a drunk about to graduate with a double major in history and anthropology." Madison turned back to the sifter. "And archeology is my passion."

Cianna didn't respond and Madison refused to look at her. Great. She really was the notorious drunk undergrad archeologist.

"Well, that escalated quickly." Liam put his hand on his hip, fully resembling a nearly bald, squat teapot. "But don't mind Cianna. She's on her period or something."

"Fuck off, Liam." Cianna crouched further over her notebook. "At least I'm not *fabulous* like you."

It was said in a cutting, homophobic way, sickening for someone who said herself she'd worked with him for nearly ten years. Liam didn't seem surprised or nearly as offended as Madison thought he should be. "I am fabulous, aren't I?"

"Hey, Mr. Fabulous." Madison picked an object off the sifter screen. "Want to take charge of the first official artifact?"

"You found something?" Mike launched out of the test pit. "Already?"

She rubbed the dirt off the object and then held it in her flattened palm. "To my highly trained eye, it's glass…from a modern age beer bottle."

Mike took it from her and studied it. "I love how, despite the fact that it's garbage, we still have to clean and catalog it. Hey, Cianna, did you hear that? We found glass. Modern glass. Can you write that down?"

"Yeah, Cianna." Liam pulled a black film canister out of his duffle bag and held it to Mike. "Unless you're too busy drawing to work. You remember work, right? That thing we do in between admiring the way the wind tussles Brad's hair?"

Madison turned, her anticipation of Cianna's response shattered by Brad yelling from the pickup. "Mike! Help me unload this second sifter!"

Her eyes shifted to the lower level of the barn, half expecting to see the curious stranger staring at her. He had seemingly left the property and yet, she still felt as if something was waiting in the stark blackness of the storage rooms. If she stared long enough, she could almost convince herself someone was in there, waiting. Watching; will her into walk inside. She shook her head to clean her thoughts and turned back to the dirt left on the wire screen. "Oh well, at least I have one fan."

Liam picked a few small dirt clods off the screen and crushed them between his thumb and forefinger. "Who? Mikey Caldwell?"

"Well, maybe. But, I was talking about that guy from earlier."

"What guy from earlier?"

"I don't know, some guy." Madison nodded toward the barn. "He was standing over there watching us this morning, and then I saw him a little bit ago in the woods. Tourists, you know? We got them all the time at Fort Pitt."

Liam frowned. "This place is shut down to tourists. The only people allowed here during the dig is us and park rangers."

She looked away from him, focusing on the sifting dirt in front of her. "Maybe it was just Brad."

"You hardly sound like someone who thinks it was Brad."

"Well, I'm easily confused."

Liam pressed his hip against the sifter, keeping her from moving it. "I don't want to sound like an authoritative bitch, but if someone's snooping around here, we need to let Brad know. The park has had a huge problem in the past with relic hunters and vandals. The last thing we need is someone fucking with our site."

"I know." She forced a smile. "I'm sure it was nothing. If I see him again, I'll flag you down."

He didn't look convinced, but let the sifter go.

She picked a few rocks and twigs out of the screen and tossed them aside. The last thing she wanted was to see him again. Glancing at the barn, she inwardly shuddered. She felt the gooseflesh spread across her arms. It didn't exactly feel like he'd left.

* * * *

Brad called it a day by five o'clock. Other than modern broken glass and rocks, they'd found nothing.

"Which is not surprising." Brad opened the passenger's side door of his pickup for her. "Tomorrow will be a better day. This is just the beginning."

Madison reluctantly crawled in the cab and let Brad close the door behind her. It reeked of thick cologne, like he'd just doused himself with a quart before letting her in the pickup. She glanced outside. Mike was in the driver's seat of the Wrangler; his eyes caught hers and he lifted his hand in a sheepish wave. God damn it, why couldn't he be the one driving her back to the hotel? She could invite him in, they could have a laugh, maybe stroll down to the saloon and grab a drink—

Brad slammed the driver's side door shut behind him. "Ready?"

"Yeah." She tore her eyes away from Mike and yanked the seatbelt across her chest. "So day one is down in the record books."

"It went like I thought it would." Brad shifted the truck into gear and pulled out of his parking place. "What did you think of the crew? They're my A-Team."

"They're great." Madison wasn't sure what was great about Cianna, other than the fact she was great at doing nothing but sitting in the shade wasting the Federal tax payers' dollars. "It seems like a good group of diggers."

"I wouldn't want anyone else on this dig with me." He glanced at her and smiled. "You are a great addition to our group."

"Thank you."

"Don't be modest. I've got four great diggers under me, all with diverse backgrounds and experiences. You being here just sweetens the pot."

Madison inwardly groaned. "Well, ah, just a reminder, I have my first rehab meeting tomorrow. It's at the college…you…ah, said you had all the information for me?"

"Yeah, it's no big deal. If you want, I can just sign off on your paperwork."

"Uh, I do need you to sign off on my paperwork, but I really need to go to the meetings." She shifted in her seat and adjusted the seatbelt. "It's kind of court ordered."

"Don't you think that's overkill?"

"Obviously. But, I want it off my record, so I'm playing along."

"Whatever you want. The meetings are in Reynolds Hall, right off the main drag. Parking is marginal, but I think most of the college kids have gone home."

"Hey, it's better than community service. I figure as long as I just answer, 'drink responsibly' I should be fine."

"I'm sure *you'll* be fine anyway."

She wanted to open the passenger's side door and jump into the ditch running beside the road. Riding in the Jeep with Mike and Liam would have been so much better. Hell, driving with Cianna would have been better than riding next to Creepy McCreepster.

When he pulled the truck into her hotel parking lot, she had to force herself from throwing the door open and leaping out before he completely stopped. "Well, hey, thanks again for the ride."

He smiled. Even that seemed oily and soaked in cologne. "Same time tomorrow?"

"Thank you, but I think I'll try and get there myself tomorrow. I have to be at the meeting by six o'clock, so I'll probably bail as soon as I can." She slid out of the cab and reached back in to grab her backpack. "At least it's only on Tuesdays."

He caught her hand and placed a business card in her palm. "I wrote my cell phone number on here. If you need anything tonight—or change your mind about carpooling—give me a call."

"I'll do that. Thanks." She pulled her hand back and shoved the card in her pocket. "Uh…have a good night."

"You too, Madison. See you tomorrow, eight o'clock sharp."

She shut the truck door quickly and waved at him, hustling across the parking lot and to the back door of the hotel. His eyes were on her—she didn't have to turn around to see him ogling her from the driver's side, it would be more surprising if he wasn't—and she couldn't get inside and up the stairs fast enough.

She burst into her hotel room and locked the door behind her, tossing her pack to the floor. What a weirdo. If he kept creeping up on her, it was going to be a long four weeks.

Once she'd showered and washed her hair, she pulled on a pair of black cropped yoga pants and gray Ft. Pitt t-shirt and flopped down on the king sized bed. Her mother had texted her three times.

Did you have a good day? How was your day? Hope it was a great day.

She swiped her finger over the face of her cell phone and entered a fast response.

Good day but I'm worn out. Motivating to walk across the street and grab some food. Dig crew is nice.

Getting into a more specific definition of "nice" with her mother wasn't worth the trouble it would cause. She didn't feel like exposing herself to the Spanish Inquisition this late in the day.

Her mother must have been sitting with her phone in hand; her response was almost immediate.

Be safe if you go out after dark. Love you!
Madison sighed.

It's not dark. Twenty people live in this town, but I promise to be careful. Stop worrying. Love you, too.

She slumped back against the pillows and sighed. Was it worth getting up and walking back down two flights of stairs, across the street, and down the road to get fast food? It had been over a year since she'd last been on a dig this involved; she felt like she'd been hit by a truck. Lounging around like a paperweight sounded entirely more desirable than moving. Or walking. Or doing anything.

A knock on the door jolted her from her drowsy relaxation. It was hesitant, almost a light rap instead of a purposeful pound.

Shit. It was probably Brad. She could just hear him, suave and coy, asking her out for dinner. Drinks. Dancing, maybe even snuggling, snogging, breakfast. Ugh, she'd rather poke her eyes out and puke.

She forced herself out of bed and to the window, pushing the curtain to the side and simultaneously steeling herself for the disastrous confrontation that was sure to follow.

It was Mike.

She snapped the curtain back in place and, nearly falling over the chair beside her, rushed to the door and yanked it open. "Hey."

"Hey." He glanced down her body, obviously taking in the yoga pants and Fort Pitt shirt. "You look busy. You're busy. I'm sorry."

"This is me not looking busy, but looking like the college bum I really am." She pushed the door back wider. "Do you want to come in? What's up?"

He grimaced and muttered under his breath. "Ugh, this sounded so much better in the car."

"Dude. Come on. You watched me nearly freeze to death standing in the shade; there's nothing you can say that could possible out embarrass that."

"Do you want to go get some ice cream?" He blurted it out like a fourteen-year-old boy asking a girl to a dance. "I was just thinking, you said you'd never been here before and I thought I could show you around town. Because I have been here before." He groaned. "I sound lame."

"You've swept me off my feet." She smiled shyly. "Let me put on legitimate pants and grab my wallet. It'll take like, two seconds."

"No cash. It's my treat."

She forced herself to close the door with restraint. It wasn't a date. It was just two archeologists going for a walk and getting ice cream and probably chatting about history. It just so happened one of the archeologists was paying for the ice cream of the other archeologist.

It kind of was a date.

Yanking on a pair of faded jeans, she shoved her feet into her flip flops as she buttoned the fly and threw herself at the door. At the last minute, she remembered to grab her room key and shove it in her back pocked. That would have been a disaster.

His eyes lit up when she opened the door. "Ready?"

"Almost forgot my key, but yeah, I think I'm set." She pulled her still damp hair back from her face and up into a messy bun. "I'm telling you, man, I'm a tornado of unfortunate circumstances. Like the little citation that ruined my life."

"I didn't want to ask about it, unlike Cianna." He started down the sidewalk, heading toward a neat row of shops and stores to the north-east of town.

"It is what it is." Madison shrugged. "My academic advisor at school doesn't seem to think it's going to impact me getting into grad school, but…who knows."

"You're got a lot going for you." He shoved his hands in his pockets, quickly glancing at her out of the corner of his eye. "I've read your journal submissions and campaign for Federal funding for Fort Pitt. Not everyone gets that kind of exposure before they even have their degree."

She flushed. "I also have a lot not going for me, namely the fact my step-father is the president of my school. He likes to constantly prove I don't get preferential treatment and, apparently, making an example of my nefarious behavior is the way he's doing it."

He guided her across the street and into a glaringly lit store. The interior was small and cramped, the far end completely taken up by the ice cream case. To the left was a shelf of knick knacks—ice cream scoops with Gettysburg emblazed on the thick, white handles—and to the right was the cash register and small coffee bar. A freckled faced blonde sat behind the counter. "Can I help you?"

"Two scoops of double chocolate fudge." He turned to Madison. "And lady's choice."

She scanned the containers of hard ice cream. "Peanut butter."

"And two scoops of peanut butter."

"I'm going to have to take up jogging or something with all these snacks you guys keep pushing on me." She awkwardly shifted from one foot to the other. It was like being sixteen again, trying to flirt with a boy and still retain some form of composure. "Not that I relish the thought of jogging. But, from what I hear, all the cool kids are doing it. Everyone I know is training for a marathon."

"Liam always threatens to run marathons. I did enough jogging to last a lifetime when I was in the Army, and I can confidently say I have no further desire to do it again." He took the peanut butter ice cream cone from the blonde and handed it to Madison. "There's a lot I miss about the Army, but running isn't one of them."

He paid for the cones and then headed back out of the shop. Madison followed, taking a careful bite of ice cream. She was starving. The ice cream was delicious, but she had a feeling she'd inhale it in approximately two bites if she wasn't careful. "How long were you in?"

"Eleven years. Well, closer to twelve. My dad signed for me when I was seventeen, but I went to basic once I was out of high school."

"What did you do?"

"I was a combat engineer." He paused and took a bite of ice cream. "It was my life for eleven years, but I got burned out after three consecutive deployments to Iraq and Afghanistan. I couldn't take it anymore."

There was something about the tone of his voice that made her desperately want to back off the subject, an underlying pain, a tense inflection that hinted to something that still shook him to his core. "So, we tricked you into the oh so lucrative business of digging in the dirt."

He laughed and when he spoke, the uncomfortable tone was gone. "I was just in the right place at the right time. I was living in DC when I finished my degree and knew Brad from an inter-departmental softball team. He needed someone last minute and, basically, I kind of fell into it. I never looked back."

"Go ahead and say it. Kind of like I fell in the test pit today."

"Well, now that you mention it…" Mike seemed to consider it. "You have the reflexes a cat. I thought for sure we were going to have to hoist you out of there."

"Notoriously, I've had that happen before." She heard a gentle tramp of footsteps and was momentarily struck by the feeling someone was walking directly behind her. Turning slightly, she realized no one was there and shrugged it off. "Not the falling in a test pit thing, but I fell through a barn floor once. It was awkward."

He laughed, but then noticeably restrained himself. "Was this a recent thing?"

"No. I was twelve. As if being twelve isn't awkward enough, throw in falling through a floor in front of all your friends." She waved her hand dismissively. "I've blocked most of it from memory, but I can assure you. I fell flat on my face. The masses howled. I wanted to change schools, but my mother said no."

Their pace was perfectly matched. He swayed slightly to the side, his free hand brushing against hers. "You're something else."

"I'm special edition."

He led her down Baltimore Street, which seemed to be the main street through town. Large brick buildings displaying a prominent brass plaques reading "Civil War Era" crowded both sides of the road. She counted five ghost tour booths before they'd reached the end of the first block. "Pretty quiet town, huh?"

"It is now. I was here last year in the summertime and it was chaos. It gets busy during the school year because of the college and the seminary. We're just in that weird time of year when the students are gone and the tourists haven't shown up yet." He pointed farther down the street. "The farther you go this way, the more shops and people you run into. Parking is a nightmare."

She glanced in a store front, scanning the display of t-shirts, hats, mugs, and pants stamped with the town name. "It's a bit commercialized."

"Don't get me started. I minored in Civil War history, so over commercialization and land development gets me worked up."

I'd like to see you worked up. She glanced behind her again. The feeling someone was behind her was pressing; she couldn't shake it.

This time, Mike noticed. "Why do you keep looking behind you?"

"I just get this feeling someone's behind me. Honestly, I'm expecting to turn around and see Brad trying to blend in with a lamppost." She hesitated. "No offense, but he's a total creeper."

"None taken, because I agree." Mike turned and looked at the path they'd travelled. "I don't see anyone."

"Neither do I. I'm just weird."

"Do you have any siblings who share in this, or did you parents think one of you was enough?"

"I have two older brothers, Jefferson and Adam."

He fell silent for a moment and then stopped walking. "Your parents named all three of you after presidents?"

"You, sir, are perceptive."

"I do my best." He fell into step beside her again. "That's actually cool."

"Well, thanks. Most of my friends, even at this stage in my academic career, don't realize we had presidents named Adams and Madison. They think my parents were just weird hippies, which actually, is also kind of true."

They stopped at an intersection. A surprising amount of traffic was clogging up the road. Mike pulled out his cell phone and checked the time. "Must be rush hour."

Before she had a chance to answer him, a woman circled around them. She was dressed in a long flowered skirt and ill-fitting black tank top, her curly black hair tucked back in a thick French twist. "Excuse me, I apologize but I had to stop you. Do you know he's with you?"

Madison exchanged a glance with Mike, but smiled politely. "I do, actually, we're together."

"Not him. The soldier."

"Again, she knows." Mike pressed his hand to her elbow and pushed her forward. "Come on, let's go this way. We can cross at the next block."

"I didn't mean to upset you." The woman fell silent for a moment, but then blurted out, "Your father died unexpectedly, didn't he?"

Madison turned on her heel and stared at her. "How did you know that?"

"Please." The woman's eyes were wide, her gaze pleading. "Just come inside, give me five minutes. I promise I won't keep you."

"Maddy—" Mike seemed to catch himself. "I mean, Madison, look, she's a palm reader. She just wants your money."

"Maybe, but she's right."

He studied her closely for several moments, his eyes locked on hers. "I'm coming with you."

The woman smiled and hustled back to the store front. She unlocked the door and motioned them inside. "I just locked up for the day. Come in and have a seat."

The interior of the store was nearly pitch black, the side windows blocked by thick, burgundy curtains.

The woman flipped on a light switch, revealing a small but comfortable waiting room with a plush black leather couch and arm chair, separated by a low coffee table. A long rectangular fish tank took up the entire far wall. It didn't look like what she imagined a palm reader's office to look like, but was somewhat reminiscent of a dentist office.

"I usually do my readings in the back room, but since the shop is closed, here is fine." She gestured for them to sit on the couch. "I apologize, my name is Lenore. I'm a clairvoyant, not a palm reader."

Mike didn't look impressed. He took a bite of the ice cream cone. "Mike."

Madison reached out to shake the woman's hand. "I'm Madison."

The woman took her hand and then stopped, clasping her other hand on top. "You're a sensitive."

"Excuse me?" Madison tried to pull her hand away, but the woman's grip was firm. "A sensitive?"

Mike stepped in. "Hey, let's take it easy. Let her go."

"I'm sorry. I'm sorry. Sit. A sensitive can hear the dead. Can speak to them." Lenore sank into the arm chair and studied her. "You were touched by death as a child."

Madison sat down on the couch, perching on the edge and pressing her hands into the dry leather to steady herself. She felt like she was in better position to jump up and run from the building. "Yes."

"You were nine."

Madison swallowed hard, but nodded.

"I feel…" Lenore closed her eyes. "I feel like you got there too late."

"My father was teaching in Boston and had a massive heart attack. We got there in time for my mother to sign the consent to pull the plug." Madison had long come to terms with her father's death, but still, the words tasted bitter. "But he wasn't a soldier; he actually was a protester during Vietnam."

"He's not the soldier who's with you." Lenore leaned forward, her brow furrowing as she squeezed her eyes shut. "You were at the Spangler Farm today."

Mike straightened a bit in his seat, but remained silent.

Madison answered. "Yes."

"Both of you."

"Yes. But how…"

"He saw you there. He says you saw him, too."

"I…" She didn't want to justify it with a response, didn't want Mike to hear what she knew was going to sound completely ridiculous. "I don't know."

"He says you can't hear him."

"He would be right."

Lenore shook her head and opened her eyes. "I can't quite…I can't quite make out what he's trying to say. He says the landscape is different now, but he remembers. He says you need to stay away."

"From what?"

"Him."

Madison looked at Mike. "Him?"

"Not Mike…Caldwell. Someone else." Lenore slowly shook her head. "I can't hear him anymore, I'm sorry. But he was very adamant. You need to stay away."

"How did you know my name?" Mike leaned forward, the tone of his voice markedly louder. Startled.

Lenore leveled her gaze at him. "The dead have a lot to say about you, Mr. Caldwell."

His eyes narrowed, and the muscles in his jaw twitched as he set his mouth in a firm line. He stood up and reached his hand down to Madison. "Let's get out of here."

"I'm sorry." She followed him to the door, but stopped short of walking outside. "I think you have me mistaken for someone else. You're right; I lost my dad a long time ago. But I can't hear the dead. Whoever I saw at the farm today was a trespasser or something, not a ghost."

"He'll try again. All you need to do is listen." Lenore's face clouded with worry, her eyes pleading. "But you need to stay away from the Spangler Farm. Something isn't right. I don't know what it is, but you— both of you—are in danger."

"We've wasted enough of your time." Mike gently placed his hand on the small of Madison's back and pushed her forward. "Thank you though."

As he guided her down the sidewalk, his hand still resting on her waist, she heard the woman call to them. "Cam says it wasn't your fault."

Mike stopped in his tracks. Madison felt him stiffen next to her and he turned back, his voice low and uncomfortably calm. "Fuck you, lady."

He nudged her forward and across the street, dropping his hand from her waist once they were on the other sidewalk. She couldn't help but feel somewhat disappointed.

They walked in silence for several minutes. Madison took a bite of her ice cream, almost afraid to talk to him. She couldn't tell if he was mad, hurt, or frustrated. He simply stared straight ahead, one had shoved in his pocked and the other cupping the ice cream cone. When she couldn't stand it anymore, she nervously cleared her throat. "Well, that was awkward."

"Yeah, I'd say so." He paused. "So...did you see someone on the farm today? Someone who shouldn't have been there?"

She nibbled on the cone. "I don't know what I saw."

"Madison. You can tell me."

"After what just happened in there?" She motioned behind her. "It's going to sound even crazier than it sounds on its own."

"Try me."

"I just..." She groaned. "I thought I saw someone watching me. He was standing in the lower level of the barn and then, later, I saw him in the woods. It was probably just my imagination. I mean, if someone was there, you'd have seen him."

"Did you mention it to anyone?"

"Liam, ah, sort of. Look, if someone was there, it was probably just a tourist or a reenactor or something. It wasn't a ghost." She glanced at him. "I thought you said you didn't believe in palm readers."

"I told you she was just after your money." He reached out and touched her arm. "If you see him again, tell me."

"It's not going to happen again."

"Well, on the off chance it does, just give me a head's up. I want to know."

She suddenly felt relieved, as if he'd lifted a burden she didn't realize she was carrying. "You don't seem like the type who'd believe in ghosts."

He kicked at a stone in the middle of the sidewalk. He missed and tried again, the toe of his shoe impacting with the rock. It skittered off the sidewalk and into the street. "I don't know what I believe anymore."

"That's okay, too."

"You're taking this all in stride. Doesn't that," — he motioned behind him, in the general area of the shop — "bother you?"

"Seeing someone casually hanging out at the Spangler barn watching me stand around being awkward bothers me. Some psychic knowing my dad died when I was a kid is weird, but I guess not entirely out of the ordinary, considering a psychic's job description."

"I was hanging out at the Spangler barn watching you, too." He paused and then groaned. "And when I say it out loud, it sounds far creepier than it did in my head."

"The difference is I liked you watching me."

She glanced at him; the corners of his lips twitched up into a poorly concealed smile. He remained silent.

"Well anyway..." She shrugged, "In my experience—and I'm quantifying my experience as time served with a prick step-father—most people are driven by the need to get what they want. They go to any length to get it. I, for example, have the need to be the best and am a perpetual overachiever. If she wanted to creep me out and add weirdness to an already bizarre day, then she got what she wanted. If her goal was to get paid or convince me of some kind of inherent supernatural powers, then no, she failed miserably. I'm not scared of the Spangler Farm. What I'm scared of is not getting into grad school and that drives me to keep going. Assuming I can actually find my way back to the Spangler Farm tomorrow, I'll be there, ghosts or not."

"If you need a ride tomorrow, I'll pick you up." He sounded shy, which didn't seem to fit his personality.

"I have my first alcohol rehab session tomorrow night. I need to leave with enough time to clean up and maybe eat. Maybe. The last thing I want is to look like

I've been rolling around in the dirt all day." She hesitated. "Otherwise, I'd take you up on it."

"Take me up on it anyway."

They'd already made it back to the hotel; the return trip seemed markedly shorter than the earlier walk down Baltimore Street. She wasn't ready for him to leave. "Okay, but only if you're sure it isn't any trouble."

"It's not." He smiled sheepishly. "You're no trouble, trust me."

"I'm lots of trouble. You just don't know me well enough yet."

"Hopefully I will soon."

She pursed her lips together in a coy smile. "Hopefully you will."

Chapter Nine

The morning dawned cold and wet. A misty haze of fog settled over the fields in the distance, the muted sun barely visible through thick clots of clouds. She felt cold and uncomfortable already. But, as long as the rain held off, the dig should still be a go. Cianna would probably stay in the car, but the rest of them could get some time in the pits.

And maybe Mike would offer to keep her warm.

She felt herself taking extra time getting ready, deliberating between a gray shirt over a white tank top or a brown shirt over a white tank top. She spent far too much time applying more eyeliner than she should have pending a day out in the rain. Dark hair pulled back into a ponytail, a subtle spritz of perfume down the front of her shirt, contacts in the correct eyes— she was ready to go.

Madison checked the face of her smart phone. Ready to go with forty-five minutes to spare. Awesome.

She shrugged a pink hoodie over her shoulders and snagged her room key from on top of the television. The continental breakfast was in a small house toward the back of the hotel complex. Since dinner had consisted of vending machine chips and a protein bar, she was ready for something more substantial. Something more free.

The building was cozy enough, with two rooms jammed full of tables and chairs and a larger room housing the breakfast food. She selected an English muffin from the bread box and, after splitting it in half, slid into the toaster. There wasn't much of a selection: egg patties, sausage patties, something gelatinous that might have been gravy, cake donuts, and a sampling of flavored yogurts. It was better than nothing—and she was starving.

Once the English muffin was ready, she assembled an egg and sausage sandwich and grabbed a container of strawberry yogurt. At the last second, she snagged two cake donuts; there was no telling how long she'd have to wait for lunch.

After shoving a spoon and napkins into her hoodie pocket, she filled a cup with cranberry juice and headed back to her hotel room. As much fun as it sounded to sit in the breakfast house and eat alone, she preferred to be where Mike could find her. After all, he could show up early. She should be there, in her room waiting.

In her room.

Madison, seriously. She chided herself. *You're two steps away from pouncing on him. Down. Down, girl.*

By the time she'd made it back to her room, her mother had texted her not once, but twice.

Good morning! Happy day two of your adventure! And the second— *Looks like rain. Dig still on?*

Up early for more quizzing. She took a bite of sandwich as she responded.

Thanks. Should be on unless we get too much rain, haven't heard it's cancelled. I'm sure I'd be the last to know.

Her mother texted back almost immediately.

Good. Do you start your classes tonight?

Madison sighed. Here we go. She had a feeling her mother had been coached by Tricky Dick to ask such a question.

Yes.

Make sure you take notes.

Thanks, Mom. I will.

She didn't have an opportunity to discuss things with her mother before she left. Her mother had at some point during Madison's teenage years decided she wasn't going to interfere with the conflicts between her and her step-father. It was easier to pretend everything was fine. Even so, Madison was fairly sure she knew what her mother would say: *I'm disappointed in the drinking, Mads, but I'm so proud you're going on a dig. You know we're proud of you—we're both so proud of you.*

Sometimes she envied her brothers for going to school as far away as possible.

She finished her breakfast and washed her hands, then took the opportunity to apply more eyeliner and mascara. As she critically judged her appearance in the mirror—pale skin, blue eyes so wide she perpetually looked surprised—she heard a knock on the room door.

Mike.

She sprinted across the room, pausing long enough to smooth down her hair and wipe her hand across her face to ensure no errant muffin crumbs were left behind. She forced herself to open the door with restraint.

His face broke into an immediate smile. "Hey, pretty lady."

"Hey, soldier boy." Her heart felt like it skipped a beat. The intensity of his eyes was enough to make her blush. "Let me just get my bag and I'm good to go. Not that I used it yesterday, but you know. Just in case."

"And your room key."

"And my room key." She unzipped the front pouch of the backpack and slid the key inside. "Forgetting my room key is becoming an unfortunate habit."

"I'm surprised Brad put you up in a hotel." He waited for her to close the door and then fell into step beside her, comfortably close as they headed toward the parking lot. "The rest of us are in park housing. And when I say the rest of us, what I mean by that is me and Liam. Cianna's college sorority sister has a condo outside of town so, of course, she's staying in the lap of luxury."

"Forgot the condo, you're in park housing?"

"It sounds far more glamorous than it is."

"I'm staying in a hotel."

"I have to fight Liam to use the shower first. It's hard to believe that two men with such minimal hair can argue who gets to shower and shampoo first, but there you go."

"Meanwhile, I'm sitting alone in a hotel room texting my mother." She glanced at him. "I'm so out of control, it's overwhelming."

He chuckled and led to her his Jeep, quickly circling around her to open the passenger's side door. "Try and ignore the mess. I swear, it feels like I live out of my car half the time, especially on digs. In compensation, I bought you coffee."

"You didn't have to do that." She set her pack on the passenger's side floor. It wasn't a typical mess; mess suggested trash and dirty clothes. The back of the Jeep was filled with a sleeping bag, two tool boxes, an olive colored duffle bag, and an assortment of books and notebooks. "But thank you. Thank you that is, unless there's a body in that duffle bag. It's ominous, man. Just a bit ominous."

"Prepare to be disappointed, because really all that's in it is dirty clothes and combat boots." He waited while she sank into the seat. "There might be one of my camouflage jackets in there. At least, there should be. That's about as exciting as I get."

"Allow me to retract the term ominous and replace it with hot." She froze, horrified she'd actually said the words out loud and not just to herself. Great. "Because…uh…all that's in my bag is snacks. Well, snacks and a paperback novel, just in case I get bored or something."

"I won't let you get bored."

She flushed again—this was becoming an annoying response to his flattery—but before she could muster up some form of witty response, she heard the squeal of tires braking behind them. She groaned as she looked up. Brad. Brad, of all the people to drop by, even after she'd flatly declined him picking her up.

He rolled down the window. His brow was knitted in a tight frown, his upper lip curled back almost in a snarl. "What the hell? Look, I thought I offered to pick you up. Do you realize you have completely wasted my time this morning? I had to drive out of my way to get here."

She exchanged a quick glance with Mike. "Well, I'm sorry you were inconvenienced, but as you may recall when we spoke yesterday, I told you I didn't need a ride. You said you understood and, in fact, told me what time to be at the Spangler Farm today. So…" She shrugged. "There you go."

Recognition seemed to register in his eyes, but he continued to frown. "Yeah, well, I have a meeting with the park superintendent this morning. I wouldn't have had time to drop you off at the site and get back to headquarters anyway."

She stared at him. What was his intention, then? To drag her along to some meeting and make her wait in the car like a puppy?

Brad dragged his fingers through his hair, then tapped them against the steering wheel. "Okay, so, I've got that meeting. I'll see you guys at the site later, I'm hoping just in an hour or so."

"We'll hold down the fort until then." Mike closed the passenger's side door, ending Madison's participation in the conversation. She was delighted. "Do you want us to split up and start another test pit?"

"Yeah." There was a pause. "Put Liam and Madison on the pit by the woods. You and Cianna stay on the barn pit for now."

"Whatever you say, man." Mike clambered into the driver's seat and jammed his key into the ignition. "Bastard."

"We're like those kids in school who get separated for talking too much." Madison picked up the coffee cup, breathing in the creamy, spicy smell. "In fact, I've always been that kid. My fourth grade report card says, 'Madison has such potential, if she'd only stop talking'. I wonder if Brad's report to Dr. Emerson will read in a similar manner."

"I have to apologize for that. I've known him a long time and I've never seen him flip out like that. He's acting like a jealous prick."

"Jealous that I'd rather spend time with you than him?" Madison rolled her eyes. "Look, he got off on the wrong foot when he couldn't carry on a conversation with me without staring at my boobs. And, get this, he offered to just sign off on my counseling sessions without me going. Because, you know, turning a forged document into the court system sounds like such an awesome idea."

"I'm not trying to make excuses for him, but I think the park is really on his back on this dig. They gave us four weeks, but I think they want us out as soon as possible." The Jeep was manual transmission. He easily moved his foot from clutch to gas as he shifted gears.

There was something ridiculously attractive about it, how he moved his legs, easing pressure from on pedal to the other. She had to look away. "He's devastated this is process and not investigation. Gettysburg never invites archeologists in. They handpicked him."

"What's his background? I've honestly never heard of him, which is a bitchy thing to say, but if Gettysburg handpicked him, he's got to have something going for him. What he do, help find the Titanic or something?"

"He works a lot with the park system. I worked with him on a dig in Chancellorsville a few years ago that was pretty big. And his notorious discovery of the cartridge rounds, of course. He's just a digger, like the rest of us, but he's got connections." Mike picked up his coffee and took a deep drink. "And what about you, Miss Madison? All I know about you is that you're an archeology girl with a drinking problem."

"I'm a paper archeologist. I have next to no experience, other than working as a volunteer with Fort Pitt and a few small digs around the Pittsburgh area. I'm an overachiever. I'm a notorious underage drinker—I turn twenty-one next week—but my archeological resume is limited to what I've published."

"You've published some amazing things. I've read your work, even before I knew you were going to be on the dig with us. Christ, you were just in *Archeology* Magazine two months ago. The Great Fire of Pittsburgh in 1845? I had no idea that even happened."

"People in Pittsburgh don't even know that happened." Madison took another drink of coffee. "It was the smallest dig you could have imagined. Pittsburgh has rebuilt since 1845, so there's virtually no sign of it. There's a plaque on the side of a building. We only got to do a half day survey when some sidewalk was replaced in front of a local church. We didn't find anything."

"Liar, I read the article. You found scorch marks. That's something."

"It's tangible evidence. The church only survived the fire because it's made of stone. There was a wooden cross on the outside wall, but they pushed it into the street to extinguish the flames. But…you knew that from the article." She ran her fingertip over the cup lid. "I also have a nasty habit of launching into historic soliloquies, as I've just demonstrated."

"I think smart girls are hot."

"It gives me something to fall back on incase this education thing doesn't work out all that well." She reached out and put the cup back in the cup holder.

Mike caught her hand in his and coaxed it over to reveal her tattoo. He ran his forefinger over the curved lines of the fleur de lis. "I still really like this."

Her breath caught in her throat. "Do you have any ink?"

"A couple. Army stuff mostly; you show me yours, I'll show you mine."

"Hmmm, well, although that's an offer I'd gladly take you up on, mine are rather well hidden by clothes right now. I mean, two alone are covered up by socks."

He sucked in a breath through his teeth. "Ah, let down."

"You'll just have to take a rain check."

"I'll hold you to it."

She was fairly certain she'd let him hold her to anything: against anything, over anything, on top of anything. Despite the fact she'd only known him two days—not even two days, just one day and roughly fifteen minutes—she liked everything about him. His looks, his physique, his personality, the way his legs moved with every release of the clutch. God damn it, he should just pull the damn Jeep over now. Instead, she said, "So, this is a completely different direction than Brad took yesterday to the site. Are you kidnapping me or something? Because I'm okay with it if you are."

"Brad doesn't know what he's doing. This is the better way." He let her wrist go as he turned the wheel around a sharp curve in the road. "I'm just cutting through the park. You said you've never been here before, so I'm giving you the full experience."

Her eyes drifted to the side of the road. A low stone wall ran parallel to the pavement, encroaching on thick woods. A figure, dressed in a dark blue jacket and dark brown slouch hat, crouched near the wall, a long rifle stretched out in front of him. He edged closer to the wall, his hand dropping to a cartridge box at his hip.

Madison glanced at Mike. He didn't seem to notice.

She looked back out the window. The soldier was gone; there was no sign of him by the wall or near the road. She inwardly shivered, then cleared her throat. "You know this park pretty well."

"I came up here a lot when I was finishing my degree. I'd set up my tent at one of the campgrounds and then hike the battlefield during the day. Since I was a combat engineer, I liked walking the terrain and thinking about logistics and tactics and that kind of thing." He glanced at her and smiled sheepishly. "Sounds kind of weird."

"Just the opposite, it's really cool. Smart guys are hot." She picked up her coffee cup. "You and I need to sit down for a nerdy history chat sometime. I bet your military knowledge would improve my overall knowledge of the battle here."

"Let's make it a date."

"Deal."

He turned the Jeep off the park road and onto a more residential looking road. "I promise I'll take you back the direct route tonight so you aren't late."

"Yeah, because you know it's going to be a totally awesome meeting." She groaned. "You know, I was *this close* to not getting caught. I hid under the bed. I would have stayed under that bed until the sun came up, but my cell phone rang. My damn cell phone, blasting out Mozart louder than I thought my cell phone was even capable of emitting sound."

He chuckled, running his hand down his chin. "Your cell phone? Man, that sucks."

"Yeah, and worse yet? It was my douche bag ex-boyfriend calling. Just to, you know, check in and see if I was ready to get back together. No. Not interested, not after he turned into a cheating scumbag. I'd rather punch him in the face. Hell, I'd rather someone punch me in the face."

"I can't fathom why someone would want to cheat on you. I mean, Christ, look at you. You're beautiful, you're smart. Was he an idiot?"

She blushed. "He was attractive and he knew it. College, for him, is a playground of hockey and girls. He's been on academic probation twice. He's a cheat and a punk, and I got tired of it. So, I kicked him to the curb and he's been trying to crawl back ever since." She waved her hand dismissively. "I'm over that shit."

"You deserve better than that." He turned the car down the lane leading to the Spangler Farm. "I'd treat you better than that."

She tried to bite back a smile, but failed. He was so sweet and attractive and…there was no way she was going to be able to concentrate on digging. She didn't even know how to respond to him. Her mind was too much a jumble to come up with even a remotely witty reply. Instead, she motioned down the driveway. "Is that Cianna's car?"

"I expected Liam to be here, but not her." He started laughing. "Liam is going to be pissed if he's had to sit with her long. Oh my God, he's going to be furious."

He parked the Wrangler next to Cianna's sporty red car, hesitating before turning off the ignition. "Is it corny to say I'm jealous Liam gets to be with you today?"

"No. I'm jealous that bitch Cianna gets to be with you." Madison chewed on her lip as she thought. "Where's your cell phone?"

Mike reached into the pocket of his brown hooded sweatshirt and handed her a cell phone. She swiped her finger across the face and located the contacts screen. "Here's my number. Text me."

"Is that offer limited to today or does that go for anytime?"

She leaned over farther than she actually needed to in order to return his cell phone. "I'll be disappointed if you don't text me. And that goes for anytime."

She heard him draw in a breath through his teeth as she slid out of the Wrangler. Good, leave him wanting more—and now he had her number.

Liam was across the parking lot before she even had both her feet on the ground. "Darling, you have no idea how happy I am to see you. I thought I was going to be stuck with that whore all day."

"Where is she?" Mike pushed the Jeep door shut behind him. "I'll be damned if she doesn't help again today. She's not going to sit around on her ass drawing pictures all day while the rest of us work."

Liam clicked his tongue. "She's in the summer kitchen. It was raining earlier—bitch will probably melt if she gets wet. Why are you so pissy?"

"Brad the Enforcer forbids Madison and me from working together."

"Bitch, please."

"He's telling the truth." Madison swung her pack over her shoulder. "His exact words were 'Put Liam and Madison in the pit by the woods'."

"Jealous much? Mikey, now he's going to hate you because you're more attractive than him and because *she* likes you better." Liam flared his nostrils. "This is just like high school. Which one of us is going to get called first to the principal's office for a spanking?"

"He had the foresight to leave me in charge, so the first thing I'm going to do is help you guys set up your sifter and get settled back there." Mike glanced at Madison. "And approximately the exact time he drives into the farm, I'll go work on the barn pit. We all know she's not going to help and we all know she's going to manipulate Brad into letting her do the least amount possible."

Liam stretched his arms over his head and yawned, an exaggerated movement that reflected boredom rather than tiredness. "Maybe it'll rain all day and we can just leave. Mikey, remember that day it rained at the Baltimore dig? We sat in the cars for like, three hours until it stopped, and then the second we got set up, it poured."

"Yeah, that was awesome." Mike cocked his head toward the summer kitchen. Madison fell into step beside him, while Liam seemed to reluctantly follow. "As I remember it, we had to cover the pits while Cianna sat in Brad's truck. With Brad."

"Lord only knows what she did in that truck to get him to let her sit out the entire dig, and yet, still get paid." Liam nudged her with his elbow. "Girl, you rode in that truck. I hope you washed your hands afterward."

"I showered afterward."

"Smart, but probably not enough. That truck, my God. My God, the things it's probably seen."

Mike rolled his eyes and ducked through the narrow door of the summer kitchen. Madison could hear him address Cianna with a scoff and a grunt, but he wasted little time in the stone building, instead pulling the second sifter outside. He hoisted it over his shoulder. "Don't worry, Liam, I've got this."

"Look how his biceps bulge." Liam clicked his tongue again and leaned closer to her. "You like the bulge, don't you? We all do. Maybe not Brad, but the vast majority of us are colossal fans. That's why Cianna hates him, because he's not wooed by her sorry excuse for tits and flat, lumpy ass. He turned her down like a bitch with a peanut allergy turns down a Snickers bar."

"Liam, dude, really." Mike turned his head slightly to the side. "I'm right here."

"I know. It's all things I want you to hear. After you're safely back on the other side of the farm, Sassy Madison and I will discuss what she really thinks about you. I'll critique."

"Just what she needs." Mike slung the sifter off his shoulder and to the ground. "Where you do want this, Liam?"

"I could care less."

Mike turned to Madison and smiled sheepishly. "I should have just asked you first."

The wind picked up slightly, ruffling the hair at her neck. She shivered, the strands of hair tickling her flesh like the soft kiss of fingertips. "Put it in the sun. I'm cold again already."

"Someone needs to buy you a heavier jacket." Liam picked at her hoodie with his thumb and index finger. "Mikey, Mikey, take off your shirt and give it to her."

"Liam." Mike adjusted the legs of the sifter until they locked in place and then pushed his weight against it as if testing the sturdiness. "Why don't you go back to the summer kitchen and get the buckets? Unless you plan on moving dirt with your hands, in which case, get to work."

Liam made an unidentifiable noise, but turned and stormed back across the field. "I'd rather dig with my hands than deal with that flat chested, blonde bitch."

Mike shook his head and again shook the sifter. "I'll go get the shovels. I figure I'll help you guys until Brad gets here."

"Sounds good to me. As far as I'm concerned, you can help us after Brad gets here too."

He crossed the short space of field between them into two easy steps. Without hesitation, he took her hands in his and brought them to his lips, breathing hot breath on her fingers. "You are cold."

"Warm me up, then."

His lower lip brushed against her fingertips. "This is probably the first time I've ever wished a dig would be called off due to weather."

"There's always later."

"Later is a long time to wait."

She looked up into his dark eyes, a shade of brown so dark it bordered on black. It was hard to tear her gaze away from his; there was so much she wanted to say, things probably inappropriate if verbalized after knowing someone less than two days. Not that she minded. Two days was better than two hours. "Good things come to those who wait."

He squeezed her hands, but didn't let her go.

The sifter pitched forward and collapsed into the roped off area of the test pit; the intimacy of the moment shattered. It was as if it had been overturned in a fit of rage, the sifting screen wrenched from the base and flipped across the ground. Madison jumped, panic racing through her limbs like an electric shock. "Jesus Christ, that scared the piss out of me."

Mike had pulled her to him; he slid his hands down her waist and steadied her. "I checked that thing twice, there's no way it could just randomly fall."

"Is it broken?" She was close enough to smell subtle hints of his cologne. It seemed to inhibit her ability to think clearly. "If it is…you know, we'll all have to work on the same pit. Or call off the dig until we can get it fixed."

"Regrettably, I have a feeling I'll be able to fix it." He guided her to the sifter and then squatted down beside it, letting his fingers trail down her arm until it was out of reach. "That's so weird. I swear it was sturdy. It didn't just fall, it sailed."

The crunch of footsteps treading across the unmowed grass behind her seemed to cross from her right to her left, then gingerly step up next to her. She turned, expecting to see Liam.

There was no one there.

Her pulse quickened. She drew in a quick breath.

The footsteps crossed back to her opposite side. For a moment, she thought she felt the pressure of a shoulder pressed against hers, the sensation of someone standing too close. She was struck by the overwhelming feeling the sifter had landed there for a reason. The wind was blowing, but in the opposite direction. It shouldn't have fallen toward the pit. It should have fallen toward them.

But it didn't.

The presence next to her shifted. She felt hot breath on her ear, like the exhalation of long held breath. A faint whisper, a muffled voice that sounded like it was speaking to her through a thick wall, begging to be heard. Desperate for her to hear. Gooseflesh rippled down her arms and she took a large step forward, ending up as close to Mike as she could without actually standing on top of him. She forced herself to sound calm. There was no way she wanted to sound like a freak in front of Mike. "Is this the kind of fix that's done in, say, a few minutes or one that takes maybe…a day or two?"

"Unfortunately, it's a quick fix. This piece just popped off." He stood and help up a wooden edge of the sifter box. "It'll only take a couple nails to get it back on. I just can't figure out how it tipped. It's as sturdy as a brick shit house. I should know—I built it."

"You certainly know how to woo the ladies. Building a sifter stand?" She cocked her head to the side. "That's an impressive skill."

"I have many impressive skills." He brushed loose strands of hair back from her face. "Just so you know."

"Tease."

"Only for now." He winked. "Anyway, I'll go get my toolbox and fix this. It'll take longer to actually walk to the car and back than it will to fix the tray."

Out of the corner of her eye, she caught a quick movement by the collapsed sifter. She stiffened and turned her head. Nothing. "Okay."

He must have heard the waver in her voice; he stopped and looked back at her. "Is everything okay?"

"Just jumpy, that's all." She forced herself to smile. "No signs of otherworldly beings, if that's what you're afraid of."

"Maybe I should be."

She nodded her heads toward the summer kitchen. "Liam's on his way back. He's even bringing shovels, so I'm obviously about to be put to work. I'm okay, Mike, if something…out of the ordinary happened, I'd let you know."

"I'll be right back."

Liam regarded him as they passed each other. "Still harassing Madison?"

"Do I look harassed?"

Liam dropped the buckets and shovels in the grass. "No, you look pale and pasty. Girl, you need blush or a cheeseburger or something." His eyes slid to the sifter. "What happened here?"

"It fell over."

"I find that hard to believe."

Madison shrugged and picked up one of the shovels. "Must have been a break in gravity or something. Satan's minions, I don't know, but we weren't even close to it."

"Satan's minion is still sitting in the summer kitchen, drawing pictures of the fireplace and whining that her hair is ruined by damp air."

"Must be nice." Madison forced the shovel into the earth and scooped a pile of dirt into one of the buckets. "No, I take that back. I'm happier playing in the dirt and not having to compromise my morals by cozying up to Brad."

"Exactly. You'd rather compromise your morals by cozying up to Mikey."

"Well. You know."

"I know. I've known Mikey for a long time, even back when he was Lieutenant Caldwell and was stomping around in uniform, all angry and masculine and intense. God, if I could be in your shoes." He glanced down. "No. Not those shoes."

"Has he been out of the service long?"

"I guess it's been almost two years. He was messed up when he came home from his last tour in Afghanistan." Liam looked back toward the summer kitchen and dropped his voice considerably. "He doesn't talk about it."

"Not even when he first came home?"

"Especially when he first came home. Something changed in him. It wasn't something I could point out specifically, but I could tell. He'd just sit and stare. He's a little better now, but I'm telling you that boy is fragile." Liam eased another shovelful of dirt into the bucket. "So, don't you hurt him."

"Hurting him isn't in my plan." Madison set the shovel down and dragged the nearly full bucket away from the pit. Mike was crossing the field, toolbox in hand. He was broken, but pieced together. She almost felt ashamed for talking about him behind his back.

I'm so cold.

The voice was audible this time, though muffled to the point it sounded like a radio station's reception fading in and out. The speaker was right beside her. Madison's breath caught in her throat. She could hear him, feel him standing next to her. His unseen eyes were locked on her. It was like the day prior, the silent figure watching her from the barn and from the woods, eyes never wavering.

She swallowed hard and glanced back at Liam. He didn't seem to notice. His attention remained focused on filling the next bucket with dirt.

Under. Under. Under.

The voice was suddenly too muffled, again sounding like someone trying to speak to her through a plaster wall. She frowned. If she was a sensitive, why was it so hard to hear anything?

"Hey."

She jumped at the sound of Mike's voice. She tried to cover it with a smile, but she had a feeling he wouldn't fall for it. "Hey, just in time."

"Is everything okay back here?" He studied her. "Other than the broken sifter. And the bald dandy over there."

"The bald dandy resents that." Liam snorted. "I'm bald because I choose to be bald. I'm so fabulous, the hairs on my head can't stand it."

Mike rolled his eyes and leaned closer to Madison. "Everything's good?"

She nodded.

He obviously didn't believe her, but crouched down next to the sifter and flipped open his toolbox. "Did Liam tell you about his hot date last night?"

"It wasn't a hot date, it was a casual meet and greet." Liam leaned against the shovel and rolled his yes. "And now I'm obligated to tell her. So, I met this guy online—"

"Wait, you agreed to go out on a date with someone you met online?" Madison raised her eyebrow quizzically. "We need to sit down and have a long discussion on the rules of dating."

"It was a legitimate dating site, not a shady gay chat room or something." Liam dumped another shovelful of dirt into the bucket. "So, we'd been chatting on the phone for a few weeks and he seemed totally legit. Until we ran into his ex at Applebee's and there was this huge confrontation that ended in my date screaming at the top of his lungs in the parking lot—of Applebee's, may I remind you—'well, you gave me herpes, so your opinion doesn't count!' It got awkward from that point."

"I'd say so."

"So, he's ready to drive me home and he's like, I was just kidding about the herpes thing. And I thought about it. I thought about it for a good fifteen seconds and said, 'No you weren't'. I left that bitch in the Applebee's parking lot and called Mikey to come get me."

"I'm like his surrogate mother." Mike tapped a nail into the wooden edging. "Mikey, come get me. Mikey, open this jar. Mikey, do you know how to get wine out of linen pants?"

Madison pressed the toe of her shoe into the dirt. "Do you?"

"Know how to get wine out of pants? No. I told him to start drinking white."

"This one," — Liam jerked his finger toward Mike — "thinks you can drink white wine with red meat. I told him you don't *do* that. Match your wine with your meat. Honestly, you'd think he was raised in a barn."

"I hate to say it, but he's right." Damp coldness felt like it was seeping through her sleeves; she rubbed her arms. "You can't mix your meats and your wines. But hey, don't feel you need to listen to me. I got my citation for too much involvement with my boyfriend Jim Beam and his cousin Jack Daniels. You can drink that with anything."

Rubbing her arms didn't help. She was overwhelmed with cold. It felt like someone had soaked her hoodie in ice water and made her wear it to a hockey arena. Her jaw shuddered as she bit back shivers from the cold, but before she could begin to worry about Mike noticing, she saw movement at the field. It was Brad, crossing from the summer kitchen and heading in their direction. Jesus Christ, could things get any worse?

"The pit looks great, guys!" He nodded in approval, a slimy smile spreading across his face. "Off to an excellent start! Probably still too near the surface to pull anything up yet, huh?"

"Only soil to document." Madison answered for the three of them. "Nothing spells accomplishment like comparing soil samples and matching them with the Munsell Color Chart."

"It sounds like an afternoon of enchantment." Brad hung back a few steps from where she stood and brushed his hair back from his head. Madison inwardly groaned. It was becoming an annoying habit of his. Cianna might find it attractive, but she'd like a take a pair of clippers to his 1990s-esq bangs. Get a sweat band.

"Look, Madison..." He cleared his throat. "I just wanted to apologize for earlier. That wasn't like me and, honestly, I think the pressures of the dig are just getting to me. I shouldn't take that out on you. How about we just start over? Wipe the slate clean."

She wasn't sure what pressures he was referring to; they were only on Day Two. If two days on a dig was enough to drive him over the edge, she hated to see him as the deadline approached and they hadn't finished all four test pits yet. But, okay, whatever. "Sure, that sounds great."

He held out his hand, an embarrassingly awkward movement. "I'm Brad. Brad Emerson."

"Madison." She wiped her hand on her jeans to be polite, then grasped his hand in the most uncomfortable handshake she'd ever experienced. She could have settled without the literal demonstration of starting over. "It's great to be here."

He looked relieved. "What else do we have going on over here?"

"The sifter fell and a piece broke off." Mike set his hammer back in the toolbox and carefully closed the lid. "It's fixed now. It set us back by all of ten minutes."

"I'm more concerned about the weather setting us back." Brad zipped his jacket up to his chin. "Jesus, it's cold over here. Keep an eye on the weather. If it's starts raining, get the pit covered up with tarps and use the buckets to secure them down. The last things we need are little pseudo fishing holes on park property."

"I'll get some tarps and bring them over. Is the park getting pissy with you?" Mike stood and stepped away from the pit, running his hand across Madison's back as he passed her. "Again?"

"The park likes good, firm scheduling. I told them we'll max out the dig at four weeks, but they'd prefer to have us out of here earlier. They're looking toward the battle anniversary in July."

"We could find Jimmy Hoffa buried out here and we'd still be done before July." Liam put his shovel down and headed toward the sifter. "Come on, darling, let's separate dirt from more dirt."

Brad jammed his hands in his pockets. "The park doesn't expect us to find much based on how small our test areas are, so I think they're writing us off. Maybe they don't want us to find anything, hell, I don't know. If they wanted artifacts pulled up, they'd have put us out in battlefield proper."

"There's still plenty of time for us to fail." Mike winked at Madison again. "Speaking of failure, what do you say you help me try to convince Cianna that break time is over? She's been holed up in the summer kitchen for almost an hour. The test pits on that side of the farm aren't going to dig themselves."

"We'll see what we can work out." Brad shoved his hands in his jeans pockets and headed back to the field. "Keep me updated, guys. I have more paperwork to push."

Mike glanced at Madison and rolled his eyes with great exaggeration and then followed Brad back across the field.

She stood still for a moment, the biting cold burrowing over her shoulders and down her arms again. The voice was in her ear, like a scream carried across an empty, open field.

She. She.

* * * *

As promised, Mike dropped her off at her hotel room promptly at 5:15, leaving her plenty of time to get ready and swing through a drive-thru on her way to the first rehab session.

"Thanks again for the ride." She unbuckled her seatbelt, hesitant at opening the door and leaving him. "I'd rather stay with you than go hang out with a bunch of other underage drunks."

"Yeah, you're a buzz kill." He chuckled, running his fingertips across her knuckles. "It's pretty easy to find the school, but if you have any trouble, call me. I'll be there."

"Keep your phone close. I can't navigate my way out of a paper bag."

He smiled at her. "So…what do you say I pick you up tomorrow? We can make a habit of this."

"Keep being so sweet to me and I'll end up just asking you to stay."

"That's something I'd gladly make a habit of as well."

She flushed. "If you show up early, I'll try and sneak you into the breakfast hut for English muffins and donuts."

"You rebel, you."

Madison laughed and opened the Jeep door, stepping out into the parking lot. "See you tomorrow."

"I'm looking forward to it."

She crossed the parking lot to the staircase and then turned back to him, clumsily waving like she was walking into her first day of kindergarten. He distracted her. Everything else—even the dig—seemed incidental in comparison to what she wanted to happen with him.

And the sooner it happened, the better.

* * * *

Madison tossed her hoodie on the bed and rubbed her eyes. The counseling class was just how she'd thought it would be — boring. There'd been introductions, an overview of the syllabus and how classes would work, and finally an ending with a dramatic description of how the human body processes alcohol. She didn't feel counseled as much as she felt her intelligence was insulted. It was going to be a long four weeks.

Her cell phone buzzed, indicating the receipt of a text. Probably her mother. She shook her hair down from the French twist and crossed the room to the sink. It was a long day, and she didn't feel like exposing herself to her mother's pep talks.

After she took her contacts out and washed her face, she returned to the bed and picked up her phone. The text wasn't from her mother. It was from Mike.

Was it as riveting as you expected?

Her heart felt like it did a move reminiscent of the cha-cha.

It could have only been improved if they'd served snacks. There's an hour of my life I'll never get back.

His response was almost immediate.

You can't have all the big fun at once. I assume you found your way back to the hotel?

You'd have gotten a frantic call from me if I didn't.

She crawled onto the bed and leaned against the headboard.

Maybe I should have called you anyway.

I'd have shown up.

The corners of her mouth twitched into a smile. It was too easy to fall for him; her simple crush was snowballing into out of control infatuation. The only question was if he felt the same way.

He texted again.

Because…I've kind of been thinking about you all evening.

He did.

Chapter Ten

By Friday, Madison determined she and Mike were reaching close to seven solid hours of texting over the course of three days. They'd spent the time getting to better know each other; he hated Brussels sprouts and was allergic to Tide. She admitted to him that, other than losing her father, the most horrible moment in her life was the realization that her step-father hated her simply because she was another man's daughter. They'd spent hours joking, flirting, and talking about nothing and talking about everything—everything but what was developing between them. She'd already known she'd fallen for him, but as the dig dragged on into late Friday afternoon, she determined she'd fallen for him much harder than she'd intended. They were far beyond what would constitute casual fling territory. And that, on its own, made her nervous.

She ran her hand over clots of dirt on the sifter screen. It was a debate which was more frustrating — finding no artifacts whatsoever in the forest test pit, or the fact she was falling in love with Mike. Her phone buzzed with another text from him.

I just found a canteen spout. Beat that.

She brushed her hands off on her jeans and texted him back.

I've found four buckets of clean dirt in less than an hour. My brutal consistency trumps your luck any day.

Don't make me come back there.

Bring it on.

She smiled. Christ, he always made her smile. He was driving her insane. He teased her, he flirted with her, he held the darn car door open for her every time he picked her up or dropped her off at her hotel. No wonder she hadn't found anything in the test pit. She was too busy trying to be witty and cute.

At least Liam didn't care about witty and cute.

She glanced at him out of the corner of her eye. He'd long abandoned her efforts on the test pit to start documenting soil and rock samples in his fastidious, uniform handwriting. Occasionally, she'd hear him mutter something about strata or the infuriating ground shift, but otherwise their relationship was relaxed, near boring. In four short days it had become comfortable to the point of monotonous.

Hoisting the next bucket of dirt above the sifter, she shook out an even layer of dirt and then shook the sifter to filter it through the screen. Loose dirt fell through to the tray below, leaving behind dirt covered clumps. She picked through the rocks and dirt clods. Nothing.

She reached for a clod at the upper quadrant of the screen and the air around her seemed to shift. The chunk was cold—not completely unusual for damp dirt on an overcast day—but it felt like she'd plunged her hand through ice water to touch it.

Dragged her. He dragged her.

She dropped the clod back to the sifter tray. The voice was as clear as if Liam had spoken to her, like the unseen figure was standing at the opposite end of the sifter tray. Madison cleared her throat. There was no mistaking the words this time. The voice belonged to a male. He sounded exhausted.

…watched…I watched…dragged her…

He was frustrated. There was a tone to the voice that sounded desperate. She cleared her throat again. "Just go slow."

"Excuse me?" Liam looked up from his plastic canisters. "If you're trying to give Mikey directions, I don't think he can hear you."

She groaned. She hadn't meant to actually say it out loud. "No, just talking to myself."

"That's nice."

Madison ignored him and forced herself to plunge her hand past the cold seemingly radiating from the dirt clod. She reached into her pocket and withdrew her pick, carefully chipping the dirt away.

The object was a little larger than a dime. As she picked the dirt away from the surface, the muted brass patina became visible, cut by the curve and arch of an eagle. It was a button.

"Liam." She tipped the button face up in her palm; the last thing she wanted was for the delicate rounded face to cave in. "I found something."

"Get out." He perked up, rising from his self-made nest of plastic containers and notebooks, and studied her outstretched hand. "Looks like your standard issue, run of the mill Federal sack coat button."

"It's better than nothing." She shook her fist at him. "Don't spoil my moment of discovery. You see an ordinary button, I see tangible proof they were here."

"We don't need a button to confirm the Federal Army was here." He retrieved a small plastic container and held steady, allowing Madison to ease the button inside. "Most historians are in agreement that the Federal and Confederate armies met here for a few days in July 1863."

"Think of it though: the last time this button was touched, it was by the Union soldier buttoning his uniform. Where was he going? What did he see during the battle? It's like a moment frozen in time; the button's journey ended here, but the soldier went on." She pulled out her cell phone and texted Mike.

I see your canteen spout and raise you a Federal sack coat button.

"Look how cute you are when you're enthusiastic and impressionable? Just wait until you're old and jaded like me." Liam patted her hand. "Call me when you find something I can't buy in one of the town shops for under ninety bucks."

"Buzz kill."

"It's like a part time job for me." He set the container in his duffle bag and jotted something in his notebook. "If you're looking for reaction, I'm willing to bet Brad will be thrilled. Anything to pad his final report and make him look like the best in his field."

"I'll pass, but thanks."

"Smart girl."

She turned back to the sifter screen and emptied the clean dirt out from the lower tray. In the silence that fell, she could hear the voice again. It was rambling and rushing, frantic and mumbled. She refilled the sifter screen with new dirt, straining her ears to hear him.

...I tried...couldn't feel, couldn't help...I tried...

What else could she do to hear him? It wasn't like she could ask him to speak louder; the more she concentrated the farther away he sounded.

...gone...I still remain...Her. Her. HER.

His final word was a near scream into her ear. She jumped back from the sifter and brushed her hand across the side of her face. She'd felt the puff of air as he spoke, his breath exhaled across her cheek. It was like he was standing next to her, against her, demanding her attention. If it was so important, why couldn't she hear him?

Liam was staring at her.

She held her breath for a moment, struggling against the trembling muscles in her body. Her cell phone buzzed in her pocket. "I'm...I'm going to take a break."

"Are you okay?"

"I'm fine." She forced herself to smile at him, but she could feel the waver in her expression. "I'm just going to flaunt my find at Mike and, you know. Flirt."

"We're done in like, ten minutes."

She took several steps backward and shrugged. "Call me a slacker, then. It's ten minutes; I'll come in tomorrow for ten minutes if you're so concerned."

Liam closed the notebook and again stood, crossing to the sifter. "Don't worry about me, then, I'll just finish this bucket on my own."

"Thanks, I owe you one." She turned around and took several steps forward, immediately hearing the shuffle of footsteps in the grass behind her.

"Madison."

She jumped, but looked back at Liam. He was again staring at her, his hands resting on the edge of the sifter. "Are you taking the button with you, or what?"

"Yeah, thanks." She hustled to his duffle bag and snagged the canister, patting his arm as she passed him. "That boy distracts me like nothing else."

"Apparently."

She ignored him this time, hurrying across the open field to where she could see Mike sitting at the edge of the test pit. He was talking to Brad, something she might otherwise have avoided. It seemed safer there, almost sunnier.

Mike's smile faded when he saw her, replaced by a look of concern that knitted his brow into a frown. "What's up, Maddy girl?"

She thrust the canister at Brad, practically throwing it at him. "Found a button."

True to form, Brad looked impressed and pried the lid off the container. "That's what, the third of the day?"

She glanced at Mike. He was still staring at her, his eyes so narrowed that he almost looked suspicious. "I texted you, Maddy."

He was right, her phone had buzzed when she was blathering at Liam. She pulled her cell out of her pocket and glanced at the face.

Unimpressed. I've got two pair so far. I bet you're bad at poker.

"I'm bad at all sports." She shoved her phone in her pocket. "Oh well, excitement over. Nothing to see here, folks. All part of the show."

"Not bad, Madison." Brad held the button closer to his eye. "Her one blows your two out of the water, Caldwell. Look at how well the detail in the eagle is preserved; yours look like marbles in comparison."

"Don't be jealous of my superior digging skills." She sat next to him, feigning it like a casual movement. What she really wanted to do was crawl in his lap and hide from whatever it was that had attached itself to her. "I'm often imitated, but never surpassed."

"If you find me a canteen spout back there, we can have a battle royale between you two." Brad slid the button back into the container. "I honestly didn't expect to find anything back by the woods. I thought it would all be up here by the structures."

"Who did you say used this as a hospital?" She rubbed the back of her neck. "I mean, more specifically than just the Union Army."

"The 11th Corps, they were positioned over on Barlow's Knoll and later on Cemetery Ridge." Brad motioned in a somewhat western direction. "Did Liam document this? If so, I'm going to put it with the other artifacts and call it a day."

"He wrote something down; what it was, I couldn't tell you."

"Great job today, guys." He spun on his heel and headed toward his pickup. "Someone let Liam know once the pit is secure, he's free to go. Mike, you've got this one under control?"

"I think I can handle it." Mike's eyes remained on Brad only until the dig head was sufficiently far away from them. He dropped his voice and leaned closer. "You can't tell me nothing happened."

"I don't know what happened." She closed her eyes. "It's just…it's this voice. I can tell it's a man, but other than that...he sounds frantic. I can't always understand what he's saying, but when I can, it's only fragmented sentences and just a generalized sense of panic. I can feel his panic."

"What does he say?"

"He repeated 'dragged her' a couple times and something about trying to help but not being about to feel. The worst was when he kept repeating 'she' and 'her'—that's what got him agitated. That's when I came over here." She hesitated. "Sometimes I feel like I can hear him walking behind me."

"Did you see him again?"

"No. But I don't have to see him to know he's there. I can feel him next to me, can feel his breath on my cheek when he talks to me. I can hear his footsteps in the grass behind me." Madison buried her face in her hands. "I sound ridiculous."

"I can talk to Brad. Maybe he'll let you and Cianna switch, so you can work with me instead." He trailed his fingers over her knuckles and then covered her hand with his. "I don't want you to be miserable for the next few weeks."

"I think—" Madison shut her mouth as Cianna exited the summer kitchen, notebooks and oversized portfolios tucked under her arm. She watched the blonde girl struggle to adjust her pack strap on her shoulder, while still maintaining the balance of her art supplies. "I'll figure something out. It'll be fine."

"That's what you always say." He lowered his voice. "And I'm worried about you."

She smiled at him, the urge to throw her arms around him and kiss him nearly knocking her off balance. "Somehow I think he is, too."

"Did you guys see which direction Brad went?" Cianna shuffled over to the test pit, digging her hand into her pocket. "I told him not to leave without me."

Mike cocked his head toward the parked cars. "I think he went back to the truck. He said we're good to go for the day if everything's locked up and the pits are secure."

"I didn't lock the summer kitchen."

"I figured as much."

"I can't carry everything, Mike, Jesus Christ." Cianna struggled to pull something out of her pocket, inadvertently releasing the pressure of her arm against her paperwork and folders. Portfolios slid free, loose papers scattered like a hailstorm.

Madison lunged to the side to stop the papers from being caught in the wind. She gathered them on top of an open sketchbook, glancing at the top page as she handed them back to Cianna. It was a simple pencil sketch of the bank barn through the window of the summer kitchen. The interior of the kitchen was shaded as if in shadow, while the barn stood out crisp and clean. "That's really good, Cianna."

Cianna narrowed her eyes. "What?"

"The barn picture, it's gorgeous. You obviously have talent." Madison cleared her throat, uncomfortable that Cianna couldn't comprehend she was trying to be nice. "I really like it."

Cianna glanced down at the paper and then back at Madison, skepticism arching her eyebrow. "You like it."

"Yeah." Madison exchanged a glance with Mike. "Should I not like it?"

"Yeah, um, I mean no." She looked taken aback and then smiled, a subtle grin that seemed to soften her perpetual scowl. "Thank you."

Madison watched her walk to Brad's pickup and then tap on the passenger's side window. For a moment, she thought Brad was ignoring the impatient window thumping and was going to drive away without her. The brake lights came on and Cianna opened the door, shoving in her papers before following suit. "Those two have the strangest relationship."

"He keeps her around because she puts out." Mike stood and reached down to pull her after him. His hands were rough and calloused, no doubt from his years in the service, and he adjusted it around her, lacing his fingers between hers. "Let's lock up the summer kitchen and go. I've seen enough of this place for one day."

"We should probably tell Liam." The pressure of his hand against hers made it hard to think. Who actually had the key to the summer kitchen? She was fairly sure it wasn't her.

"Liam!" He cupped his hand by his mouth. "Brad split."

"It's about God damned time."

Mike let her hand go long enough to pull the exterior kitchen door closed and locked it. He jammed the key back into his pocket. "Ready?"

"The weekend awaits." She peered in the direction of the test pit. "Have a nice weekend, Liam!"

"Stay out of trouble, Sassy! No drinking."

Mike reached over and slid his fingers around hers. He led her to the makeshift parking lot and opened the Jeep door, trailing his fingertips down her back as she got in the passenger's seat. She watched him circle around the front of the vehicle. His gait was smooth and relaxed, the curve of his biceps pressing against his shirt fabric in a way that was far more distracting than it should have been. Jesus Christ, she'd sell a kidney to find out what it felt like to be held by those arms. Pinned down by those arms.

She exhaled sharply. *Focus. Keep it together.*

He climbed into the driver's seat and started the engine. "I'd say that wasn't too shabby a start to the dig. No unexploded ordinance but, hey, Brad can't win them all."

"I get the distinct impression we're already falling behind his strict timeline."

"Oh yeah, definitely." He backed out of the parking area and drove down the lane, the Jeep bumping and swaying on the uneven road. "Four weeks is not nearly enough time for a dig like this. We've spent more time surveying yards the size of utility sheds. The park expects to find bullets and buttons and general military paraphernalia. No one is going to be surprised at our finds so far."

"I'm used to cataloging nail fragments and sitting around hustling grant money. In comparison, this is like finding the Titanic."

"You're cuter than Bob Ballard."

"So…I was thinking…" She hesitated. "Do you want to hang out tonight? As much as I enjoy my fortress of solitude at the Inn, having company for dinner might be a nice change of pace."

Mike was silent. He slowed the Jeep to a stop at an intersection and glanced both ways before turning onto a battlefield lane. "I actually have plans tonight."

"Oh." She could hear the disappointment in her own voice. There was no point in trying to act like it didn't sting. "Okay, well, that's cool."

He again fell silent.

Madison felt like she might throw up. Had she misjudged the entire situation? He'd flirted with her for nearly a week. He'd held her hand today for God's sake. No, there was no way she'd misjudged anything…was there?

"I'm sorry, look…" His voice trailed off and he exhaled deeply, as if trying to expel a thick burden clotting his throat. "I see a counselor. Twice a week, Tuesday and Friday; every week, no exceptions—not even holidays—for the past year and a half. I…I had some issues when I came home from Afghanistan the last time."

"Okay." She glanced at him. His knuckles were white from the force of gripping the steering wheel. "So…what you're saying is, tomorrow would be better?"

"Seeing a counselor isn't normal."

"It isn't abnormal."

"It's been a year and a half."

"It doesn't make me want to be with you less." She flushed. Way to play it coy. "Okay, so you see a counselor and we can't go out tonight. We'll go out tomorrow. Or another night. Whatever."

"You're not upset?"

121

"There's no reason to be upset. My brothers and I saw a counselor after my dad died. I'm in counseling now for being a drunk. It is what it is." She shrugged. "You could see a counselor twice a week for the rest of your life and I wouldn't think less of you."

He was again silent. She glanced back at him. The color had drained back into his knuckles so he must have relaxed a little. His eyes were focused on the road ahead, his legs working the gas and the clutch as he switched gears. Well, this was awkward.

She inwardly grimaced and turned her gaze back out the passenger's side window. The curve of Cemetery Hill was to the front of the car. There was nothing remarkable about the hill and nothing out of the ordinary; it was dotted with stone monuments like the rest of the battlefield. People milled between artillery pieces and took pictures in front stone markers commemorating units and brigades, yet, something was unsettling. She stared at a barren patch of land, devoid of markers or monuments. A heartbeat pounded in her head, but her own pulse remained steady. The hint of a shadow, nothing more than a faint interruption in the otherwise clear landscape, caught her eye. It sank toward the ground and then was gone.

The heartbeat stopped.

Madison held her breath and dropped her gaze to her lap. Her hands trembled. She clenched them together and forced breath steadily in and out of her lungs. This had to stop. Something had to make it go away.

"Madison."

She jumped, embarrassed she'd been so distracted by her thoughts that she'd tuned out Mike's voice. "Yes. Sorry, I'm looking at the artillery pieces and monuments. Touristy, I know. What battery is that?"

"The one by the road is the 4th US Battery B and, I think, the one down by Howard's monument is New York Battery I. I think, this was all the 11th Corps. Howard's headquarters were over there."

"And they got all the way to the Spangler Farm?"

He nodded. "We can debate the maneuverability of the 11th Corps all you want later, but I was wondering... I mean, if it's too late you can say no, but I'll be done with the counselor at seven or seven-thirty. I can pick you up and show you around the battlefield. Uh, if you want. Or we can just hang out or...whatever."

Or...whatever left a lot open for her imagination to fill in. She suppressed a smile. "I wouldn't classify seven-thirty as too late. Text me when you're on your way, and I'll make sure I'm presentable. Or, at least, wearing adequate shoes."

"I think you're beautiful now."

"Well, I...um..." She blushed. "You're sweet, but I'm fully aware I smell like sweat and bug spray, not to mention the fact I look like I crawled out from underneath the bank barn."

"I wasn't going to mention the smell, but if you're going to bring it up..." He chuckled and turned the Jeep into the hotel parking lot. "I'm kidding."

"I'm not. I'm offending myself."

He slowed the Jeep to a stop and shifted it into park. "I'll text you as soon as I'm finished. I'm only over in Chambersburg, so I can be back here in less than half an hour."

"Sounds like a plan." She unfastened her seatbelt, hesitating before opening the door. Something felt left unsaid, as if she should say more to him. He still sounded like he was apologizing for having to go to a counselor.

"Hey." He caught her arm and gently pulled her back to him, pressing his lips to her cheek. "Thanks for understanding."

Invite him in. The idea sounded ridiculous and presumptuous; it was exactly what she wanted to say. Instead, she restrained herself, pursing her lips into a coy smile. "I'll see you tonight."

"Yes, you will."

She felt like she could do cartwheels the whole way back to her hotel room. It was like some kind of kitschy musical. The fact he'd kissed her on the cheek was far more meaningful than it probably should have been. They were adults. Yet, she felt like she did the first time Joey Clarke kissed her in their church's kitchen when they were twelve. Giddy. Stupidly smiley. Propensity of walking into walls.

She forced herself to walk across the parking lot at a respectable pace, turning to wave to him before scampering inside the building. There were only a couple hours to kill before he'd be back. Quick shower. Quick dinner. Then, just a marginal amount of time to waste waiting for his text, time that she could maybe fill up with a crossword puzzle or paperback—a sentiment that made her feel closer to seventy-one than twenty-one.

The hot water and steam of the shower was relaxing, enough to kick the butterflies in her stomach into submission. Her muscles ached. The tendons and ligaments in her upper shoulders and back throbbed as if she'd been moving heavy furniture all week instead of throwing her weight against the screen sifter. It was just another brutal reminder that, although she was thin, she was pathetically out of shape.

She stood under the unrelenting water, craning her neck from side to side in an attempt to work the muscles loose. Maybe Mike could crack her back for her. She smirked. Now that was a pickup line she'd have to remember: say, care to get on top and crack my back?

Once the conditioner was rinsed out of her hair, she turned the faucet off and reached for a towel. Her hair was getting long. It seemed like she'd need to use two or three of the thin, white hotel towels to sop up the excess water. No matter, she could resort to using the room's hair dryer and, in forty-five minutes or so, the feeble little machine might get her hair dry. Damn it, of all the things to leave at home. She hadn't planned on needing to look as attractive and desirable as humanly possible. If she had, she'd have brought along a better selection of makeup.

She towel dried her hair enough to keep water from trickling down her back, and then wrapped another towel around her body. It was a good thing she'd done a load of laundry the previous day. Not that she had "date" quality outfits with her, but she was fully aware which pair of jeans accentuated her curves the best. She pulled on a red vintage style t-shirt emblemized with a grayed out Union Jack. It was casual and cute, though she was reasonably sure her clothes were the last thing on his mind.

The steam from the small bathroom had filtered out into the sink area, fogging up the mirror and giving everything a generally damp feeling. She wiped her hand across the condensation covered mirror. In the unobstructed reflection she could see a figure, a man, standing directly behind her.

She bit back a shriek and jerked around. There was no one there; the room was empty.

"Shit." The words felt as if they bubbled out of her throat, pushed out by her rapid heartbeat. She gripped the countertop with one hand to steady herself. The reflection in the mirror was clear and crisp. It wasn't a shadow or the light playing on the steam from the shower. It was a man. It was him, the man who'd been watching her for days. He'd stood and watched her at the Spangler Farm. He'd breathed on the back of her neck, whispered in her ear as she worked in the test pit.

Now he was in her room.

Madison swallowed hard, peering into the main section of the hotel room. It was empty. Nothing was out of place, no one was watching her from any corner of the room; yet, she didn't feel completely alone. He was still there.

Her hand faltered on the countertop and she sank backward, half sitting, half leaning against the sink. The air in the room felt soupy and stale. Gooseflesh rippled down her still damp arms and across her back. What in Christ's name did he want from her?

She felt him next to her, his breath on her shoulder. *Please.*

Could he hear her when she spoke to him? It was worth a try. "I'm not sure I know how to help you."

But she knew someone who did.

* * * *

It took her far longer to get dressed than it should have, as she'd made the clumsy effort to keep her towel around her while pulling on underwear and bra, but she was out the door and down the stairs in less than ten minutes. She hadn't wasted time drying her hair, though she realized she should have. It was brushed, but hung down to her mid-back in dripping tendrils that left her shirt increasingly damp. Ridiculous. Part of her felt like a child; running away from a voice in her head, from things she couldn't explain. Maybe she was crazy, maybe it was all in her head, but she felt the desperation in his voice better than she could hear it. Something was wrong.

The windows of the palm reader's shop were dark. She slowed her pace considerably, almost to a stop and studied the front door. Too late. Shoot, how had she missed her? Closed. The sign in the front window was almost mocking: too slow, Madison. Always too slow. Always missing out. She exhaled loudly, pressing her palms to her forehead. Maybe there were weekend hours.

As she stepped toward the store front, the door opened. Lenore's eyes widened and she shifted her bag and stack of books to her other arm. "I figured there was a reason I was running late this evening."

"I can hear him now." Madison heard the waver in her voice. "And I don't know what to do."

Lenore's expression softened and she motioned her into the store. "Does Mike know you're here?"

"I'm sorry for what he said to you."

"Mr. Caldwell is more complicated than you are. I didn't take his sentiments personally." She set the stack of books on the counter. "Do you want a cup of tea? I have spice and chamomile."

"Oh, no, please, I don't want to keep you. I just have a few questions and…I guess…" Madison hesitated. "I need advice."

"I'll help you as best I can." Lenore flicked on the waiting room lights and sat down in the arm chair, tucking one of her legs beneath her. "You've come a long way in a few days if you can hear him now."

"I can hear him, I can feel him, I can see him." Madison sat down across from her and again pressed her palms to her forehead. "Even when I can't exactly hear him, I feel like I can hear him in my head. He's always there. And…the more I actually verbalize it, the crazier I feel."

"You're a sensitive, Madison. It's a gift, not a curse. Though," — Lenore sighed — "sometimes it isn't necessarily a blessing."

"But, why me? Of all the people who crawl all over this battlefield and all the people who *know* they're sensitive and *know* how to use their gift, why did he pick me?"

"That's not something I can answer."

"Well, that's not something he can answer either."

"Did you ask him?"

Madison stared at her.

"You should ask him. I highly doubt he wouldn't tell you, if he could." Lenore adjusted several oversized, gold bracelets over her wrists. "There are two types of hauntings, residual and intelligent. Residual hauntings are like a broken record, just a blip of action or speech pattern the spirit continuously repeats. They can't see you, they can't interact with you. They aren't necessarily cognizant that it's even happening."

Madison thought of the soldier she'd seen on Culp's Hill, crouched down and sliding toward a stone wall. Perhaps he was reliving—in death—the last moments of his life.

"Intelligent hauntings, however, are the opposite. They know what's going on. They can see you, talk to you, and—if they're strong enough—can touch you. These spirits don't always know they're dead. I think your spirit does, though. He doesn't sound confused. He sounds like he's frantic to get his point across."

"I still don't understand why he picked me." Madison slouched back against the couch cushions. "I wasn't trying to be sensitive to anything; I was just there to do my job."

Lenore tented her fingers in front of her face, pressing her fingertips into her lips as if she was deep in thought. "So, you've never dealt with a spirit before?"

"Never. I worked on the Pittsburgh Allegheny Cemetery commission two years ago and spent five to six hours a day in a cemetery. Nothing strange or out of the ordinary happened in the three months I worked on the project."

"Do you have family who fought here at Gettysburg? Could it be someone in your family or a direct ancestor?"

Madison shook her head. "My father's side didn't emigrate from Germany until the 1880s. My mother's side had two brothers who served, but they fought in the Western Theater, mainly in Tennessee."

"There's something about you, though, something so strong that he's attached himself." Lenore tilted her head from side to side. "He won't answer me anymore. He's wholly focused himself on you."

"I feel useless to him. Part of the time he sounds like he's underwater. Other than that, he sounds like he's screaming at me from two miles down the road." Madison squirmed in the seat, cracking the knuckle on each finger individually, one at a time. "I get like, one or two words at most that I can hear well."

"But you've seen him."

She nodded. "I've seen him so well I can make out the features in his face. He's young, probably my age or a little older. His eyes are wide, panicked almost, and he looks...he looks sad."

"Has he told you his name?"

"I didn't ask."

Lenore leaned forward and reached for her hand. "Ask him now. I'll help you."

"No...I, I can't." Madison looked away, focusing her attention to the stack of books on the counter. "I feel like an idiot."

"Just try." Lenore grasped her hand and turned it over, palm up. "Focus your mind on him. Open yourself up, close your eyes if you have to, but try and empty your mind of all thoughts; of Mike, of the dig, of feeling silly. Picture your mind as a blank slate. Let him use your energy to answer you."

Maybe this was the point in the evening when Lenore shoved a soldering iron through her skull. She didn't like the vulnerability of sitting there with her eyes shut. Curiosity won out. She felt like a fool, but closed her eyes, trying to will panicked thoughts out of her mind. She focused instead on the darkness, expelling thoughts and distraction with each exhaled breath. "Can you tell me your name?"

Silence.

She frowned and took a deep breath, holding it in her lungs until she couldn't go without oxygen anymore. Exhaling slowly through her mouth, she tried again. "Please, tell me your name."

He was next to her, standing over her and looking down at the top of her head. She could feel him lean down closer, as if he was trying to whisper in her ear. *Ben.*

"Ben." She repeated his name. There was something about knowing his name that made him seem more concrete. He wasn't an imaginary figment, he'd been a person. He'd had feelings and desires and hopes until one day, sometime over the course of three days in July 1863, it all ended. He'd ended, but something—no doubt whatever it was he was trying to tell her—made him stay. "I'm glad to know your name, Ben."

Madison...please... His voice faded and then was suddenly too garbled to understand.

She groaned, opening her eyes to study Lenore. "He was completely clear and then faded into mumbling. Why does that happen?"

"It takes an incredible amount of energy for him to speak to you, let alone become visual. Most spirits can only contact through tapping or light manipulation. Full figured apparitions, like you described, are rare. He's exhausted." Lenore paused. "And he's obviously desperate."

"You said he can feed off my energy." Madison chewed on the inside of her lip and frowned. "How can I help him do that?"

"Practice. Work on honing the technique you just used now. Make yourself open. Physically relax yourself—tighten and release your muscles—from the top of your head to the end of your toes. Empty your mind, strengthen your focus, and you'll get there. He'll help you." Lenore hesitated, briefly looking away. "Keep in mind, though, when you open yourself up, he's not the only spirit who might come in. There are innumerable spirits in Gettysburg. The air is saturated with them. Residual, intelligent, what have you, but they're here. They'll feed on that energy as well."

"And hurt me?" Her voice cracked. Ben was one thing, but a vindictive spirit manipulating her or attacking her was horrifying.

Lenore seemed to consider it. She spoke slowly. "I don't feel as if there are dark spirits here. There are troubled spirits, those who are confused and scared. They don't know they've passed and don't understand what's happened to them. They're the panicked, the persistent. They can be overwhelming."

"All of this is overwhelming."

"It is, but you'll handle it." Lenore hesitated again, as if there was something she wanted to say but couldn't bring herself to utter the words. "If you trust someone enough to help you, you can always consider long-standing contact methods, like glass divination. Be careful though, as with that amount of energy, you'll be open to any number of earthbound spirits."

"I trust you." Madison shrugged. "Why can't we try it now?"

"Ben is connected to the Spangler Farm. If you try something like glass divination, you'll get the best results there. He'll be strongest there." She hesitated again, a habit which was quickly becoming an irritant. "You need to be careful. "

"I thought you said there were no dark spirits in Gettysburg."

"I said I don't think there are dark spirits here." Lenore's eyes fluttered shut. She inhaled deeply and then exhaled slowly, turning her palms up. "But I feel there's darkness at the Spangler Farm. It's not Ben radiating it, it's coming from other voices. I feel it…at least two distinct spirits are in agreement. They're chiming in, they keep saying 'she, she, she'. Do you know what that means?"

Madison shook her head. "No…but he's said that to me, too."

"Three spirits, one message." Lenore leveled her gaze, her face as expressionless as solid marble. "One warning. Whatever is wrong at the Spangler Farm, you need to be careful. It will find you. And when it does, no one—not Mike, not Ben—is going to be able to stop it."

Chapter Eleven

Madison slid her finger across the face of her cell phone. Ten minutes had passed since Mike texted her. He'd told her the trip from Chambersburg would only take him about twenty minutes, but it felt like she'd gotten the text four hours ago. After her chat with Lenore, she really didn't feel like being alone. The hotel room seemed stifling and stale, so she decided to wait for him outside.

Outside, though, didn't feel much better. Maybe "opening" herself up to Ben was a mistake. She felt vulnerable, as if unseen eyes were staring at her. Sizing her up. Testing. Watching.

Waiting.

She slid her finger across the face of the phone again, this time pulling up the web browser. Entering the search term "glass divination", she tapped her finger against the first web address that came up. The method sounded simple enough.

Long used in séances to contact the spirits of the dead, glass divination is typically performed with two to five people. Participants gently rest their fingertips on an upturned glass, focusing their energy and minds on the spirit(s) around them. The spirit is queried by manner of yes or no questions, urging the spirit to contact and answer through direct tapping or manipulation of the glass. As the energy force increases, the spirit should be able to move the glass over and across the tabletop without direct manipulation from participants. See Ouija Board.

She looked up from her cell phone. It seemed doable. It also seemed vaguely illegal, considering the fact Lenore suggested actually going to the Spangler Farm to perform it. It wasn't going to be easy to convince anyone—especially Mike—to help her break into park property for a glorified séance.

Most likely.

Tucking the phone back in her pocket, she slouched farther down the bench and shut her eyes. There were so many positives to this dig, namely actual archeological experience and the possibility of sex with Mike, but she didn't feel like being a sounding board for a desperate, lost soul. She couldn't do anything for him. Really, how could he expect her to help him when she couldn't hear him most of the time?

He was with her. She could feel him standing over her as if he were staring at her face. Concern and uncertainty seemed to radiate from him. The hairs at her temples tingled like he was brushing his fingertips across her brow. His voice was in her ear. *Help...help like I couldn't...I need you...*

She answered him out loud before she could stop herself with a whisper, no more than a murmur. "I don't know how to help you."

He was too strong. I wasn't. I wasn't. You are. You can help me, can help her. Her. Her.

Madison squeezed her eyes tighter. What did it mean? "Ben...who are you talking about?"

Madison. He sounded drained, his voice growing fainter with each syllable. *Her. I can't. Too late...I was too late...*

Her eyes fluttered open. She could still hear him, but his voice was too far away to understand his words. He was talking, rambling almost as if he was telling the whole story to her, yet she still couldn't hear him. She still couldn't hear him.

A familiar white Jeep Wrangler stopped in the traffic on Steinwher Street, turn signal blinking in the direction of the hotel lot. Mike. She felt her lips spread into a ridiculously wide smile. For a while, at least, she could focus on something other than the dead. *Sorry, Ben.*

"Hey, Maddy girl." He leaned his head out the window. "Ready?"

"I'm beyond ready." She jumped up from the bench and crossed the sidewalk to the Jeep. He'd leaned across the seats and opened her door. "It's been a strange afternoon."

"Maybe I can help improve your evening."

"I need it improved."

"He came back, didn't he?" Mike circled the Jeep around the parking lot and pulled out onto the street. "The Spangler Farm...thing."

"Yeah, we've really been getting to know each other today, he and I. His name's Ben. He may have watched me take a shower this afternoon." She shuddered. "He's very persistent."

"Did he tell you why he's so bent on contacting you?"

"No. No, that's the one thing he hasn't gotten around to telling me yet. He's frantic. I think he saw something he couldn't stop, but other than that, he still just repeats 'her' over and over again. I don't know if I'm 'her' or if someone else is and, even if I did, I don't know what I'm supposed to do with that information." She sighed. "I saw him, though. Plain as day, right there in my hotel room."

"Does he scare you?"

"No. He frustrates me." She glanced at him out of the corner of her eye. He seemed relaxed, his arm propped up on the open window and his fingers bobbling with the movement of the car. "How do you feel about séances?"

"I think if Abraham Lincoln endorsed Mary Todd's séances in the White House, I can endorse yours."

"How do you feel about breaking onto the Spangler Farm and trying glass divination in the summer kitchen?"

"I think," —He slowed to a stop at an intersection and leaned over, pressing his lips to her cheek — "you should stop thinking about it."

"Are you offering to distract me?"

"I'm offering to do my best. That's why I'm taking you to one of the best places in the park."

"I hope they serve alcohol."

"Naughty girl." He turned the Jeep onto a battlefield road. "It's better than that. Well, I think it is; you might end up seeing some kind of ghost regiment and we'll have to go back to the hotel."

"Tell me again why that's a bad thing?" She hesitated. "You know what scares me the most is that it's just in my head. All of it, that there's no one watching me or trying to tell me something."

"That palm reader seemed to pick up on it, so why couldn't it be true?" He shrugged, turning the Jeep into a thickly wooded area. The terrain was hillier than before, the setting sun nearly obscured by thick overgrowth. "I don't think it's hard to believe. Tragedy never leaves a place, it leaves a mark. And…I can tell you from experience, that mark doesn't go away. Ever."

"I just wish I knew why he picked me."

"Who wouldn't pick you?" The hill crested and he pulled the Jeep into a parking area on the left side of the road. "You caught my attention from the moment you stepped out of Brad's truck."

He didn't give her time to respond, instead climbing out of the Jeep and circling around the vehicle to open her door. "Come on, I want to show you something."

"Little Round Top?"

"It's the best place in the park to watch the sunset." He laced his fingers around hers and led her up a steep paved path. Enormous boulders—one topped with a brass statue of a man overlooking the valley below—bordered the winding trail to the crest. "I used to come up here in the fall, just to think. It's too loud up here in the summer, too many bus tours and people, but in the late fall it's usually pretty deserted."

In the distance, she could see the enormous rocky outline of Devil's Den. The hillside itself was covered in fallen rocks and thick weeds. "I can't imagine trying to take this hill."

"The soldier in me can't comprehend it either. Trying to charge this hill, scramble over these rocks, while the Union soldiers here were firing down on them? It's suicide."

"It's beautiful now." She could hear chatter behind her, mumblings she knew came from the dead. *...Hazlett's dead...right flank is weak...* She tried to tune them out. "But sad. I can't imagine what it took to see death staring you down, to know chances were good you were going to die, and still make the decision to march forward anyway."

He climbed onto a boulder and pulled her up after him, then sank down to a seated position. "It's not all that different from now. You're one of a group, you're marching together. Somehow that takes away part of the trepidation."

"Do you think your military experience gives you different perspective on archeology?"

"Sometimes, if it's trying to understand why things are where we find them." He pulled her down next to him so she was leaning against his chest. "Archeology is just one big game of Russian roulette. You dig a quarter of an inch in the wrong direction and you never find what's buried. That's what's going to happen at the Spangler Farm, you watch. We put our test pits in random places to 'preserve' the integrity of the site, but it seems too haphazard."

The movement of his lips tickled loose strands of her hair. She shivered.

"Are you cold?" He wrapped his arms around her, pulled her closer to him. "I have a sweatshirt in the Jeep if you want it. I can't guarantee it's clean, but it's there."

"I'd rather you keep me warm."

"I can do that."

She held her hand up to the sky. "I once saw on a survival television show you can measure how much daylight is left with your hand. You put your hand up to the horizon and each finger represents fifteen minutes. So, basing my guess entirely on that assumption, I'll wager there's about half an hour to go."

"Do you plan on being put in a survival situation where you'd need that kind of logic?" He tightened his arms around her waist. It seemed like such a casual movement, like they'd been together for years.

"No, but even paper archeologists theoretically could end up with their backs against the wall."

"What if I had your back pressed up against the wall?"

"Why don't you try it and find out? I'm fairly sure you won't hear me complaining."

He chuckled. "Don't you want to watch the sunset? It's beautiful, it's romantic. How many opportunities do you get to be here, on Little Round Top, watching the sunset over the battlefield?"

"Unless something catastrophic happens with my archeological career, I'm assuming tomorrow would be the next opportunity." She sighed. "I guess I should say something more catastrophic. My alcoholic reputation precedes me."

"I think you'll be fine." He paused. "Because, you know, I'm the poster child of archeologists without problems."

"They almost threw me out of school."

"Eh, I remember a time in my younger days when I got wasted at my annual training with the Army. I was so hung over I was lying under a five-ton truck puking my guts out. 'They' told me I'd never amount to anything. And 'they' eventually promoted me to lieutenant. So, see. Idle threats."

"I guess I don't technically need my doctorate. I mean, worst case scenario." She leaned her head back against him and looked up at the sky. He was right, the golden hues of daylight melting down into the horizon was pretty.

"You don't even need to have a masters. I have mine because the Army paid for it, but I had my job right out of school. Granted, that was because I knew Brad, but still." He paused. "Brad doesn't even have his doctorate."

"It's just always been my plan: go to school, get good grades and my degree. Then the real world hits and I meet Cianna, an archeologist who doesn't even have a degree related to the field and still has more experience than me."

"I wouldn't compare you to her. She doesn't even measure close."

They fell into a comfortable silence. His breath was hot on her neck and, as much as she wanted to try and enjoy the beauty of the setting sun, he distracted her. It was a sunset. It looked like every other sunset she'd ever seen. People wandered around the path next to them. She occasionally heard a faint whisper she couldn't explain, but her focus was on him. The way his lips brushed against her neck. The way she seemed to fit perfectly in his arms and the way he smelled like musky cologne; forget the battlefield and the sunset and voices from the dead. Forget Normandy. Hell, forget it all.

He brushed her hair away from her neck and pressed his lips to her skin. "So…you want to go check out some monuments?"

"Is that a euphemism?"

"We have to head in that direction anyway." He stood, pulling her up after him, and led her back to the Jeep. "Might as well show you my favorite."

He pulled the Jeep back onto the main road, circling around the craggy formations of Devils Den and around sharps turns leading into the woods. The road dipped and wound around more sharp bends, the headlights reflecting off marble monuments in unexpected bursts of light. Each stark white explosion was like a new terror, as if the headlights were reflecting off the glow of the dead.

She tapped her fingers against the passenger's seat. "The sunset was nice, by the way."

"It was my feeble attempt to impress you."

"I was already impressed, but you scored points for romantic thematic elements."

He slowed the Jeep and eased it to the side of the road, stopping in front of a monument tucked into a thick overgrowth of trees. Madison's eyes had adjusted to the dark and, in the glow of the headlights, she could see the marble was fashioned into Celtic cross. A stone wolfhound was stretched out at the base of the cross, his head tucked solemnly between his front paws.

"It's to the Irish Brigade." He tapped his fingertips against the steering wheel, craning his head to better see out his window. "Call me sentimental, but it's my favorite. Over thirteen hundred monuments and memorials in the whole park, and this one gets me every time."

"Did you have ancestors in the Irish Brigade?"

He nodded. "Jacob Bowser, he was in the 63rd New York Infantry."

"That's really cool. I have a few ancestors who fought in the Western Theater, but my family was too new to this country for the most part. We were still slumming around Germany until the turn of the century."

"It's another one of my quirks, I guess you could say." He shrugged and opened the driver's side door. "I got a free trial period to one of the family history databases online and conveniently forgot to cancel before they started charging my credit card. By that point, I had to get my money's worth and spent 'you don't want to know' how many hours researching my family tree."

She waited as he circled the Jeep and opened her door for her. "As quirks go, that's not a bad one. I like to read science fiction and eat cheese. It could be worse."

"We're kind of nerdy, you and I."

"Nerds are cool." She stood on her tip toes to better see the wolfhound. "It's a beautiful monument."

"The wolfhound is life size." He trailed his fingertips across an inscription below the dog's paws. "That's what it says here, anyway. At the dedication ceremony in 1888, Father Corby called the cross an 'emblem of Ireland'. They were decimated at Antietam and Frederickburg and barely had enough for two companies each once they got here, but they still fought like hell back at the Wheatfield."

"You'll have to bring me back here in the daytime to see it better. Honestly, I can't see much of anything right now."

"I know." He turned and caught her in his arms, pressing her gently against the base of the monument. Cupping the side of her face with his hand, he trailed his fingertips down her cheek and along her jawbone. "I had ulterior motives."

"Oh, really?" The corners of her lips tugged up into a smile.

"I have a confession." He cradled her in his arms, his lips impossibly close to hers. "I'm...I'm falling in love with you."

"I think it goes without saying that the attraction is mutual." Her pulse raced like she'd just gotten the acceptance letter into graduate school, except, she knew she wanted Mike more. "Just as long as you don't think I'm easy."

"You don't seem like the type of girl who looks back." He tilted her chin down and brushed his lips against hers. "But, I didn't want to lead you on. Incase...you know...you didn't feel the same way—"

"You had me at Pennsylvania bank barn." She rose up onto her tip toes and kissed him, letting her teeth nibble on his lower lip. "If you'd played your cards right, you could have had me *in* the Pennsylvania bank barn."

"I could take you back to your hotel room." He kissed her again, flicking his tongue against hers, taunting her by pulling away instead of kissing her deeper.

"Yes, you should."

"You have your key, right?"

"I'm fairly sure I do." She pulled him back to the Jeep and they both climbed inside. "And if I don't, you can just fuck me in the parking lot."

He laughed, swerving the vehicle back onto the main road. His hand slid to her knee, his fingertips lightly trailing down the inside of her leg.

Her breath caught in her throat. "If you're going to do that, you're going to need to drive faster."

"I'm incapable of breaking the speed limit in a national park. I physically cannot shift out of second gear and tempt fate." He chuckled. "I probably shouldn't even be out of first gear, but I'll admit you push me into second gear, baby."

"That's oddly complementary."

"Well, you know, I'm still trying to woo you."

He parked the Jeep in a public parking lot a short ways from the hotel, looking somewhat apologetic. "I'm a stickler for free parking."

"Free parking and second gear?" She raised her eyebrow quizzically. "I knew you were an old soul, but I didn't think you were actually an old man."

He circled around the vehicle and opened her door, pulling her out of the seat and into his arms. "Says the girl who never remembers her room key."

"I have many more redeeming qualities."

She led him across the street and up the two flights of stairs to her room and, with much satisfaction, produced the room key from her pocket. "You'll have to excuse the mess. I'm...well, frankly, I'm a slob. And I left in a hurry."

"I'll try not to openly judge you."

She hesitated as she opened the door, sliding her hand in the room to switch on the light before strolling inside. The room was, of course, empty—but she wasn't convinced he was gone. *Please, just leave me alone for like, fifteen minutes. Maybe twenty. With my luck it'll be ten.*

Mike closed the door behind them and caught her wrist, pulling her back to him. He brushed his lips against hers. "So…nine tattoos. If I can find them all, what kind of reward do I get?"

"You can have me."

"Can't I have you anyway?"

"Well, yeah. But making you work for it makes me seem less easy."

"I don't think you're easy." He scooped her up in his arms and carried her to the bed. "I mean, it's not like we just met. We just met a week ago."

"I bided my time." She kicked off her flip flops. "Such a lady."

He pulled her wrist to his lips and kissed the fleur de lis tattoo. "One."

"Too easy."

He pushed up the legs of her jeans away from her ankles and studied two large watercolor tattoos stretching from the base of her toes to well above her ankles. A magpie was etched on the top of each foot, surrounded by a tangle of faded greenery and dull blue and purple flowers. He pressed his lips to each ankle. "Two and three."

"One for sorrow, two for joy." She was blabbering and she knew it. "It's from an eighteenth century nursery rhyme."

"I'm not surprised." He crawled up on the bed beside her and unfastened her jeans, sliding them down her hips and off her legs. Large, black centered red poppies were tattooed from her right knee, to well above her hip bone, the vibrant color a stark contrast to the faded, watercolor style on her feet and ankles. He trailed his lips from her knee to the edge of her underwear. "Four."

He eased her shirt up and over her head to unveil an orange and yellow phoenix on her right side. "Five."

Latin underneath her left collarbone. Alis volat propriis; she flies with her own wings. "Six."

Black lace and filigree on the top of her left shoulder. "Seven."

Song lyrics in between her shoulder blades, *but the fighter still remains.* "Eight."

He had to search for the last one, a tie dyed colored peace sign on the back of her neck, just below her hairline. "Nine." He kissed the back of her neck, trailing his kiss to her jawbone and then to her lips. "I win."

"Winner takes all."

He kissed her, cradling her face in his hand and caressing his tongue against hers. He moved slowly, almost deliberately, sliding his hands from her face to her back. His palms were flat against her skin and he pressed them underneath her bra and down her sides, as if he were acquainting himself with her curves from ribs to hips and back again.

She dug her fingertips into the fabric of his shirt and tugged it upwards. He pushed himself up into a sitting position and yanked it off the rest of the way, tossing it to the floor. As he reach down and unbuckled his belt, Madison let her eyes drift across his chest. He was trim and muscular; on his left peck was the tattoo of a skull in an Army beret, encircled by the words US Army. She could see what looked like a red castle on his left bicep and what might have been a black keystone on his right. The keystone was cut by a thick scar. With her eyes, she followed it up his arm until she lost it at the top of his shoulder.

His gaze met hers. He shimmied out of his jeans and briefs. "Don't worry about that."

"I'm more worried about a ghost watching us."

He slid her underpants down and, once off, nudged her legs apart with his knee. "I can turn the light off."

"Leave it on."

He smirked and kissed her again, lowering himself down on top of her. With a gentle thrust of his hips he was inside her. He let out a little moan against her lips and fumbled with her bra, finally yanking it up over her breasts so he could get to them.

Her breath caught in her throat. She moved her feet to his calves, pushing herself up to better match his rhythm. "You feel amazing."

"Jesus, a week was too long to wait for this." He caught the underside of her knee and pulled her leg up, pinning it under his arm. "I might have to make this one up to you."

"I'm not timing you."

He touched his forehead to hers and kissed her, his light laugh soft against her lips. "Good, well, just do me a favor and stop arching your back like that."

"Like how? Like this?"

"Exactly like that." He bit his lip and again kissed her, mumbling against her lips. "God…Madison…you're…"

He looked at her for a moment, as if he was going to say something else, but instead buried his face against her shoulder, dragging his teeth across her skin. As far as she was concerned, whatever he had to say didn't matter. All she cared about was that he kept making her feel the way she did. She could feel it from the pit of her stomach to the tips of her toes. Every movement he made sent sizzles of electricity down her spine, made her want him to slow down so the feeling didn't stop. Fuck graduate school. This made getting thrown off the Normandy dig entirely worth it.

* * * *

After they'd showered, he perched on the edge of the bed and watched her brush out her hair. "Your tattoos are beautiful, by the way. Not as beautiful as you. But they're stunning."

"I spent more time getting inked than I've ever spent studying." She dropped her hand to her thigh and idly traced a tangle of poppies. "This one was the worst. It took forever. My ankles were the most sensitive because of the bones, but this one was so damn big, I had to do it in like, five sessions."

"Do you think you'll get any more?"

"It's an addiction, so yeah, once I figure out the next piece." She pulled her hair back into a ponytail and crossed the room to him. "I'm particular. Not to mention poor, since the stipend on this gig wouldn't cover a tat the size of quarter."

He pulled her into his lap and kissed her. "I guess I should get going."

"I think you should stay."

"Well, I did want some of that continental breakfast you've raved about."

She laughed and kissed him. "Get into bed."

"You drive a hard bargain."

She turned the light off and hustled through the darkness to reach the bed, snuggling against him under the covers. She felt safe. Secure. Whatever was prowling around in the dark would have to get past Mike to get to her and, irrational as it sounded, it made her feel better. He was real beneath her fingertips. He wasn't a dream. He wasn't an echo from the past. He was hers. She was his.

He was silent beside her for so long, she'd convinced herself he'd fallen asleep. But then he spoke, his voice barely above a whisper. "I have to tell you about the scar."

She looked up at him, even though she knew she couldn't make out the features of his face. "No, you don't."

"I want to tell you what happened." His arm tightened around her, but she could feel a tremor in his fingertips. "I don't want to hide it from you because...whether I like it or not, it's me. And I trust you, I know you'll understand."

"Okay."

He fell silent again before taking a deep breath. "The scar isn't just on my arm. It's in my head. When I got home, after it was all said and done and they'd pinned medals on our chests and told us we were heroes, I couldn't shake it. Everything that happened seemed to fester in my brain like a splinter festers under your skin."

She remained quiet.

"We were on patrol outside Fallujah. One of my buddies, Cam, and I were doing a sweep of this house. We'd been past it a thousand times, these two little girls were always on the front stoop. It was just like any other house. They all started to look the same after a while. In and out. There were two rooms in the back of the house. We'd been playing poker all afternoon and Cam owed me two hundred bucks, so he gets this bright idea and says, 'You know, Lieutenant, I don't have two hundred bucks to pay you. How about I let you pick left or right and we call it even?' I told him he was a cocksucker. He said he'd let me pick and he'd spot me fifty bucks next hand. So, I stepped in front of him and went left with Dennings and Stormer, and he went right with Martinez and Baker. And...the next thing I know, the entire center wall was blowing up in my face. Everything went black for…God, I don't even know how long I was out for, maybe a minute or two. I was lying on the ground. My arm was ripped open, my ear was bleeding from the percussion of the explosion. Dennings lost an eye. Stormer's legs were blown apart. Then this firefight broke out and…there were shots coming from everywhere. People yelling in what seemed like a hundred different languages. I just remember crawling through the rubble and finding Cam—"His voice broke and he cleared his throat, hesitating for a beat. "Dennings and I had to drag Stormer back to the trucks. I still don't know how we did it. I could barely lift my M16 to fire and Dennings was half blind. But even then I knew. I *knew*. I was the one who made the choice. I should have gone to the right. I'd taken a step in that direction but when Cam put the option out on the table, I just mindlessly went to the left. And he died. Because of me, he went into that room and got blown up by some fucking kid with explosives strapped to her stomach. It should have been me."

"You couldn't have known. It wasn't anybody's fault." She didn't know what else to say. Saying nothing probably would have been the better course, but at that moment, he seemed so vulnerable. The guilt and devastation seemed to weigh in his voice, like it was pulling even the tone and tenor down.

"No, it wasn't my fault. But you know what they called me? They called me a hero." He rubbed his free hand over his eyes. "The Army, in their infinite wisdom, gave me the Bronze Star for 'a heroic and meritorious achievement in service' in dragging Stormer back to the trucks with one hand and evidently shooting a bunch of militants with the other. I saw it as an award for killing my best friend. Then, they gave me the Purple Heart for almost getting my arm ripped off, which I saw as further confirmation I was too weak to have saved Cam anyway. I tried to kill myself in the hospital and I couldn't even get that right. My enlistment was up and I told them all to go to hell, but even if I hadn't, they put a medical flag on my record for behavioral health issues and I couldn't have re-upped if I'd wanted. I was honorably discharged and sent home as a hero. All I really wanted was to not feel anything anymore, for the ground just to swallow me up and make it all go away."

"Did you go home to family?"

"Thank God I did, or else I probably would have tried suicide again. My mom, she saved me. I hated her for it at first, but she kept her eye on me. She got on my case when I drank too much, made sure I wasn't alone when I was down, and forced me to go to counseling sessions. It's been almost two years, but if I close my eyes, I can see his face. He...he looked surprised, like he didn't expect to see them—"

His voice broke and he exhaled, his breath ragged. He dragged the back of his hand across his eyes and then squeezed her against him. "Now that I've effectively ruined the moment."

"I don't think so." She leaned up and pressed her lips to his. "What happened isn't anything to be ashamed of; it makes you who you are. And, if I can be so blunt, I really dig who you are."

"That makes me happier than I can describe." He cupped her face in his hand. "There's something about you I just can't shake. I've never been able to talk about Cam, but with you, it's easy. Like it's okay."

"And I'm a good time."

He chuckled. "And you're a good time, but you're more than that—to me, anyway."

She snuggled against him, the silence surprisingly comfortable, and listened to his breathing grow increasingly deeper as he drifted to sleep. Everything seemed ridiculously perfect. She was falling in love with a brutally hot man. She had an impressive gig at an archeological site, though, the boy far outweighed the job. It was enough to make her smile in the dark.

She felt pressure on the bed next to her, as if someone had braced their hand against the mattress to lean over her. Something moved; a pressure, a movement so subtle and soft that slid strands of her hair from her neck. His voice was stronger this time; his breath tickled her flesh. *He's the one who will understand.*

Chapter Twelve

For the remainder of the weekend, Mike left her room only long enough to pick up clean clothes, his toothbrush, and Chinese takeout for dinner. He reported that, despite his efforts not to rouse Liam's suspicion, Liam was suspicious and accused him of fucking her. Mike hadn't denied it. Liam's response was, reportedly, "Well, it's about time."

"I think it's a better utilization of resources for you to stay here, anyway." Madison tossed her book bag into the back and crawled into the Jeep. "Gas prices as they are. Granted, you're not receiving the same miniscule stipend I am, but still. You have to think about the big picture."

"I think I'm spoiling you." He sounded unusually playful. "Shouldn't I make you miss me? Wouldn't that make you want me more?"

"Not a fair tactic."

"I'm not saying I'd actually go through with it, because that'd keep me from getting what I want. That's counterproductive."

"You, sir, are enjoyable to have around." She hesitated. "Besides, when you're with me, he leaves me alone."

"Who, Brad?" Mike shifted the Jeep into drive and pulled out onto the main street. "Oh. You mean *him*, him."

"Unless I've been too distracted to notice."

"Not to brag, but I have been pretty distracting, haven't I?"

"You're surprisingly spry for an old man."

He reached over and squeezed her knee, then rested his hand on her thigh. "Despite your age discrimination, I'll guess I'll stick with you instead of Liam. I'm pretty sweet on you and, really, he just has a nasty habit of stealing my t-shirts."

"To be fair I, too, have stolen one of your t-shirts."

"You had to wear something to the ice machine. Flip flops and a smile weren't going to cut it." He chuckled. "I mean, I was completely okay with it, but that family of four across the hall might have disapproved."

She laughed and slid her hand into his. It was different with him than it had been with Anthony, or any other previous boyfriend for that matter. Mike could look into her eyes and tell her how crazy he was for her or tease her and tell her ridiculous jokes. Either way, she always felt like she was the center of his attention. Anyone could be passionate, but with Mike, she felt like she was home: happy, relaxed, just herself. Nerdy, history obsessed Madison—and that was who he wanted.

He slowed the Jeep at an intersection and flicked on the turn signal to make a left hand turn. Madison leaned forward in her seat and squinted, staring across the street at a small, family run diner. "Is that Brad?"

"I'm willing to bet that Cianna he's intertwined with."

Brad's arms were wrapped around a petite blonde, her head tucked awkwardly underneath his chin. As Madison watched, the stance only looked more awkward and unnatural. His hands were locked on his own wrists instead of cradling her body, and his stance was stiff.

His eyes suddenly shifted and he seemed to see her watching their embrace. He locked his gaze on her and slid his hands into the woman's back pockets.

Madison looked away. "He creeps me out."

"I'm telling you, he's just using her. Again. Liam and I tried to 'do the right thing' the last time this happened, but she didn't want to hear it. She insisted he loved her. Then when his marriage broke up—"

"He was married?"

"Baby, you have no idea the shit that went down. It was like a train wreck. We wanted to look away, but we couldn't stop watching. His wife found out about Cianna—and no doubt all the other Ciannas that had come before—and she showed up at the dig site with two suitcases of his stuff. She didn't say a word, just threw them in the back of Brad's truck and left. I've never been so uncomfortable in my life. Well, that is, until Brad broke things off with Cianna and we had to live through that whirlwind of emotion."

"I didn't know archeology was so salacious."

"It's of control. I know he's only doing this because he can't have you." He let go of her thigh only long enough to shift gears, then replaced it. "I'm surprised he hasn't thrown me off the team yet."

"Maybe he doesn't know."

"I doubt that. I have problems keeping my eyes off you."

"Well, then maybe he doesn't care. Maybe Cianna has him satisfied enough that he's moved on from saying inappropriate things to me."

Mike made a noncommittal grunt in his throat and exhaled loudly. "Look, I know we've only been, you know, together for a couple days, but promise me you won't let him get you alone. I'm being irrational I know it. But…just don't let that happen."

She swallowed hard. "I won't."

"I mean, he's a good guy and all. I'm probably just over protective."

"No, I'm completely comfortable with staying on the opposite side of the Farm from him."

Mike nodded. His eyes flicked down to his cell phone and he frowned, idly tapping his index finger against her thigh. "He's a bastard. What does that text say?"

Madison picked up his cell phone from the floor, where it was tethered to the charger cable connected to the cigarette lighter. She swiped her finger across the face. "I'm running late this morning, so head up the front pits on your own. Put Liam and Madison on the pits by the woods. Cianna will be in later."

"Oh good, he's back in Cianna's pants so now I have to head up the dig." Mike snorted. "I'm sure he won't share his salary in return."

He turned the Jeep down the dirt road leading to the Spangler Farm and parked in the shadow of the bank barn. The sun already felt oppressively hot, which didn't bode well for the rest of the day considering it wasn't yet nine in the morning. She couldn't imagine how unbearable it would be in July.

"Seeing as how I'm in charge until Brad manages to find his way in, I'll get the front pits uncovered and start moving some dirt around." He leaned his head against the headrest and closed his eyes. "It's going to be a long day."

"You act as if Cianna's participated in the past."

"Excellent point, she hasn't, but at least when she was here there was the faint glimmer of hope she'd do more than sit in the shade. Or stand in the shade. Or draw pictures in the shade."

"She made a phone call one time that was work related." Madison looped her backpack straps over her arm. "And she stacked those papers and put them in a file folder. That's something."

"That's being overly appreciative of her abilities."

"She's being judged on abilities in completely different categories than we're being judged in." Madison stepped out of the Jeep and cupped her hand over her eyes. The sun felt like it was singeing the tip of her nose already. "I'm not even getting college credits for this gig! I'm here for the sheer love of the field."

"To be fair, you're getting laid too."

"Touché."

He leaned over and pulled the neck of her shirt out slightly, planting a kiss on her bare shoulder. "I hope you were expecting the Spanish Inquisition."

Liam was charging across the field between the bank barn and the woods, his short legs pulsing like pistons through the tall grass. He pointed at Madison. "Time for a bitch session. Michael, if you'll excuse us."

"Bitch session?" Madison raised her eyebrow. "I'm not fielding complaints today."

"Yes, bitch session." He nudged her toward the test pit at the tree line. "I'm a bitch and you need to dish. Toodles, Mikey."

Madison turned to Mike and smiled, shrugging her shoulders in defeat and allowing herself to be herded to the pit. "We have to get set up."

"I knew you'd say that, so I took it upon myself to get in early and get set up. It was an astounding amount of effort, what, putting out some shovels and buckets. Oh, and the sifter too but if you recall, I'm the one who muscled it—alone—to the summer kitchen on Friday. You're fucking Mikey."

"You make it sound so dirty."

"Was it dirty?"

"It was delightful." She paused and picked up a shovel. "And that's all you get."

"No, no, that's like saying, 'Hey, I went to Fort Lauderdale and was the only guy who got in the hot tub with clothes on' and just leaving it at that. I insist—no, demand—more detail. It's Mikey. I simply cannot rest until I know he's being properly taken care of."

"You've offered a rather specific example there, buddy. I assume you were that kid with clothes on in the hot tub?"

"Shit, girl, I went into the hot tub with a sweater and sweatpants on. Do you see this body? No, of course you don't and neither does anyone else." He pursed his lips together. "Stop changing the subject."

"I'm not changing the subject. I just refuse to give you sordid details of a delightful weekend." She looked between the two sections of test pits. The far pit, closer to the woods, seemed to draw her in. "In summary, he was there and I was there and it was exactly what you'd thought it would be. He was very well taken care of and he returned the favor....several times."

"I simultaneously hate you and want to be you." Liam snorted. "But if I were you, I'd use a little more self-tanner."

"I had no complaints from Mike."

"Bitch."

Madison snickered and edged towards the test pit. There was so much work left to be done and so much more they could accomplish—if only there was more time. One entire week was finished. They only had three weeks left to finish the entire survey. It wasn't fair.

...Her...

The test pit felt colder than it should, as it was situated in the direct sunlight, and for a moment, she stopped, her shovel still poised over the ground. Something didn't feel right. The air around her was vibrating and she could hear Ben whispering, his voice frantic, but the words were impossible to understand. He was too far away.

"The pit isn't going to dig itself." Liam peered over the edge of the pit and raised his eyebrow. "Lost in reminiscences of the weekend? Because if that's the case, I'm happy to help talk you through it."

"Nope, I'm good." She plunged the shovel into the dirt and dumped the soil into the bucket. "Unless you'd like to look at the rug burn on my back. Do you think that kind of thing can get infected?"

He narrowed his eyes, studying her as if he were debating whether or not she was being serious. "Hilarious."

"Loose lips sink ships."

"Please. There's nothing you could possibly say that would scandalize me. I'm asking only on the basis of possible titillation."

"You'll just have to use your imagination."

"Bitch."

Madison bit her lip to suppress a smile. She thrust the shovel into the dirt again and pulled out another load of soil. Ben's chatter was increasing to a dull roar in her ears, almost like the muffled buzz of a seashell when held up to her ear. He seemed to be all around her at once; pacing, tugging on the hem of her shirt, but she still couldn't make out anything he was trying to say.

As she went to plunge the shovel into the ground for a third time, something made her hesitate mid-movement. She wasn't sure if it was a trick of shadows overtaking sunlight or if she actually saw something move across her line of vision, but it was enough to slow her to the point where the shovel barely skimmed earth.

The chatter stopped.

Madison pulled the shovel back and looked into the hole, opening and closing her eyes several times to wet her contact lenses as if it would better help her see. Something was in the hole, just barely unearthed from her abbreviated shoveling. It looked almost like a garbage bag: black and flimsy, nearly shredded from being underground.

She set the shovel down. "Do we have any spades?"

"Over here." Liam cocked his head toward his duffle bag. "Did you find something?"

"I think it's just garbage, but I want to be careful before I tear into it."

"Smart girl."

She retrieved the spade from Liam's bag and stepped back down into the pit, crouching over the unearthed item. It wasn't a garbage bag. It was heavier, with an almost rubbery texture, and seemed to extend a distance underground. A tarp of some kind, maybe?

She decided to backtrack and instead of using the spade to dig down, she dug over the item. The soil was dry and easily crumbled. It didn't take long to lower the top strata of dirt down in a twelve inch by twelve inch section. Time had disintegrated portions of the black material but it still looked more or less intact. She trailed her finger over it: smooth and rubbery. Bizarre.

Movement at the edge of the pit caught her eye and she looked up. For an instant, no longer than a heartbeat, she saw him. He was looking down into the pit, his eyes focused on the strange black material. Even after he was gone, she could feel his pain — devastation so deep it felt like it would physically pull her down. There was something about what she'd found. Something he was looking for, something he was fixated on.

She looked back down at the material. At a second glance, it seemed like it was doubled over on itself. Something was barely sticking out from underneath, obscured almost entirely by the fabric around it.

Madison leaned closer and lifted the material up. It was decayed enough around the edges that it moved easily, revealing what it was covering.

Bone.

She scrambled backwards, her hand hitting the spade to the side. Her knuckles throbbed from the sudden impact, but she barely noticed. Had she just found Ben's remains? Was this why he'd been following her, persistently leading her to his final resting place? It almost seemed too easy.

"Liam." She almost didn't recognize her own voice, it waivered and cracked like an uncertain teenager. "Can you…I need…come here."

He huffed. "I thought you said it was garbage. We still have to bag it and tag it, even if it's a Styrofoam burger wrapper from 1994. That's how this game is played."

"No." She pawed her cell phone out of her pocket. Her fingers were shaking so badly she could barely type the message to Mike.

You need to get over here.

"No it's not garbage, or no you're not bagging it?"

She swallowed hard. "I think it's human remains."

She heard the sifter stop and, almost instantly, Liam was peering over the side of the pit. "Are you sure? Because it's usually not remains. It's usually a rock or a stick or something."

"I've taken anatomy classes, Liam, I'm pretty sure that's a bone."

"But human remains?" He didn't look convinced. "It's probably a rat or a chicken or something."

"I don't think so."

She pursed her lips together. Before she could fire back, Mike jogged over to them and smiled. She could see a hint of concern in his eyes. "What's up, guys? Did you break something again?"

"She thinks she found human remains." Liam crossed his arms plaintively. "I told her that usually doesn't happen."

Mike glanced at her. "You think it's him, don't you?"

She nodded.

"Wait, who's him?" Liam looked back and forth between them. "You two are hiding something from me. What's going on?"

"Maybe nothing." Mike stepped down into the pit and picked up the edge of the fabric with the tip of his index finger. "Maybe something. You know what this is, don't you?"

Liam again huffed. "Maybe you could speak with a few more generalities."

"It's a gum blanket, or what's left of one. Standard issue for the infantry during the war as a ground cover, but soldiers often used them as something like a poncho. It's just canvas covered in vulcanized rubber. Goodyear patented it in 1844." Mike paused. "You can't deny it's wrapped around something, Liam. Bone or no bone, there's something under there."

"I'll get some more spades."

Mike held up his hand. "Hang on, I'm going to call Brad and see what he wants to do."

"False. We'll do what we need to do."

"Dude, we have to at least let him know." Mike slid his finger across the screen of his phone and then held it to his ear. He frowned. "Straight to voicemail."

"We all know who he's doing." Liam wrinkled up his nose as if he'd just caught the scent of spoiled milk. "Disgusting."

"We're not going to sit and wait until he calls you back, are we?" Madison heard the panic in her voice. Ben could rest—or whatever lost spirits do—just because they'd found the remains, right? Or would they actually have to excavate and rebury him? The rule system for this type of thing didn't seem particularly well laid out.

"Hey, it's Mike, call me as soon as you get this. We found something." Mike ended the call and then rubbed his temple with his fingers. "He'd want to be here for this."

"He should have been here two hours ago, but he wasn't." Liam crossed his arms. "I vote we dig."

"Liam's right." Madison chewed on the inside of her lip. "It's not like he's in a meeting or out to the store to buy more supplies. He's screwing a pathetic groupie. We can't just leave whatever this is partially excavated. We run risk of further damage from rain, from wind, heck, even just from being exposed to all this oxygen in the air."

Mike tapped the cell phone against his forehead. "I know, baby, I know."

"Pathetic groupie is the meanest thing I've ever heard you say." Liam smirked. "You're a catty bitch like me after all. Mikey, she's a keeper."

"I know." Mike winked at her, then again turned serious. "Let me try him one more time, then we'll dig."

"I'll get the shovels." Liam headed toward the duffle bag. "We'll have this whole thing excavated before that douche even has his pants back on."

Mike rolled his eyes. Looping his finger through Madison's belt loop, he pulled her to him. "I don't want you to be disappointed if it's not him."

"I'm sure you'll help me find a way to pick up the pieces."

"You say that now." Mike touched the screen of the cell phone and held it to his ear. "God damn him. Yeah, dude, it's Mike again. You need to call me the second you get this. Madison found something in the test pit in the woods. I can confirm it's a gum blanket, maybe something else, so we're going to move forward with excavating at this point. So just…you know, give me a call. We need you here." He shoved the phone in his pocket. "I hate him. I really do."

"I'll leave the final decision up to you." Madison glanced down at the square of black fabric unearthed from the soil. "But you know what I think."

"I agree with you, Maddy girl." He pressed his lips to her forehead. "Not just because you're cute, but because that's what needs to be done. We can't put the dig on hold because he's busy."

"Distracted."

"Yeah." He ran his finger down her jawline. "But a girl also has me distracted. I'm still here."

"Enough with that." Liam pushed a spade into Mike's hands. "You humped on each other all weekend. Come up for air for God's sake."

Madison ignored Liam. "So, how do you want to do this?"

"A gum blanket spread out measured around 46x72 inches." Mike's eyes scanned across the test pit. "Even if it was spread out flat, I doubt it's going to be intact. It looks like it's tucked down around the bone—or whatever that is—so I say, let's level it down first, then work from the open area to the back. We'll set up our dig line with the lines of the blanket. Take it as it comes."

"What about sifting?" Liam nodded toward the duffle bag. "I'm assuming we're skipping that for now."

Mike glanced from the pit to the duffle. "Skip it. Let's keep any loose dirt to one area. If we need to come back to it we can sift, but for now let's focus on getting this out and protected. Maddy, this is your find. Do you want left or right?"

"I'll take the right side."

"Liam, you take left. I'll document and help you both." Mike took a deep breath. "We've got this, right? We can handle this?"

"Like there was any doubt." Liam sank to his knees and started picking at loose dirt at the leftmost edges of the gum blanket. "Tell me one thing that douche bag has done for this site, other than the customary paperwork and occasional acquiring of pizza and hoagie sandwiches. Please. I'm over his bullshit. This is the kind of shit that puts a digger on the map. And where's he? What's he doing?"

Madison crouched next to the right side of the gum blanket. Her hands felt shaky, almost numb. Was it really that easy to end his suffering? A little over a week on the job as a sensitive and she'd already put him to rest? If that was the case, the rest of the dig would be smooth sailing.

Madison.

She tried to focus on the excavating. How did you suggest a soul make its way to eternity? Was there some kind of final speech she needed to give? She'd found remains. Wasn't that enough?

Her…her…her….

Madison set her spade aside and picked up a toothbrush. It would be easier to work around the delicate edges with the small brush instead of the clumsy spade. Maybe concentrating harder would block out his voice, his desperation. This was it, right? This part was over.

Mike sank down on the ground next to her and spread out a map. He made a mark over a well-defined quadrant. "You know, everything else we've found fits the prescribed spectrum for a Civil War site. Buttons. Canteen spouts. Bullets. This body shouldn't be here."

"It was a hospital." Madison picked at a stubborn clump of earth. "Isn't it more out of the ordinary that we haven't found any remains until now?"

"Not really. I mean, you know that big gas station down on Route 30? Camp Letterman, one of the biggest field hospitals, was in that general area. Yet, when we did the survey of the area, we didn't find a single bone shard. Nothing. Not a bone, not a fragment, nothing." Mike looked up from his map. "I was in college. It was one of my first digs, but I remember it like it was yesterday. We found artifacts and debris, sure, but we never found remains. We know men died at Camp Letterman. But we never found a single trace of them in the ground."

"Maybe the Spangler Farm was different." Liam's eyes remained fixed on his dig line. "Camp Letterman was set up after the battle. The Spangler Farm was more immediate. Maybe there was no chance to move the casualties."

"We have the surgeon's records, though. Almost all the dead are accounted for: those who were sent home and those who ended up in the national cemetery."

"We know about most of them, but not all of them." Liam motioned around the test pit with the tip of his spade. "Maybe this one was different."

"He'd have to be, if he's here by himself. Something set him apart."

Liam flicked a clot of dirt across the pit to Madison. "So, tell me, Sassy, who you think this is? Obviously he's set apart in Mikey's mind, since Mikey can't fathom a randomly placed grave, but you were set on edge. Family? Friend? Bastard child?"

Madison laughed lightly in response, but kept digging. "If only it were that easy."

"Mikey won't mind if you tell me."

Madison stared down into the dirt, the clumps of earth veritable road blocks between her and the truth. The boys were listening now, but how long would that last? "I'm just super motivated."

"Not a legitimate answer."

"Liam." Mike glanced up from his map. "Dude, lay off."

"I'm just saying, I distinctly heard you ask her if she thought it was him. That would lead one to believe she had a specific him in mind."

"And I'm saying you wouldn't believe me if I told you." Madison picked a rock free from the dirt and set it aside. She forced her hand to stay restrained and dig slowly. Deep down she just wanted to tear into the pit and find out what was underneath the gum blanket.

"We're all friends here. Try me."

She used the back of the toothbrush to loosen another rock. "I...okay, for argument's sake, do you believe in ghosts?"

"No."

"This conversation is going to go nowhere then, let me tell you."

"Okay, fine, I'm sorry. Ghosts, yes." Liam didn't look up from digging. "When I was seven, I stayed in my great-aunt Ruth's antebellum house outside of

Charleston. I was lying in a four poster bed when this big, orange orb floated into the room, settled on the ceiling above the bed, and disappeared."

"I'm not talking about orbs. I'm talking about full body spectral…specters."

"You mean like that nonsense about the ghost unit on Little Round Top? An entire company of long dead soldiers drilling in the field of death, then just vanish into nothing?"

"No, I'm a bit more specific, as in one dead soldier."

Liam finally looked up, motioning at her with his spade. "When we started this dig, you said you saw someone watching you from the bank barn. I told you this site was shut down to the public and you tried to brush me off. You think it was a ghost?"

"I told you that you wouldn't believe me."

"I'm not saying I don't believe you." Liam looked back down at the pit. "Everyone and their brother has seen a ghost in Gettysburg. There're books devoted to ghosts in Gettysburg. There're forty million ghost tours out on the main drag in town. You aren't the first person to see a shadow and think it's the spirit of the undead."

Tears pricked the back of Madison's eyes. She blinked them back quickly—what loss was it to her if Liam thought she was nuts? She couldn't shake the feeling of defiance though, as if it were her job to protect his spirit. "His name was Ben."

"Excuse me?"

"I talked to a psychic in town and she said I was a sensitive. She helped me talk to him and he told me his name is Ben. He's young, probably not that much older than me." She kept her gaze on Liam steady, as if she were challenging him. "He looks lonely. Lost."

Liam looked from her to Mike. "Did you know about this?"

Mike shrugged, scraping dirt away from the edge of the gum blanket. "She knew about Cam. She…ah…she said Cam doesn't blame me for what happened."

Liam glanced back at Madison, his jaw set in a straight line. "And you think these are his remains." It was a statement, not a question.

"I don't know." Madison scooped out a handful of loose dirt and set it aside. Something didn't feel right, something she couldn't quite put her finger on. "It makes sense it would be him. I just feel like he's been pushing me to this spot since I got here. The sifter practically landed on this spot last week and every time I'm back here, I'm cold. I can always feel him, sometimes hear him."

"All right then. I'm skeptical, but I'll believe you." Liam leaned back and retrieved a small pick and toothbrush. "If I were you, I wouldn't mention this to Brad."

"There's a better chance of me discussing my last gynecologist visit with him."

Mike stood and held his cell phone over the test pit, taking a picture with the camera. He then crouched down to take a closer picture of the gum blanket. "He's going to be pissed he missed out on this."

"Probably, but what's he going to do? Fire us all for doing our jobs?" Liam picked at the earth with the back end of the toothbrush. "Get mad because he was too busy humping a blonde windbag?"

"That's exactly what he's going to do." Mike sank down into the dirt next to Madison. "I have a buddy who's a law enforcement ranger here. I wonder if I should call him and have him come out and take a look at this."

"Maybe he should be here in case Brad pops a gasket." Liam laughed. "Remember that time in Baltimore when the tow company came to take his car? I thought we were all going to end up arrested."

Mike chuckled. "I remember him waving his cell phone in the air. 'Do you have any idea who I am? I'm going to call my lawyer and have him come down here and explain it to you'. Oh, God, it was out of control."

"You guys make him sound like this hideous ogre of a man that's going to crush my bones and make soup out of my spleen or something." Madison brushed loose dirt off a section of gum blanket. So much seemed intact, it didn't seem possible. "I'm starting to get worried."

"He's all bark and no bite." Liam leaned back on his heels and drew his arm across his forehead, wiping away the sheen of sweat. "You've got Mikey anyway now, bitch. I'm the only one of the three of us currently residing alone. Because, you know, I get this distinct feeling he's only going to show up again to get clean clothes."

Mike's lips twitched in a suppressed smile, but he didn't look up at either Liam or Madison. "Let's change the subject."

"So, here's my question." Madison scooped another handful of dirt free from the pit. "I'm finding a lot of this blanket intact. My guess is because of the makeup of the rubber?"

"It's synthetic, so more than likely parts of it will never decompose," Liam said. "That's why landfill tires are going to destroy the planet. They'll take thousands and thousands of years to disintegrate and, frankly, that's just disgusting."

"Please don't get him started on ecology and saving stray cats and dogs." Mike snickered. "That'll last longer than a tire will in the dirt."

"Make sure you only buy free range chickens." Liam pursed his lips together. "And grass fed beef. Always local. Never shipped."

Madison bit back a smile, instead focusing on the edge of the gum blanket. They were close, so damn close. Now it was only a matter of time.

* * * *

The entire section of excavated gum blanket was over nearly five feet in length. It was sparse in places, have partially decomposed, and the entire bottom portion had rotted away completely—or, had been cut off by the original owner. The width of the blanket was hard to estimate. It seemed to be tucked down into the earth on one side. With careful excavation, they'd managed to loosen the opposite side and, theoretically, would peel that back to reveal what was underneath.

Mike's phone started ringing.

"Jesus Christ." Mike dragged his finger over the face of the phone, leaving a trail of dirt across it. "It's about damned time. Seriously, Brad? Where are you?"

He paused, rolling his eyes at whatever the excuse was coming from the opposite end of the connection. "Yeah, well, this is huge. You need to fucking get down here. Maddy found something. So far we've got around five feet by two feet of infantry gum blanket excavated. Madison. Yeah, well, I fucking called you three hours ago and you're just now calling back? Bull shit. Bull fucking shit. Anyway, look, something's under the gum blanket. We're not sure."

Liam elbowed Madison and handed her a cold bottle of water. "He's so hot when he gets angry."

"I know, right?" Madison cracked open the cap and took a swig of water. "He's pretty hot when he sleeps, too."

"Have I mentioned how much I hate you?"

Mike's forehead was creased in a frown. "Yeah, I know. Okay. We'll see you then. Yeah, dude, just get here, okay?" He hung up the phone and looked at them. "He wanted to know why we didn't call him when we first found something."

"He's an asshat." Liam studied his fingernails. "I assume he's bringing the princess with him?"

"He said they'd be in here in less than ten minutes." Mike sighed. "He said not to do anything else until he gets here. Because, you know, at this point his reputation is on the line."

"Was he pissed?" Madison grimaced, not sure she really wanted to know.

"No, he was cocky." Mike rolled his eyes and accepted a bottle of water from Liam, "Like I owed him some kind of explanation. Meanwhile, back here in the real world we had a dig to work. He forgets that our worlds don't revolve around him, like Cianna's does."

"Oh, things are going to get interesting." Liam tipped his head back and finished his water. "Let's just peek under the blanket now and get it over with before he gets here."

"I wish." Mike sank to the ground next to Madison and nudged her with his elbow. "Hey, cutie."

"Hey yourself. Are we having fun yet?"

"So much fun you won't have to rock me to sleep tonight." He closed his eyes and sighed deeply. "Wake me up when he gets here."

"I'm sure you'll hear him coming." Liam snorted. "It'll be like a sonic boom. The horror of the whole thing will consume us all. The horror being the whore, that is."

As he'd estimated, Brad arrived at the farm in less than ten minutes. The pickup truck roared down the dirt lane, throwing rocks and dust into the air like a windstorm. Madison felt her stomach churn in ugly anticipation. As much as she wanted to see what was underneath the gum blanket, she didn't want to share the moment with Brad and Cianna.

Mike seemed to sense her trepidation. He squeezed her thigh as he crawled to his feet. "Ah, the sweet sound of the executioner arriving."

Madison wrinkled up her nose. "You're hilarious."

"I'll make it up to you later."

"You'd better."

Brad charged across the field like a runner on the way to the finish line, his body at full tilt. Cianna, on the other hand, trudged behind him with her arms folded across her chest, clearly unhappy to have been pulled away from her private day with the dig leader. Even from the distance she was at, Madison could tell the blonde didn't want to be there.

Fingertips trailed across her neck. She looked up for Mike, but he'd already headed toward Brad. There was no one beside her. No one she could see; she knew who was with her. She could feel his presence.

Madison…please…don't let….

"Hey team!" Brad's smile was a little too broad. "So, tell me what's going on. What did we find?"

"Well, Madison found a gum blanket." Mike nodded toward the excavated pit. "She was right about here and ran into the outer edge. It's smaller than the standard issue blankets were, but it's logical to assume it either rotted away or was cut."

Brad looked taken aback. "When you said you found a blanket, I thought you meant it was folded.

That's why I couldn't figure out why you said you had a five by two section dug out. Why would it be spread out like this?"

"That's what we thought." Mike hesitated, glancing at Madison. "We think it's covering something."

"So you said earlier. Why do you think that?"

"We can see something down at this end." Mike cocked his head toward one end of the blanket. "We...ah...we think it's a bone."

"I doubt that." Brad looked over the blanket, the smile spreading across his face again. "This is fantastic! Look at this, you guys! Madison, what a great job. Seriously, you are phenomenal."

"Well, thank you." She felt her cheeks flush. "I'm interested to see what's underneath it."

Brad didn't respond to her. "Did you document everything?"

"I took pictures with my phone," — Mike slid his finger across the phone face and pulled up the picture reel — "and I have it documented in the binder. Times, strata, color, everything."

"Excellent." Brad flipped through the pictures. "Guys, this is huge."

"We'd really like to see what's underneath the blanket." Mike reached across Brad and searched for a picture. "Here, this is what we could see from the bottom."

"It's a stick, Mike."

"No, it's definitely not a stick. Liam and I checked it out as well and we both think it's a bone. Obviously we can't tell if it's human or animal...which is why we need to get under there."

Brad looked at the picture, resizing it with the tips of his fingers. "Well, I mean, anything's possible I guess.

We need to get this up and out of here. Did you bring the trays and the bags down?"

"They're right over there."

Brad squatted down in the dirt and examined the edge nearest him. "This goes down deeper. We need to get down to the edge so we don't damage it further. It could crumble at any minute; the rubber's still here, but I bet the canvas is long gone."

"We'd really like to see what's under it." Mike shoved his phone in his pocket. "Who would have left something like this laid out flat? There's no logical explanation for it, other than it was used to cover something up."

"Or set something on." Brad straightened and stepped back from the pit. "Someone could have been resting on it and had to leave in a hurry. It's not out of the question."

"I can't imagine someone just leaving this here because they didn't have time to pick it up."

"Mike." Brad pushed past Cianna to retrieve a spade; she looked crushed. "We dig."

With four of them digging—Cianna sat in the shade of a tree and "took notes"—they were able to dig out the edge of the blanket in less than forty minutes. Brad dragged a metal artifact tray to the edge of the pit and lined it up with the top of the blanket. "If we fold it back on itself, we can slide it onto the tray and carry it out. We'll use its weight to help support it when we lift. We go slow and we go on three. Only take it back on itself, no further. Ready?"

Liam and Madison took one end of the blanket, while Mike and Brad took the other. Brad looked down the line and nodded. "Just like folding a blanket. Well...I guess it is a blanket. Okay, everyone move together. One. Two. Three."

They eased the blanket backwards, the rubber stubborn to move from its stretched, flat position. It felt so delicate beneath her fingertips that Madison was at first afraid it would crumble to pieces before it was folded back. It didn't. It moved as Brad hoped it would, folding back like a blanket. "Don't crease it back, let's get the tray."

No one responded.

Madison looked down to the squat, square of earth they'd uncovered. Bones. Two rows of light white bones, easily identifiable as tibia, fibula, and femur, stretched upward toward the curved remains of a pelvic bone. She could see the edge of a spinal column disappearing underneath the gum blanket. "Shit."

She glanced at Mike. He smiled at her, his face lighting up. "You were right, Maddy baby. You were right."

"We have to call this in." Brad gaped at the remains and slowly shook his head. "We have to get someone down here. Do you know how huge this is? We...this is really happening. My god, this is actually happening."

"I believe you now, Madison." Liam stared into the pit, his words barely more than a mumble.

"Mike, is your buddy in LE still around?" Brad dug his phone out of his pocket. "I'm calling park headquarters to get someone down here. You get LE on the phone and get a ranger down here now."

"Got it."

"Cianna, you start photographing this. I want every inch of this documented." He pressed the phone to his ear as he walked away. "Hi, Jim? Brad Emerson, down here at the Spangler Farm. My team found something. You're not going to believe this."

"It's okay, Brad, we'll just standby." Liam rolled his eyes. "Bitch, do you know what this is going to do for your career?"

"Not just mine." She shook her head. "We did this together."

"You found it first."

"Like it or not, you helped."

Mike touched her elbow as he passed. "Drew's on his way down. Why, I'm not entirely sure. I'm assuming it's because we need to get this checked out and make sure this isn't a more recent burial site. Not that Drew can do that."

"They'll have to call an osteo-archeologist or forensic anthropologist." Liam crossed his arms. "As big as this park is, do you think they've got one on staff?"

"If not, Washington's just right down the road."

Madison cracked the knuckles in her fingers, individually moving from one finger to the next. She wanted to throw her arms around Mike, to celebrate what they'd found, but something still didn't feel right. Something was wrong. What was it?

Brad returned to the test pit. "The park superintendent is coming down himself. He's down at the visitor's center right now, but will be here in about ten minutes. Mike, did you get ahold of LE?"

"He'll be here any minute. He was down near East Cavalry Battlefield."

"Good, okay." He rubbed his hands together. "I'm thinking they'll call in forensics, just to make sure these remains date back to the war. We can't do that on our own."

Madison glanced at Liam. He mouthed the words, *Told you.*

"Then what?" Cianna spoke for the first time since she'd gotten to the site. "Are they going to call in National Geographic or something?"

"They might." Brad brushed his hair away from his face. "Even Roger Frye said this was huge. They haven't found remains on the field in over fifteen years. This is almost intact. That's…that's beyond incredible."

Madison shuddered. The remains were once a person; they all seemed to be forgetting that fact.

Flashing lights coming down the road caught her eye. A green and white park service SUV pulled into the parking lot, slowing to a stop almost in the grass, and a ranger hopped out. He plopped his hat on his head and began making his way across the field toward them.

"There's Drew." Mike cupped his hand close to his mouth. "Hey, Carson!"

"Hey, Lieutenant!" the ranger called back. "Are you still causing trouble?"

"You didn't tell me the LE was an old Army buddy." Liam looked intrigued. "And I thought we were friends."

The ranger was young, probably Mike's age, with a square jaw and a beefy upper body that was indicative of a man who lifted weights like it was a profession. He extended his hand to shake Mike's. "Glad you called me. You've got some remains?"

"Roger Frye's on his way down." Mike nodded toward Madison. "She's the one who found them. This is Madison Monroe. Maddy, this is Drew Carson. We served together in Iraq back in 2003."

"So, you're Madison." Drew smiled sheepishly. "It's nice to finally meet you."

"Ah, thanks. I think." She glanced at Mike. He shrugged innocently, but she didn't believe it for a second.

177

Brad pushed his way over. "Thanks for coming out, Drew. I wanted to make sure the site was secure. We're just waiting on Superintendent Frye to get down here to decide what to do next. There are protocols for this, of course."

"Of course." Drew peered into the pit. "They're intact. I didn't expect that."

"Neither did we."

Drew rested his hands on his belt and stepped back to the group. "We'll see what Frye wants to do, but we can get someone posted down here if he wants. Get them on a rotation or something, that won't be a problem."

"Thanks, Drew. I appreciate it." Brad brushed his hands on his jeans and straightened the collar of his shirt. "I'm going to head down to the lot and meet the superintendent when he gets here. Brief him on what we've got. Cianna, make sure everything is photographed and documented. We'll need to turn all the books over to him."

"But I thought maybe I could come with you."

"Nope, just get everything together in case he wants to check our records from last week." Brad headed back across the field, not once looking at Cianna.

Madison glanced at the blonde. The hurt was etched across her face, but she seemed to soak it in, instead turning back to the pit with her camera. Poor thing—she was being used. And she knew it.

"Is that guy for real?" Drew spoke softly. "Lieutenant, I can't imagine you putting up with that kind of shit."

"I'm a different kind of guy these days. More laid back, you know?"

"Still, do you really think I need to be here? Don't get me wrong, I love sitting at East Cav Field as much as the next guy, but I don't think we're going to have fight any looters or pillagers today."

"The day's still young." Mike winked at Madison. "This one's trouble, anyway."

"You've told me a lot about the charming Miss Monroe, but nothing that would lead me to believe she's trouble." Drew adjusted his hat and reached into his pocket, pulling out a small notebook. "I'll have to file a report, pending confirmation of the age of the remains. I'm sure it goes without saying you documented everything?"

"Photographed and logged."

"I hate to even ask, Lieutenant, but you have permits from the park service? I just need to jot down the numbers. You know. Protocol."

"Yeah, right here." Mike flipped through the log book and pulled out the site permits the park service issued prior to the start of the dig. "Signed by Frye himself."

"Hold on to that, man. I think he's getting ready to retire." Drew jotted down the permit numbers in his notebook, then handed it back to Mike. "He published a couple books last year and, word on the street is, he's vying for park historian. Less work, no pencil pushing. Just living the dream."

"Oh, no, if he wants to live the dream, he wants to come work with us." Mike snapped the binder shut and stepped back to Madison, running his hand across the small of her back as he brushed past. "There's a lot of peril in archeology. Obviously, lots of excitement."

"I think he's looking for less excitement. He had to reorder seven thousand brochures last week because *McPherson* was spelled wrong on the ones we got."

"We can accommodate lots of sitting. It's a pretty flexible profession."

"Let's ask him now." Liam nodded toward the parking area. A white sedan pulled into the lot; Brad was already circling it like a turkey vulture. "I'm a little bit panicked. I've only met him once and I spilled apple juice on myself. Not on purpose, mind you, but suave and elegant nonetheless."

Madison watched Superintendent Frye cross the field, with a somewhat strained and lumbering gait. He was tall and stocky, with thick lensed, round glasses that seemed to dwarf the rest of his face. His pace was rapid but he walked with difficulty, like someone who had perpetual trouble with his knees, and the effort was noticeable in his face.

Brad motioned in their general direction. "Mr. Frye, this is my team. They're the ones who actually discovered the remains when I was indisposed this morning."

The superintendent reached his hand out to shake theirs. "I almost didn't believe Mr. Emerson when he told me you'd found remains out here. Commendable work, this is an exquisite find. Mr. Caldwell, it's a pleasure to see you again. I remember you from last summer. And you, sir?"

"Liam Stanish."

"Liam." Mr. Frye shook his hand and then turned to Madison. "It's a delight to meet you, my dear. You are?"

"Madison Monroe." She shook his hand. It was sweaty and damp. She had to restrain herself from promptly wiping her hand down her jeans. Gross.

"Madison, Liam, and Michael. You just put yourselves on the map." He looked into the pit, adjusting his glasses as if to see better. "Let's get the rest of the gum blanket up and see how intact the remains are. The condition of the femur and pelvis are remarkable. Some of the smaller tarsal bones appear to be missing, but the larger bones seem to be in place."

"Liam and Madison, you take that side; Mike, you help me on this side." Brad crouched down next to the edge of the blanket. "We'll take it slow, like last time, and set it on the tray if we can. Ready?"

He didn't wait for an answer. They lifted the blanket free from the ground and eased it to the waiting artifact tray. The weight of the double folded blanket seemed to make it sturdier and Madison was thrilled it actually made it from the ground to the tray without falling apart. Now it could be preserved. Protected.

She turned back to the pit. They'd uncovered the skull; its gaping eyes sockets stared back at her from the ground, the jaw open as if frozen in unspoken final words.

Now...now...now...

Frye was silent for several moments. His eyes were locked on the skeletal remains. He rubbed his fingers together, tapping the pads of each finger to his thumb in quick succession. He shook his head. "Shut it down."

Brad opened his mouth to speak and then promptly closed it. He tried again. "Excuse me, sir?"

"Shut the dig down." Frye turned on his heel and headed back in the direction he'd just come. "Now."

Chapter Thirteen

Mike pressed her up against the back wall of the shower, the sudden shock of cold like electricity against her skin. Her breath caught in her throat and she arched her back in attempt to squirm away from the wall, but not from him.

He chuckled, pinning her in place with his hip. "Do you like that?"

"You I like. The cold freaking wall I could do without."

He kissed her again and cradled both sides of her face with his hands, guiding her underneath the stream of hot water. "I wish we had more time before dinner. I'd like to take this to the next level."

"You didn't have to tell Liam yes."

"I was caught up in the moment."

"You can have me after dinner." She kissed him, dragging her teeth over his bottom lip. "It's not like we have to get up early tomorrow or anything."

"Eh, it's only for a couple days while they date the remains. Then we'll be back to work." He trailed his lips down her neck to the hollow between her throat and shoulder. "I can think of other ways to spend the day."

"What if they shut the dig down permanently? It could happen. I'm sure it's happened before."

"Over remains? Nope, won't happen. And if it does, you can spend the rest of the summer with me." He straightened and kissed her deeply, pinning her against the wall. "On further consideration, we have time. Liam can wait."

"Liam won't wait."

"Then he can eat by himself." Mike slid his hands down her thighs and lifted her up, pushing her against the wall for better balance. He entered her with one thrust, drawing in a sharp breath through his teeth.

Madison's legs flailed awkwardly behind him and she crossed her ankles to lock herself in place. She giggled against his lips. "This is so dangerous."

"You like it."

She kissed him in response, wrapping her arms around his shoulders and trailing her fingertips down the nape of his neck. It was almost dizzying, his steady rhythm, the clouds of steam, the fear of falling; she let her eyes drift shut and kissed him. It was perfect. He was perfect.

The phone started ringing.

Mike dropped his face to her shoulder, burying it against the side of her neck. "God damn it."

"Don't stop." She locked her legs around him. "Voicemail will get it. That's what voicemail's for."

"That's the ring I have set for Brad. If I don't answer...and he calls you and you don't answer...he'll figure out that we're not answering together." He pulled her away from the wall and set her on the floor, holding her steady until she checked her balance. "Let me get rid of him."

"You can always call him back."

As if in agreement, the phone stopped ringing. Mike pressed his clenched fist to his forehead and groaned. "I fucking hate him."

Madison followed him out of the bathroom, dragging a towel over her arms. "Delayed gratification is good for you."

He didn't respond, instead catching her wrist and pulling her into his arms. He tossed the towel to the floor and picked her up, setting her down on the counter and nudging her legs apart with his hip. "Remind me to thank him later, then."

She lightly moaned against his lips as he entered her again. Neither of them spoke, focused on each other, on touching and exploring. When she opened her eyes, he looked at her and smiled, kissing her deeply. His eyes slid to their reflection in the mirror and he watched for several moments. After a beat, his eyelids fluttered and he pressed his face to her shoulder. "Shit."

He thrust several times and then relaxed against her, exhaling against her skin. "Sorry...that, uh, was my fault. Lesson learned though. It's not a good idea for me to watch in the mirror."

She leaned her head back against the mirror and took several deep breaths, trying to slow down her heartrate. "I think if you're going to fuck me like that, you can watch in the mirror anytime you want. Now get back in the shower."

After a markedly shorter, uneventful shower, they toweled off and started the slow process of getting ready for dinner. Madison pulled on a black bra and hot pink panties, then stood in front of the dresser. "So...do you know where we're going for dinner?"

"Your birthday was yesterday. You wouldn't let me celebrate."

"Still doesn't answer my question. Is this like, a shirt and jeans kind of place or...mini skirt and shirt kind of place? Because, honestly, that's about all I've got here: jeans, shorts, and one skirt/slutty boot combo that just seemed appropriate."

Mike pulled his jeans on and buckled the belt at his waist. "Skirt and boots. Like it or not, Liam and I are insisting on celebrating with you. Birthday, most momentous dig in the history of the Spangler Farm—"

"Only dig in the history of the Spangler Farm."

"Anyway." He stepped behind her and kissed the top of her shoulder. "I got something for you."

"Mike." She turned around in his arms, pursing her lips together in a coy smile. "You didn't have to get me a present. We've only been officially breaking all the rules of professional relationships for four days."

"I know, but I can't be a bad boyfriend after four days." He suddenly looked sheepish. "If that's what the kids these days still call it."

"I imagine so." She pushed up onto her tip toes and kissed him. "But you still didn't have to. I wasn't expecting you to do something."

"Which is exactly why I did." He reached around her and pulled his hoodie off the top of the dresser. Digging into the large front pocket, he withdrew a flat, square box. "Happy birthday, Maddy baby."

She picked the lid off the box. Inside was a silver fleur de lis, attached to a black choker necklace. "I love it! Thank you, Mike, seriously. This is sweet."

"I saw it when I was, ah, on my way home from the counselor Friday night." He took it out of her hands and fastened it around her throat. "I thought of you."

The fleur de lis hung in the hollow of her throat. She loved it. Throwing her arms around him, she hugged him tightly. "You're adorable."

"I do my best."

A knock at the door made them both jump. Mike ran his hand through his hair and sighed. "Either he's early, or we took ample advantage of what little time we had."

Madison shrugged on a tight, black short sleeved shirt and her denim mini skirt. "Possibly."

She crossed the room to the door and, without checking out the window, opened it. "Hey—"

Brad.

It was Brad, not Liam, on the other side of the door. Madison dug her fingers into the door to restrain herself from slamming it in his face. "Um, hey, uh, Brad. What are you doing here?"

"Huge news, I've been trying to get ahold of you for the past hour." He held his phone to his ear. "I can't reach Mike either. He's not picking up."

Madison froze. "Don't—"

Mike's phone, inside the hotel room, still resting on top of the television, started ringing. She heard him curse under his breath and the phone shut off.

Brad stared at Madison silently, lowering the phone and sliding his finger across the screen. He pushed the door open wider. "Mike?"

Mike jerked a white V-neck shirt over his head and cleared his throat. "Hi, Brad."

"Okay." Brad looked back and forth between them, a frown etching across his forehead. He shoved his phone in his pocket. "Okay, uh, wow. This is awkward."

"You wanted to get ahold of us." Mike shrugged. "We're both here."

"Yes, you are." There was a tone to Brad's voice that made her feel uncomfortable. They were all adults—whatever she and Mike wanted to do together was their business. He looked accusing, hurt, angry; all ridiculous reactions for someone who was already sleeping with another digger on the team. She wanted to punch him. "You're together. *Together*, together."

Mike crossed his arms. "And?"

Brad seemed to snap back to reality. "Frye's been on the phone since he left the Spangler Farm. He's called in a forensic anthropologist and an osteo-archeologist from Washington D.C. They're coming tonight, which on its own is huge."

"Great, so we can get back to work soon?" Madison tugged on the bottom of her skirt, wishing she could lengthen the hemline. Brad's eyes seemed to be everywhere at once.

"Uh, no, we're shut down indefinitely." He paused. "Well, not indefinitely. Only until they determine the age of the remains. If they're modern, so to speak, we'll have to turn it over to federal law enforcement. If they're to the period, we'll be allowed back on site, but not in those pits. Those pits are done. It's a burial ground."

Madison finally realized what it was about Brad's behavior that gnawed on her psyche. He sounded condescending, like a father who just caught his daughter having sex with a boy in the backseat of his car. The idea of him being insulted she's picked Mike over him was ludicrous. He was a louse. He was louse who was already fucking Cianna—just because he could.

"But, they'll at least let us finish the dig." Mike recrossed his arms in front of him. "They're not throwing us off the farm."

"Well, no."

"Sounds like business as usual. This happened at Chancellorsville. Remember, that other team found the femur bone?"

Brad's face clouded. "Yeah, Jim Miller's team. I remember that. But, this time, it's us. And it's not just a femur bone. It's practically an intact skeleton."

Madison glanced at Mike. Practically intact was an exaggeration. From what she'd seen, only the thicker, denser bones were left. The delicate bones of the feet, hands, and ribs were long gone.

"The park wants us to make a statement." Brad took a deep breath. He was nearly quivering with excitement. Madison wasn't sure she'd ever seen someone quiver. "And after that, Frye warned me that media outlets are going to explode. We're talking national news. He wants us to be ready for a press conference."

"Seriously?" Mike groaned. "Talk about ruining the sanctity of the site. It's going to be a circus out there. Can't the park's public relations department handle that shit? I mean, come on, we've got work to do. We only have a few more weeks to do it before they shut us down for tourist season. Oh, God, can you imagine what a madhouse that will be if they let tourists out there?"

"He's already thought about that. They'll have law enforcement rangers monitoring the farm and they'll shut down through traffic to the site." He rubbed his hands together. "They won't hold the press conference until after the remains are dated. But, when they do, we're all going to be there and we're all going to be happy, right?"

"Yeah." Madison again exchanged a look with Mike. "Right."

As she spoke, she saw Liam round the corner of the exterior corridor. He saw Brad standing half in her room and half out and stiffened, trying to duck back around the building before Brad noticed him.

His effort was too late. Brad looked up and waved. "Hey, there's the other digger I was trying to track down. What are you doing here?"

"Oh God." Liam looked frantically from Mike to Madison, as if he were watching an out of control tennis game. Mike shrugged. "I'm...we were going out to...ah...what are you doing here?"

"I was coming to tell Madison how huge our discovery was today." Brad cocked his head inside the room. "I found this loser here with her."

"Isn't that special?" Liam picked at an invisible piece of lint on his shirt. "So, what's this epic announcement? Do we get our own wing in the visitor's center? A monument dedicated to our supreme archeological prowess? And, side note, why did you see it fit to tell the heterosexuals and not me?"

"I called you, man. Fuck you that you didn't pick up." Brad ran his hands through his hair. "Frye wants us to make a statement. Once the remains are dated, they want us to have a press conference. This is the most exciting discovery in park history."

Liam adjusted his collar, still not looking directly at Brad. "Here's a statement. Quote. Three archeologists discovered human remains at the Spangler Farm. End quote."

"He's going to have us do it in front of the press."

"I fail to see the difference between that and a press conference."

"We'll take questions at the press conference."

"Terrific." Liam dug the toe of his shoe into the pavement. "So, here we all are…"

"I know, and it's perfect, because I was thinking we could head out to dinner and celebrate." Brad's smile seemed forced. "All of us. Come on, Cianna's in the truck waiting."

"We can just meet you there." Mike nodded toward Madison. "She's not finished getting ready yet."

"She can finish. I'm parked out front." He backed away from the door and clapped Liam on the shoulder. "See you in five minutes. Come on guys, look excited. It's my treat."

Liam watched him walk away and then pushed his way into the hotel room, shaking his head in disgust. "I bet that was uncomfortable."

"Which part?" Madison headed back to the counter and pulled out black eyeliner. She glanced down at the countertop and blushed; oh the things that counter had seen. "The part where he insinuated he helped discover the remains, or the part where he discovered Mike, shirtless, in here with me?"

"You weren't wearing a shirt?" Liam pursed his lips together. "I'm literally irate I missed out on that."

"He handled it better than I thought he was going to, don't you think?" Mike stepped into his tennis shoes and leaned over to tighten the laces. "I mean, yeah, at first he looked like he'd just taken a drink of rank milk, but once that passed he didn't seem bothered. Much."

"He's still a creeper. He stared at my legs the entire time, despite the fact he'd figured out we're sleeping together." Madison applied a thick layer of eyeliner on her upper and lower lash line, followed by an equally thick coating of mascara. "But, considering the alternative and giving the tantrum he threw when he saw us together in the car for the first time, I'd say we're in for a completely relaxed and comfortable evening."

"Girlfriend, I'm even staring at your legs." Liam snorted. "I had no idea you were all tatted up like this. You sassy little rebel!"

"I don't wear shorts often."

"You should, look at you. Mikey. Mikey, tell her she has acceptable legs for a scrawny bitch."

"She knows how I feel about her legs." Mike walked behind her, sliding his hand across her lower back, and reached for his cologne at the edge of the sink. "Liam, correct me if I'm wrong, but after Miller's team found the remains in Chancellorsville, didn't the park service release the statement? I don't remember any press conferences."

"You don't remember them because there weren't any. The park released a statement and *Archeology* magazine had an article." Liam shrugged. "I think CNN had a two minute interview with Miller and that was it. Madison, are those the boots you're wearing? That's the hippest thing I've ever seen you wear."

"I clean up well." She pulled the sides of her hair back into a clip, letting the rest hang loose down her back, and then shoved a tube of lip gloss in her pocket.

Mike elbowed her playfully. "With some help."

"Shut up." She elbowed him back.

He caught her wrists in one hand and pulled her to him. He smiled, revealing his dimples she adored so much, and pressed his lips to her forehead.

"Ew, gross, seriously?" Liam huffed. "Save the face sucking for later. I'm hungry and that bastard is paying. Let's go."

Mike stuck a room key in his wallet while Madison sprayed perfume down her shirt and retrieved her purse from the table.

Opening the room door, Liam stepped outside. "I cannot imagine anything more uncomfortable than going to dinner with those two."

Madison zipped up her boots and followed him outside. "Hey, I'm twenty-one now. Maybe he'll buy champagne and I'll be too tipsy to notice how horrifying the evening is going."

"I'm keeping you on the wagon." Mike slid his hand around hers and pulled her to him. "I'd hate to see you ruin all those important life skills you've learned in your rehab classes."

"I'm filing it away with what I learned about algebra in high school. Look, yet another day has passed and yet another day I haven't used algebra. There's not a big demand for quadratic equations in real life situations."

Brad's truck was parked in one of the spaces at the front of the hotel. Madison could see him leering at her over the steering wheel, his eyes locked on her hand intertwined with Mike's. Great. First he was a creeper, now he was morphing into a jealous creeper.

If he noticed, Mike didn't seem to care. He opened the back door of the quad-cab and boosted her up.

Liam circled around the cab and crawled in the rear passenger's side. "Skinny bitches sit in the middle."

Madison slid to the center and waited while Mike crawled in beside her. He put his hand on her knee and pulled it against his. "So, where are we headed?"

"I figured we head out toward Hanover. There's a nice Italian restaurant there we could go to for dinner, and a few clubs we could hit later if you want. Oh, wait, Madison. You're underage."

"My birthday was yesterday."

"Happy belated birthday!" He glanced at her in the rearview mirror. "You should have said something."

"It's not really a big deal."

Brad pulled the truck out onto the main street. "Does everyone here like Italian? That place I was talking about, La Tavola, has calamari that's out of this world."

"I'm a vegetarian." Cianna was dressed in a low cut, silver tank top and tight, black pants. She looked ready to hit the club, dinner or no dinner.

"I already made reservations."

Madison inwardly groaned. If only they'd left before Brad had gotten there. If only she hadn't opened the door and instead dragged Mike back for a longer shower. She could be naked back in the hotel room instead of being trapped in the truck with creeper Brad and insipid Cianna.

It was going to be a long night.

* * * *

As if dinner wasn't bad enough, sitting at the bar at a half dead dance club was worse. Madison tapped her index finger against the glass of Jack and ginger. The hour and forty-five minutes they'd spent at La Tavola's was a lesson in patience. Brad kept hinting for information on Mike and Madison's sex life, Mike would try to change the subject to the dig, and Liam would order more wine. It felt like the worst inquisition known to man and, worse yet, Cianna spent the whole of the time visibly growing more and more upset that Brad was ignoring her.

Madison threw back her drink. It was time to go back to the hotel and fuck Mike again. This was mind-numbing nonsense.

"You need to slow down." Mike took the glass away from her. "You've had three more drinks than you should have had."

"It's my birthday." She pouted, though she was fully aware it would have no real effect on him.

"Cianna's dancing." He slid his arm around her and kissed her neck. "Want to dance?"

"I want to go back to the hotel room."

"I personally didn't want to leave the hotel room." He sighed, pulling her to him. "Because, you know, there's nothing more fun than sitting over spaghetti and meatballs discussing your sex life."

"That's why I started drinking wine." Madison's liver had enough experience that she didn't immediately feel the effects of the Jack and ginger. "But, I can tell you, it didn't help. That was still excruciating."

"I'll call a taxi." He trailed his fingers down her jawbone and tilted her chin downward, touching his lips to hers. "We'll just get out of here and do our own thing."

"We should be celebrating." Madison pulled him back to her, kissing him again. "I mean, Brad only said it forty-seven thousand times. We made the discovery of the century."

"I can think of other ways you and I could celebrate."

"Then call the cab."

Mike wrapped his arms around her waist and pulled her against him, planting his lips against her throat. "We can't abandon Liam like that. No man left behind, they were very specific about that when I was in the Army."

"We'd have more fun alone."

"Just wait until I get you back to the room and I'll prove it." Mike slid his hands down her hips, guiding her against him. "Unless you want to find a secluded bathroom."

She closed her eyes. The effects of the alcohol were starting to cloud her judgment. "Stop teasing me."

"I'm not teasing you, I'm serious." His breath was hot in her ear. "You look fucking amazing tonight. I'm ready to take you into the bathroom and just pull that little skirt up."

"Is that so?" She tilted his head back to hers, kissing him gently at first, but quickly deepening it. "Brad's probably watching us, you know that right?"

"Fuck him."

"I'd rather you fuck me."

"Oh, I will." He slid his fingers up her thighs, pushing the edge of her skirt upward. "But you have to wait."

"I'm not a patient person."

"As much as I want to, I can't just flip you onto the bar and have my way with you."

"Buzz kill." She squirmed away from him and pulled him to his feet. "I love this song. Dance with me, come on."

"How about no?" Mike seemed to be letting her drag him to the dance floor. "I'd rather just watch you."

"Nope. You passed on your chance to take advantage of me in the bathroom. Now you can dance. And you can enjoy it."

Mike chuckled and pulled her against him, sliding his hands down her hips as she danced. He swayed with the music, occasionally singing along, but he seemed far more preoccupied with kissing her neck and touching her than actually dancing.

Liam danced over. "Don't be jealous of my dance skills. And no dancing queen jokes because, seriously, I'll knock you right over."

"So, this is how archeologists celebrate the find of the century." Madison lifted her arms up and reached behind her, pulling Mike's head to hers. "Reasonably mediocre Italian food and a lame dance club."

"We're living the dream, baby!" Mike's breath was hot in her ear. "Bad food and entertainment is how we roll."

"You're damn right we're living the dream!" Liam swayed with the music, lifting his arms in the air. "Honestly, you bitches think it gets better than this?"

Mike spun Madison around and kissed her, cradling the back of her head with his hand and locking her in place. When he pulled away, he touched his forehead to her. "I'm pretty sure it doesn't."

She could see Brad over Mike's shoulder, seated alone at the bar. He was glaring at them, anger knitting his brow in deep furrows, and holding a shot glass to his lips. His eyes were fixed on her, his gaze steady. He threw the drink back.

She ignored him. Touching her lips to Mike's, she smiled. "Agreed."

Chapter Fourteen

Ten minutes before seven on Wednesday morning, Mike's cell phone rang. He cursed and, without lifting his head from his pillow, fumbled on the nightstand for his it. "What?"

Madison rolled onto her back, pawing her hair out of her eyes. What a night.

"Are you kidding me? Well, no, I wouldn't expect it to be official at this point either." Mike pushed himself up into a sitting position. He rubbed the side of his face. "What do you think? Yeah, she's right here. If they're not done, why are they calling us in already?"

Madison reached for her glasses on the nightstand and shoved them on her face. In theory, whatever Brad wanted was important. If nothing else, it was enough to get Mike fired up. It was kind of hot.

"We'll be there. Dude, I said we'd be there." Mike rolled his eyes. "Whatever. Yeah, I'm sure it's awesome."

He hung up the phone and tossed it on the bed. "So, apparently the park superintendent called Brad at six o'clock this morning to let him know the osteo-archeologist found something."

"Something as in, the remains are modern and the dig is shut down permanently." Madison paused. "Or something as in, they identified the remains?"

"I have no idea. Brad doesn't even know." Mike stretched his arms over his head and yawned, craning his neck from side to side to crack it. "He said they worked all evening Monday when we were out celebrating and all day yesterday. Nothing official, but they wanted to talk to us."

Madison laid back down against the pillow and pulled the blankets to her chin. "Part of me is excited, but the other part of me remembers we didn't go to sleep until two in the morning. I'd rather stay in bed."

"Well, the bad news is they want us at park headquarters by nine." He picked up his phone again and slid his finger across the face. "The good news is that the park went ahead and released the statement to the press this morning. He said it's online."

"Twenty bucks says we're not even mentioned by name."

Mike tapped his finger against the side of the phone. "Here it is: For immediate release, archeological team headed by Bradley Emerson discovered human remains at the Spangler Farm site on Monday. The remains are currently being investigated by a forensic team brought in from Washington. The national park service will hold a press conference Friday at noon. No further information is available at this time."

"And, I'm not surprised."

"At least we didn't have to stand there while Brad read some kind of prepared statement." Mike leaned over and kissed the top of her shoulder. "I'll run over and bring breakfast back for us. You start getting ready."

"Make sure there's lots of coffee invited back to the room with you."

"I can do that." He crawled out of bed and crossed to the dresser, pulling out clean boxer briefs and a dark green shirt. As he dressed, he glanced back to her. "So…after we're done at park headquarters, what did you want to do?"

"What did you have in mind?"

"I thought maybe I could take you around the battlefield and then out to a nicer dinner than Brad took us to Monday." He slid the room key into his back pocket and then walked back to the bed, leaning over to kiss her. "Because, as much as I'd rather be in here making love to you darlin', you have physically worn me out."

"Get a protein bar on your way back."

"I guess you'll just have to love me for my mind for the time being and not my body."

She giggled and swatted at him. "Get out of here."

"You're only saying that because you know I'll bring you back donuts." He chuckled and headed to the door. "I'll be back."

She blew him a kiss and then slid back under the covers as he closed the door, stretching her arms out over her head. God, she loved him. Everything about him was intoxicating, from the way he held her, made her laugh, fucked her, teased her—even just sitting around talking about nonsense with him was amazing. She was becoming one of those girls who just gushed and gushed about their boyfriends. It was an odd feeling, considering how toward the end of her relationship with Anthony, she didn't even admit she knew who he was.

The mattress lurched slightly, as if he had just sat down at the foot of the bed. She smiled and rose up onto her elbows. "Did you change your mind?"

No one was there.

Her mouth ran dry. She pulled the blanket closer to her breasts and sat up, glancing around the room. She'd felt the bed move, as if Mike had sat down again. The hairs on her arms pricked up; she knew she wasn't alone in the room. Impossible.

"You...you're supposed to be at peace." She whispered, staring at the foot of the bed where she felt his presence. "I found your remains. You can...rest now." Was there something specific she had to say? Something to prompt him to cross over…or whatever lost spirits had to do.

Madison…

"I know you're here. I don't understand why." She closed her eyes and tried to focus her mind on him, letting her body relax from the top of her head down to her toes. "I thought you wanted me to find your remains."

…save her…

She held her hand out, palm facing the wall. After a moment, she felt a pressure on her hand, like the warmth of a palm pressed against hers. "Who are you trying to save?"

He sounded far away, as if the strength to touch her exhausted him. His touch waivered and for a moment, he disappeared completely. When he came back, his touch was stronger than before. *…Keep you safe…*

"Tell me what I need to do. I want to help you."

Body…the body…now bones…

"I found your bones." She shivered. Why did this have to be so damn difficult? "We found them, we'll bury them properly now. You deserve that."

I failed.

"You didn't. You didn't fail. Were you part of the 11th Corps? The Union won the war, Ben, your sacrifice saved them." She fumbled for something to say. What was she missing?

I was part of the 11th. But, I failed…I won't…again.

"You led me to the bones, I know you did. You knocked the sifter over and showed me where to dig." She could feel him fading. The pressure of his hand was diminishing. "Isn't that what you wanted? Did you want me to find you?"

Save you. Madison...you know I can't stay long...
"If you need to go, it's okay. You deserve rest."
I can't rest...until...

His voice faded and, in an instant, every trace of his presence was gone. She couldn't feel him physically or mentally.

Madison sighed and buried her face in her hands. Couldn't rest until what? What else did she have to do? Granted, it was the forensic anthropologist and osteo-archeologist who were actually removing the bones from the site. But, that aside, if they found him and buried him as he should be buried—the park service would do that, right?—wouldn't that qualify as saving him? What else would he need?

She leaned over the edge of the bed and found Mike's under shirt where he'd dropped it last night. Pulling it on, she slid off the bed and walked to the bathroom. It felt appropriate to cover up, just in case he came back, but she had a feeling it didn't matter. If he'd been in the room earlier...well, it was suffice to say he'd seen it all anyway.

Her reflection looked paler than normal. She turned the water on to warm it and then dipped her hands in, scrubbing her face. It wasn't that she didn't want to tell Mike about seeing Ben, but there really didn't seem like much of a point to it. He couldn't do anything but tell her it was going to be okay. They'd found the remains, so, in time it was probably going to sort itself out.

She dried her face off and then put in her contacts lenses. Yes, it would sort itself out. There was no reason to tell him.

As she applied her eyeliner and mascara, she could see the reflection of the door behind her. It swung open and Mike walked in, carrying two Styrofoam cups of coffee and two plates of food. She wasn't entirely sure how he managed to unlock and open the door. "Here, let me help you."

He glanced at her and grinned. "If that's what you're wearing today, I approve."

She flushed. "Well, you know. Cold as always."

"You look pale."

"I always look pale." She took a drink of coffee and smiled. "Did you get any donuts for you?"

"Hilarious. This plate is yours. Keep your grimy little hands off mine." He popped a piece of bacon in his mouth and winked. "I thought we'd come back here after we slum around the battlefield for a while. Shower, get ready to go out, that kind of thing. I was thinking…you know, maybe you could wear that little skirt again."

"Oh you think so?" She pursed her lips together coyly. "I thought you were too tired for such naughty behavior."

"Bacon is very energizing."

She laughed and took a bite of donut, carrying the pastry back to the counter with her. "I can just wear jeans today, right? Because if I need to dress up, we're going to have to go shopping first."

"Right. This is probably going to be the least official thing you've ever gone to in your life."

Madison's cell phone started ringing. She ignored it. "You only say that because you've gone to them before."

"Not exactly like this, but I'm assuming it's the same as most of the 'unofficial' artifact meetings I've been at." He paused. "Your phone is ringing."

"Noted. It's my mother."

"You should answer it."

"Trust me, you don't want to witness the carnage if I do."

"Tell her we're on a schedule." He picked up the phone and handed it to her. "And tell her I said hi."

"She'll want to talk to you if I do that." Madison slid her finger across the face of the phone and then held it to her ear. "Hello, Mother."

"Hi, Madison!" Her mother sounded overly excited, like she was preparing to coach Madison into having a great day. "I saw the press release this morning. Was that your dig?"

"Yes, that was us." Madison pulled open the dresser and fished through her clean shirts, finally pulling out a hot pink tank top and a tight black shirt. "Pretty cool, huh? We're on our way to talk to some experts on what we found."

"Rick and I are so excited for you, sweetie."

Madison strongly doubted Tricky Dick even acknowledged the press release existed. "I'm excited too, Mom. This has been so much more amazing than I thought it was going to be."

"And your counseling sessions?"

"Well, they're as one would expect them to be. Pretty much a waste of time."

"You shouldn't say that, Madison. You have to learn—"

"I know, Mom. I know." She rolled her eyes and searched for her flare legged jeans. "I'm learning my lesson just like the court wanted. Since I'm twenty-one now, you'd think they'd just go ahead and drop those charges."

Mike cleared his throat and nodded to the floor. Her jeans were in a rumpled pile, along with her bra and panties. "You left those there last night."

"Is someone with you, Madison?"

"Uh, yeah, someone's with me." Madison shook her fist at Mike as she retrieved her jeans.

He chuckled.

"Oh, you're making friends. That's good."

"Mom, I'm not a social outcast, even when I'm at home."

"No, honey, no I'm not saying that at all. I'm just saying I'm glad you're not spending all your time being serious. Or *drinking*."

"Nope, not drinking." She pulled clean underpants on one leg, and then the other, as she pressed the phone against her ear with her shoulder. She shimmed them up her body. "Just working and having fun."

Mike sat in the chair and slouched down to watch her dress. He cocked his head to the side. "I don't think that's *all* you're doing."

She widened her eyes and him, unsuccessfully attempting to hold back a smile.

Her mother fell silent for a moment. "Is that a *male* you're with?"

"Yup, that's a male I'm with." She snapped her fingers at Mike and pointed at the phone. "His name's Mike."

Mike waved at the phone. "Hi, Madison's mom."

"He says hello."

"Madison." Her mother again fell silent, as if she were searching for the right thing to say. "Is he on the dig with you?"

"Yes."

"You barely know him."

"Well, he's pretty amazing." Madison nibbled on her bottom lip. "And, really, Mom, I have to go. We have to be at park headquarters in like, an hour. I still have to get dressed."

Mike snickered.

"Ugh, I mean, I still have to get ready." Madison pressed her fist to her forehead. That slip was going to go over well. "I'll talk to you later."

"Madison." Her mom drew in a sharp breath. "Just have fun. Be careful, have fun. And...tell him I said hello, too."

"Thanks, Mom. Love you."

"I love you, too. Bye, sweetie."

Madison hung up the cell phone and tossed it to the bed. She pointed at Mike. "You, sir, are trouble."

"I'm only pretty amazing?" He pouted. "I retract my previous statement denying you my donuts, if it offended the lovely Miss Madison."

She crawled into his lap, straddling him, and kissed him. "What did you prefer I said? Something more along the lines of, 'Yeah, Mom, he's sexy, got an amazing body, and is phenomenal in bed?'"

"Well, I don't want to brag." He slid his hand under her shirt, flicking his finger over her belly button ring. "It's good that you talked to her. You usually don't."

"I usually don't have much to say to her." Madison shrugged her shoulders and then pulled her shirt off, tossing it to the floor. "If there was a Madison Monroe fan club, she wouldn't be a charter member."

"I'd be the president."

"Biased." She gave him sufficient time to take in the curves of her body and then slid to the floor, walking back to the counter to finish getting ready. "Anyway, she's been fairly apathetic to my general behavior since she married my step-father. It's a strained relationship but, hey, I'm trying. Right?"

"I think you're trying to do a lot of things right now."

She ran her tongue over her bottom lip and then turned back to the mirror, leaning over to finish applying her eye makeup. "Possibly. What about your parents? Are they cool?"

"Yeah, I always had a good relationship with them growing up. They were insanely supportive when I came home from Afghanistan with my...ah...issues. But, Maddy, I joined the Army when I was seventeen and moved out permanently when I was eighteen. I'm used to being on my own and they're used to me being away. It's just different."

She tugged her jeans on and then fastened her bra around her shoulders. "I always wonder if things would have been different if my dad hadn't died. Maybe we all would have been...I don't know, happier or something. Better people."

"I think you turned out fine."

"Well, thanks." She smiled at him. "It means a lot to me."

"You hog the sheets though."

"Seriously, dude?"

He laughed and walked behind her, wrapping his arms around her waist. "Come on, beautiful. Let's hit the road."

Madison finished getting dressed and pulled her hair back, then followed Mike down to the Jeep. "Before I forget, my mother said hello."

"See? She likes me already."

He pulled the Jeep out onto the main street and drove north out of town, through the tighter, congested streets of the tourist areas before heading out onto the highway. The park's headquarters were contained in an antebellum farm complex and tucked back far off the main road, much like the Spangler Farm. Several smaller administrative buildings were dwarfed by a large farmhouse and bank barn.

Mike pulled the Jeep into a space beside Liam's car. Liam was out of his vehicle and around to Mike's window in an instant. "What the hell are we doing here?"

"I take it Brad gave you about the same amount of information he gave us." Mike pulled off his sunglasses and tucked them in his visor. "I'm trying to muster up the appropriate amount of excitement for whatever it is."

"He mentioned something about results, but not results they're ready to make official yet." Liam huffed. "What kind of results can they find on remains? A minie ball lodged in the skull? A bayonet through the sternum—not that I'm even sure that's physically possible—or some kind of cache of unexploded ordinance? I mean, unexploded ordinance just rains down on the douche like manna from Heaven."

"I would find all of those results to be absolutely fascinating." Madison flashed a thumbs up sign at him. "Sign me up."

"Where's Brad?" Mike craned his neck as he looked around the lot. "And, of lesser concern, Cianna?"

"It's not nine yet." Liam shrugged. "He'll be here."

"We can only be so lucky."

Liam leaned over and studied Madison. "Are you feeling any better?"

"Uh, yeah?" She said, uncertain what exactly he was talking about. "I wasn't aware I was feeling bad."

"No, I mean better about the remains."

"Being him, you mean?"

"Okay."

"It's been a lot to process."

"This has been the strangest dig I've ever worked." Liam ran his hand over the back of his head.

"Brad's acting like a loon, the dig has been simultaneously dull and completely out of control. I need a sedative."

Mike drummed his fingers against the steering wheel. "I thought it's been pretty good so far."

"You would. You've been getting laid nonstop for over a week."

"Don't get mad at me, man. You could have gone out with that guy again, you just chose not to."

"Mikey. He said he had herpes. At *Applebee's*." Liam huffed and then abruptly straightened. "Here comes Brad. I can't tell if the bitch is with him."

Brad maneuvered the pickup truck into a nearby space. He jumped out of the cab with far more energy than Madison felt was necessary for that time of morning and headed in their direction. "You guys ready for this?"

"So, what's the deal?" Mike stepped out of the Jeep, closing the door behind him. "What'd they find?"

"No idea." Brad started walking toward the farmhouse. "I think it's going to change everything for us, though. I think it's huge."

Madison circled around the Jeep to Mike and Liam. She watched Brad hustle to the farmhouse. Cianna, who'd been slow to slide out of the truck cab, was hurrying after him, trying to simultaneously swing a huge, designer purse over her shoulder. It was almost— almost—sad. "I get the feeling he's going to take credit for this."

"Hell yeah he is." Liam adjusted the collar of his shirt. "His name is on the dig. We're just the muscle. Well, Mike's the muscle. I'm the personality and Madison's the sexpot."

"Uh, okay." Madison glanced at him. "Usually I play the role of drunk or bookish weird girl."

Mike slid his arm around her and pulled her against him. "I agree with Liam's assessment. Which, take note, because that'll never happen again."

They followed Brad and Cianna to the farmhouse. Although the outside resembled any other farmhouse in the area, the interior of the building had been refurbished into an office space. There were large paintings depicting the 1863 battle in Gettysburg displayed on the walls and a huge, awkwardly placed green fern shoved in one of the corners. It reminded Madison of the reception area in a funeral parlor. The furniture looked comfortable, but ill-used and the heavy burgundy curtains looked like shrouds in a church.

Superintendent Frye was waiting for them, shuffling through a file folder splayed open on the secretary's desk. "I'm glad you all could join us on such short notice." He shook Brad's hand, but nodded congenially at the other four diggers. "We have everything set up in the archeology suites. Follow me."

He led them back outside the farmhouse and to one of the larger outbuildings. It was a modern building constructed to complement the other structures in the complex, with similarly painted siding and blue shuttered windows. The inside of the building was more like a gynecologist's office, with steel tub sinks and groutless tiled floor. An examination table was in the center of the room, and beside it stood a man and a woman, both wearing khaki slacks and white long sleeved shirts.

Madison realized these were the heralded experts, the two brought in to confirm what she, Mike, and Liam had pulled from the ground. The man looked to be in his mid-fifties, tall and lanky with a thick beard and stringy blond hair. The woman appeared about ten years younger. Her hair was short, dark brown streaked with gray, and she peered at them through thick, round glasses.

Superintendent Frye raised his hand in greeting to them. "Team, I want you to meet our osteo-archeologist Jan Williams and forensic anthropologist, Scott Spada. Scott and Jan, this is the archeological crew brought in for the survey. This is our dig head, Bradley Emerson. You may remember him from his discovery of the unexploded cartridge rounds from Allegheny Arsenal."

Introductions were quick and rushed, with lots of hand shaking and repetition of names. Madison was fairly sure the two experts fell suit with Superintendent Frye—only acknowledging Brad's participation in the dig—until Scott held on to her hand for an extra beat. "You're the one who found the remains."

She flushed. "Yes, sir."

"Excellent job, Miss Monroe."

He let go of her hand and crossed back behind the examination table. He nodded at the osteo-archeologist. "You go ahead, Jan, since it was mostly your effort."

The remains were laid out as in physiologic order, showing just how much actually had survived the passage of time. Jan pulled on examination gloves. "The condition of the remains is remarkable, considering how long they'd been in the ground. We're attributing that to the rubber blanket that was over it. In theory, the rubber repelled water to a certain extent and protected the bones from substantial deterioration. We did a standard examination of the remains. It's my professional option, based on all our testing and both physical and elemental observation, they are period to the Civil War."

She started at the top of the table and gestured to the skull. "The wear on the subject's teeth give a developmental age of between age eighteen and twenty-four. There was evidence of cavities. One of the back molars is missing."

Madison shuddered. She wasn't sure how comfortable she felt with Jan referring to the remains as 'the subject'. 'The subject' had once been a person. 'The subject' once was Ben.

Scott handed her a laser pointer. She leveled it at the spinal column. "We found a bullet lodged approximately between the 2nd and 3rd thoracic vertebra or, rather, what was left of the vertebra. The impact of soft lead would explode bone outward, sending bone shards into the surrounding tissue. Clearly, this would have been the cause of death. Moving downward, we measured the length of the femur and determined the subject stood an estimated height of five foot three inches."

Liam cleared his throat. "That's below average for the period, isn't it?"

"You have people at all ends of the height spectrum, of course." Scott pointed both index fingers at Liam, like he'd just told the punch line of a joke and was waiting for response. "But that's what we thought, too."

"I measured the pelvic bones probably a dozen times." The pitch of Jan's voice rose, her excitement growing. "I had Scott verify twice. The subject is female."

Impossible.

"Female?" Brad repeated. His voice sounded strangely uncertain, devoid of his typical arrogance. "You're sure?"

"I checked, and then I rechecked." Jan dropped the laser pointer in her pocket. "Pardon my candor, but this is huge. It's definitely female. The structure of the skull is more feminine than the typical brows we see in males. The confirmation is in the pelvic structure. There's no doubt it's female."

No one spoke.

Madison stared at the remains on the examination table. It wasn't Ben. After all this, the remains he'd dragged her to, the body he'd helped her discover, wasn't him. It was a woman. Instead of answering her questions, it seemed like the revelation only spurred more. Why was there a woman buried at the site of a military hospital? Who was she? How did she get there?

Liam was the first to verbalize what everyone was no doubt thinking. "Are you saying we discovered the remains of a female soldier? That's not huge…that's like, the first ever. That's monumental."

"Off the record," — Frye extended his hand to Brad — "this is the biggest archeological discovery in the history of the park. Congratulations, Brad. You're going to feel the echoes of this one for a while."

Brad whooped, pumping his fist into the air. "That's my team! Way to go, guys!"

There were hugs and congratulations all around. Madison even awkwardly hugged Cianna, despite the fact she hadn't lifted a finger over the entire course of the dig, but when faced with Brad, she froze. "Way to go team."

He opened his arms to her. "Come here, Madison. We're celebrating."

Reluctantly, she let him hug her. His embrace was too tight and too long; his entire body seemed to excrete sweat and the overpowering reek of cologne. She quickly pulled free, stepping backwards against Mike.

He looped his arm around her waist, leaning his head close to hers. "That's my girl. This one's all yours."

"Hardly. You and Liam did just as much as I did."

Jan held her hands up. "We can't officially confirm that the female you found was, in life, disguised as a soldier and lost her life in battle. It's conjecture."

Madison cleared her throat. "I found a federal sack coat in the same test pit, not too far from where we found the remains."

"She was covered with a gum blanket so, yes, there's a lot of evidence that she was somehow affiliated with the Army." Jan shook her head. "Unfortunately, with no records and no specific evidence proving she disguised herself as a male, we can only surmise why she was buried there. She could have been a civilian."

"I have to disagree with that." Mike broke in. "If a female civilian was killed in military presence, we would have had records of it. Look at Jennie Wade in town. I mean, that was a huge deal. She baked bread for soldiers and died in the process—we know the whole timeline."

"If she wasn't a soldier, why did she have a federal gum blanket over her body?" Liam tugged on his lower lip. "Someone had to have put it there on purpose."

"I wish I could tell you what that purpose was." Jan held her hands up, almost in a sign of helplessness. "Unfortunately, I can only tell you what the bones tell me. I can tell you what her diet most likely was, I can tell you possible diseases she carried that scarred her bones, but I absolutely cannot tell you why she was where you found her. We all know she shouldn't have been there, yet, she was."

"It doesn't detract from the importance of the find." Superintendent Frye spoke quickly. "I just want you to be prepared for that question, because you know it will be asked at the press conference—probably more than once. It will be the park's stance that it's reasonable to assume that she was one of the few female soldiers who fought in the war, but without hard evidence proving it, it remains just a theory. She could have been anyone.

Unfortunately, most likely we'll never confirm her identity."

Madison chewed on the inside of her lip. They might not be able to identify the remains, but she knew of one person, one soul, who could.

Chapter Fifteen

The parking lot for the press conference was filled to maximum capacity.

"Jesus Christ." Mike slowed the Jeep down and scanned row after row of parked cars. "I told you this was going to be a circus. We're early, too—can you imagine what this place would look like if we were late?"

Liam was squeezed in the back of the Jeep. He peered between the driver and passenger's seats. "Let's bail."

"After you forced us to buy clothes for today?" Madison gestured down at the short, pale gray dress and beige duster he'd insisted she needed. "No. No, Mike, park on the sidewalk."

He pulled his cell phone out of his pocket and slid his finger over the face. "I'll get us a spot. Don't you worry."

"I'm more worried about you plowing into a parked car."

"I was a combat engineer, this is nothing." He lifted the phone to his ear. "Hey, Carson, what's going on buddy? Are you still working the press conference?"

"I've never seen the visitor's center this packed." Liam offered Madison a mint. "This has all the makings of a disaster."

"Why did they have it here?" Madison kept her voice low, so as to not interrupt Mike's call.

"Because it's got an auditorium and sound system equipment and, prior to seeing this, I had the assumption it had ample parking."

Mike turned the wheel with one hand, backtracking to the lot entrance. "Around back? You mean, back next to the field or back next to the cyclorama? The cyclorama, okay, be there in about a minute. Thanks, man." He ended the call and shoved the phone back in his pocket. "He's going to hook us up."

"Sweet." Madison picked the edge of her dress, wishing it was a few inches longer. She didn't regret her tattoos, but she didn't want to be a media spectacle right off the bat. "I was under the assumption that four or five people would be here."

"Discovery of the century, baby." Mike maneuvered the Jeep down the windy road leading to the back side of the visitor's center. Ranger Carson was waiting beside a small patch of what appeared to be employee parking. He motioned for Mike to pull the Jeep into an empty spot in between two luxury sedans.

Once the car was parked, Carson opened Madison's door and reached his hand in to help her out. "It's delightful to see you again, Miss Madison. Are you ready for the big show?"

"False." Madison stepped out of the vehicle and tried to force a sunny smile. "I can think of about a million things I'd rather be doing. Jury duty. Root canal. Kidney donation."

He slid a parking pass onto the front dash. "It might not be that bad. Right, Lieutenant?"

"No, it's probably going to be worse." He circled around the back of the Jeep, opening the back so Liam could squeeze out and to the ground. "It's going to be a circus, especially when it's announced the remains were female."

"Female?" Ranger Carson fell into step with him. "You think she was disguising herself as a man to serve in the military?"

"If she was, she'd the first remains ever discovered. We have no idea how many served or how many were killed. Just speculation."

"And God knows we can't speculate." Liam rolled his eyes dramatically and then smoothed down the front of his shirt.

Carson ushered them into the auditorium. Madison had pictured a school auditorium like at her junior high school—this was substantially smaller. Five rows of six folding chairs were set up in front of a long, head table. Paper placards were placed in front of each seat to designate where each dig crew member was to sit.

Madison immediately noticed she was as far away as possible from Mike, seated next to Cianna.

"You don't think Brad had a hand at setting the table up, do you?" Liam tapped his finger against his chin. "Mikey, he hates you so much."

"Yeah, well, he can suck it."

"Madison, did he ever actually ask you out?" Liam pulled his chair out and sat down, adjusting the name placard to line up with the edge of the table. "Or, is he anti-Mikey on principle?"

"No, but he did stare at my boobs for a high percentage of the time we were together."

"We've all done that, Sassy."

"And on that note," — Carson stuck his hand out to shake Mike's — "I'll catch you guys after the press conference. Have fun."

Reporters slowly drifted into the auditorium, filling the folding chairs from the front to the back. Some were scribbling in notebooks or typing on tablets even at this point, obviously already preparing the first exclusive story of the dig results. Madison started to feel sweaty. It was the same physical reaction she got when delivering a speech in school: pulse pounding, nerve wracking, knee shaking panic. It was a good thing her name was written out in front of her; she had a distinct feeling her panic would reach the height where she'd need prompting for simple answers.

Maybe she'd just fade into the background and Brad could run the show. He'd probably like it better that way, anyway.

He and Superintendent Frye were in secluded conversation near the front of the room, no doubt discussing what could and couldn't be said about the dig. Brad's arms were crossed in front of him, with one hand extended upward and cupping his chin. He looked calm and serious, like he was preparing to deliver his acceptance speech for some prestigious award he'd waited his whole life to get. Hell, that's probably exactly what he was thinking.

Cianna stormed into the room and pushed past them, taking her seat at the table. She glanced up at them, immediately defensive. "I'm late because there was nowhere to park."

Liam looked around the room. "Unless I'm wrong, we haven't started yet. You're not late."

"Parking is a nightmare."

"We had the same problem." Madison took her seat next to her. *Be nice. Don't call her a whore.* "I'm glad Mike drove, because I'd have had a nervous breakdown. I might still have a nervous breakdown, because I see nothing desirable about this press conference."

Cianna regarded her. "Me either."

Brad took his seat at the table, his smile a little too big and exaggerated. "Hey, guys! Everyone here? Are we ready for this?"

Madison shook her head. Liam made some sort of indeterminate noise in his throat.

"We're going to do great." Brad winked at Madison. "We've got this. The hard part's over, right?"

Madison choked back the urge to throw up.

Superintendent Frye stepped to the front of the table and raised his hand in the air, signaling the journalists and photographers to fall silent. They complied. "Good afternoon, ladies and gentlemen, and welcome to Gettysburg National Military Park. As we previously released, on May 11, human remains were discovered during an archeological dig at the George Spangler Farm, the site of the Federal 11th Corps hospital. The remains are currently being analyzed by forensic anthropologist Scott Spada and osteo-archeologist Jan Williams. Ms. Williams released her initial report of the remains this morning, confirming the subject was a female, approximately between the ages of eighteen and twenty-four."

Murmurs rippled through the crowd and several journalists put their hands in the air to signal questions. The room was peppered with flash bulbs, like little bursts of lightening above the reporters.

Frye raised his hands again to silence them. "I have with me today the head of the archeological survey, Bradley Emerson, and the members of his crew: from right to left, we have Liam Stanish, Michael Caldwell, Cianna Simon, and Madison Monroe. I'll turn our discussion over to Mr. Emerson. Brad?"

Brad cleared his throat, adjusting the microphone in front of him. "We're going to open the room up for questions on the dig, the site, and the overall process of archeology. Until the final reports are issued from the forensic examination, I won't be able to give much detail on the state of the remains other than what's indicated on Dr. Williams report. First question?"

A man in the front row stood. "Hank DuFour, Gettysburg Chronicle. Will the remains be returned to the Spangler Farm and, if so, what future does that hold for the remainder of the planned survey?"

"As for the remains, no specific plans have been made for internment at this point. Once the examination is complete, the park service will determine when and where the remains will be laid to rest." Brad paused, adjusting the pages of notes in front of him. "Our survey of the site will continue once it's cleared by the park service. We will not continue any further excavations in the test pits where the remains were found, but will fall back on the other three pits we had set up. We hope to still complete everything on schedule."

He nodded at a woman a few seats down. She stood, pen poised above a pad of paper. "Carol Vanek, Harrisburg Sun. Who found the remains? Specifically."

Brad's eyes shifted down the table. "That would be Miss Monroe."

The reporter nodded and turned toward Madison. "As a woman in a field dominated by men, tell me what it's like to have discovered the remains of a woman who, quite possibly, hid her sex to fight in a war also dominated by men."

Madison shifted her weight from one hip to the other and twisted a sterling silver ring around her finger. Shouldn't Brad be answering all the questions? Her mind went blank, but she forced herself to answer. "Well, um, I don't think that archeology is a field dominated by men. Look at our crew: we're evenly matched two women and two men. I think we all have equal opportunities to be awesome. I just…happened to be in the right place at the right time. It could have been any of us; it could have been none of us. That's just how fickle field archeology is: one quarter of an inch off and you find nothing but dirt."

"But how did you feel finding remains? No one has found remains here in over twenty years."

"She wasn't who I expected to find." Madison grimaced. *Idiot.* "I mean, we weren't expecting to find remains. We found buttons and brass and canteen spouts but this...this was different. This was a person. Regardless whether she was a soldier or a civilian, she was someone. She had a life and friends and family and...it's just all very sobering. It makes you think about what's really important and what's not."

Brad motioned to a reporter in the second row. "Next question?"

"JJ Schmidt, Archeology Magazine. This question is also for Madison: how does this experience compare to other digs you've worked?"

"I haven't been on any other digs like this."

"What's your degree in?"

"I don't have a degree." She blushed and looked at the back of the room. This was ridiculous. "I'm still in college."

"How did you end up on the dig crew, then?"

"I'm applying to graduate school and this is part of the requisite field experience. Previously I worked at Pittsburgh's Fort Pitt and helped on small surveys at Allegheny Cemetery and the site of the 1845 Pittsburgh Fire." She hesitated, not sure what else she needed to say to get the attention off of her. "I'm from Pittsburgh."

"What school do you go to?"

"Monongahela University of Western Pennsylvania."

"Are you a good student?"

"I'd like to think so." She shrugged. "I'm somewhat of an overachiever."

"Favorite class so far?"

"Survey of World War I Trench Warfare with lecture series of archeology of extant trenches."

"Why do you think they selected you for this dig?"

"Other than my stunning wit and charm?" She shrugged again. "Another example of the right place at the right time, I guess."

"I think you're being modest."

"I think I'm just really bad at interviews."

A chuckle rumbled through the seated journalists. Mr. Schmidt wrote something on his pad of paper and then smiled. "Last question: has your impression of archeology changed since you discovered the remains?"

"Yes. I think it's even more important and imperative now than I did before."

Another journalist stood. "Will you finish your degree now?"

"It would be a waste of money not to finish my degree, not to mention a big waste of three years studying and learning and testing on all the minute historical fact you could be interested in, or, not interested in as the case may be. I tried to learn Latin because I thought it would help, but that was a disaster."

Still another journalist. "What's next for you, Madison?"

"Other than Latin? I'm one class shy away from a minor in French. Other than that, school starts again in the fall and, pending anything out of control, spring will be my last semester. Graduation after that, the start of grad school in the fall, you know. Living the dream."

And another. "Do you think this experience has changed you?"

"No, I'd hope I'm the same socially awkward nerd I was before, the girl who likes science fiction, a good cheese, and crossword puzzles."

The group of journalists chuckled again. Another journalist took his turn. "Do you think you're the new face for the field of archeology?"

Madison groaned. God, she hoped not.

* * * *

Although a few of the questions were directed to other members of the team, Madison felt like the overall onslaught of questions was directed toward her. This was precisely what she wanted to avoid.

Mike led her to the car, his fingers tightly laced around hers. "You're a media darling. I like how you did the majority of the press conference while Liam and I got to sit back and count ceiling tiles."

"That was the worst thing I've ever had to do."

"I thought you were delightful." Mike squeezed her hand. "Charming, funny, politically correct in every way possible; they ate it up. You're, like, the media whisperer or something."

"Consider this my retirement from the sport."

He opened the passenger's door for her and then circled to the rear of the Jeep to open it for Liam. She watched them in the side view window, nervously twisting her ring around her finger. As easy as it was to get caught up in the present, her mind easily slid back to concerns of the past. The remains in the test pit were female. It was a woman—a girl her age—entombed in the Pennsylvania soil, not Ben. He'd dragged her to the pit, he'd prompted everything she did, whether she fully realized it or not. After all that, how could it not be him? Why was he still trapped in eternal limbo, some hazy point of existence in between life and death?

What was he trying to tell her? And, more importantly, why was she too dense to figure it out?

Mike slid into the driver's seat and jammed the key into the ignition. "Okay, so, what do we want to do now? Lunch? Update our resumes? Sit around and do nothing?"

"I vote lunch." Liam noisily shifted around in the back of the Jeep. "Go somewhere where I can get a scotch."

"You answered about two-thirds of one question."

"I'm flustered."

Mike chuckled and then stopped, touching his finger to Madison's cheek. "Why so down? Come on, it wasn't that bad. Besides…it's over now."

"It's not over." She hesitated and then sighed. "*That* part is over. But, I still don't know why Ben wanted us to find her. Or, why he's still lurking around now that we have."

"Wait, you saw him again? When?"

"When you went to get breakfast this morning. He acted like he was trying to tell me something. I still can't understand him or, hell, I can't even hear him half the time. I'm not strong enough. Neither is he."

"I'm not sure those are questions you'll ever be able to have answered." Mike pulled the Jeep out of the parking space and drove toward the main road. "It's not like calling him on the phone. You can't just redial or ask him to repeat himself.

"We can ask him if we have a séance."

Liam scoffed. "You want to have a séance? Are you serious?"

"Yes, and I want you to be there." She turned and faced Mike. "I just think, if there's the three of us trying, all the combined…psychic power or whatever it is can amplify him. It would be like plugging a guitar into an amp. Sure, the guitar works without the amp, but plug it in and it's even better. It's louder."

"You've given this a lot of thought."

"I've relied heavily on internet searches because I have no idea what I'm talking about."

Mike sighed. "Look, I understand where you're coming from. I do. But, what happens if it doesn't work? Or, worse yet, you don't get the answer you're looking for?"

"At least we'll have tried." She glanced at the rock clotted green battlefields. "I just feel like we need to try."

"Feasibility aside…" Liam paused, as if he were choosing his words. "I assume you'd want to have a séance at the test pit—which we can't do. The next best thing would be the summer kitchen, which we also can't do, because the entire farm is shut down. We'd get arrested if they caught us trying to get on site. Hell, I'm fairly sure we'd get arrested trying to get on site even if it wasn't shut down."

"I'd want someone to do it for me, if I was in his shoes."

"I'm game if you are, Liam."

"You're fucking her, Mikey. I think that precludes you from having a choice."

"Fair point, I'll give you that." Mike shrugged. "But, after all this, I'm interested to see what will happen. It can't hurt. Worst case scenario, we sit in the dark for a while and go home. My only requirement is that we wait until we're cleared to go back into the site. Somehow…somehow I feel like that will slightly diminish the possibility we'll get arrested."

Madison smiled. "I owe you one."

"Yes, you do, and I already know how you can make it up to me."

"Seriously, guys, I'm going to require lunch if you're going to talk like this for the rest of the afternoon. I can't suffer through this on an empty stomach." Liam clapped his hand on Mike's shoulder. "Look, the Turnpike Restaurant is right there, right by Cemetery Hill. I'd eat a hamburger."

"Look how full the parking lot is!"

"It seats a lot of people and I'm sure everyone drove separately." Liam nudged Madison. "You want the Turnpike. Trust me. Best late night eatery around."

"Liam, it's 11:45 in the morning."

"Just trust me."

Mike groaned, but slowed at the intersection at Cemetery Hill. "I'm not paying for your food, Liam."

"You say that now."

Madison giggled. Her smile quickly faded as something demanded her attention from the hill. Something she couldn't pinpoint or see, but something that tugged on her soul.

Time is running out.

Chapter Sixteen

The park service reopened the Spangler Farm the following Monday morning, with strict instructions the test pits near the woods remain roped off and untouched. No decision had been made on what to do with the remains, but Jan William's report was official and in print: the remains were a five foot, three inch tall woman, whose cause of death was a bullet wound to her thoracic spine. The report deferred from an opinion of whether or not she was a soldier, but as far as Madison was concerned, it seemed more unlikely that she wasn't.

By Monday afternoon, journalists were gathered outside the farm entrance, now barred and guarded by Law Enforcement Rangers. Madison's cell phone was ringing off the hook from a reporter from *Archeology* magazine. When she didn't answer, he left her a voicemail. Three times.

"How did he get your phone number in the first place?" Mike moved a full bucket of dirt to Madison's side. "I mean, other than possibly the internet."

She dumped some dirt onto the sifter tray. "No, he had it already. It's the reporter who interviewed me about the Pittsburgh Fire. His name's Jack Kornick. He's a prick."

"Tell me how you really feel."

"I think things soured between he and I when, following the interview, he asked me out for a cup of coffee and then a romp in bed. I declined. He told me I didn't have the proper motivation to further my career."

"You attract a really bizarre type of people."

"I'm actually more worried he's calling for an interview and not a date."

"Interviews are a good thing, right?" Mike stepped back down into the test pit and began shoveling. "Miss paper archeologist?"

"You're pretty mouthy over there. Interviews are usually a good thing, but this feels more like a freak show. Just wait until they start labeling me as a drunk who got thrown off an international dig." She plucked a rock from the tray and tossed it aside.

"We won't let that happen."

"Or they start a smear campaign against you because we're together."

Mike rotated his shoulders and craned his neck from side to side. "Eh, so then all the men of the world hate me for my sexual prowess and my dreamy good looks. There are worse things in life."

Her phone started ringing again.

"Oh, for God's sake." She jammed her finger across the face of the cell phone, leaving a trail of dirt behind. "Hello."

"Madison."

She wanted to shove the sifter over. "Yes, this is Madison."

"Hey, it's Jack. Uh, Jack Kornick? I don't know if you remember me…"

"Yes, actually I do remember you." Try to be nice. Try to be nice. "I see you called a few times."

"I've been trying to get ahold of you. One of our reporters was at the press conference last week and, let me tell you, your discovery is…well, it's beyond words."

"Thanks."

"No, really, you're nowhere near the girl I met last year."

"Okay, thanks, but look I'm kind of in the middle of the dig here." She brushed loose strands of hair out of her face, no doubt leaving streaks of dirt across her forehead. "We're behind as it is."

"I know. There's a bunch of us here by the road. The damn rangers won't let us up to the farm."

"Wow, creepy, Jack." She jammed her fist against her forehead. "Can I help you with something or are you just calling for some kind of weird, verbal status update?"

Mike snickered.

"Yes. Yes, I'm calling to see if we can get together."

"I'm seeing someone now, Jack. But thanks."

"That's good to know, but I meant in a professional setting." He spoke rapidly, as if he was being sincere. He wasn't. "I wanted to interview you for *Archeology*. Not just interview, we want a cover story."

Her stomach lurched; no, this wasn't even remotely appealing. "Thanks for the offer, but we're so busy up here trying to catch up—"

"I know, and that's totally fine. I thought maybe after you were done for the day. Maybe dinner?"

"That's sweet, really, but like I said I'm dating someone right now. She took a deep breath. "Besides that, I wasn't the only one who excavated the remains. We're a team."

"But you're the one who found them."

"I'm really busy, Jack."

"Wait, wait, okay, so bring your crew with you. We'll do dinner, drinks." He paused. "My buddy Ed is here with me. He's with *National Geographic* and he wants an interview too."

"Really."

"Yes, really. Madison, do you realize how huge you are? You're trending on Twitter."

She didn't know what to say. That was a little on the impressive side.

He continued to talk, as if he hadn't expected her to respond. "You're the biggest name in archeology right now and, honestly, I want the first interview. Ed can have sloppy seconds."

"Uh, okay?" She wasn't going to impress anyone with self-confidence. Hopefully he wasn't taking notes. "When and where? I have to get back to work."

"Tonight at six o'clock. We already made reservations at Toliver House."

She vaguely remember Toliver House, a huge mansion turned restaurant perched on the edge of the battlefield. Liam had remarked that despite the reviews, he wasn't about to pay forty-five dollars for a steak. "That's a bit out of my price range, Jack. I'm living on a stipend here, not an inheritance."

"*National Geographic* is paying."

"I'm bringing two other diggers with me. This was a team effort."

"Fine, fine. Be there at six."

"Six o'clock." She hung up the phone without giving him the opportunity to respond. "Great."

"When you say you're bringing two other diggers," — Liam fluttered his eyelashes — "you wouldn't happen to be talking about us, per chance?"

"Why, yes, yes I am." She shoved her phone in her pocket and turned back to the sifter. "I hope you don't have plans, because you two are going on a date with me, *National Geographic*, and *Archeology* Magazine."

"A threesome." Liam clicked his tongue. "Hot."

"I'm sure Jack would love that. But, no, it's far worse. He wants dinner at Toliver House and not one, but two interviews. One with *Archeology* and one with

National Geographic." Madison felt like she was reading off her own sentence of execution. She didn't want the spotlight on her. She wanted the spotlight on the field and on the importance of their discovery. They found a person—someone who once lived and breathed and loved—not the ruins of some long decrepit building. Christ, why didn't anyone get that?

Liam glanced at Mike. "Yeah, that sounds horrible."

"They're going to pay for our dinners."

"Oh." Liam blinked. "In that case, are we getting ready at your place or mine? I wonder if I have anything with an elastic waistband. I want to get my eating on tonight."

"This is good for you, Maddy." Mike stepped out of the test pit and set another bucket of dirt beside Madison. He leaned over and pressed his lips to her cheek. "Really, whether you like it or not, this is going to make your career."

"I'd rather make my career the old fashioned way, through hard work and diligence."

Mike reached into the sifter and plucked out a round object. He picked at it for a few moments and then discarded it. Another rock. "You're a dying breed then, baby. It won't be that bad. I mean, yeah, it probably will be, but look at the bright side. You'll get a free dinner and so will we."

"When was the last time you had to suffer through this kind of nonsense?" She poked her index finger into his chest. "Huh, big shot?"

He caught her hand in his and pulled her to him. "After the Chancellorsville dig. And the Baltimore dig. And after a dig last year in Sweden. It happens to the best of us, Maddy baby. You answer a few questions, smile for a few pictures, and then you go home. Lucky for you, you get to go home with me, so it's completely a win-win situation."

"Do the interview for me and I'll blow your mind."

He playfully smacked her ass. "I'll take my chances."

As he let her go, she saw Brad sauntering over from the summer Kitchen. She had a feeling he'd seen the whole interaction between her and Mike and, though she cared little of his opinion, she was a little concerned of his reaction. He seemed nonchalant. "Important phone call, Madison? We usually don't take personal calls during work hours."

She flushed. "No, it wasn't a personal call. It was related to the dig, just a reporter wanting an interview."

"Oh?" Brad picked up a film canister and pried off the lid, easing a metal thimble out into the palm of his hand. "This is a nice find, guys, keep it up. What magazine, Madison?"

"*Archeology* and *National Geographic*." She sighed. "I'm not looking forward to it."

Brad was silent for a moment, studying the artifact in his hand. When he finally spoke, he sounded too calm. "That's got to be a good feeling, being interviewed by two of the top leaders in the industry."

"I'd be happy just to go back to my room and relax."

"With Mike?" Brad squeezed his eyes closed and checked himself. "Sorry, that was inappropriate. Well, good luck to you, Madison. That's a big honor."

"Something like that."

He didn't respond, instead turning to Mike. "I'm going to need you to run some files up to park headquarters. Superintendent Frye has asked for daily reports."

"Me?" Mike frowned as he picked up his shovel. "You usually give him the reports."

"I have to run Cianna to Chambersburg to pick up her car." Brad shrugged. "Oil change."

"Whatever, man."

Madison glanced back down at the sifter, if only to avoid having to look at Brad. Another feeble attempt at "punishing" Mike for being in a relationship with her. Did he have the authority to punish them? Was making Mike do menial tasks an actual punishment?

"Since you have plans tonight, Madison, why don't we go ahead and shut down early?" Brad looked at his watch. "It's almost four o'clock, anyway. What difference will an hour make?"

"It can make a lot of difference." Liam picked the thimble out of Brad's hand and reinserted it into the canister. "She's not in that big of a hurry."

"Liam's right, I don't have to be there until six o'clock." Madison forced a confident smile. "It's not a big deal."

"Please, it's a huge deal. Mike, the files are in the summer kitchen. You head up to park headquarters. I want you to discuss the broken probe tip we found near the barn with him. Run our idea past him of a triage station in this general area." Brad marked off a grid on a map and handed it to Mike. "It's not a lot to go on, but he's aware of that."

"Uh, okay?" Mike glanced up from the map. "Can this wait until we're done here? I'm Madison's ride back to the hotel. She can just come with me."

"Nope, you need to go now. Frye's only there until five and he needs this today. He's heading into Washington tomorrow to meet with a joint staff of authorities from the Smithsonian and the Department of the Interior." Brad headed back toward the summer kitchen. "Now, Mike, not in five or ten minutes."

Mike waited until Brad was well out of earshot. "Bastard."

"I'll drive her back to the hotel." Liam didn't look up from his meticulous documentation. "Get it over with so we can focus on more important things. Like, if we'll be getting steak or elk tonight. Did you know Toliver House's specialty is elk? Have you had elk? Shit, what wine do I pair with elk?"

"Whisky goes with elk." Mike leaned over and softly kissed Madison. "I'm not presenting anything to Frye. Stick with Liam. I'll meet you back at the hotel."

"Okay." She tightened her grasp around the sifter handles. Getting mad only gave Brad the reaction he was evidently looking for. She wouldn't give him that satisfaction. "I'll wait to shower until you get there."

"You'd better." He hesitated for a moment and then headed toward the parking area.

Madison looked back down at the sifter and picked out a few more rocks and decaying twigs. She wanted to throw up. First she was talked into a miserable dinner with a horn dog, and now she had to watch Mike leave without her. Brad's apathetic punishments were more like irritants, like shards of glass embedded in the sole of a person's foot. Annoying. Grating.

"Seriously, guys, let's shut it down for the day." Brad walked back up to the test pit. "Liam, take these buckets into the summer kitchen for tomorrow. You can start with them in the morning."

"Um." Liam glanced up from his notebook. "She can have them done in a few minutes. We can just finish them up now and do something else in the morning. Progress, remember, that's what's driving us much like it drove the pioneers as they headed West with Manifest Destiny and shit."

"Liam, man, really, just accept the fact I'm being nice and go with it! I won't be this benevolent next time." Brad chuckled as if there were something funny about it. "Take the buckets to the summer kitchen. I'll bring the sifter over. Once we secure the pits, we'll head out for the day."

Liam grunted, but did as he was told. "I'm keeping the logs in my car."

"Yeah, yeah, you do that." Brad watched him lug two buckets down the hill toward the small, stone building that was the summer kitchen. As Madison started to follow, he held up his hand. "Hang on there, lady. I just wanted to make sure you had a ride back to your hotel room."

She stepped backward, if only to increase the distance between them. "Yeah, I'm good. Liam said he'd take me back."

"I'll drive you. It's no big deal, I'm headed that direction anyway."

Madison hesitated. She hadn't heard Ben's voice all day, but out of nowhere he filled her ears with frantic, incessant chatter. She couldn't understand him, couldn't interpret a word of what he was trying to say, but she could feel his desperation. Panic crept up her arms like the gentle brush of fingertips. "No, really, I'm good. Liam will take me."

"Yeah, but after Mike, Liam's next in the chain of command and I'm going to have him secure the site. He'll lock everything down." Brad cocked his head toward the parking area. "Come on. He'll probably be another ten or fifteen minutes. Cianna's down at the administrative building and I need to go get her. I'll drop you off on the way."

Ben's chatter swelled. Madison felt fingertips tug on her elbow. "I appreciate it, Brad. Really, but I really feel like I should help Liam. I'll just catch a ride with him."

"Are you sure? Because…you know, I'm leaving now. You can start getting ready for your interview."

"Thanks, but I'd rather get this tray finished." She forced a smile and turned back to the sifter. "I don't mind waiting. The longer I'm here, the longer it is until I have to suffer through an interview."

"If you're sure—"

"I am." She broke in quickly. "You can leave if you need to, Brad. I'm okay."

Out of the corner of her eye, she saw him linger next to the test pit. He finally mumbled something under his breath and turned, sulking off to the parking area on his own.

Madison exhaled slowly. Thank God. If she could only avoid one undesirable thing today, being alone with Brad was a good one.

* * * *

A few minutes before six o'clock, Mike pulled his Jeep into a parking place at the rear lot of Toliver House. He pulled the key out of the ignition and sat still, starting out the windshield in silence. After a moment, he ran his finger under the short hemline of Madison's miniskirt. "I'm sure you know to expect the Spanish Inquisition."

"I'm anticipating being hit on and to suffer through an inappropriate barrage of sexual innuendo." She studied him. "Is something wrong?"

"I'm just tired, that's all." He slid out of the Jeep, first circling to the back to let Liam out and then opening Madison's door. "If you want to talk about us being…you know, us, I'm cool with that. And if you don't, I'm cool with that, too. It's up to you."

"I want to get this over with so we can get back to just being us." Madison fell into step next to him. Toliver House, despite being a restaurant, still carried the façade of a turn of the century mansion. The exterior was hewn in stone, with tall, lead lined windows reaching into pointed peaks to the slate roof. The greenery on the outside seemed overgrown and rambling, yet at the same time looked to be carefully cultivated to complete the picture of a somewhat dilapidated English manor. The more she looked at it, the more it seemed out of place pressed up against a Civil War battlefield.

The interior of the building had the same, strange elegance. The front room was sparsely furnished with nothing more than a chaise lounge and several ceiling high bookcases, jammed full of dusty, cloth covered books and what appeared to be several, thick Bibles. The room was lit with electric lights, but they seemed like they were set to emit no more light than a candle.

A man in a dark suit stood behind an ornately carved stand. He regarded them. "Do you have a reservation?"

Madison cleared her throat. "We're part of a larger party. I'm assuming it's under the name Kornick. Jack Kornick."

"Ah, yes, Mr. Kornick." He motioned through an archway leading into the heart of the house. "Right this way."

They followed him down a hallway and to a small alcove. A heavy oak table was crowded up against a fireplace, with equally heavy looking, straight-backed chairs spaced around it. Although there was electric lighting well hidden in the corners of the room, most of the light came from the fireplace and thick, pillar candles in the center of the table.

She recognized Jack immediately, his blond hair pulled back into a short ponytail and scruffy beard somewhat unkempt looking compared to his black button down shirt and black leather jacket. He looked like he belonged in a rock band, not a top reporter with *Archeology* Magazine. He was attractive and he knew it.

He looked up as they approached, quickly standing and extending his hand to Madison. "There she is, Madison, it's great to see you!"

"You really didn't have to do all this." She smiled. "I'm just a college kid with simple, no-frill tastes."

"Shut up, you're being too modest." He motioned to the man seated next him, an equally trendy dresser with thick, spiked brown hair and black plastic glasses. "This is Ed Agosti. He's with *National Geographic* and, let me tell you, they want you to order whatever you want. Everything is extravagant and frilly for you tonight, my dear."

She made a noncommittal noise in her throat and shook Ed's hand. "It's nice to meet you."

"Thanks for agreeing to come on such short notice. This asshat thinks the ambush technique gets him better interviews, whereas I prefer scheduling and reservations."

"Either way, we're here." Madison stepped backwards and nudged Mike in front of her. "This is Mike Caldwell and Liam Stanish. I'm part of their team. We excavated the remains together."

Mumbled greetings ensued and Madison was fairly sure Mike and Liam were only there because she had insisted on it, not because either reporter was interested in what they had to say. She took a seat next to Mike, sliding into the chair rather than trying to drag the ornate carved monstrosity away from the table. "We've driven past here several times, but never stopped. It's…it's ostentatious."

"It was a private residence until the mid-90s, when an art director bought the place from the original owners and turned it into a restaurant." Jack motioned to the paper menu on top of her plate. "Order whatever you want; appetizer, dessert, everything. I recommend the pan seared sea bass."

Madison glanced at the menu and almost choked. Eleven dollars for a cup of lobster bisque? Mother of god.

She heard Mike exhale next to her. Obviously, his impression was the same as hers.

"So, off the record Madison," — Jack leaned forward — "do you think you'll finish school after this or just start looking for a job? I'm sure the bid wars to get you on an established team will be insane."

"You're a reporter. It's never off the record."

Jack chuckled and glanced at Ed. "All the same."

"Well, Jack, I've put a lot of time and a lot of dollars into my education. It'd be a little silly to quit now, when I only have two semesters left." She shifted in her chair. "I have to repay my student loans either way."

"What about graduate school?"

"What about it? It's an application process and I still have to submit my portfolio."

"I thought there was talk of you going on an international dig?" Jack looked up as the waiter stopped next to the table. "Drink orders, anyone? Madison, I'm sure they have a list of chocolate or fruit mixed drinks, unless you'd rather wine. Ed and I already started a tab."

"I'll have a scotch." Madison chewed on her lip. How was she going to explain the Normandy dig? "Better make it a double. And the lobster bisque."

Once the waiter had taken drink and appetizer orders, Jack turned back to Madison. "Anyway, when we chatted about the Pittsburgh Fire last summer, you'd mentioned applying for an international dig this year for field experience. What happened with that?"

"It fell through." She shrugged casually. "These things happen."

"Not often."

"Well, it's not often that human remains are found on a Civil War battlefield, but as the last few weeks demonstrated, that happens too."

"Now that the remains are excavated, studied, analyzed, tested, the whole works," —Ed paused and pulled out a small notebook and pen — "what do you want done with them? If it were up to you, of course."

"I'd like to see them buried, properly, either back on the farm or in a formal cemetery." Madison adjusted the lineup of three forks and two knives next to her plate. "Honestly, I don't think it matters if she was a soldier or a civilian. She was a person. She deserves to be buried."

"I think you'll lose that wide-eyed innocence the more digs you're on. You have to separate yourself from the human aspect; otherwise you won't be able to handle the sheer nature of it. Think of the archeologists pulling out the bog people in Europe. Those remains are mummified; you can still make out the detail of their faces, even down to their eyelashes." Jack held his wine glass to his lips, but didn't drink. "Though, I'll say there's something inherently seductive about someone so strong in their opinions."

Mike cleared his throat. "I don't think sensitivity to the human 'aspect' as you call it, is necessarily a bad thing. I think we become desensitized to our profession. We see femurs and skulls and bits of bone and see them for their individual pieces. She sees the bigger picture.

That's not a mark of inexperience, it's a mark of maturity to remember the grand scale of what happened here."

"I'm sorry, you're who again?" Jack narrowed his eyes. "Why does the name Caldwell sound familiar to me?"

Liam waved down the waiter. "Sweetie, bring the lady another scotch. I need gin and tonic, easy on the tonic."

Ed tapped his finger against the edge of the table. "Unlike this junior reporter to my left, I actually did a little research prior to this evening. First Lieutenant Michael Christopher Caldwell, enlisted as a private at age seventeen, rose through the ranks at a rapid pace due to a higher than average deployment rate, what, the Balkans, the Middle East, even a stint in Korea? Went to Officer Candidacy School when you were twenty-four and awarded both the Purple Heart and the Bronze Star for a combat incident in Fallujah two years ago and, if memory serves correctly, you resigned."

"They offered me promotion to Captain and I turned them down."

"Anyway, it looks like somewhere in between Officer Candidacy School and being awarded the Bronze Star, you got your degree and started working with Bradley Emerson." Ed paused. "As a side note, does that guy have any other experience than literally falling into those cartridges?"

"He's led a lot of digs, actually." Liam took a drink of his gin and tonic. "Mostly down in Virginia, but we work in Maryland and here in Pennsylvania on occasion. It's a private operation, not one of those public free for alls."

"You, I couldn't find anything about." Ed consulted a slim tablet next to him. "Not even as much as a speeding ticket."

"I'm an enigma, bitch. I like to keep my name out of the papers."

"What does this have to do with anything?" Madison picked up her scotch and held it, half temped to toss it squarely in Ed's face. "I mean, so what if he's got a Bronze Star and Liam, possibly, leads a double life? I thought this interview was about the remains and the dig site."

"Should you really be drinking so much, Madison?" Ed raised an eyebrow. "I found some interesting information about you in the criminal court system. Seems you have a record."

"I have a citation for underage drinking."

"Is that what happened with your international dig?"

"I don't think that's any of your business." Mike's voice was soft, but firm. "I think if you don't want to talk about the site or the remains, we can just leave. Liam can stay, but she and I will split."

Jack held up his hands, almost in a defensive position. "I have to agree with Mike, that's not really why we're here."

"Sure it is, she found the remains." Ed shrugged. "Look, sweetheart, you're playing in the big leagues now. This isn't your little survey of some lame fire that no one's heard of in a city no one cares about. Like it or not, everyone knows your name right now and they're going to know everything about you. Even the bad things, the things you think you left hidden in the back of the closet or buried somewhere. If you think people won't find out, you're wrong; they're going to find out and they're going to hold you to a completely different standard than they're going to hold someone else against."

"What do you want me to say then, Eddie?" Madison leaned back in her chair and took another sip of scotch. "I stole my neighbor's bike when I was twelve. I kissed a girl in eleventh grade. Last month, the cops found me sloshed at a fraternity party and issued me a citation which, yes, got me thrown off the Normandy Dig and almost got me put on academic probation no doubt in part to the fact my step-father is the school president and already holds me to a different standard than the twenty-five other students who got citations that night. The chair of the history department took pity on my poor, pathetic soul and got me put on this dig, in hopes that maybe, just maybe, I'd scrape together enough field experience so I can get into graduate school."

"I'd say you've got enough experience for graduate school now."

"I'd say you're damn right." She threw back the rest of the scotch and set the glass on the table. "Don't try to bully me, man. I don't have any intention of becoming some kind of archeological superstar. All I want to do is dig in the dirt and try to piece together the past."

Ed nodded, looking somewhat impressed. "You hold your own pretty well."

"It takes a lot more than inappropriate questions to scare me."

The waiter returned to the table with a refill on drinks and took their entrée orders. Madison stared at the menu for several minutes, realizing she'd been too busy staving off questioning instead of deciding what she wanted to eat. She ordered the prime fillet and Boursin potatoes and then ran her finger around the lip of her water goblet. Would it be inappropriate to order another drink? She needed something to get her through the next barrage of questions.

Jack plucked a roll from the bread basket and then passed it to Ed. "Madison, I'm not sure you realize the scope of this discovery. I've interviewed some of the biggest names in the field and, let me tell you, they could have only wished for a start like this. You're not going to need a degree. You're the girl who found the first documented remains of a female soldier—and at Gettysburg, nonetheless. That's like, the Holy Grail of Civil War finds."

"It's only speculation she's a soldier. She could have been a civilian."

Jack shook his head. "You don't believe that. Look at you; you know she was a soldier. Why else was she buried at what is a documented military hospital site and covered with a military issued blanket?"

"There could be a lot of reasons." Madison pulled a warm roll from the basket and passed it to Mike. He ran his fingers down hers as he took it. "Granted, they aren't good reasons. But we can't officially call her a soldier if we don't have official, hard evidence that she was."

"And off the record?"

"There is no off the record."

"Humor me."

She sighed. "I don't know. Maybe? I just think if she was a civilian, they wouldn't have just buried her in a pit. They would have left her with other civilians."

"Maybe she was a camp follower." Ed reached across the table for the butter dish. "Maybe she wasn't worth the trouble of hunting down a civilian who would help."

"Burying Confederates wasn't worth the effort. They left them rotting on the field."

"What else did you find in the test pit?"

"Our survey isn't finished yet and we haven't released the official report." Mike broke in. "You can't ask her that kind of question and you know it."

"Uh huh." Jack ran his tongue over his teeth, as if preparing a decent response, and then tried again. "So, you didn't think you'd find a body in the pit."

"Not a woman." Madison caught herself. "That's like finding a needle in a haystack."

"But you're insinuating you expected to find a man?"

"I'm insinuating I didn't expect to find anything." Madison's mind raced. She had to start watching her mouth. "Look, this was supposed to be a survey. We weren't supposed to find anything and, if we did, it was supposed to be the typical battlefield finds: bullets, canteen spouts, maybe an errant bayonet or belt buckle. Not a body. And not as much as we found."

"Do you think this changes the game? For women I mean."

"Are you saying that archeology is an all-boys club?" Madison crossed her arms in front of her. "That's pretty chauvinistic, even for you."

"Maybe, but think about it. When kids think of archeology, who do they think of?" Jack studied her, his eyes drifting from her face down to her shoulders and the cut of her shirt. "They're thinking of Indiana Jones."

"He's a fictional character."

"The point is, they're not thinking of women." Jack finally looked back up into her eyes. "How many notable female archeologists can you name?"

"Gertrude Bell, Harriet Boyd Hawes, Dorothy Bate—"

"So you know a few."

"Dorothy Garrod, Virginia Randolph Grace, Alice Kober, Mary Leakey." Madison paused. "I can keep going if you want."

Liam snickered from the far end of the table. "Bitch."

"So, put your name into that list. Now what?"
Jack leaned forward. "You said you have a boyfriend. Is
he going to let you run around unsupervised in the
Mediterranean digging up entire cities and making all
kinds of notable discoveries, maybe opening a wing
dedicated to you in a history museum in London?"

"I think you make it sound like he would be
emasculated by me pursing my career." Madison
pointedly looked at Ed. "Is this the 1950s or something?
I feel like you boys think a woman's place is in the
kitchen."

Jack shrugged. "Or the bedroom."

Madison rolled her eyes. "Seriously? You're
really going to go there? It's the twenty-first century,
Jack. I don't have to pretend to be a boy to be an
archeologist. I can get a degree and I can own property
and, hell, I can even vote."

"You can do more than that." Jack raised his
eyebrow. "I've given you the chance once."

"And I told you I wasn't interested. I'm still not."

"Your boyfriend doesn't have to know."

"That's enough." Mike set his water glass down
hard on the table, the liquid sloshing over the rim and
sinking into the white tablecloth. "Seriously, man, back
off."

Jack's eyes widened and then he checked himself,
leaning back in his chair. He motioned between them.
"Oh, I get it. You two are a thing. My bad, my bad, hey
no offense meant, buddy. I blew my chance with her last
year."

"How about you change the subject?"

"We could talk about your Bronze Star." Ed
suggested, running his finger down the face of the tablet.
"I'm looking at some press releases from the Department

of Defense about what happened and, honestly, that looks like a story *National Geographic* would like."

"Off limits."

"It's not a secret, the story's right here—"

"I said, it's off limits." Mike glanced at Madison. "Look, you invited her here for an interview on the remains. Interview her on the remains, or the Spangler Farm, or the articles she's published, but stop with the questions on drinking and sex and, most off all, about my past. I won't answer them."

Jack rolled his eyes to Liam. "What about you?"

"I'm just here for dinner." Liam dug another roll out from the basket. "But, I'll talk about my sex life if you want. It's like the Holy Grail: no one has seen it in centuries."

Madison turned her head slightly and caught Mike's eyes with hers. She smiled.

He smiled back and looked, somewhat, relieved.

Before either reporter could start a new question, the waiter and an assistant returned with the entrees. She'd never been so happy to have a plate of food set in front of her and, for several moments, the table fell into complete silence as everyone tended to their meals. It was the best cut of meat she'd ever had, tender and juicy, with a delicious crust on the outside. The square serving of potatoes could only be described as potato lasagna: a layer of creamy potato followed by a layer of delicate cheese and then repeating. It was almost worth sitting through a horrific interview with two disgusting pigs.

"Back to the Spangler Farm, how much longer do you think the survey will last?" Jack plunged his fork into a piece of sea bass. "Is it based on park service schedules or on the progress of the dig? The question is open to anyone."

Mike wiped a napkin across his mouth. "I'd say it's a combination of both. The tourist season is right around the corner and they want the farm scrubbed down and open for tours. Supposedly, I mean, I don't know if our finding remains changes that."

"After the dig is finished, where does everyone go next?" Ed nodded down the table. "What about you, Enigma?"

"I'm going to sleep in a bed with a decent mattress until the next job rolls around." Liam smirked. "Maybe I'll find a nice man to keep me company."

"What about you?" Jack stared at Mike. "Just going to bum around until the next dig falls in your lap?"

"No, there are artifacts to clean and catalogue and reports to write. By the time all that's done, Brad will have the next site set up. That's how it's worked for the past few years."

"Are you happy letting Brad run the show?" Ed asked. "I mean, really, from what I can tell, the two of you have more field experience and dig time than he does."

Mike shrugged. "He's good at what he does."

"Is he, or are you just saying that?"

"Take it as you will."

"How about you, Madison?" Jack leaned forward and picked the salt shaker off the table. "If this dig is done by the first of June, you'll still have, what, two months before school starts?"

"I'm sure I'll find ways to keep busy." Madison didn't want to acknowledge the fact the dig had to end. If she did, she'd have to start figuring out how she could stay with Mike as long as possible and still manage to start her final year of college at the end of August. "I like cataloging artifacts. There's a certain catharsis to putting everything in its place."

"I assume you'll be turning something in for your graduate school portfolio? Do you think this field experience will be enough to get you in?" Jack punctuated his sentence with a thrust of his fork.

"I hope it's enough. I mean, it still has to go up in front of a board and they review a lot more than just the dig. It's based on my grades and my entrance essay and…you know, everything."

"Somehow, I don't think they'll be judging you on more than this dig."

"I'm not going to try and get excited at that prospect."

"Well, I'll tell you right now." Jack took another bite of sea bass. "I've talked to a lot of diggers and so-called authorities in the field over the last few years. You impress me, Madison, you really do. I think you've got what it takes to bring archeology to a whole new level. You're young, you're fresh, you're—no offense meant, Mike—gorgeous. And, moreover, you stood up to this prick's interrogation. That's impressive."

"Well, thanks."

"You stay smart and stay sharp and you'll be at the top of the field in no time." He scribbled a few more notes on his pad and then pushed it aside. "I think I've got all I need for a decent cover story. We can send a photographer out to the dig site tomorrow around lunchtime if that works for you."

"Is a photograph completely necessary?"

"Actually, yes. We're running a magazine here."

She groaned. "They'd better make it fast, because we only break for an hour for lunch. I'd like to spend part of that time actually eating lunch."

"I'll let them know nothing dramatic." He rubbed his hands together. "I have just enough room for dessert and more drinks. Anyone else?"

Madison wasn't going to say no to dessert. The conversation was pleasant enough from that point on, but despite the fact she tried to distract herself with warm Whiskey Caramel Toffee Cake, she could tell Jack was still staring at her. Even with Mike beside her, the douche was still ogling her. His foot brushed against hers several times; maybe an accident once but not three times. She was ready to sit on her feet to keep him from reaching under the table to touch her. Creeper—even more so than Brad, and she thought he was the Creeper King.

Once dessert was finished and drinks were refilled and quickly consumed, the group broke up. Mike looked irritated, Liam was drunk, and Madison was plain tired of Ed's cockiness and Jack's wandering eyes. She couldn't get out of there fast enough.

Jack walked with them as far as the edge of the rear parking lot. "I'm going to push this into production as fast as I can. I'll call you and let you know when it's ready so I can get a copy out in the mail to you."

"Thanks, man, that sounds great." It didn't and she couldn't care less if she saw a copy. She just wanted him out of her face.

"You're tough, kid." Ed reached out and shook her hand. "I'm going to see about doing an online feature on top of the story for our print edition. Keep up the good work. I'm going to be keeping tabs on where your career takes you."

"I appreciate it."

Jack extended his hand to Mike. "No hard feelings man."

"Yeah." Mike slowly reached out and accepted the handshake. "Got it."

"It's always a pleasure to see you, Madison." Jack turned to her and took her hand, holding it far longer than she could stand. "I'll be in touch."

She tried to restrain an outward shudder. "Thanks, Jack. Take care of yourself."

Looping her arm around Mike's, she snuggled against him and pulled him toward the Jeep. "Get me out of here."

"That was excruciating." He kept his voice low, holding her tight against him. "If he came onto you one more time, I was going to slam him against the wall."

"You're sexy when you get angry."

He smirked.

Liam flopped dramatically against the Jeep, rubbing his palms against his face. "My God, that was the best food I've ever eaten. If I die now, I'll die happy. Seriously."

"Get in the Jeep, Liam." Mike nudged him toward the back of the vehicle. "I want to go back to the hotel."

"I know *why* you want to go back."

"Fine, then we're all on the same page and understand the urgency of the situation."

"I can almost forgive your friend Jack for being a dirty bastard." Liam half fell, half rolled into the back of the Jeep. "He was beautiful. Hairy, but beautiful."

"You'd probably get lice if you humped on that mess."

Mike turned the key in the ignition and stared at the steering wheel. He rested his hand on the gear shift but made no movement to the clutch with his foot.

"You're not still mad, are you?" Madison touched his arm. "He's harmless. I think. Don't let him get to you, though, because then he wins."

"It's not that." Mike sighed. "I think...I'm just blowing something way out of proportion."

"Tell me."

"It's just been bothering me all night." He shifted the Jeep into reverse and pulled out of the parking place, working his legs against the clutch and the gas in perfect synchronization. "I went to park headquarters tonight to drop off those files for Brad. But...Frye just wanted to review them. There wasn't any meeting with joint staff of the Smithsonian or the Department of the Interior. It was just him."

"Maybe he was meeting with them later."

"No, I asked him because I thought it was strange that the Department of the Interior would want menial, daily reports from the dig. It didn't make sense. Frye said that Brad must have misunderstood."

"He seemed pretty sure of himself to me."

"I know." Mike shifted gears and then turned and looked at her. He was frowning. "That's the part that bothers me most."

Chapter Seventeen

…Can't get there in time…

Madison opened her eyes, her heart pounding in her chest with such force she could feel the percussion up her throat and into her cheeks. His voice was loud, so close; it was like he was talking to her from inside her head. There was something he was trying to tell her and, even in the state of deep sleep, her subconscious couldn't hear him.

She rolled to her side, being careful not to wake Mike, and squinted at the alarm clock next to the bed. 3:00 am. Still three hours until she needed to get up. That wasn't too bad.

Settling back down against the pillow, she closed her eyes and forced herself to take slow, deep breaths. In. Out. In. Out. He was watching her. She could feel his gaze locked on her face as if he was crouched down next to the bed. His face seemed only inches away from hers, a stance so close and intimate she could almost convince herself she felt the soft exhalation from his lungs, the gentle kiss of his eyelashes as they brushed her cheek.

She opened her eyes.

Nothing.

She let her eyes fall shut again, this time concentrating on the darkness around her. "I know you're here."

You found her.

"I thought I was going to find you."

Her redemption was her innocence.

"I don't know how I can help you, Ben. What's left to find? We pulled her out of that pit; we know it was a woman. Tell me who she was. Why is it so important that I know?"

...save you...save me...

"Save me?" She frowned. "There's nothing to save me from, Ben. I'm fine."

Anger....he knows...anger, anger, anger.

"Knows what? Ben, I don't understand what you want me to do."

Be...be...

Be what? Be mindful? Be thankful? He sounded so desperate, so bitterly impassioned. His effort was overwhelming; she could feel the vibrations in the air around her. It felt like it was popping and pulsating. He was with her, so close she felt like she could reach out and hold him.

...Be...afraid.

The light on the nightstand beside her switched on.

She jumped into an upright position and scrambled backwards, slamming her hip into Mike's shoulder as she moved. She wanted to disappear into the headboard, to hide from the voice—the touch—that haunted her.

Mike was awake and looked far more alert than she felt. "What's wrong? What are you doing?"

Tears spilled over Madison's cheeks. He looked so concerned, so in control despite being woken out of a dead sleep by a kick to the shoulder. "He was here, he was right beside the bed talking to me and trying to tell me something. The only thing I could understand was 'be afraid' and the next thing I know the light turns on—"

"Hey, hey slow down." He cupped her face in his hands and brushed her tears away with his thumbs. "He told you to be afraid."

She nodded. It made her want to throw up.

"Of what?"

"I don't know."

"Do you think of him?"

Madison fell silent, searching her mind and trying to reach out to Ben with her being. "No. I think he's trying to warn me."

Mike wrapped his arms around her and pulled her against him. "Then, you're okay. It's something else."

"That's what bothers me. I feel like he knows something bad is going to happen to me, but he can't muster up the energy to explain what it is." She rubbed her eyes. "I don't know what to do anymore."

He leaned over and kissed the top of her head. "Then…then I guess we do your séance."

"Really?"

"Baby, I don't want you to feel like he's stalking or taunting you. If you think a séance will help—and it does—then it's worth it, in my opinion. We'll drag Liam with us."

She relaxed in his arms, but couldn't bring herself to close her eyes. "Thank you for not thinking I'm a loon."

"I'm just worried about you." He stroked her hair back with his fingertips. "This can't happen again. Look at you. He has to know he's hurting you."

"I think whatever it is that he wants trumps that." She shivered. "But, yeah, this pretty much sucks."

"Just get some more sleep. Sleep will help."

She shivered again. The thought of lying there, asleep and vulnerable, wasn't appealing in the least. He could do anything he wanted while she slept. She couldn't stop him. "That's not even remotely appealing, actually."

"I'll stay awake." He leaned over and grabbed the television remote. "You know, just keep an eye on things."

"You don't have to stay awake for the next three hours."

"Sure I do." He yanked the sheet and comforter up, tucking it around her. "I like late night television and, moreover, I like looking at you."

"There's a certain creepiness factor to that, buddy." She looked at him and smiled, then turned serious. "But…thank you."

"You don't have to thank me. You just need to sleep." He pushed her head against his chest and hunkered down against the pillows. "I won't let anything happen to you, Madison. I swear."

Madison was fairly sure sleep wouldn't come easily. She tried to focus her attention to Mike, to the soft, gray Army PT shirt he was wearing and the faint smell of his cologne that seemed to emanate from his skin. He was so sweet, so caring; he never judged her despite the fact he, most likely, didn't believe half of what she was saying….

….She opened her eyes and stretched out her legs, arching her back as she tried to relax her knotted up muscles. "How long did I sleep?"

"Almost three hours." Mike leaned over and kissed her forehead. "I kept an eye on you and, I can confidently report, you didn't move once."

She crawled into a sitting position and stifled a yawn. "Please tell me you got a little sleep."

"I may have dozed once or twice."

"You should have just gone to sleep once I fell asleep." She pulled the elastic band out of her hair and shook it loose over her shoulders. "I'm going to feel bad when you fall asleep face down in a test pit."

"Nah, I'm good. My mom said even when I was a baby, I just never needed sleep. It's those kind of qualifications that helped me excel in the Army. Fire watch, guard duty, sentry, whatever. I'd stay up all night and still get up for PT."

"As a child and teenager, I routinely slept in until lunchtime."

"It's called beauty sleep and you're gorgeous." He leaned over and kissed her. "Do you know what you're doing tonight at the séance?"

"You're still willing to do that?"

"I wouldn't have offered if I didn't mean it."

"Uh, no, I actually have no idea what I'm going to do." She slid off the bed and crossed to the dresser, rifling through her clothes for a t-shirt. "I read about glass divination on the internet. It sounds easy enough."

"Hear me out on this." He joined her at the dresser. "When you're contacting a spirit, how do you know you're limiting to him? I mean, couldn't any spirit in the vicinity drop by? Or a demon? Or…whatever's lurking around out on the field."

"I have no idea." She stripped her sleep shirt off and pulled on her bra. "I'm just under the assumption Ben will be there. He's always with me. No matter where I'm at or what I'm doing, he's there. Watching. He's always trying to talk to me and, honestly, I'm hoping that with three of us trying to help him, I can at least figure out what he wants. Maybe then he'll leave me alone."

"I just don't want you to be disappointed, especially if Liam and I turn out to be useless."

Madison stared at her reflection in the mirror. "And I don't want to be disappointed in myself anymore."

* * * *

They arrived at the Spangler Farm parking lot just in time to catch what appeared to be the tail end of an argument between Brad and Cianna. Her back was pressed against the closed tail gate of the pickup; Brad was leaning over her, forcefully pointing in the direction of the bank barn. She wasn't looking at him.

"This sets a great precedence for the day." Mike pulled the Jeep into a parking place. "He's going to be in a fantastic mood."

Madison unbuckled her seatbelt but hesitated before opening the door. "You know, let's go back to the room. Jack's photographer is going to be here this morning and, frankly, I'm not interested. I don't want caught up in whatever that mess is over there and...and, no. Let's just bail."

"He's already seen us."

"Tell him I had the sudden urge to vomit. It's not that far from the truth."

Mike chuckled. "Just because you're my archeology princess doesn't mean you get to sit back Cianna-style and coast through the rest of the dig. We still have a competition going on. Yes, quality of finds, you're winning. But quantity? Ha, lady, there's no way you're going to catch me by the end of the dig."

"You have a good point. I mean, really, you've found enough rocks and nail bits that you could construct a monument to me." She forced her legs to move, plodding along beside Mike toward the dig site. "Site of the world famous discovery by the world famous Madison Monroe."

"Archeology princess comma Army veteran seductress." He shrugged. "It's true. You totally took advantage of me."

"False. You took advantage of me." She playfully shoved him. "I'm just a sweet, young college girl. You're an old man who can't keep his hands to himself."

"I think it was you who dragged me back to your room."

"Maybe."

He smiled, grabbing her wrist and pulling her against him, and acted as if he was going to lead her right past Brad and Cianna. If that was his plan, it was quickly thwarted by Brad. "Hey, Mike, I need you to run me down to park headquarters. I have some reports to file."

"And you need me to go with you because…"

"Frye wants a couple trays of our artifacts dropped off in their facilities, since it's more secure than just leaving them in the summer kitchen. I guess that osteo-archeologist wants to take a look at what else we pulled out of the pit."

"She's going to be disappointed. We only pulled a button and the gum blanket out of that pit."

"Dr. Spada's been examining the blanket." Brad pulled two trays out of the back of the pickup and headed to Mike's vehicle. "Dr. Williams is too busy basking in the glow of her report on our remains. She took our work and made it her lifetime achievement."

"It's been like, a week." Mike squeezed Madison's hand and smiled at her. "I'll see you later."

"She's already been picked to give the keynote at the Smithsonian's gala next month." Brad cocked his head toward them. "Hi, Madison."

"Hey there."

"You and Liam can work on the barn pit today. Expand it a little more toward the actual structure."

"Got it." She watched them load into the Jeep, Brad grumbling the entire time about Dr. Williams, and then lumber back down the farm road. His sudden, adamant hate of Jan Williams was a little surprising. She was an authority called in to assist. It wasn't like she'd been picked over Brad to work on the remains.

Cianna cleared her throat.

Madison looked back at her. "Did you need something?"

Cianna looked down at the dirt parking area for several moments and then, finally, lifted her eyes to look at Madison. "Mike's a good guy."

"Yes, he is."

"I hate you." Cianna crossed her arms over her chest, rapidly running her hands up and down her flesh as if to warm herself. It made her look helpless, like she was holding onto herself for protection. "Just so you're aware."

"Good to know." Madison walked away. Further response would have simply been a waste of her time.

* * * *

Three hours later, Brad and Mike still hadn't returned to the site. Cianna simply left for the day.

"You know, I'm getting paid a stipend of seven dollars a day." Madison used the bristles of a toothbrush to clean dirt off a small chunk of white porcelain. "She's getting paid how much to not work?"

"It's more than seven dollars a day." Liam dropped his shovel in the dirt and crossed to his backpack. "I think Brad tried to dump her today. They were screaming at each other in very impressive whispers before you and Mikey got here."

"I got the impression we were walking into the middle of something delicate."

"Bitch, please, he called her out for being the whore she is." He squirted a small dollop of sunscreen into the palm of his hand and then rubbed it into the top of his head. "Don't judge me."

"I'll be honest—"

"I'm bald, I get it."

"No, not that." She suppressed a giggle. "I was just going to say, this is not what I expected the life of an archeologist to be. I pictured...I don't know. Less drama. More digging."

"More like Howard Carter finding Tut's Tomb in 1922."

"Something like that." Madison's cell phone buzzed in her pocket. Maybe it was Mike texting her, maybe with some kind of scandalous report of what was going on at park headquarters. Maybe something more like Tut's Tomb in 1922.

It was a text, but she didn't recognize the number.

Hey, Madison, it's Ranger Carson. Mike's Army buddy? I'm up here at the entrance to the Spangler Farm with some questionable looking guy named Jack Kornick. He's got a photographer with him and says you're expecting him.

Madison groaned. Great, just when the day couldn't get any worse. "Liam, just hit me in the face with the shovel now."

"I don't think Mike would appreciate that."

"Not only is that stupid photographer from *Archeology* Magazine here, but somehow Jack Kornick invited himself along for round two." She fired off a response to Ranger Carson. *Yeah, regrettably I knew they were coming. Don't let them near the site. I'll be down.*

"I wouldn't meet up with him alone, if I were you." Liam paused. "But, if I were me, I'd meet up with him. Alone. Teams. Whatever."

"If you were you?" She cast a sideways glance at him. "There's an LE Ranger down there. I'll live."

"Drew Carson?"

"Maybe."

"Bitch."

"Hey, I've got Mike." She eased the piece of porcelain into a plastic container and then headed toward the parking lot. "Feel free to do as you wish with the other dudes up there. Especially Jack, take him as far away from me as possible."

"If only."

Madison wiped her hands on her jeans as she walked down the dirt driveway leading to the main road. What a waste of time. She had work to do. Test pits to dig, experience to leech off Liam and Mike and to a lesser extent, Brad. Somehow, instead of being a boost to her career, finding the woman's remains was turning out to be a huge stumbling block in the way of getting anything done. She wanted to punch someone in the face.

Namely Jack.

He was leaning casually against a sporty black car, his hands flailing about as he talked about whatever nonsense he was discussing with Ranger Carson. She didn't care. One picture, one quick handshake or whatever pleasantries needed to be exchanged and she was done. Check, please.

Jack's eyes lit up and he noticeably straightened from his casual position. "There you are. You're a hard person to track down."

"I'm usually here or at my hotel."

Ranger Carson rested his hands on his belt. "How are you, Madison? Sorry for the text. I tried to get a hold of Mike first and he gave me your number."

"That's okay." She smiled at him. He was a nice guy, she had to admit.

"We won't keep you long, Madison. We just needed a few pictures for the article." Jack extended his hand to her. "It's nice to see you again."

"Thanks."

The photographer was female—disputing Madison's assumption that only men were getting jobs in the area—and she nodded in the direction of a split rail fence bordering the property. "Maybe you can stand there to start."

Madison trudged to the fence and awkwardly shoved her hands in her back pockets, looking back toward the site. There was so much work to do. "I can't take too long of a break. We're...shorthanded today."

"It won't take long." The photographer lowered her camera. "That one's actually really pretty."

"See, Madison, you make this easy." The oily quality of Jack's voice was almost more offensive than if he'd simply walked up and stuck his hand down her shirt. "Beautiful girl, beautiful scenery."

"So, uh, Drew..." Madison brushed her hair out of her face. "Did Mike mention when he's coming back?"

"He said they were just finishing up."

"Good. It's hard to excavate three test pits with only two diggers."

"Can we get some shots of the test pits?" Jack patted the pockets of his blazer and then pulled out a pad of paper. "That would be so great for the article."

"You'd have to ask Brad about that. I don't really have that kind of authority."

"Come on, Madison, just a few pictures. We're not going to touch anything."

There was a certain creepiness factor to the way he said it, almost like he wasn't talking about the site at all. God, she hated him, almost as much as she hated Anthony.

"Mr. Emerson will be back any minute." Ranger Carson shifted his stance. "I'm sure if you really want the pictures, you won't mind waiting."

"That's cool, I don't mind." Jack narrowed his eyes. He did mind. It was obvious.

"Maybe you could try leaning against the fence?" The photographer frowned. "Or, maybe, better yet, sit on the ground there and lean back against that central post."

Madison groaned. It was borderline degrading.

The camera whirled and whizzed as she snapped the photographs. Madison stared off toward the road, not even attempting to smile. Somehow one picture from the cover was turning into one roll of film.

Finally, like the sound of the bell at the end of a day of high school, she heard the familiar rumble of Mike's Jeep. He slowed as he pulled into the drive, bringing the vehicle to a stop next to Drew Carson's white and green park service SUV. "Well, hey there team."

Madison scrambled to her feet. "Good, my ride's here. Do you have enough shots for the cover?"

The photographer nodded. "I can make something work."

"Drew, it's always nice to see you." Madison glanced at Jack. "And then there's you, Jack. Just let me know when the issue is out so I can send a copy to my mother."

"I'll bring over a few personally." He caught her hand in his and squeezed it. "I'll call you."

"Great." She pulled away and hustled to the Jeep. Time to make a getaway so Jack could stop molesting her with his eyes; too bad Drew couldn't arrest him on that alone.

Mike leaned out the open window and raised his eyebrow. "Looks like you're having a blast."

"I'm going to cross supermodel off my list of things to fall back on if this whole archeology thing doesn't work out." She glanced at Brad, firmly planted in the passenger's seat. It didn't appear he was going to offer her a front spot next to Mike. "Hi, Brad."

He glared at her, his jaw set in a firm line. "What's all this?"

"Jack's from *Archeology* Magazine, remember? He demanded pictures to go with the story."

"This kind of thing shouldn't be going on during work hours, Madison." He swallowed hard. "I'm sorry, but I'm going to have to reflect this in your evaluation at the end of the dig."

"If you're upset about the time I missed, I just won't break for lunch today."

"That's not the point. We're not paying you to have your picture taken, Madison, we're paying you to excavate a site. So, you're not only wasting our time, but you're wasting our money."

"Jesus, man, lay off." Mike's voice oozed authority, probably the same tone he'd taken when he was giving orders in the Army. "Cianna has spent most of her time not working and you don't say shit to her."

"Well, Cianna's off the dig. And unless Madison wants off the dig, too, she needs to get back to work."

"Wait, what?" Mike stared at him, his mouth gaping slightly. "Why is Cianna off the dig?"

"That's none of your business."

"You fired her?"

"She resigned." Brad turned his stare to Drew. "This area is private property, Ranger Carson. Can you show these people the way out?"

Drew glanced from Brad to Mike. Mike tipped his head down in a quick nod.

"Okay, folks, thanks for stopping by." Drew motioned to Jack's sports car. "Time to go."

Jack started to speak. "But, can't we—"

"Jack, now's not a good time." Madison tried to plead with him with her eyes. *Just shut up, idiot.* "Please."

He looked at her and took a few steps backwards. "I'll call you, Madison."

"Whatever." She looked back to the Jeep and to Brad. He was staring straight ahead toward the Spangler Farm, his face seething with anger. It was as if she and Mike had completely faded from his sight and he was only focused on one thing, his obvious hatred.

She knew without asking: that obvious hatred was directed at her.

Chapter Eighteen

At one o'clock on the dot, Mike pulled the Jeep down an unlit farm lane leading to a small, stone house. Madison had tried to pay attention to the winding battlefield roads they'd followed, but in the dark, the moon hidden by thick cloud cover, and without any street signs, she was lost almost instantly. "I have no idea how you can find your way around this park in the dark."

"I'm good with maps or, rather, the lack thereof." He shrugged. "When I was overseas, we had operators who drove the up-armor vehicles for us, but I could remember our routes even after only one circuit. It's a good skill to have when you're in a firefight and trying to get the hell out of there."

"I once got lost on my own college campus."

"That happens to freshmen sometimes."

"True, but I was a junior." She rubbed her hands up and down her arms. The night air was crisp and the cold seemed to soak through the sleeves of her hoodie. Maybe it was nerves, the unbridled excitement of possibly contacting Ben—and how illegal the whole thing was. The park closed at dusk.

The farmhouse was small and squat, two windows on the upper floor and two windows on the lower floor, evenly spaced around a red painted door. Electric candles glowed in the windows but, otherwise, the house looked deserted. "This is park housing?"

"This is it." Mike slowed the Jeep to a stop. "If that little jerk is in there sleeping, I'm going to drag him out by his face."

"Tell me again why we've been staying in a hotel room verses a stone farmhouse in the middle of the battlefield?"

"Well, namely, because the hot water in here lasts about ten minutes before it runs out and our showers....typically last longer than that." He pulled out his phone and fired off a quick text. "And, second, because it's supposedly haunted. I never saw anything, but you…"

"Good call."

"That's why they pay me the big bucks." He looked down at his phone as the screen lit up with a text response. "Drew says he's down at the farm. As long as we stick to the main roads, we should be fine. We're lucky it's on the outskirts of the park, otherwise, they have all the gates locked down this time of night."

"It was nice of him to come out again tonight, after being at the site all day." Madison twisted a silver ring around her index finger. "He didn't have to do that."

"Drew's a good guy. He…uh…he knew Cam too."

"So, what exactly have you been telling people about me?" She turned in her seat to look at him. "He always looks at me like he knows this big time secret, like that time I slid down a pile of gravel and ripped open the back of my pants, resulting in having to walk to my mother's car backwards so my friends didn't see my underwear."

"Weird things happen to you, Maddy baby." He slid his fingers down her thigh. "I just told him I met this girl and…and I'm kind of crazy for her."

"You're sweet."

"I also told him you can do a really hot back bend in bed."

Madison's jaw dropped. "You *told* him that?"

"It might have come out in a conversation." Mike paused. "Or two."

"Oh my god."

"He thinks you're gorgeous. I told him to back off, because you were spoken for." Mike tapped his finger against the steering wheel and then cocked his head to the house. "There he is."

Liam held his hands in front of his face as he exited the house, blocking the headlight beam from his eyes. He crawled in the back of the Jeep. "Christ, do you think you could turn the high beams off?"

"Oops, sorry, Liam." Mike got back into the driver's seat and shifted the Jeep into reverse. "Did you bring the glass?"

"Yes." Liam held out a clear drinking glass. "Maybe after we're done talking to the dead, we can fill this baby up with some whiskey. You know, to celebrate not getting arrested."

"Oh, there's still a chance we're going to get arrested." Mike turned back onto the main road. "I have discussion points prepared in case the cops or more LE rangers show up, but I'm not sure how believable, 'I forgot my cell phone and just happened to have a glass with me' is really going to be."

"See how much we love you, Madison?" Liam patted her shoulder. "We're willing to put our professional reputations and personal freedom on the line so you can talk to a ghost."

"I wouldn't want to share a jail cell with anyone else."

"Well," Liam sniffed, "let's just hope it doesn't come down to that. I want to meet men, but not convicts. White collar crime, maybe, but I don't think you can categorize this as white collar."

"You've got to get your priorities straight, man." Mike slowed to a stop in front of a stop sign, then turned onto a larger road. The road they'd been following led into the heart of the battlefield; it was blocked by a padlocked gate. "What happened to the guy you met from San Francisco? Kevin? Keith? Something like that."

"Nothing like that, his name was Al." Liam grunted. "See how much he pays attention to me, Madison? No, I couldn't deal with him anymore. He had mother issues. And, when I say mother issues, what I mean is that he lived with his mother and he'd text her through our dates just to 'check in'. There were enough red flags with that boy to lead a parade."

"Did you meet him online, too?" Madison stifled a giggle. "Because you need to meet men the right way. You know, the grocery store. The book store. Archeological digs."

"Believe me, I've tried. Mikey, remember that guy in Guam a couple years ago?"

"Yeah, what was his name? Jose?"

"Jose, ah, now that was a man." Liam sighed deeply. "He made these pork tacos you'd sell your soul for."

"What happened?"

"He was a summer fling, like a camp boyfriend or something nonsensical. I left my heart in Guam. And my figure too, because girl, I gained twelve pounds while we were there."

Mike turned the Jeep onto the dirt lane leading to the Spangler Farm. He switched the headlights off. "If anyone is having second thoughts, they need to speak up now. Once we're in, we're in."

Neither Liam nor Madison spoke.

"Good." He drove at a slower than normal pace, making the pot holed road seem that much more bumpy. Even in the dark, Madison could see the outline of a white and green park service SUV. The headlights flicked on and off.

Mike did the same with his lights and kept driving.

Liam was the first to speak. "I am scared shitless."

"Not half as much as I am." Madison reached for Mike's hand. She could see movement in the dark, faint echoes of souls long departed still moving about the farm grounds. The barn seemed like it was buzzing with activity, faint moans and groans easily audible, even from her position in front of the vehicle. "They know we're here."

Liam cleared his throat. "Who?"

"All of them." She tightened her grip on Mike's hand. "It's like this place is alive with the dead. So many lives ended here, so many souls left wandering."

"Can you see them?" Mike drove past the parking area, stopping the Jeep as close to the summer kitchen as he could without actually pulling onto the grass. "Or just hear them?"

"Both." She felt the panic building in her chest, fear shooting down her arms like rain down a window. "I'm not sure I can do this."

"I'm right here." He turned the Jeep off, leaving the key in the ignition, and then took her other hand in his. "But if you really don't want to go any farther, we won't. It's your call."

She swallowed hard. "I'm okay."

He squeezed her hands. "If at any point you want to stop, just say so and I'll get you out of here."

"Okay."

She slid out of the Jeep and eased the door closed, being careful not to slam it or make any more noise than needed. Eyes were watching her; she could feel them in the darkness. There was movement on the farm, the residual imprints that replayed like a broken record, but there were other intelligent spirits in the dark. They knew she could feel their presence and it seemed like they were waiting. Watching.

Fumbling her way around the Jeep, she grabbed onto Mike's arm and shuffled through the grass next to him, sticking as close as she could without actually having him carry her. She could hear Liam tramping in the grass on the other side of him. The summer kitchen loomed in front, a squat shaped building barely visible against the trees at the rear of the property.

From behind them, in the general direction of the bank barn, a loud slam echoed through the night air. Madison jumped, stumbling backwards into Mike. "You heard that, right?"

"Jesus Christ." Liam hissed. "Did that come from the barn?"

"It could have been, or maybe from the main road." Mike didn't sound convincing. "It was probably the main road. Just keep walking."

Stone pavers in the ground seemed like a path, leading around the outside well and to the door of the summer kitchen. Mike pulled a key out of his pocket and jammed it into the padlock, flicking his wrist and deftly unlocking it. He opened the door, hesitating before finally stepping inside. "You guys are freaking me out."

The floor of the summer kitchen was modern hardwood, the interior walls white painted plaster. The far corner of the room had once been a fireplace and part of the plaster had fallen from the interior, revealing decayed red bricks. The dig equipment was stored inside the kitchen: two sifters and a myriad of shovels and trays were stacked against the wall nearest the door.

It was colder inside the kitchen than it should have been.

"Supposedly Confederate General Armistead died in here." Liam slunk inside, pulling her in after him. "I once read that a park maintenance worker walked in here and saw him, leaning against the wall and looking out the window toward the bank barn."

"Stop it, Liam." Mike swung the door shut. "Okay, Maddy, this is your show. What do we do?"

"Did you bring the glass, Liam?"

"What do you take me for?" He handed her the drinking glass.

"Okay, so, granted all I know about glass divination I learned from the internet. The theory behind it is that our combined spiritual energy will magnify his and…and assuming that's correct, he'll be able to speak louder or be more physical. In most cases, spirits can't audibly speak, but they can manipulate lights or knock to respond to yes or no questions. I brought my cell phone because, I figured, maybe he could press the button and turn the light on to answer us."

Liam sat crossed legged on the floor. "You've talked to him before, so why can't we just assume he'll talk back?"

"I'm not getting my hopes up." Madison sank to her knees on the floor, setting the glass upside down on the hardwood. The cloud cover had parted significantly, the moonlight illuminated the floor just enough so they could see what they were doing. "We just need to put our fingertips on the glass, like this." She rested the tips of her fingers on the flat, smooth glass bottom.

Mike sat next to her and leaned forward, doing the same.

Liam scooted into the circle. "Like a Ouija Board."

"Yeah, but instead of spelling stuff out, the theory is the spirit can move the glass." She shrugged. "God, I feel like an idiot."

"Just do it." Mike prompted. "You're not an idiot. We're with you on this, right Liam?"

"Right. Totally onboard."

Madison took a deep breath. "Close your eyes and try to empty your mind, directing your energy to where your fingertips meet the glass. Just relax. Listen. Don't talk and just…we'll see what happens."

She closed her own eyes and forced herself to relax, physically quieting the muscles in her body as she focused her mind on the glass. "We're here, Ben. We want to talk to you."

Nothing.

She inhaled cold air into her lungs until they burned and then slowly exhaled. "I know you're here, Ben. I can feel you. Let us know you're here…knock on the walls or move the glass."

The glass slid to the side, jerking across the dusty hardwood.

"Liam, did you do that?" Mike muttered.

"No."

Madison's heart pounded. "Who was buried in the grave in the woods?"

Silence.

"Can you knock on the wall if you can hear me?" She sighed. "I know you can hear me, Ben. I know you're there, why won't you talk to us? Use us somehow, if you have to, but I need to know Ben. I need to know who she was. You led me to her, but why?"

The silence burned her ears. The glass moved slowly from one side to the other, but more like the lazy movements of someone playing with it, not trying to communicate.

She took another deep breath, forcing her breathing to become slow and even. Getting irritated wasn't going to get him to talk to her. "Talk to me, Ben. Please, I need to know who she was...who she was to you. I'm going to open my eyes. If you can, hit the button on my cell phone to turn it on. Let me know you're there."

She opened her eyes and looked at the cell phone. Nothing.

Out of the corner of her eye, she caught movement in the dark. She looked up; he was standing in the doorway, as if he'd just stepped through the closed door and had stopped to look at them. His eyes were fixed on her frame and he drifted in like an afterthought, slowly circling behind Mike and Liam.

Madison.

"Ben?" She looked up into his eyes. He seemed so clear—so vibrant and real—and she could easily make out his features. Large blue eyes, a thin patchy beard across his chin, hollow cheeks. "I can...I can see you."

He watched her. Silent.

She was vaguely aware of Mike's voice, as if he were speaking to her, and in that flicker of inattention Ben's figure wavered. Madison stared at him, focusing on his shape, as if the harder she tried to see him, the more he could draw from her. "I want to know. Tell me what happened."

He stared at her, but took a step closer. *Can you hear me?*

"I can always hear you. Why?"

My soul is bound to yours. He sank to his knees beside her and held his hand up as if he might touch her. *And always will be.*

"Why me?" Everything around her seemed faded, washed out. The more she concentrated, the closer he seemed, but the further reality drifted away.

"Why not you?" His lips moved as he spoke and she could hear him. His voice wasn't in her head now, it was real. It was audible in her ears, his breath soft against her face. "You're the only one who heard me. You're the only one who can help."

"I found her. Who was she? You know how she got here, I know you do. Let me help her, too."

"She's always had rest, always had peace while I remained. I was the last who knew." He touched his hand to her cheek, cradling her face in his hand. "Until you."

The warmth of his touch was startling. She could barely hear the whisper of the present, of Mike's voice, but the desire to focus on it was gone. "Please tell me, Ben. Please."

"The circle will break, my time is short." He edged closer, his hand firm on her cheek. "Do you trust me?"

"Yes."

He leaned closer, as if he was going to kiss her, but instead touched his forehead to hers. His skin felt so real against hers, his body so close. He sighed and as he did, her breath caught in her throat. It was like she'd caught his sigh inside her, holding his last breath in her lungs. He was against her, inside her. Her eyelids felt heavy.

"Trust me."

She let them close.

They reopened. She was vaguely aware it wasn't the physical act of opening her eyes. Instead, it was something inside her mind switching on, strengthened by her connection with Ben.

He was standing next to her now, protectively holding onto her hand. He was dressed in light blue wool trousers and a stained white linen shirt. Despite the Union kepi on his head and leather cartridge box around his waist, he wasn't how she pictured a soldier to look.

He turned and looked at her, almost sheepishly, responding as if she'd asked him out loud. "It was hot in July."

"Where are we?" The landscape was unfamiliar, an overgrown hillside sloping down in front of them. There was a structure off to one side and in front of her, she gradually became aware of a constant flow. Movement; the marching of an Army.

"It's the last thing I remember." He watched them walk. The pace seemed so frantic, so hurried, but they moved so slowly. "We'd marched so long. So far. She always fell behind."

"Who?" Madison watched a soldier stop next to her, aim his rifle, and fire.

"I don't know her name." He nodded toward a solitary soldier, smaller than many of the men running past. "She had few friends among us."

It registered that his statement should make sense, but she couldn't remember why. The battle around her seemed clear, but faded, like an old reel movie projector sputtering to a stop. "Were you her friend?"

He was silent for a beat. "It felt like our lines were falling apart here. The hill was steep. If you ran too fast, you'd fall. Our artillery was behind us. I couldn't hear anything."

"Who was she?"

"She was brave. She kept to herself, so we wouldn't know her secret." He hesitated. "But they knew. They figured it out."

Madison watched the woman quickly reload her musket, jamming the ramrod into the barrel to tamp down the round. Her back was to them, so she couldn't see the woman's face.

"When they found out, they forced themselves on her. One held her down and covered her mouth. They took turns." His voice broke and he stopped talking, staring forward at the delicate, but tenacious soldier in front of them. "I found her afterwards."

Madison could see him in battle, not far from the woman. He was dressed in life as he was beside her in death. No jacket, no vest, just calculated firing and reloading his rifle. He was quick. Accurate.

"She was going to bring them up on charges of rape." His voice was quiet. "But then we got moved forward and the battle blew up in front of us like two colliding steam engines."

"She was killed."

He shook his head. "They found out."

"That she was going to tell?"

"I don't know how, but they did." He spoke quickly. Madison could feel urgency around her, something tugging on her. They were running out of time. "I can't remember them, their faces. It's always been her. Always. Until you."

He touched her face with his free hand and guided it forward. A soldier was making his way to the woman, his gait confident. Determined. As he drew closer, he lifted his musket and leveled at the girl's back.

He fired.

The bullet impacted low on the back of her neck—thoracic spine 2 and 3—and she pitched forward. Madison flinched, crying out as the girl fell face first into the ground.

The faceless soldier pressed on, kicking her shattered frame as he passed.

Madison looked at Ben. His large eyes seemed to brim with tears, his forehead creased in obvious despair. She turned back to the battle in front of them. The living Ben had seen what happened to the woman. He ran to her, crossing in front of men, weaving in between firing soldiers to reach her side.

But then he stopped. He stumbled.

"No." The words slipped out of her mouth before she could stop them. She realized what was happening.

He righted himself, his hand clutching his throat. With each step, blood oozed between his fingers. It coated his neck like paint, dripping down the front of his shirt. He sank to his knees beside the woman and let go of his neck, trying to pull her backwards. With each exertion, blood pulsed from his throat. Blood was everywhere. He pulled her, dragging her with his fading strength toward the rear. His blood flowed freely now. It dripped down onto her motionless body.

He stumbled and sank down onto his elbow; the blood flow seemed slower now. He rolled to his back and stared up at the sky, his arm reaching up to passing soldiers. Trying to stop them, trying to wave someone down to help him.

She heard him speak next to her. "I met death faster because I tried to save her."

A soldier stopped next to the crumpled figures on the ground. Madison saw him lean closer to Ben, no doubt in an effort to hear a voice that was rapidly fading. The soldier grasped the woman underneath her armpits and began dragging her to the rear.

Madison looked at her Ben. "But we found her body. She didn't live."

The battle seemed to melt away in front of them, replaced by an open field shrouded in darkness. The echoes of gunfire were silent.

"No, she didn't." Ben's voice was barely above a whisper. "But they did. I watched them follow the hospital wagon to the farm. I left my body on the hill and followed them here. And here I stayed."

Madison watched a faceless soldier emerge from the shadows. He dragged a body to a pit, unceremoniously kicking it over the edge. Another soldier dropped the gum blanket over the body, pushing the canvas around her thin shoulders and legs. Together, the men began filling in the hole.

Ben's voice sounded far away. "I was alone until I found you."

The landscape around them changed. Trees grew while others faded away. She saw herself walk past the buried woman, glancing over her shoulder as she spoke to the man behind her.

Mike.

"Madison."

She looked up at Ben again, but it was hard to see him. "Ben? Don't leave me."

His hand was on her cheek again. "There's one more thing. You must—"

She could still feel his touch, but his face was fading. "Must what? Ben? Ben!"

"Madison." Ben's voice melted away, replaced by a voice that seemed familiar. She couldn't place it. "Madison."

Blue eyes faded to brown. His touch was so warm, still so real.

"Madison, look at me."

She squeezed her eyes shut and then opened them, rapidly blinking to try and clear the haze. Ben's face was replaced by Mike. He was gone.

Mike cradled her face, pressing the pads of his fingertips into her temple. "That's a girl. Are you okay?"

"I'm fine." Her eyes clouded with tears and she couldn't hold them back. They spilled freely over her cheeks. She struggled upright into a sitting position and covered her face with her hands. "I'm sorry, I have no idea what happened. I...I can't stop crying."

"Hey, baby, it's okay." Mike leaned over and wrapped his arms around her, pulling her to him. "You were in some kind of trance or something. You just faded out right in front of us. I couldn't get you to wake up."

"I saw what happened." She glanced from him to Liam. "I could see him as clearly as I can see you. He was wearing light blue pants and a white shirt with suspenders. His kepi had a red crescent moon badge on the side. He had...he had a cartridge box on a leather belt around his waist. And she was there, too, they were in battle together. She was murdered."

"Murdered?" Liam sounded skeptical.

"Ben said other soldiers found out she was a woman and raped her. She was going to bring them up on charges, but they were called into battle before she could. One of them just walked up behind her and shot her." She looked down at her hands. "Ben was hit too. He died on the field."

"Which field?" Mike tipped her chin up so he could look at her. He didn't look judgmental or critical. He looked almost like...he believed her.

"I haven't the faintest idea. It was a hillside." She frowned, trying to remember the faded images in her mind. "There was a building off to one side; it looked like it was shaped like a thick H."

Mike was quiet for several moments. Finally, he said, "Cemetery Hill. You saw the entrance to Evergreen Cemetery."

"He said the men survived the fight and followed the hospital wagons back here. They buried her and thought they got away with it. But Ben knew—and now I know."

Liam and Mike were silent. Finally, Liam said, "But I'm not sure you can prove it."

"We might be able to narrow down who Ben was, if we dig into regimental records and see who was listed as killed in action here," Mike said slowly, "but do you even know what company he was in? He was in the 11th Corps, a red crescent on his kepi means he was probably first division, but…if we don't know much more than that, it's going to be hard. Extremely hard, I mean, you're looking at thousands of men. We only know his first name."

"And he didn't know her name." Madison sighed. For as much as she now knew, she still felt lost. "No one knew her real name, maybe the male alias she used, but unless a miracle happened, I'm not sure we'll ever really know who she was."

"Did he say anything about her? Where she came from?" Mike chewed on his lower lip. "Did he mention a town or an area they might have come from?"

"He just said she was brave." Tears welled up in her eyes again; she tried to blink them back. "And…there was something else."

Mike looked at her.

"Right before I came to, he said there was something else. It seemed important. He tried to tell me but I woke up too fast." Madison squeezed her eyes closed and tried to think. "The last thing I heard was 'you must'. I have no idea what that even meant."

"Was it a warning?" Mike leaned forward. "Do you think he was warning you about something here?"

The light on Madison's cell phone switched on, as if someone had pressed the button on the face.

"Is it something here at the site?" Madison looked around the room, hoping she would see him again. "Is there someone else here I need to be afraid of?"

The light switched on again.

It faded to black, then flicked on again.

And again.

Chapter Nineteen

Madison stretched her legs out in front of her, tilting her head back so the sun shone fully on her face. Mike was lying on his back with his head on her lap, eating an apple. The site was quiet. Brad was off doing whatever it was that Brad did during the day, and Cianna was still off the dig. Despite what had happened—and despite whatever Ben had been warning her about—she felt more relaxed than she had in well over a week.

"I took it upon myself to research what happened to you." Liam picked green peppers off his hoagie and disposed of them in a plastic baggie. "Since you two were too busy, you know, fucking or whatever it is you do in the hotel room."

Mike took another bite of apple. "We took a shower and went to bed. She was tired."

Madison thought for a moment. "Well, technically…"

"Anyway, Liam."

"Anyway, so, I did some pretty in-depth research online this morning, probably a good ten minutes or so, and I think you had an out of body experience. The cool kids call it an OBE. I mean, in lieu of actual clinical exam findings or CT scans. I think that would be more definitive, but based on what I saw, it was definitely an OBE."

"I didn't die, Liam." Madison ran her fingertips over Mike's spikey hair. "I thought you had to be dead to have an out of body experience."

"No, apparently you can have a psychic out of body experience anytime. Most people have them in the deeper stages of unconsciousness, like REM sleep, but there's a select few who can have them willy nilly."

Liam set his sandwich aside. "I knew a girl in college who could orgasm just by squeezing her legs together. I'm assuming it's the same as this."

"Probably not." Mike took another bite of his apple.

"I can see an out of body experience, maybe, if I was wandering around Cemetery Hill as it is today, but I wasn't." Madison shook her head. "I saw the last things Ben saw in life. If it was an out of body experience, it was one taking place in the past."

"I'm not sure there're specific hard and fast rules when it comes to psychic experiences." Liam picked up his sandwich again and took a bite. "The website said OBEs are more vivid than dreams. You experience sights, sounds, and smells. You move freely, smoothly; you live the moment. It's not like dreaming where you aren't in control."

Madison considered it. She remembered the feeling of Ben's hand on her cheek and the sulfur smell of artillery or musket fire. It felt real, but often her dreams felt real. How could she tell the difference? "Everything was clear. I could see him, every detail of his face and what he was wearing. He didn't fit what I pictured the classic Civil War soldier to look like: dark blue trousers, jacket, hat. He had on light blue trousers and just a stained shirt. He said it was because it was hot in July."

"It makes sense to me." Mike rolled slightly to his side and set the apple core in the plastic bag the hoagies came in, then rolled back flat. "I've always speculated soldiers took off their gear and left them behind lines. I can't imagine the artillerymen loading and firing artillery in wool jackets. I'm sure they stripped it all off."

"I'm not convinced my subconscious works that way."

"Maybe, maybe not. Did he say anything else to you?" Liam set his sandwich down again, wiping a paper napkin across his face. "Other than the generalities of what happened during the battle?"

"He...um..." Madison looked into Mike's eyes. She wasn't sure he was going to like this. "He said his soul was bound to mine."

"What the hell does that mean?" Liam huffed. "Mike? Thoughts?"

"I have no idea. I understand why he picked her, though."

"Okay, fine, if you two are happy just letting bygones be bygones fine." Liam ground the toe of his tennis shoe into the dirt. "I still think it was an out of body experience."

"Personally, I feel better knowing who she was and how she died." Madison looked over her shoulder, toward the test pit turned grave. "Even if no one else would believe me."

"I believe you." Mike slid his hand up and caught her hand in his, lacing his fingers around hers. "I might not understand what happened last night, but I saw what it did to you. His story sounds plausible. We just can't prove it."

"I'm going to run through the 11th Corps roll sheets and see if I can narrow down documented casualty lists from the Gettysburg campaign. Ben is a common name. So, you know, next time he's around to chat, see if he'll tell you his last name." Liam stuffed the remainder of his sandwich into a plastic bag and knotted the top. "That would make it *that* much easier and I'm going to tell you right now, if his last name is Smith or Jones I'm going home. I can only do so much for you."

Madison didn't know what to say. "Thanks, Liam. That means a lot to me."

"We're a team aren't we?" Liam pursed his lips together. "Wasn't it Benjamin Franklin who said, 'We must all hang together, or assuredly we shall all hang separately?'"

"Only when they signed the Declaration of Independence."

"Well, put your words into actions, bitches. Here comes Brad." His expression softened and he smiled broadly. "Hey, buddy."

"Hey, crew." Brad smiled at them and tossed Madison a magazine. "Check out what came to park headquarters today."

She looked at the cover. *Newsweek.* "This isn't what I was expecting."

"Turn to page nineteen."

Madison flipped to the correct page number. The article was small, only a quarter of the page, but there was her name in bold.

First recorded remains of a female Civil War soldier found? Maybe, but Gettysburg National Military Park isn't confirming either way. So far, the only official reports from the National Park Service indicate human remains were discovered by **twenty-one year old archeologist Madison Monroe***, of Pittsburgh, Pennsylvania. The remains are confirmed as female, but without concrete evidence to support she was a soldier, she will remain yet another nameless tragedy associated with the three day, bloody battle in July 1863. One name we'll take away from this discovery though, is Miss Monroe, a vibrant, fresh face to a somewhat dull and dusty profession. Humble, sweet, and personable, Miss Monroe is just the kind of woman you want on your dig team. We want to be archeologists too.*

"Yikes." Madison handed the magazine to Mike. "Do you guys think I'm sweet? Because, you know, I think I always come across as bitter and sarcastic."

"This is phenomenal, Madison." Brad smiled broadly at her. "Look at you! The new face of archeology. I'm proud of you, really. This is the kind of discovery we need to get our field on the map. Before you know it, you're going to be running digs and giving presentations. My uncle is going to be very, very impressed with your work."

Madison stared at him. He seemed genuine. Happy. This was not the same man that had snapped at her the previous day in front of Mike and Jack. This man seemed thrilled for her success. He seemed happy to see her. "Thanks, Brad."

"No, really, I called him this morning to fill him in. He already knew. I guess it's all over the news in Pittsburgh. He said you're the best thing to come out of the Steel City since Sarris chocolate."

"Meriwether Lewis and William Clark started their famed Corps of Discovery expedition in Pittsburgh." Madison glanced between Mike and Liam. "It's a very, very fantastic city. We have a lot going for us."

"Other than Lewis and Clark and chocolate?" Liam raised his eyebrow quizzically. "Bitch, please."

"No, no, really. There's a lot there." Madison sighed. "I will campaign for the glory of Pittsburgh, even if the rest of the world fails to see its grandeur."

"The Steel City and the home of the world famous Madison Monroe." Mike squeezed her thigh. "If people didn't care before, they will now."

"Please, I've got better things to do."

"No, you don't." Brad leaned over and patted her shoulder. "Madison, you are headed straight to the top. My uncle said he's convinced you'll get waved into graduate school, no questions asked. Shit, they'll probably want you to start teaching graduate level classes."

Madison blushed. "That's okay. I'm happy just getting my degree and doing some digging. Pittsburgh is already on the map, firmly to the right of Harrisburg, and we're good with that. We've got Super Bowl Rings and Stanley Cups and…and a functioning baseball team. They don't need me to be the face of the Steel City. Really."

"Well, my dear, I don't think you have much of a choice." Brad smiled at her, an act that made her more uncomfortable than if he'd physically touched her. "You're our It Girl."

"Did the park service decide what they're doing with the remains yet?" She tried to change the subject. "I'm hoping they don't just want to throw her in storage like some kind of specimen."

"They're still debating. Frye wants her buried in the National Cemetery, but there's a lot of red tape to get through before they'll approve that request." Brad sat next to Liam. "He's filed the paperwork for it, though. I submitted a letter as well."

"She deserves to be in the National Cemetery." Madison nodded her head slowly. "I'd rather see that than leaving her here."

"The other option is on the other side of the fence, in Evergreen Cemetery." Brad shrugged his shoulders. "I think putting her back in the ground here is last on their list."

"Good." Madison stiffened, trying to keep herself from outwardly shivering. "I don't want her to stay here. It seems too, I don't know, anonymous."

"I wouldn't worry about it. The whole world knows about her now. They're going to make sure she's given the burial she deserves. We may not be able to prove she was a soldier, but we have enough evidence to at least assume she was important to this battle. Her story won't end at this farm." Brad hesitated. "That being said, I have some bad news for you guys."

"They cut funding?" Liam broke in. "We have to shut down now?"

"No, I actually wish it was that easy." Brad took a deep breath. "Jan Williams was in a car accident last night. They found her car in a ditch outside of Chambersburg. She was pronounced dead at the scene."

"Oh my god." Madison gasped. "That's horrible."

Mike sat up, pushing his sunglasses up onto his head. "What was she doing out near Chambersburg? I thought she and Scott were headed back to Washington yesterday morning."

"The police don't know. From what I heard at park headquarters today, they're looking into it. She left about the same time we did yesterday, Mike, and told them she was going to visit a friend here in town before heading home. Her car was en route to Hanover, so it's anyone's guess at this point." Brad shook his head. "I'll be honest, guys, they're looking into toxicology results at this point. It wasn't a bad accident, all things considered. One thing is for sure, she wasn't wearing a seatbelt."

Madison shuddered. How awful.

"Anyway, the park wants to have a brief memorial service tomorrow morning. Nothing elaborate, just something small to highlight the work she'd been doing in the past week." Brad pushed his hair back. "God, this is such a punch in the face. I mean, who doesn't wear their seatbelt? She did so much work on the remains and one stupid mistake ends it all."

"Jesus." Mike settled back down in Madison's lap, pressing her palm against his chest. "It's a shame she drove out that direction at all."

"I knew a guy back in college that took a turn too sharp and rolled his pickup." Brad outwardly shuddered. "He wasn't wearing a seatbelt and slid out the open window. The truck rolled on him and killed him instantly. The cops said if he'd been wearing his seatbelt, he would have walked away from the accident without so much as a scratch. Life is precious, guys. Let's remember that."

Madison closed her eyes. She'd gone from the top of her world to the proverbial pits of despair. Jan was a nice lady with a fantastic career. What a waste.

Chapter Twenty

"Something's bothering you."

Madison tilted her head up and looked at Mike. His cheeks were still flushed from mind-blowing sex, followed by a relaxed but somewhat too hot shower. He wasn't looking at her, but was staring up at the ceiling. She rested her hand on his chest. "What makes you think that?"

"I can tell. I know you, Maddy."

She sighed, snuggling against him. "Maybe. I don't know. I guess it's just everything. The dig, Ben, now Jan and the car accident. I mean, seriously, at this point all I want to do is hole up in here with you and not have to face what tomorrow brings."

"Meaning…"

She closed her eyes. "I don't want the dig to end, because that means I have to go home to Pittsburgh. What I want is to stay here with you."

He sighed, rolling to his side to face her. Cupping the side of her face in his hand, he pressed his lips to her forehead. "It's been in the back of my mind this week, too. The more we get done on the site, the sooner we're finished. Then the reports get turned in to make everything nice and tidy and official. That's the last thing I want. Maddy, I'm not going to lose you. We'll figure something out."

"God damned graduate school."

Mike chuckled. "Don't think about it. Look, we still have a test pit to finish up, two if you count the fact we've only done about half near the bank barn. As far as I'm concerned, the amount of time we have left at the Spangler Farm is indefinite. But, I'm not thinking about that. I'm thinking about now. You, here, with me. That's all that matters."

"When this whole convoluted mess started, I was sure my citation ruined me finally achieving my goals." She nuzzled her face against his. "What it gave me, though, was more than I could have dreamed."

He pulled her to him and held her tightly, tangling his fingers in her hair. "I love you, Maddy baby, so much more than I think you know. Just because the dig ends, doesn't mean we end. You're stuck with me, whether you like it or not."

"I love you, soldier boy." She nuzzled her face against his. Finally! She felt like she'd been waiting eons for him to say it. "I'd gladly give up my degree and graduate school to have you."

"No, no, you're going to finish up your degree. You said it yourself, you've paid for it so you might as well finish it up." He pulled back and studied her. "You're going to have a great career in archeology, Maddy. I'm just excited to be with you, watching it unfold."

"Or I'll just be awkward and trip over things."

"That too." He kissed her. "Stop worrying. Focus on now: you're naked, we're together. Nothing else matters."

"Well, other than Ben's warning."

"You still have no idea what kind of context that was in."

"A warning is a warning, no matter what context."

"I know, baby. All I'm saying is, it could be completely unrelated to the dig, right? I'm going to keep you safe. Drew has his eye on the site and, height requirements aside, Liam's a scrappy kid. Nothing's going to happen to you."

"Something happened to Jan. Now she's dead."

Mike exhaled deeply, cradling her in his arms. "I know, but that was an accident. They don't know what happened. Alcohol, drugs, falling asleep behind the wheel, over compensating poor driving skills, texting; we won't know until the investigation is done. Whatever it was, I won't let it happen to you."

"I feel helpless, that's all. I thought I'd help Ben by finding the remains, but he was still here." Madison buried her face against his chest. "Even though he's told me about her, I just get this feeling he's still with me. I can feel him."

"I'd rather you feel me."

"Strangely, he's shared his opinion on a lot of things, but never on you." Madison thought for a moment. "He did tell me he thought you'd be the one who would understand."

"Understand what?"

"I don't know. There's a lot he says that I don't fully comprehend." Her mind drifted back to her experience with him. *My soul is bound to yours.* What did that mean? How did it even happen? "I just want him to find peace. He tried so hard to save her, both in life and now in death. I don't understand why he isn't able to cross over, or whatever it is spirits do. What's keeping him here?"

"He seems pretty devoted to you."

"Maybe."

"You sell yourself short too often. Like with this dig, you deserve all the credit for discovering the remains, yet, you keep insisting Liam and I had just as much to do with it. We didn't. As I recall, Liam tried to talk you out of it."

"I'm not in this for fortune and glory or whatever it is people think I should be trying to get." Madison traced her fingertips over the tattoo on his chest. "I just really love the field of archeology. I like knowing that, even after we're gone, we leave a tangible trace of our existence behind."

"God, I love you."

She blushed. "Talk about selling yourself short. You could have had anyone, but you wanted me. Some college kid from the slums of Western Pennsylvania."

"I've never met anyone like you, Maddy."

"Is that good or bad?"

He pulled her against him, burying his face against the hollow between her shoulder and neck. "Better than you can imagine."

"You had me from your initial, rambling description of the Spangler Farm. Falling in love with you was easy." She wrapped her arms around him. "I was afraid keeping you would be the hard part."

"It won't be."

Madison was ready to pull the covers up and call it a night, when Mike's cell phone buzzed on the table beside him. He let her go for a moment, reaching over to retrieve the phone and review the text. He was silent and instead of speaking, he placed the phone back on the nightstand.

"Is everything okay?" Madison looked up at him, trying to catch his eye with hers. "Who was it?"

"No big deal." He pulled the covers up to her shoulders, tucking it around her frame. "It was just Drew."

"Did he want something?"

"Nope, not really."

Madison rested her head against Mike's chest, but her mind whirled. He never acted like that with texts, not even with phone calls for that matter. Whatever the text said, struck him.

But it was the fact he wouldn't tell her what it said that made her nervous.

Chapter Twenty-One

The viewing hours and funeral for Jan Williams were held in a local funeral parlor in her home town of Frederick, Maryland. The early calling hours and early service were too much for Madison and her team to commit to, so they instead opted to drive down later on in the day for the evening calling hours. They'd skip the service and graveside completely.

It was open casket.

Madison shuddered. The last funeral she'd been to was her father's. Mike didn't look anywhere near how relaxed he'd looked the past few days. He held on to her hand tightly, his back pressed up against the wall of the parlor. He looked around and softly said, "I'm not a fan of big crowds. Combat mindset kicks in: back to the wall, check the exits."

"At what point do we feel confident we've paid the appropriate amount of respects and can leave?" Liam loosened the knot of his necktie. "Because look, I know five people here. Two of them are you. Nobody cares we're here."

"It's the right thing to do." Madison scanned the crowd. As far as she was concerned, as soon as they saw the park superintendent and Brad, they were safe to go. Make it known they were there and then split.

Mike closed his eyes and tilted his face upward, resting his head against the wall. His foot tapped against the floor at a frantic pace. "Have you ever been to Harpers Ferry, Maddy baby? It's right down the road. John Brown's Raid and all. It's very exciting, and I will take you there right now if you want."

"We just need to say a fast 'what's up' to Brad and Superintendent Frye. Then we're good to go. Trust me, that's how these games are played. My step-father does it all the time. He goes to these important school functions just long enough to get his picture taken with committee members and then goes and hides in his office." Madison held on to Mike's hand with one hand and rubbed his forearm with the other. "I've learned from the best."

"Well, someone needs to find them now."

Liam straightened his collar and brushed invisible dirt off his sleeves. "I'll go mingle. You stay here and try to keep your hands to yourself."

"Dude, I'm just trying not to throw up." Mike kept his eyes closed, his grip on her hand tightening. He finally sighed and rolled his head toward her. "I'm sorry. I just…I have a hard time with this kind of thing."

"It's okay." She scanned the mob of people tightly packed in the small parlor. "Do you want to go outside for a couple minutes?"

"No. That's letting it beat me." He took several deep breaths and then opened his eyes. "I'm all right. Really."

"We can just chill here and critique people's funeral attire." She rested her head on his shoulder. "Check out that girl's shoes. I mean, really—blue and hot pink sequined stripper shoes at a funeral? I'd trip and fall on my face."

"I can't imagine you in stilettos." He pouted. "I guess that's a fantasy I'll have to file away for my dreams."

"Oh, wait, those are platforms, which make them even worse." Madison leaned forward slightly, trying to peer past a slim woman wearing a large black hat. "Oh, wait. That's Cianna."

"Well, that's surprising."

"Not really. She knows how to play the game."

Cianna was standing by herself, also scanning the crowd like she was looking for someone. She turned just enough to catch sight of them and, with a general look of annoyance, started walking in their direction.

"Shit." Mike tucked his head down by Madison's. "Try to blend in with that wall sconce or something. I can see this conversation going two ways: excruciating or unbearable."

"I'll spill something on myself and cause a scene." She giggled. "You run for the door."

Cianna showed marked prowess in flouncing across the room in stripper shoes. She glared at them. "Have you seen Brad?"

Mike leveled his gaze at her. "It's nice to see you too, Cianna."

"Cut the shit. Where's Brad?"

"Contrary to popular belief, I'm not his personal secretary. I've had to manage the dig in his noticeable absences over the last few weeks, but I've washed my hands of keeping track of who he's doing and when." He paused. "What are you doing here?"

"Same thing you're doing here, I assume." She looked over her shoulder. "Is Liam here, too?"

"You're not that dumb, Cianna. What do you think?"

She narrowed her eyes, her upper lip twitching as she seemed to restrain a snarl. "It's sad about Jan. That's a bad stretch of road."

"It's an empty stretch of road, so there was no one around to tell the cops what happened." Mike pulled Madison closer to him. "Maybe she was texting or something. Wasn't she on her way home?"

"That's the wrong road to be on if you're heading to Frederick. But, yeah, I heard the car was found at the end of an S turn. She was driving fast."

"No seatbelt."

"No seatbelt." Cianna shrugged. "What a waste. It's pathetic when people have loads of book smarts, but no common sense."

"Speaking of common sense, why'd you quit the dig?" Mike matched her glare for glare. "We asked Brad, but he pretty much told us to fuck off."

"Who needs me when you have the magnificent Madison?" Cianna switched her gaze to Madison, her stare cold and somewhat critical. "I saw the article about you in *The Times*. I bet you're proud of yourself."

"I really don't care about it. I'm happy just to play in the dirt."

"And with Mike."

Madison shrugged. "What do you want me to say, Cianna? Do you want me to apologize that Mike fucked me because he loves me and Brad fucked you because you opened your legs? I wouldn't give you the satisfaction."

"This was nowhere near as bad as Baltimore was, yet you were there to the bitter end, public spectacle and all. I can't figure you out." Mike closed his eyes. "You just gave up free money."

"I couldn't take his shit anymore."

"He's the same prick he's always been."

"This was different." She looked over her shoulder again. "Look, I don't want to get into it. I quit. I quit the team and I quit his shitty excuse for a dig company so I can be done with all his disgusting drama. Is that good enough for you, Mike? Does that answer your question?"

"Nope. It just gives me a hell of a lot more."

Cianna ground the toe of her shoe into the carpet and picked at the ends of her white blonde hair; for a split second, Madison thought she noticed her lower lip quiver. Her composure was quick. She looked over her shoulder and, straightening considerably, grumbled, more to herself than to either Mike or Madison, "There he is, fucking bastard."

Madison followed her line of sight and saw not only Brad, but Superintendent Frye and Liam. She wasn't surprised to see Brad and Frye together. Brad seemed to latch onto him, always cornering him in conversation and no doubt talking himself up with accomplishments he didn't even achieve. He was like a walking resume.

She turned to Mike. His eyes were already open. He slowly edged away from the wall and stepped forward. "The sooner we get this over with, the sooner we can leave."

They followed Cianna through the crowd of mourners. Mike kept his hand firmly around Madison's and when they reached the group, he extended his free hand to Brad. "Hey, man."

"Thanks for coming out, guys." Brad shook Mike's hand and then reached over, gently squeezing Madison's upper arm. "Are you doing okay?"

"Yeah, it's just kind of a shock." She turned to Superintendent Frye. "She was very kind to us."

"I'm just stunned she'd act so foolishly." The superintendent shook his head. "I've known Jan for over twenty years. She wasn't the type of woman who would use her cell phone while she was driving or leave without a seatbelt. It's like she was in some kind of hurry."

"Do the police know who she was calling?" Brad leaned over and ran his hand down Cianna's arm. "Are you doing okay, sweetie?"

"I'm fine." She jerked her arm away from him, but didn't move away from where he was standing. It was like she couldn't quite bring herself to break the cycle of what no doubt was emotional abuse.

"The police said the battery on her phone was dead." Frye rubbed his chin. "She must not have realized and was busy fiddling with it, when she should have been watching the road. I can't imagine what could have been so important. She'd filed her official reports on the remains. I know she was lining up quite a bit of speaking engagements and a few high profile interviews, but she'd used my office for that all morning. There was no reason to be using a cell phone to do it at ten o'clock at night."

Madison stared down at the tops of her shoes. "Sometimes one mistake is all you get to make."

"It's a strong reminder on how much we all take for granted. Even I'm guilty of using my cell phone when I drive." Frye looked genuinely moved by Jan's death. "I'll be keeping it in my briefcase from now on."

"Madison, I was just telling Mr. Frye about the article in *The Times* and your recent interviews with *National Geographic* and *Archeology* Magazine." Brad smiled. "It's important to keep our eyes on the future and the scope of what Jan was working on."

"We're expecting good things from you, Miss Monroe. Jan was a prolific supporter of women's advancements in the field. I wish the two of you could have spent more time together." Frye smiled at her. "I'll tell you right now, with what you bring to the table, next time we have a dig at the park, your name will be first on our list."

Mike squeezed her hand.

"That's very kind, thank you." Madison glanced up at Mike. "Right now I'm more focused on living in the present. I'm looking forward to seeing what the rest of our work at the Spangler Farm brings."

"Overall, I'm willing to declare the survey a success. Once you've finished your survey—and we do want you to finish the survey, despite what Brad thinks—we're going to get it set to open to the public the beginning of June. There's so much interest in the farm right now. We have to get it open as soon as possible."

Mike cleared his throat. "Why would Brad think you didn't want the survey finished?"

"I just thought they'd want the site cleared and open for tours sooner, maybe by the end of the month." Brad shrugged. "I was willing to shut it down now."

"Uh," — Liam exchanged a glance with Madison — "that's news to us."

"And it's nothing to worry about, because as gracious an offer as it was, we want the site completely surveyed. Keep on schedule and have the final report turned in by May 31st. Cover up the pits, clear out your equipment, and we'll get everything landscaped and roped off for public viewing by the first weekend of June. Madison, we'd be thrilled to have you give a few remarks at the visitor's center the morning the farm goes live to the public." Frye turned to Brad. "That's sufficient time, don't you think?"

"It's more than enough time to take care of everything." He looked distant for a moment and then slowly nodded. "No loose ends."

"Excellent. Your team does impressive work, Brad." Frye reached out and shook his hand, then clapped him on the back. "Madison, stop by my office sometime next week. We can talk about a possible lecture or brief appearance when the site opens."

"I will, sir, but I'd rather the focus be on the site and not on me." She flashed what she hoped was a sincere, sweet smile. "If you'll excuse us, we...uh...have some work to get back to at the farm. Keeping on schedule, you know."

"Of course. Thank you for coming out, I know it means a lot to the family." He patted Mike's shoulder. "It's always nice to see you, Mr. Caldwell. Keep up the good work."

"Thank you, sir, likewise."

Madison tugged on his arm and, brushing past Cianna, led him through the mass of people still crowded in line to view the casket and straight to the exit. She wanted to kick the front door open and pull him out into the sunshine. "I'm going to categorize that as one of the more awkward conversations of my life."

"What the fuck does he mean Brad wanted to shut the site down?" Liam fell into step next to her. "We're basically handed four weeks to dig in Gettysburg and he wants to just say, nah, we're good here. You keep these extra two weeks and we'll just go home and crochet scarves or something. Does he have something better to do? No, no he doesn't. He's got nothing and he knows it."

"He's trying to cover his ass." Mike twisted his tie loose and pulled it over his head. "Frye knows he wasn't at the site when Madison found the remains. We had that whole pit excavated before he strolled back to the farm. He figures if he's the one who makes the decision to shut it down, he's still the one in charge."

Madison ducked into the passenger's seat of the Jeep. "Frye doesn't seem to care."

"Frye doesn't care who found it. He just cares that it was found, it was a woman, and the whole archeology community is practically lactating over it." Liam slouched down behind Madison's seat. "Hey, Mikey, maybe we won't have to write the final report on this dig?"

Mike snickered. He looked more relaxed now that they were back in the Jeep, away from the mob of people and the oppressive feeling of death. "The last, what, five digs we've done, Brad's dumped the responsibility of writing the final report off on me and Liam. He's far too busy with more important things."

"We submitted the first report under his name, but we've just been leaving the rest in our names." Liam scoffed. "I don't think he notices and, if he does, he doesn't care."

"He only cares about two things: advancing his own career and getting pussy." Mike glanced at Madison. "Sorry."

"We all know it's true."

"Well, now that Cianna's has dried up, I get the feeling we're going to be stuck with him." Liam paused and seemed to consider his own remark. "Actually, he hates Mike because he's fucking you, and he hates you because you're not fucking him. That means I'm going to be stuck dealing with his whining and incompetence."

Madison snickered. "I know you said incompetence, but my ears heard incontinence."

"Bitch, I'd be in the car and on the highway. He can go straight to hell."

Mike worked the clutch and gas pedal and pulled out of the parking lot. "I've said it before, Maddy, but I'll say it again. I don't want you alone with him. As much as I hate her, I don't like how he treats Cianna and…and I just don't want you with him."

Liam cleared his throat. "For what it's worth, I don't either."

Madison stared at the window, not sure how to respond to them. It went without saying that she didn't want to be around Brad. She would be perfectly happy to finish out the dig with just Mike and Liam, but that wasn't going to happen. There were only two weeks left.

And she had a feeling they were going to be a fast two weeks.

Chapter Twenty-Two

They officially shut down the test pit beside the barn by mid-week. Although the park service still wanted the test pit where the remains were found left open—in case the decision was made to return them to their original grave—Mike and Madison started to fill the barn pit back in. It felt like solemn work, of burying untouched possibilities and artifacts that would always remain lost to time.

"This brings back memories of when I was enlisted." Mike dragged his arm across his brow, wiping the sheen of sweat away. "When I became an officer, I critiqued trenches dug by other soldiers. But when I was enlisted, man, we honed our ditch digging ability. Foxholes, latrines, trenches, sometimes the occasional ditch to see if we were capable of digging a good ditch, you have no idea how much time we spent moving dirt from one side of the course to the other."

"Does the Army still actually employ trench warfare?" Madison dumped another shovelful of dirt into the hole and then retrieved her water bottle. They had to pick the warmest day of spring to fill in the pits, it only figured. Even the fact that evening was setting in wasn't helping to lower the humidity.

"No, actually, but just in case the need should arise, we're very well trained."

"Two pits down, two to go." Madison took a quick swig of water. "This feels like how my car handles a tank of gas. I drive for thousands of miles until I hit a quarter of a tank; then it just drops to empty after a tenth of a mile. That's how this dig has felt, this last week is just flying past."

"I know." He sighed. "Next week is going to be miserable. The dig being over, having to deal with Brad finalizing all the paperwork and the final report I may or may not still have to write…figuring out how to stay with you as long as possible."

"We still have time to make some other kind of fantastic, once in a lifetime discovery, right?" Madison spoke rapidly, as if focusing on something else would keep the inevitable flow of tears from preemptively starting. "If it can happen once, surely it can happen twice."

His lips twitched into a smile. "What exactly are you planning on finding this time?"

"Let's aim high. An entire, intact artillery piece."

"I'd definitely quantify that as aiming high."

She handed her water bottle to him. "You never know. Who'd have thought we'd find human remains?"

"Who'd have thought I'd be lucky enough to find you?" He took a quick drink and then set the water bottle down. "Come here." He touched his finger to the underside of her chin and tilted it up, gently pressing his lips to hers. "Stop worrying."

"I can't help it."

"I'll help get your mind off it later." He kissed her again, deeper this time. "You're wearing those jeans again. You know they drive me nuts, the way they hug you in just the right places."

"I should wear them more often."

"You should. I'd like to take them off you more often."

She stood on her tiptoes and kissed him. Over his shoulder, she saw Brad hustling over from the parking lot. She couldn't see his eyes, but she was fairly sure he'd been watching them the entire time. "Here comes Mr. Personality."

"Terrific." He let her go and again picked up his shovel. "I liked him more when he was fucking Cianna and too busy to show his face here."

"Hey, team!" Brad called down to them. "Wait until you see what I have."

Liam strolled over from the summer kitchen. He leaned over Madison's shoulder. "It's probably syphilis."

She snickered.

Brad held a manila envelope in the air. "Your friend Jack was up by the road. He said he called you several times."

"Aw, colossal let down." She rolled her eyes. "My phone is the Jeep charging."

"He wanted me to give this to you. It's an advance copy of *Archeology* with your cover story." Brad handed her the envelope. "Open it up."

Madison groaned and brushed her hands off on her jeans. She opened the flap of the envelope and pulled out the magazine, immediately dismayed to see her figure on the front cover. After a second, more critical evaluation, she decided it wasn't a half bad picture. It was one of the first the photographer had taken. She was looking over her shoulder at the bank barn, one hand on her hip and the other tucking her hair behind her ear. *Magnificent Madison: How two women changed the rules at Gettysburg.*

She half groaned, half gasped.

"I think they airbrushed a tan on you." Liam peered over her shoulder. "You don't look nearly as pasty as you normally do."

"It's porcelain, thank you." She flipped to the article. "I totally rock porcelain."

The article was accompanied by a smaller inset picture of her, a close up of her face and upper body as she leaned against the fence. "Awesome, it looks like my senior picture. Though, in my senior picture I was holding a lacrosse stick."

"You played lacrosse?" Liam snorted. "I can't imagine that went well."

"I'm surprisingly swift. Getting walloped with a lacrosse stick hurts, so the faster you can run to the other side of the field and score, the less bruises and battle scars you end up sustaining." She scanned the beginning of the article.

She hasn't yet earned her undergraduate degree, yet twenty-one year old Madison Monroe has made one of the most important discoveries in the history of Gettysburg National Military Park. She's found the remains of what may be the first documented female soldier of the American Civil War, a woman who stood a few inches shorter than Madison stands; a name that's long lost to history. The student turned archeologist breaks the mold of the stuffy, vanilla diggers. She's beautiful, vivacious, and sports an unconfirmed number of tattoos that would scandalize some of history's most notable authorities in the field.

"Yeah, I'm done with this." Madison handed the magazine to Mike. "This reads more like the introduction of a beauty pageant contestant. Vivacious? Really?"

"Look, Liam, he mentioned us here." Mike cleared his throat. "She's flanked by two of the other diggers on her crew: sullen Army veteran Lieutenant Michael C. Caldwell—a recipient of the Bronze Star and Purple Heart—and Columbia University graduate Liam Stanish."

"You get to be sullen and have your rank listed, while I only get my name and school? Seriously?" Liam huffed. "I was the vivacious one. Let's be completely honest here."

"You were the drunk one."

Brad started reading aloud. "She's just the type of sass this tired field needs: energy, passion, determination. It's people like Madison who are going to change the face of archeology. We here at *Archeology* Magazine look forward to watching her career develop."

"I think I'm going to throw up." Madison groaned. "This is the type of thing my mother will copy and mail to my grandmother, but the kind of thing that's going get me laughed out of school."

"I think it's fantastic." Brad handed her the magazine. "Good for you, Madison. That's the kind of exposure we all want."

"The stakes and expectations just got that much higher." She put the magazine back in the envelope and tossed it on top of her hoodie. "That nickname has to go. The first person here who calls me 'Magnificent Madison' is going to get punched in the face."

Mike chuckled. "It sounds like the slogan for the welcome center in Madison, Wisconsin."

"Or a stripper." Liam twitched, as if he were holding in laughter. "Do you like Marvelous Madison better? Maybe Magical Madison?"

"Memorable Madison?" Mike chimed in.

She playfully shoved him. "Stop it. Now they all sound like stripper names."

Brad had fallen silent. He was staring up at the bank barn, his brow knitted in a deep frown. His eyes seemed distant, as if he was concentrating so intensely on one thought that he'd completely tuned out the three of them.

Madison...

She froze. Ben; it was almost impossible to hear him, but the tone in his voice was unmistakable. He was panicked, almost desperate.

...don't...don't...Mike...

She felt an unmistakable tugging on her elbow. The grip was firm at first, but quickly dissipated. He didn't have the strength.

...please...

"Mike, I need you to do me a favor." Brad shoved his hands in his pockets, slowly running the toe of his shoe through the dirt. "I need you to run some paperwork up to park headquarters again. I have some files and the rest of the artifacts from the barn pit that need stored up there. We might have to take the second sifter up there too. I just don't see the point of keeping it here when we're down to only two pits."

"It would fit better in the back of your truck." Mike retrieved his shovel and pitched a few loads of dirt into the hole. "We can ride over together if you want."

"My truck's in the shop. I'm using a little compact rental that makes Liam's shoebox look like a tank."

"I resent the implication my car looks like a shoe."

"Anyway, I have to run up to Harrisburg tonight on a personal matter. I'll be back in the morning, but these files need checked in with Frye tonight."

"Okay, man, whatever." Mike tossed another shovelful of dirt into the pit. "Do you want me to take the sifter or what?"

"Yeah, I think that's best. We might as well shut the kitchen pit down in the morning." Brad consulted his watch. "It's almost five. Mike, I'll get you everything you need to take up to headquarters. That way you can get back to the hotel early. I'm sure you and Madison have plans. Liam, you finish locking everything down here."

Mike handed his shovel to Liam and then cocked his head toward the Jeep. "Come on, Maddy, I have to give you your phone before you leave."

She fell into step next to him, the nagging chatter of Ben's voice still searing through her mind. He was talking too fast to understand. "Did we have plans?"

"I don't know what he's talking about." Mike slid his hand down her back and let it rest on her hip. He pulled her to him, lowering his voice considerably. "I'm going to have Drew stop by the room. He's done at six and, if this takes as long as it did last time, I'm not going to be done until closer to eight. I'd just feel better if he checked on you until I get back. Maybe twice."

"Is something wrong?"

"Just a shell shocked old Lieutenant's nerves getting the better of him." Mike tightened his hold on her. "Make sure Liam drives you back to the room. I'll give you Drew's number if you need him."

He opened the door to the Jeep and reached in, pulling out her cell phone and handing it to her. He fumbled on the top of the dashboard and in the cup holders. "Shit, I think I left my phone down by the barn."

"It's okay. He's texted me before, remember?"

"That's right." Mike sighed and pulled her into his arms. "I'm freaking out over nothing. There's just this part of me that's fiercely overprotective to the point I'm ridiculous."

"I'll be fine." She smiled at him, but the corners of her mouth wavered. "There's nothing to worry about and besides, you'll just be down the road. I'll get all dolled up for when you get back and you can, you know, help me relax."

"Don't worry about putting your clothes back on if that's your plans." He kissed her. "I'm sorry I'm so negative all the time."

"You're fine."

He hugged her again, cradling the back of her head in his hand. "I'll be back as fast as I can. I'm not fucking around this time, no matter what Brad thinks needs to get done tonight."

She clung to him. Something just didn't seem right, something she couldn't quite put her finger on.

Ben's voice was in her head, a faint whisper she could barely hear. *...Stay...stay...Madison...*

Bound.

Chapter Twenty-Three

"Are you sure you don't want me to come in and hang out until Mike gets back?" Liam pursed his lips together. "Madison, be reasonable. I'm not going to try to seduce and take advance of you. I'm gay. Yes, I know. It probably comes as a surprise to you."

"Liam." She giggled. "I'm going to be fine. I'm going to walk up to the room, lock the door, and wait for Mike to come back."

"I can keep you company."

"If someone is out to get me, they'll have to break down the hotel room door and that's a pretty noticeable thing. I won't answer the door, even if it's a little Girl Scout selling cookies or, more horrifying, Jack Kornick asking me out on a date."

"You have my cell phone number?"

"You gave it to me three times before we even left the Spangler Farm parking lot."

"Call me if you need me."

"I'm not going to need you, but I appreciate the thought." She leaned over and kissed his cheek. "Mike will be back here in like, twenty minutes. I can survive twenty minutes without him, contrary to popular belief."

Liam didn't look convinced.

"I'll text you when I get to the room so you know I'm safe." Madison rolled her eyes. "You're worse than my mother. You guys are freaking out over nothing."

"I'm afraid Mike will pummel me if something happens to you." Liam paused. "Though there's a certain sexiness to the thought that I can't deny."

"Good night, Liam." She crawled out of the car and waved at him. "Go home and take a cold shower."

"I'm going to push the car home."

She laughed and headed up the stairs to the room, promptly texting him as soon as she had the door closed.

Thanks, Mom. I'm in the room, the door is locked.

He texted back.

Have fun playing with Mikey. Bitch.

I always do.

She tossed the phone onto the bed and pulled the elastic hair band out of her ponytail. The thought of a hot shower to relax her aching lumbar muscles sounded amazing…but waiting for Mike to get back and shower with her sounded better. She leaned over and unlaced her shoes.

Her cell phone buzzed.

She flopped back on the bed and picked it up. It was Mike.

Hey, can u meet me back at the farm? The battery in the jeep died and I need a jump.

She raised an eyebrow.

That sounds like a ploy.

I wish.

She hesitated. He seemed unusually cold.

Can't Drew swing down?

Can't reach him.

Weird.

I need you, Maddy. Come on, I'll make it up to u.

She sighed and leaned over to retie her shoelaces. When she straightened, she fired back a text.

I'll be there in like ten minutes.

Thanks, babe.

He was acting strange, but admittedly, he'd been acting weird since Brad asked him to run the files to headquarters. She grabbed her car keys and room key off of the top of the television and headed to the door.

Something made her stop. Incessant chatter in her head, words she couldn't understand, hit her psychic conscious with such strength, she had to hold onto the doorframe to steady herself. Ben seemed frantic, but no matter how hard she tried, she couldn't understand what he was saying.

She pressed her fingertips to the face of her cell phone.

Is everything okay? You seem strange.
It will be once u get here. I'll explain.

She shrugged off the feeling and opened the door, stepping out into the rapidly cooling evening air. She couldn't abandon him, because tone of voice didn't translate across text messages. Besides, if she didn't leave now, it would be too dark—and there was no way she'd find her way to the Spangler Farm in the dark.

As it was, she missed two turns and had to turn around in two residential driveways before she stumbled on the correct road. It was almost completely dark by the time she turned onto the bumpy dirt road leading to the barn. It loomed above her, like a still, silent monolith watching her every move.

...wait...Mike...

The parking area next to the barn was deserted.

Her hands tightened around the steering wheel. Where else would he have parked? Was this some kind of stupid joke? If it was, it wasn't funny.

Her phone glowed on the seat next to her.

Sorry, I'm down in the summer kitchen. I have the sifter wedged in the door. Can u come help me get it out? I feel like an idiot.
Where did you park?

She hesitated.

Why are you acting so weird?

I told you, I feel like an idiot over the sifter. The jeep's up behind the barn. I moved some shit up there for Frye. Go check if you want.

I'll be down.

Madison shoved her phone in her pocket and slid out of the car. The night air felt like it was tinged with ice. It was colder than it felt when she left the room. As she trudged through the grass toward the kitchen, she felt a presence beside her. Ben. He seemed stronger and was slightly, though not yet completely, easier to hear.

Can't....trust....can't...Mike.

"Can't trust Mike?" She almost stopped walking, but forced herself to breathe deeper, to try and reach out to him. "I don't understand that at all."

...like her...too late...I can't...save...

She let her attention drift to listening to Ben's crackling voice, straining her ears to try and hear as much as she could while trying to mentally fill in the breaks to figure out what he was saying.

Madison...stop before it's too late.

She looked up a moment later than she should have.

Brad stepped out from behind the summer kitchen. "Hi, Madison."

"Brad." She stopped short and took an uncertain step backwards. "I thought Mike was down here. Is...uh...is he with you?"

"No, Madison. Mike isn't here." His hands were behind his back and he casually stepped closer to her. He looked calm. "I was actually waiting for you."

"Why?"

"I think you know why, Madison."

"Humor me then." She slid her hand to her hip, trying to dig her fingers into her pocket to hit the phone button. Where was Mike?

"Get your hand away from your phone, Madison."

"I don't understand what's going on." She took another step backwards. "I want to talk to Mike."

"You know, Jan Williams was a lot easier to shut up than you are." He reached his left hand out. "Give me your phone."

"What happened to Jan?" Madison had a sinking feeling in her chest, the distinct feeling she knew what happened. She didn't want to hear it from him.

"Jan Williams tried to take our discovery and make it her own." Brad walked closer to her, his hand still extended. "The field shouldn't extoll bottom feeders like that. I handled her. I was telling you the truth when I said my truck was being worked on. The bumper of her car cracked the front grill when I ran her off the road."

Madison's heart sank. "You killed her?"

"The car accident killed her." He shrugged casually. "I just helped her along. It's funny, it's so hard to distinguish injuries sustained in blunt force trauma. Was it from the accident? Was it from a tire iron? So hard to tell. Now, give me your phone like a good girl."

"Brad, no."

He moved his other arm out from behind his back and leveled a handgun at her chest. "Don't make this any harder than it has to be, Madison. Give me your phone."

She swallowed hard, shakily reaching into her pocket and pulling her cell phone out. She handed it to him.

He put it in his pocket and motioned at her with the gun. "Walk back to the car."

"Please, Brad. Don't do this."

"I'm going to ask you again nicely. Don't make me hurt you preemptively." He pushed her forward with a tap of the gun barrel. "Let's lay down some ground rules. If you scream, I'm just going to shoot you now. I don't want to have to do that, Madison, I really don't. There's a lot of houses around here and that's a lot of innocent people we don't need involved in a personal matter, right?"

"Right." She could hear Ben's footsteps in the grass beside her. He was still with her. He was helpless to assist, though.

Once in the parking lot, Brad reached his hand out again. "Give me your keys and get in the passenger's seat. That's a girl, nice and slow."

She handed him her car keys and crept to her car, fumbling to open the passenger's side door. Every fiber of her being told her not to get into the car with him, but what other choice did she have? He would shoot her. Fuck, he was probably going to shoot her anyway.

He pointed the gun at her. "Seatbelt, Madison. We don't want what happened to Jan happening to your pretty face."

She fumbled with the seatbelt, but slowly drew it across her body and latched it. It felt like she was just strapping herself in to die.

He rounded the car and slid into the driver's seat, adjusting it to better accommodate the length of his legs. The car roared to life as he turned the key into the ignition, and he easily pulled out of the lot and back to the main road. Nobody had seen them. Nobody knew she was with him, trapped in her own car.

She had no idea what roads he was following, but she quickly realized he was taking her deeper into the battlefield. The beam of light from the headlights glanced off monuments as they passed, shadowy stone spectators of her plight. Statues couldn't help her. Mike couldn't help her at this point; the battlefield was too big. He was as helpless as Ben was; hell, she didn't even know where she was. How could Mike possibly find her, even if he knew she was in trouble?

"You know, you brought this on yourself." Out of the corner of her eye, she could see him look at her. "You couldn't leave well enough alone."

"I was doing my job."

"Oh, sure, that's what you were doing. The job I so graciously gave you. You're a marginal archeologist with marginal technique. Diggers like you are a dime a dozen. You have no experience and yet, you still manage to stumble on the greatest discovery this god damned park has seen in twenty years. Now you're the belle of the ball! Magnificent Madison, the best god damned thing to happen to archeology. You're going to single handedly save the field." He pounded his fist into the steering wheel. "Meanwhile, I play gopher for the park service. I file all the permits and I make sure all the work is done correctly and reported to headquarters two god damned days before they need it, because they expect it to be done two weeks ahead of schedule. They don't want results. They want it done. And who's the one who put the test pit in the woods? Madison. Who discovered the remains of a female soldier? Madison. Who is the poster child for archeology? Madison. Every waking breath of my life is devoted to this god damned field and what do I get? Nothing. I get nothing."

"Please just let me out of the car." She forced her breath in and out of her lungs evenly, trying to stay calm. Trying to feign confidence.

"I'm not letting you out of the car."

"If you let me go, we can just forget any of this happened. I'll just resign from the dig and go home—"

"You're not going home!" His voice was at a near roar. He lifted the gun from his lap and motioned at her. "You're more trouble than you're worth. We're going to end this now."

Tears pricked the back of her eyes. She blinked them back, holding her breath in her lungs in an attempt to ground herself. Being afraid wasn't going to stop him. Trying to appeal to reason wasn't going to stop him. He seemed to feed off her weakness. She wasn't going to give him the satisfaction.

"It didn't have to be like this." He balanced the gun on his lap and slid his hand to her knee. "You should have made it easy like Cianna. She understood what it takes to get ahead. That could have been you; you could have just breezed through this dig. I'd have raved about you to my uncle and got you into grad school. Now you're forcing me to have to tell him how devastating it is to lose such a bright girl with so much potential."

She shoved his hand away. "Mike won't let you get away with this."

"Mike was your first mistake. In fact, I should have thrown you off the dig once you started fucking him. But, if you think he's going to show up and save you," —Brad set the gun on his lap and fished in his jacket pocket, pulling out a cell phone and confirming what she'd already figured out — "you're wrong."

"How did you get it away from him?" Panic welled up in her throat. "Did you hurt Mike too?"

"Christ, what do you take me for? You think I'd mess with some battle scarred hot head?" He snorted. "I took it when he so gallantly took you back to the Jeep to get yours. And, once you and I are finished, I'll leave it with you. That way, the police can give it back to him after they find you."

The road wound around a sharp curve; as it straightened, the car's headlights illuminated two figures standing in the middle of the road. Madison's breath caught in her throat. They were the dead: two soldiers, black empty orbits focused on the approaching car, their uniform jackets flung open as if in leisurely relaxation. She could see them so well, could see each detail of their uniforms and accoutrements.

"What the…" Brad leaned closer to the steering wheel, his brow furrowed. She knew he saw them too, just as she did. They stood still and stared, never moving or flinching, never wavering from their position in the road.

Brad slammed his foot to the brakes. The gun slid from his lap to the floor as the car slowed; it impacted with a dull thud.

It had to be enough.

In one fluid movement, Madison wrenched the seatbelt from around her waist and opened the passenger's side door, throwing herself out and tumbling to the asphalt below. Pain seared across her lower extremities, across her hip, through her knees. She was falling, rolling, landing. Gravel and shards of branches ripped into her palms as she hoisted herself upward and tested her footing. Shaky but firm. She launched forward and into the consuming blackness of the woods, half expecting him to grab her from behind or her legs to give way beneath her.

He howled in the car, an unearthly combination of a roar and a scream.

Blind from the inky darkness around her, she half ran, half fell through the thick underbrush. She kept her hands in from of her, a feeble attempt to keep from slamming into a tree. It was impossible to tell where he'd taken her. She could be anywhere on the battlefield. Brad was right. Mike was never going to find her in time. She didn't know where to run, didn't know if there was a place to hide.

And Brad was right behind her. He had to be, she sounded like a grizzly bear crashing through the woods. Terror seized up her throat, and tears she'd fought to hold back spilled over her cheeks. She couldn't stop, couldn't think. The blackness around her was dizzying, pulsing; she was running to nowhere. She couldn't stop.

Slow down.

The voice was beside her. It was inside her head at the same time, his heartbeat pounding as if it matched her own. She could feel his hand encircle her wrist, softly at first like the gentle kiss of a breeze, but with a sudden tug.

They'll delay him as best they can, but you need to slow down. Hide. Here, now, you have to trust me.

She could hear him so clearly, like her desperation somehow amplified his voice. It registered in her mind, the words he'd spoken back at the summer kitchen: our souls are bound.

She slowed to a stop. There was no other choice.

The tip of her shoe hit pavement. Maybe the road circled around back on itself. Maybe if she followed it, she'd be able to figure out where she was. Brad was nearby; he'd stopped moving, but his scream pinpointed him still behind her. Still with the car?

Here. You won't make it if you run.

She crept forward in the dark, allowing the tug of his hand and voice to lead her through the darkness. She couldn't see him, but she could feel him. It seemed like he was all around her, next to her; she wouldn't die alone.

Her fingers brushed against cold marble—a monument.

Behind it. Go.

She wrapped her arms around the monument and slid around to what she hoped was the back. Her shoulder seemed to slam into a brick wall, she stopped.

A firm force on her shoulder pushed her down to her knees.

Ahead, she saw a brief flash of light. The unmistakable shriek of her brakes sounded more like the scream of the dead, a warning. He was coming; he'd given up chasing her by foot.

Madison held her breath and pressed her forehead to the cold marble base of the monument. The damp earth beneath her knees soaked through her jeans. She tried to ink into the marble, to form her body to the hard lines of the squat, rectangular shape. One shadow would betray her. One movement, one sound—it would be over.

Something crashed through the woods ahead. The car picked up speed, the taillights quickly disappeared around the bend and the rumble of the old engine faded into silence.

She exhaled slowly, whispering into the night. "Where am I?"

Culp's Hill.

"How do I get back to town?"

"Ahead, behind him."

"What if I go the other way?"

Rock Creek. Town is forward, safety is forward...but so is he. His voice sounded like it was drifting away, like it was trapped in a sudden undertow pulling him away from her. *Can you hear me? I can't feel you anymore.*

"Please don't leave me." Fresh tears pricked the back of her eyes. He couldn't leave her alone now, but the effort to pull her through the woods must have drained him.

I'm so tired.

"It's okay." She braced her body against the monument and hoisted herself to her feet. Culp's Hill,

Mike had driven her through there before. The narrow road through the woods emptied out onto a main throughway beside Cemetery Hill. There were restaurants on the other end of the hill; stores, an Irish pub. She could make it. She just had to be careful and she'd make it. She'd track down Mike or Liam or Drew. Someone would take her to the police or them, and it would all be over.

She crept onto the road, her knees wobbling beneath her. Her eyes had adjusted to the dark to an extent, but the thick tree cover kept the light of the moon from filtering to the road below. Voices called out around her, some directly addressing her, but most stuck in the endless repetition of the last moments of their lives. Ben's voice was lost among the roar of the others. They drowned him out completely.

"Just stay calm." She spoke out loud, as if somehow hearing her own voice would ground her in the present. The taillights seemed to be long gone. Maybe he was up to the main road by now, maybe he'd just given up.

She rubbed her hands up and down her forearms. The nearby presence of the dead made the air feel like a freezer. She felt unseen figures pass by her, could feel their fingers brush against her flesh. They knew she felt them. They were tired of being unheard.

The road seemed to curve in front of her. In the distance, she saw the faint glow of an interior dome light. Maybe a tourist? Maybe someone searching out the presence of the long dead?

Realization smacked her like a punch to the face: the lit dome light, a car door propped open. It was her car.

He'd stopped.

She froze, her feet planted into the pavement beneath her. Squeezing her eyes closed, she forced herself to concentrate on the present, to weed through the shriek of voices around her. The woods seemed silent.

She took a step forward in the dark. She strained her ears to listen for him, for any sound to reveal where he was in the woods. Was he hiding in the car? Was he betting she'd approach it in a desperate search for the keys? Maybe she should just track back and follow the road deeper into the heart of the park. He wasn't expecting that. He might still press closer to town, knowing full well that was the direction she had to go.

Another step.

She could see the console and, beside it, illuminated by the dome light, her keys were in the ignition.

Another step.

The light only stayed on for twenty minutes, then the factory setting kicked in and shut if off to prevent the battery from draining. She could wait twenty minutes. If he was hiding in the woods by the car, she might be able to slide in and floor it before he grabbed her or, worse yet, fired on her.

"Madison! You mother fucking bitch! Get out here!" His voice echoed off the trees and rocks, the frustration and anger oozing from each word. It sounded like he was behind her. Surely she had to be right, the sound had to be from behind; he'd looped around.

She leapt forward, digging her feet into the pavement and pushing off with explosive force. The car was close. It was so close, the door was right there—

Her feet left the pavement; she was again running in the dirt. She could still make it. She had to make it.

The tip of her shoe hit a rock and she stumbled, pitching forward, falling in the dark. She felt herself falling forward and braced her hands in front of her, a desperate attempt to catch herself. Her hands slammed into a hard, rocky surface and seemed to catapult her forward. A sickening crunch echoed in her ears as her head impacted with the hard surface of a rock or monument. In her last moment of consciousness, pain seared from her temple and radiate through her skull, the dull roar of the dead dissipating around her as if she was being pulled under water.

She blacked out.

Chapter Twenty-Four

Her eyes fluttered open. Her heart was pounding.
Each thud seemed to rocket off of her brain like someone
was physically hitting her. It felt like the skin on her
head was vibrating from the pain.

She touched her fingertips to her forehead and
flinched. There was a gouge in her forehead, reaching
back into her hairline, and it was wet—no doubt from
blood. It trickled down her face. She fitfully wiped it
away from her eye.

The woods around her were silent.

She crawled into a sitting position, bracing her
hands against the monument she'd hit her head against to
help her stand. Her body swayed like she was standing
on a child's teeter totter and she nearly fell again. She
didn't trust herself to move with any coordination. She
could barely stand.

Go.

He was beside her again, pulling her forward,
prompting her to move even though she was sure she
couldn't. She stumbled forward, fumbling for the trees
around her to steady her as she crept through the dark.

"Madison!"

He seemed like he was still behind her, like he'd
run in the opposite direction she had. She staggered
onward, stumbling and tripping over rocks. It felt like
her legs couldn't coordinate their movements, her head
was buzzing with pain.

The trees suddenly gave way and she broke out
into an open field. The glow of Gettysburg was in the
distance; she could see the lights of traffic on the road
ahead. The Turnpike Restaurant was down the road. She

could see the glow of the white and green sign from where she stood.

She stumbled again, forcing herself into a run. Each step radiated through her head. Her vision was peppered with the bright bursts of light. She had to keep going, she couldn't stop.

Behind you, he's behind you.

"Madison! Fucking stop! You're only making it worse!"

She sprang forward, her legs wobbling and threatening to give out beneath her. Blood flowed freely into her eye and she was half blinded, running on instinct alone. Each step was sheer agony. All she wanted to do was sink to the ground and give up. She was dead already, so what was the point? There was no way she'd make it.

She was vaguely aware she'd run across the road, but was too afraid to stop running. Stopping gave him a change to catch up. Stopping was giving up.

Ben was pushing her forward.

She scrambled up the slight incline of the hill, frantically trying to determine which way to run. Her ankle twisted and gave way beneath her and she pitched forward, collapsing on the ground in a heap. Her vision clouded and she felt her consciousness waiver. It would be so easy just to roll over and sleep. Her eyelids were heavy. She teetered on the edge of reality.

Someone stopped in the grass beside her. Her head pounded, but she rolled to her side. Maybe it was Brad. Maybe it could all just be over now.

It was Ben. She could see him clearly again, as she had the night in the summer kitchen. "Where am I?"

It occurred to her how handsome he was, but how his face was clouded in sadness.

This is where I died.

Panic welled up in her chest; she could feel dread seep into her bones like blood into a rag. She rolled to her side and forced herself into a standing position. Her ankles trembled as she stumbled forward, swaying against the darkness that blurred the edges of her vision. He was still next to her, still so real and whole.

Stay with me.

"I can't." Blood trickled into her eyes from the gash on her head, making it even harder to scramble across the field. The terrain in front of her seemed to dance and sway. Nausea washed over her and she dropped to one knee. "I can't let him do this to me."

Let me save you.

The sleepy feeling was winning, the darkness was pulling her in. She struggled to her feet and lurched forward. Brad could be anywhere on the road or in the field behind her. She had to get help. "Dying won't save me."

Our souls are bound. You can be with me now.

"I want to be with Mike." Her head swam, her eyes threatened to roll back in her head. The Turnpike seemed farther away than it had before. There was no way she could make it; maybe Ben was right. Maybe it was easier that way, just to slow down and let peace settle over her. Rest, just rest. Just a short rest and everything would be fine.

He's coming.

Madison dug her fists into her eyes and wiped the blood out of her face. Her hand brushed against the swollen cut on her temple and she gasped, the pain searing through her head and down into her feet. Her skull pounded, but the wash of pain grounded her. "If he gets me, he'll kill me. You know that. Just like before, just like how she was killed."

I love you, Madison. I've always loved you.

"Then save me." Tears spilled over her cheeks and she lurched forward, a pathetic half run, half fall that almost didn't feel worth the effort. Her left ankle nearly gave out again, but she staggered on, pushing herself to cross the field. She couldn't give in to the comfort of his voice, that pull of his spirit. She could feel him wanting her, dragging her toward him. She didn't want Ben. She wanted Mike.

She knew she wasn't going to make it. She knew she wasn't going to see him again.

The thought seized up her throat and she choked back a sob, her tears mixing with the blood dropping into her eyes. She just hoped he wouldn't be the one who found her. "Mike…oh, God, I'm sorry."

Ben seemed to hesitate next to her. His footsteps seemed to slow and he was gone; a beat later and he was again next to her. She could feel him steady her.

Say you love me, too.

Her tears flowed. It felt like all the energy was draining out of her body, but the restaurant was there. It was just straight ahead—this close, only to fail. This close, only to die trying. "I love you, Ben. I do."

He was gone.

Madison forced her legs forward, left and then right. Left and then right. Forward, not back. She gasped for breath and the burning pain of exhaustion radiated through her lungs. She was alone. The crushing, empty feeling was numbing; it was almost enough to bring her to her knees. Why had he left? Was just her verbalization of her affection enough to put him at peace?

Her mind searched for him, screaming, crying out. No, no, not now. He couldn't leave her now.

"Madison!" Brad's voice was almost a roar, bordering on frantic scream and furious howl like he was ready to tear her apart. There wasn't a trace of rational thinking in his voice. Whatever it was, whatever she'd done to slight him, had pushed him over the edge.

She didn't waste time turning to see where he was at; she broke into a run. The impact of her feet on the ground rocked her skull with each step, like stabs of ice picks jamming into her brain. Pain almost blinded her, her vision blurred and hazy, but she kept running. Step after step, painful tread after painful tread. Her eyes were locked on the door of the restaurant.

There was an explosion behind her, the sound of his gun blasting in her direction. She screamed, covering the back of her head with her hands as if that would somehow help protect her from the bullet.

He missed. Fired again.

Miss.

She launched forward, panic enough to propel her the last several yards to the parking lot. Ducking around light poles and parked cars, she threw herself at the front door of the restaurant and yanked it open. She fell inside and kicked at the door, fully realizing she was wasting precious moments trying to shut behind her.

Pushing back from the door, she stumbled backwards and slammed into someone. She nearly fell, but the man grabbed her arms and steadied her. "Oh my god, what happened? Did you wreck your car, sweetie? Are you okay?"

"He's...he's...trying..." She couldn't catch her breath; she could barely get the words out. Damn it, she needed to calm down. "I need...I need you to call the police."

The entire restaurant seemed to fall silent. Several people stood up and looked in her direction; one or two actually got up from their tables and began making their way to the front. The host standing behind the front counter reached for the phone.

The door burst open behind them and Brad sauntered in, his breathing as labored as hers. She could tell he was trying to look relaxed, but his eyes were large and round. Panicked. "There you are, baby, I didn't think I'd catch up with you. Come on, let's not fight anymore."

Madison scrambled behind the host's stand, slamming into the man still holding the phone receiver in the air. Why hadn't he dialed? Damn it, why did it feel like everything was moving in slow motion? "No. He's trying to kill me. Someone call the police."

"Just calm down." Brad smiled at the customer she'd run into. "We had a little argument and she fell and hit her head. Poor thing doesn't know what she's talking about."

"I do fucking know what I'm talking about. You're trying to kill me." She yanked the phone out of the host's hands. "He's got a gun."

A murmur went through the customers in the restaurant. Brad sighed, almost as if the entire situation was a hassle to him, and pulled the gun out of an interior jacket pocket. He leveled it at her. "Okay, Madison, let's do it the hard way. Come on. You're coming with me."

The man she'd run into stepped forward. "Hey, buddy, calm down. Put the gun down."

Brad whirled toward him, aiming the gun at the man's head. "No, you calm down, fucker. Back up. She's coming with me."

"No." Madison heard the waver in her voice. She clung to the side of the host's stand, her knees wobbling as a tremor wracked her body. "I'm not going with you."

"Then I'll shoot you here."

She stared at the barrel of his gun as he pointed it at her face. From this close proximity, there was no way he would miss her this time. She swallowed hard and set her jaw in a firm line. So, this was how it was going to end. Tears slid down her cheek, but she made no effort to wipe them away. "Then do it. You still won't win."

He hesitated for a moment and then slid his finger to the trigger. "You should have just left well enough alone."

Madison held her breath.

The door to the restaurant flew open and a figure bolted inside, jerking Brad around as he squeezed the trigger. The unexpected movement caught him off guard and he obviously couldn't compensate for it. The bullet smashed into a wall sconce, exploding the iron and glass harmlessly to the floor.

Mike.

He balled his fist, slamming it into Brad's mouth. The archeologist stumbled backward, but Mike grabbed him and held him by his throat, punching him again. Wrenching the gun out of Brad's hand, Mike threw him to the ground and leveled the barrel at his chest. "Give me one fucking reason why I shouldn't just shoot you now."

"We both know you won't do that." Brad spit blood on the floor. "I'm your friend. Your mentor. You wouldn't be who you are without my help."

"Try me." Mike's grasp on the gun was steady, his body relaxed. He kept it trained on Brad's chest. "I'm a damn good shot. You try to run, I'll still fucking get you."

The restaurant door opened again and Drew Carson slid in, his gun also trained on Brad. He reached to his belt and unhooked a pair of handcuffs. "I got him,

Lieutenant. You, buddy, roll over on your stomach. That's it, nice and slow."

Carson tucked his gun into his holster and wrenched Brad's arms behind his back, securing his wrists in the cuffs. "He's good. Get your girl."

Mike flicked the safety on the gun and handed it to Carson. He was around the host's stand in an instant, pulling her into his arms and holding her against him. "I thought I'd lost you."

"You almost did." The sound of his racing heartbeat sent a wash of chills down her spine. She didn't want him to let her go—not now, not ever. "How did you find me?"

"Shit, look at your head. We have to get you to the hospital." He cradled her head in his hands, his eyes searching hers. "Carson, radio for an ambulance."

"Already done, Lieutenant. ETA less than five."

Madison swayed again, leaning her full weight against him. Nausea twisted her stomach and she pressed her hand to her mouth. As if she hadn't humiliated herself in front of a restaurant full of people already, the last thing she wanted to do was throw up in front of them.

Mike scooped her into his arms and carried her to a small waiting area at the opposite end of the entryway. He set her down on the cushioned bench and steadied her. "What happened?"

"He stole your cell phone and texted me, pretending to be you. I didn't figure it out until it was too late." She hesitated. "Ben helped me get away. I jumped out of the car when Brad was distracted and he got me through the woods, up on to Cemetery Hill. I just ran."

"I wouldn't have shot her." Brad craned his neck to see her. "We could have just talked this out."

Carson groaned and nudged him with the tip of his boot. "Buddy, I'm trying to read you your rights. Do we need to go back to the 'right to remain silent'? Turn your face back over here before I do it for you."

Mike kissed her temple and held her against him. "I have never been so scared in my life. God, Madison, why did I leave you like that? I should have gone with my instinct that something was wrong."

"He killed Jan. He told me he ran her off the road."

"Don't worry about him right now. We have to get you to the hospital and get this looked at. You're going to be okay, you'll be fine."

"Stay with me." She fought back another wave of tears. "I'm scared."

"I'm not planning on leaving you again."

She could see the flash of red and blue lights outside the building and the door opened again. This time policemen and paramedics filed into the restaurant. It was over.

She clung onto Mike's hand and took a deep breath. It was over for the most part, but there was still far too much left unresolved. Still too many questions left unanswered.

Her head throbbing, she sank back against Mike and closed her eyes. There was only one question she cared about at his point. And the answer was Mike.

Chapter Twenty-Five

The next morning, after providing police statements and confirmation she wanted to press charges against Bradley Emerson, Madison was discharged into Mike's care. She was diagnosed with a skull fracture and a grade two high ankle sprain. She was bruised and battered, but she'd live.

She still wondered how.

Instead of agreeing to go back to the hotel room like she'd promised the doctor, she conned Mike into taking her back to Cemetery Hill. He helped her limp to the area where Ben said he'd died and, together, they sat in the grass overlooking the field where in 1863, the 11th Corps fought.

Neither spoke. Madison stretched her legs out in front of her and looked around the field. The woman, her name long lost to time, had been shot just feet in front of where they sat. Ben had bled to death in the dirt where, she too, had almost died. She didn't even feel like she was living the same life anymore. Before the dig, she'd been a carefree, paper archeologist. Now, she'd barely gotten out of her first dig alive. "So…now what?"

"Well, the dig is pretty much shut down permanently." Mike swept her hand into his and kissed her palm. "I told them I'd write a final report of what we found. They're not in a hurry to get it."

"Are they kicking you out of park housing?"

"Eh, I wouldn't call it kicking us out." Mike shrugged, lacing his fingers around hers. He squeezed her hand. "The dig's over, just like all the other digs I've done before. Time to start applying again."

Madison chewed on her lower lip. She felt lost, like she was standing at the split in a road. "I'm not sure

I want to go back to school. Somehow it was easier being a paper archeologist, you know? None of this jealousy and exploitation."

"Don't say that. You've got talent, not to mention the fact you made the so called discovery of the century here. No one can take that away from you." He trailed the fingertips of his free hand down her cheek. "I think you'd be a damn good archeologist. Hell, you are a damn good archeologist. Like it or not."

"Regardless, I don't want to go back to Pittsburgh yet. My mother is having a fit. God knows what my step-father thinks, but I couldn't fucking care less." She drew her good leg back and rested her forehead against her knee. "Dr. Emerson left me this big, long apologetic message, but I didn't call him back. God, I don't even feel like the same person I was when I left."

"So, stay with me." Mike studied their intertwined hands. He stammered nervously, though Madison suspected he'd been rehearsing what he wanted to say. "I live near the battlefield at Antietam. It's not the nicest apartment you'd ever see, but…honestly, I'd be lost without you. I don't want to think about not being with you. "

She blushed.

"When I thought Brad…ah…when I thought the worst had happened, I was ready to explode. It ripped me apart. You mean the world to me and, look, Madison, I love you. Come stay with me, whether it's just for the week or until you go back to school or forever. I just don't want to lose you. Not again."

She leaned over and pressed her lips to his. "If you're making me choose…then I choose to stay with you forever."

He wrapped his arms around her and pulled her against him, kissing her with such intensity it took her breath away. When the kiss ended, he didn't let her go. "Carson told me Brad wants to file charges against me for assault and battery."

"I don't think that will stand up in court."

He chuckled. "Doubtful. And, despite what Brad thinks, he's not getting away with this. Attempted murder of you aside, he killed Jan Williams. He tried to defile this park which, in this area anyway, is a crime in itself. We said it jokingly before but, damn it if his jealously didn't drive him over the edge."

"How did you find me?" Madison sat up and looked at him, turning his chin toward her to force his gaze to hers. "I could have been anywhere in the park. I ran from Culp's Hill to here and, if you'd been half a second later, he would have pulled the trigger."

Mike hesitated. "Nobody was at park headquarters when I got there. It was deserted. I was going to drive to Brad's place and find out what was going on, but Cianna showed up in the parking lot. She told me what Brad was planning to do, so I took her to LE headquarters instead. Carson and I started looking for you."

"But how did you find me at the Turnpike Restaurant?" Madison sighed. "Even if Cianna had known he was taking me to Culp's Hill, she couldn't have known I'd get away and run down Cemetery Hill."

Mike stared at her. "It was him."

"Who?"

"Carson and I were down by Spangler Spring. He'd pulled over to radio headquarters and see if they could send some rangers up to Little Round Top and Devils Den to look for you. When we were stopped, I heard…I heard him. Ben." He paused. "Your Ben."

"He got me off Culp's Hill. He led me here."

"I know. I couldn't understand everything, but I heard him say…" He hesitated again. "Cemetery Hill. Save her like I couldn't. I heard the shots when we got closer and, when I didn't see anyone in the field…somehow I just knew you'd made it to the restaurant. It was like…it was like he was pushing me in that direction."

"I thought he left me."

"I think he saved you."

She rested her head against Mike's shoulder. Ben had saved her. He'd given her the chance to live the life he hadn't. She owed her life to him, to a man who died over one hundred and thirty years before she was born. Maybe he was right. Maybe somehow their souls were bound together. Even so, she hoped that by helping save her, he somehow would find the peace he was searching for.

"Come on, let's get out of here." He stood and reached down to help her up. "Liam wants me to tell you we should go in business together. Something about how we can be the Lazarus Society, archeologists and a sensitive/archeologist not only finding the dead, but putting them to rest. He's very big in Victorian Spirituality, so I have a feeling that's where this is stemming from."

"Sounds interesting." She let him pull her to her feet. *Goodbye Ben.* "But…maybe not today."

"Agreed. Besides, you're with me now."

She froze, almost hoping she'd misheard him. "What?"

"You're with me now." Mike raised an eyebrow and stared at her, a flicker of concern meeting his eyes. "Liam can wait."

"Oh, yeah, exactly. Just you wait until I get my strength back, then I'll rock your world." She smiled at him, but her pulse began pounding in her ears. *With me now.* Ben had said it, too, and he'd said it more than once.

Shaking the thought from her mind, she slid her hand into Mike's and let him lead her back to the Jeep. He reached down to unlock the door and, as he did, Madison looked back to Cemetery Hill. She could see him, standing where they'd just been. His eyes were focused on her and he nodded his head, as if he somehow understood what he'd meant to her.

Part of me will always be with you.

"Are you okay?" Mike looked back at Cemetery Hill and then switched his gaze to her. She knew he didn't see him. Not this time.

"I'm good." She stood on her tiptoes and kissed him. "I love you."

"I love you too, Maddy."

Being careful to not hit her head on the doorframe, she eased down into passenger's seat and looked back to Cemetery Hill a final time.

He was gone.

The End

www.heatherhambelcurley.com

HEATHER HAMBEL CURLEY

Evernight Publishing ®

www.evernightpublishing.com